Destiny's Call to Arms
Dragon Heart Chronicles, Book One
Kathleen L. Shay

Shay, Kathleen L.

Destiny's Call to Arms by Kathleen L. Shay

"A Dragon Heart Chronicles book."

Summary: A young girl named Josephine Drageon is born with the power of a Dragon and must learn the ways of the Dragon Hearts to help save her world with the help of her Ice Dragon partner Aurora and fellow Dragon heart friends.

Hard Cover Second Edition ISBN-13: 979-8-9992032-0-5

Paperback Second Edition ISBN: 979-8-9992032-1-2

Ebook-Kindle edition-2025

Contents

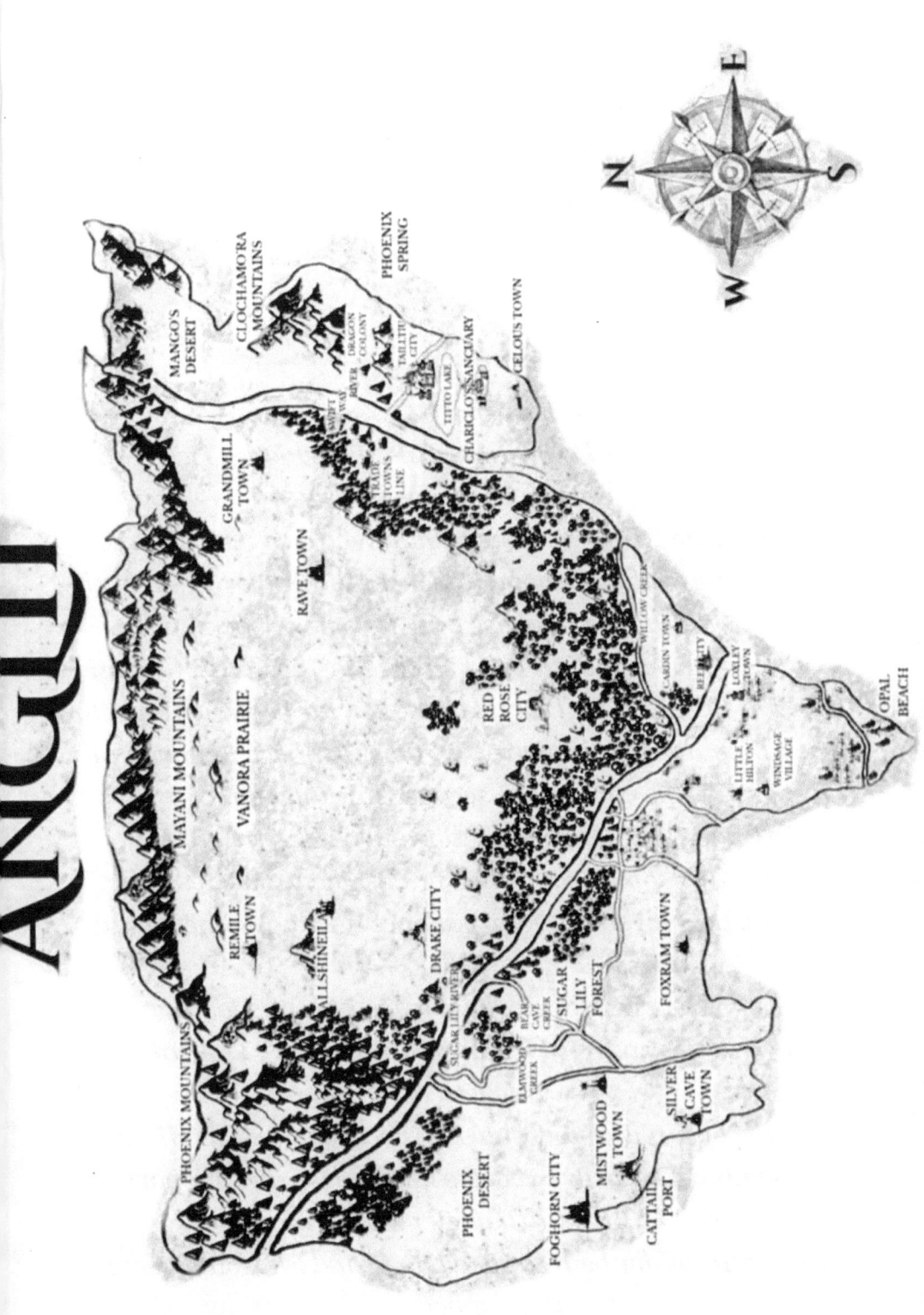

This book is dedicated to

My Mum, who let me dream (but only after I fed the cats),

My Dad, who helps me make sense of the world and its idiotic movements,

To Jessica Moyer, who found my notebook when it was stolen,

My dear friends Meghan, Misty, Jenn, and Katherine for believing in me,

To Allie, My Master Editor, girl b.f.f./soul sister, fellow Twilighter and Harry Potter fan, real-life Princess Ticka (you rule on so many levels),

To Michelle R., my Master Editor, who saw through the rocks and saw the diamond underneath, thank you so much for all the great advice and Zero hour back up,

To fellow writer and my other great Master Editor Christina, YOU ROCK SO MUCH, Thank You for helping me get to the finish line and begin my greatest supporter though all this editing the second time around,

To Cheyenne, the student who surpassed the master,

To my awesome original cover designer/map designer Sarah, thank you for your patience and awesome digital skills,

To Leigh, for the help to get me started,

To my other wonderful friends, Tim D., Steve D., Leah, and Chelsea,

To the original 36 followers on Facebook (a.k.a. all my friends and family), thanks for the love and support,

To Brandi, the Bella to my Alice,

To Michelle W. for being a good friend and awesome photographer,

To the memory of Dr. Sheraw, the great Professor of humor,
To my ex-coworkers at the library,
To the former members of Thunder, Gamer's Guild, and
Inklings,
To my dear friends and critics, Erik, James, Heather, and
Alyssa.
To especially Erik, my awesome last–minute Mapmaker,
And (Of course) to my magical advisor/b.f.f./soul brother
Tim Shartle (also known as Timacus the god of video
games, Tim-kun, Zuul, and Timmy the Great)
I thank you all.

Prologue
The Beginning

I, Fair Lady, from the land of Francia, have been given the great honor to record my story in the book known as the *Dragon Heart Chronicles*. Generations upon generations have written the stories of their service in the extraordinary group of warriors known as the Light Dragons of the Crystal Alliance. The history that the Chronicles gives is not only of the birth of the Alliance but also when on the continent of Anglii, came forth the most wondrous... the greatest creatures ever known to the world: *Dragons!*

When the world formed, a spark of life came from six stones in the earth. Some say it was a wizard; others claim the elements themselves sang to the stones, but regardless, from the six precious jewels rose the first Dragons. The great scaled beasts of power and fire, with bat–like wings, keen eyes, ruthless claws, and cunning minds. Dragons cutting through prey with ease with their large sword–like teeth. The color of their scales and size reflecting their elements. The first dragons came to be known as:

From the Ice of Opal, Wise Glen,

From the Wind of Diamond, Noble Windro,

From the Water of Sapphire, Sweet Marina,

From the Lightning of Citrine, Clever Amerina,

From the Fire of Ruby, Fierce Farra, and

From the Earth of Amber, Sturdy Nori.

As time went on, the dragons, like other living beings, grew curious of the world. Many cultures matured and moved around, mastering the waves of the seas to find refuge from their homelands full of turmoil. Many of them found Anglii to be the land of new beginnings, to create a new life.

The Dragons reached out to their surroundings, even becoming the masters of tongues, able to communicate with all in any language. But even so, they found it hard, for the land was full of dangers, war, plagues, and fear of the unknown. As life grew, so did death, darkness, and treachery. It was not safe to travel across Anglii, Francia, or any other continent, not even for the dragons, for a darkness was rising, and not even the most powerful could fight against it.

A creature came forth from the dark folds of the earth. No one knows how they were created, only that the creature was attracted to harsh emotions and blood. It spread throughout the land of Francia. Their bodies made of smoke, eyes like silver mercury. Their mouths hidden until they withdrew the life from their victims. The creatures' preferred prey being humans, with their emotions of fear, anger, and hate. Wars helped the creatures breed and grow to plague–size proportions. The creatures thus called Shadows.

Humans with magical talent and dark intentions discovered they could twist the will of the creatures and use them for nefarious purposes. Shadow magic took hold of the earth. Shadow magicians creeped in from the far reaches of the world to manipulate entire kingdoms and bring them to chaos and blood. The magical powers of the Phoenixes and the Unicorns, with their purifying fire and light, were the only ones resistant to the black magic of the Shadows.

The Dragons saw this, knowing this would destroy all of creation. They fought against any who dared to trespass upon their territory, to protect themselves from all. For years, all creatures, two-legged or four-legged, fought against the shadows and anyone else not their own kin. It seemed the world would tear itself apart, with wars creating rivers of blood, families torn apart from one another. The land becoming black from the devastating evil that gripped it.

Turmoil continued for many years until, one day, a human child named Taranis was born. His eyes were the same shape as a dragon's. Because of this, people feared him, including his own kin. As he grew, he found his strength and senses were beyond those of the others. His mother, though proud of her son, worked hard to shield him from harm, but Taranis discovered he could defend himself.

At nine-years old, a Shadow creature attacked Taranis in the mountains. As it lunged at him, he felt something inside himself, a spark. He grabbed the monster and in a flash of lightning and smoke; it became dust.

As this happened, in the rocky Clocha Móra Mountains, an abandoned dragon egg hatched as the spark of Taranis's lightning hit the Shadow. The dragon's instincts pulled at him and left his nest, roaming through Anglii until one day Taranis and the yellow lightning dragon met in a field. They both wished to stop the Shadows and the pointless killing.

The dragon said to Taranis, "Give me a name and the two of us will become brothers. With our bond we can bring understanding to our clans and stop the endless killing."

Taranis gave his Dragon partner the name of Quick Strike. The two became skilled warriors, who over time found five other humans with Dragon powers and Dragon partners, representing the elements of fire, water, earth, ice, and wind. By banding together, the friends fought and defeated the greatest Shadow magician, named Zankeno.

With Zankeno defeated in the first Shadow War, Taranis and the other five, who called themselves the Dragon Knights, founded the Light Dragons of the Crystal Alliance. Their first act was to create a peace and a partnership between the Dragon clans and the Human kingdoms. The humans brought compassion while the dragons brought their fierce fighting abilities, sealing the bonds of the Dragon Knights. Bringing promise that more Dragon Knights would be born.

Those with the souls of dragons and their dragon companions trained with the six masters to learn how to use the gifts given to them to protect. Thus began the Dragon Knights, called Dragon hearts by the common folk, as they possessed the hearts and souls of the mighty creatures.

The Dragon Knights made their home in the main human kingdom of Red Rose at Red Rose City, Anglii. Even though the Alliance held council there, they were in their own order, separate from all kingdoms. Answerable to only the innocent.

To help spread peace throughout all the lands, the Dragon hearts permitted others to join them, the human kingdoms of Red Rose and WarWink, the Tuatha Dé Danann kingdoms, the Centaurs, Unicorns, and many others. Over time, the Dragon Knight Alliance fought to keep their lands safe from the dark practices of Shadow magic and promote peace between the kingdoms. Everyone in the Alliance helped make the lands safe for the innocent. They fought anyone who dared to defy law and order. Few thieves, Shadow magicians, or crooked lords went without notice or punishment.

This is how the Dragon Knights came to be. Recorded in the book of records, the *Dragon Heart Chronicles*. Thanks to the hard work of the Alliance, peace would reign for ages.

But then our peace came crashing down around us, our lives forever changed, destroyed.

This is where my tale starts when the Dragon Knight Alliance fell. I make this record in my own words for the Chronicles, hoping that when future generations read our story, they will learn from history in ways we did not, and not repeat our horrible mistakes.

Chapter One
Josephine Drageon

Wind Sage is a simple country village with a mill, blacksmith, inn and various other little businesses that any respectable town would have. Located near the southern coastline of Anglii, it boasted fair weather and fair people. As the sun touched the dew on the tree leaves, the inhabitants of the town rose to begin their chores.

Josephine Drageon walked towards her family's stables. The wind tickled her raven hair, making it glitter in the early morning light. As she reached for the door of the stable, someone called out to her.

"Morning Josephine!"

She turned to see her childhood friend Jake, sitting tall on his brown stallion. He was sporting dirt already on his plain black shirt and brown trousers.

"Morning, Jake!" she said, smiling as she unlocked the big lock on the doors.

"Where are you off to today?"

"I'm going with Starlette for an early ride. Thinking about going to visit with your cousin and the others at the mill later. Maybe we'll have a lifting contest," she smirked as she opened the stable doors wide to air it out.

Jake rolled his brown eyes, ruffled his already wind brushed hair.

"You are the strangest girl I've ever met."

"And don't you forget it!" she laughed.

"Oh, I won't. I can promise that much. If you're done with your chores, I've got a few in town to do. Want to tag along?" Jake smiled, picking up his horse's reins in his large, calloused hands.

"Only if that includes a race!" she called out from the barn.

"Of course. I'd never bother asking because I know you wouldn't come along if there wasn't a promise of that!" said Jake.

She laughed, reappearing in the door frame with her arms folded. Josephine was donning her normal riding out-fit: black leather pants, knee-high brown leather boots, and a blue, long-sleeved tunic.

"You know me so well. Sure, I'll tag along. Let me get Starlette up and going. But I don't know why you bother to challenge us. Willy won't win. A regular horse will never be able to match the speed of a unicorn!" Josephine told him.

"Doesn't stop us from trying, though." Jake grinned; his eyes gleaming.

As Jake rode back over to his house to pick up the mill parts from his father, Josephine walked into the stable to pull her saddle. As she did, she thought about how Jake called her strange. It made her smile. It was true, she didn't wear dresses unlike the other girls (not for lack of trying by her aunt and mother). She rode horses like any other man, and she hated being inside for longer than five minutes.

She pulled out her brown leather saddle and wiped it down, making sure there was no saddle soap leftover from cleaning yesterday. From the top of the pommel to the wooden stirrups, she inspected it. Once satisfied her saddle was in order, Josephine turned to place her supplies back when a horse neighed behind her. The family's largest stallion, BlackStar, gazed at her with big eyes. He nudged his feeding trough. Josephine smiled, then shook her head.

"I fed you this morning already! If you keep eating without end, you'll be too fat to do anything," she informed the horse in a disapproving voice.

BlackStar ignored her comment, nudging the tray again. She laughed and went and got a scoop of oats and gave it to the horse.

"Fine BlackStar, but this is all the more you are getting or Father will have both our heads."

The horse clicked its teeth as though thanking her before eating the oats with disgusting gusto. Josephine patted the stallion's soft, black head. Her family was tenth generation horse trainers and breeders. Out of the four children, her older brothers being Matthew, Timothy and Ronald, she had a genuine gift with the horses. Josephine could calm down BlackStar when he was scared or was being stubborn and won't let anyone put a saddle on him. The horses responded well to her touch and voice. She patted BlackStar for another minute, then returned to her saddle.

Josephine went to the old cabinet and pulled out her riding blanket, and walked over to Starlette, her unicorn. Her pearly white coat shimmered like a rainbow in the bright sunlight. Her mane of hair was long and fine. Josephine braided it for her to keep it neat. Starlette had a silver, star-shaped birthmark right on her forehead between her sunny yellow eyes.

Starlette was still asleep. Josephine, with a soft touch, placed the blanket, then the saddle up onto Starlette's back, her mind going back to what Jake had called her.

True, she never cared who was marrying who or what the latest fashion was. She loved listening to Dejen telling stories of the ancient Dragon Knights, or what was the latest news from other lands. Josephine knew more about other continents than any other young girl in the entire village.

Though it wasn't only her personality that made her different; it was also her looks. She was not only the tallest girl but also the strongest. At six foot one, Josephine towered over all the girls, and even a few of the men. She could lift equally to the strongest man in the village, which was Jake's father who runs the local mill. Her strength and height came in handy when dealing with the larger horses.

Josephine finished tightening the billet strap on Starlette.

The unicorn continued to doze.

Josephine wiped the dirt off her face with her sleeve. She pondered over the one thing that made her stand out the most from even her own kin: her eyes. Her father had nicknamed her kitten because of her narrow pupils. Josephine was the only one in her family whose eyes glimmered like ice in the sunlight. She liked that thought, being unique. Her grandfather always had spoiled her more than her brothers. He told her she should always be proud of who she was. He even encouraged her brothers (to her mother's and aunt's disapproval) to teach Josephine how to fist fight.

Josephine shoved her wandering thoughts away when Starlette jerked up as she finished putting on her bridle. She poked Josephine with her short silver horn.

"You know, it's rude to saddle someone whiles she's asleep," she muttered.

"I'm sorry, but you looked so exhausted I didn't want to wake you until I finished," Josephine apologized, pulling out an apple to make up for being rude.

Starlette chopped it down, swallowing in one gulp.

"Well, considering I had to help you with those two ridiculous mares yesterday, are you surprised? Honestly," she snorted in an indignant tone.

Josephine laughed at the comment. Starlette had such a proper personality. She figured that's how unicorns acted. Neither of them knew, for Josephine found Starlette when she was six years old, huddled under a tree during a nasty thunderstorm. Starlette had no memory of her parents or even how she got to Anglii. Unicorns lived on the continent of Francia, and far as Josephine knew, there were no herds in Anglii. From that day on, Starlette became Josephine's friend and riding companion. She would help them with training the horses by talking to them when not even Josephine could.

"Feel up to a race against Jake and Willy?" Josephine inquired, smiling. Josephine pulled her long raven hair into a ponytail as she walked, with Starlette rambling right behind her.

"I suppose I would be willing to do an early morning sprint around the village. The weather is fine," Starlette said.

Josephine saw the excitement of a race beating away Starlette's sleepiness. As she pulled the doors closed, Jake rode up riding Willy. Like her and Starlette, Jake and Willy had grown up together. Even though Jake couldn't talk to Willy like Josephine could to Starlette, they both acted the same way; fun loving but wary of anything that would risk them injury, such as jumping over high fences like Josephine loved to do.

Jake was neither a curious person nor someone who enjoyed taking risks; he preferred keeping both of his feet and Willy's four hooves on the ground always. Starlette did not mind jumping high; it gave her an excuse to show off her skills. Regardless, she did not relish going where she believed no unicorn had a right mind to poke their noses into. Josephine, however, was filled with endless curiosity and the need to try everything that came her way.

"First stop, Blacksmith?" asked Josephine.

Jake nodded, turning Willy to face the west side of town, where Main Street stretched out towards a part of the surrounding forest. Josephine inhaled deep the fresh air, the last of traces of doziness gone.

"Race you there!" she challenged.

Jake shook his head.

"Running through town will raise a few eyebrows," remarked Starlette.

"That's my forte!" Josephine said, a mischievous grin on her face.

The unicorn and the teen boy both rolled their eyes but didn't argue. Josephine gave a gentle nudge to Starlette's side. Starlette spurred off with Willy behind her into town.

They raced past the houses, the Duke's Inn, and Mr. Marcy, the local grocer, to come to a halt in front of the blacksmith.

"Tie!" said Jake, kicking up dust as he pulled on Willy's reins.

"I think we won by at least a foot, but out of the goodness of our hearts will let you think that, Jake," teased Josephine.

Jake snorted. He dismounted, going off to drop off the broken tools and to pick up a part. Josephine stayed mounted on Starlette as he did.

Josephine sighed, pulling her ponytail tight. A constant battle for her hair being silky fine.

Giggling came from behind Josephine. Two girls were coming up the road. Josephine recognized the one with the pale red dress and cream lace umbrella as Bibi Benoit. Beside her was Denise Larouche in a green dress without as much lace but still childish looking. She could not see the appeal of having pale skin or wearing so many layers of clothes you cannot tell there is a person underneath it. Josephine chuckled to herself as she wiped dirt off her trousers, admiring the slight tan of her skin.

Bibi and Denise were well-to-do daughters of the local Lord and the town's mayor.

"Good morning!" said Josephine in a cherry voice as the two walked past.

Bibi raised her eyebrows as she glanced at Josephine's appearance.

"Yes, Good Morning," said Bibi. The other girl said nothing. Once they were a few paces away from Josephine, the two giggled again. Despite their whispering, Josephine could hear the unpleasant conversation.

"That unicorn should have better than a girl who looks as though she's been digging in the ground like a troll!" chipped Denise.

"You would think her family was poor from her look. Not even wearing a dress!"

Bibi clicked her tongue. "It's all well she dresses like a man. She's too tall and tan to be a respectful woman! She might as well become an old maid now; men dislike women who are taller than them!"

Josephine and Starlette snorted. Josephine smiled, seeing something out of the corner of her eye. She called out to the girls, "Oh! Bibi!"

The two twirled around, Bibi flipping her curly brunette hair as she did.

"What?" she demanded in a snotty voice.

"Just wanted to tell you how lovely your dress is..." Josephine said, keeping her face as neutral as possible.

Bibi blinked in surprise, her mouth forming an "O".

THUD!

The two girls squealed as the blacksmith's son, Gratien Lafevre, ran into them, unable to stop in time due to their sudden stop. He had been carrying a large bucket of ash he probably was going to dump out in the woods.

Josephine and Starlette both laughed under their breaths as poor Gratien tried to help the silly girls. However, his ashy hands only made the situation worse for the dresses. Bibi was screaming and yelling at the apprentice, but for her part, Denise did not seem to mind as much as her companion. He looked at Denise with an apologetic look. Bibi was oblivious to the pair as she ranted about filthy blacksmith shops.

"Come along, Denise!" snapped Bibi, grabbing her friend's arm and dragging her off.

"Sorry!" yelled Gratien again.

"Freak thinks she can laugh at us!" snapped Bibi.

"Yeah…" grumbled Denise.

Josephine rolled her eyes at the freak comment, then stared at Gratien who was still staring at the two girls.

"You cannot seriously like Denise. She's got lower intelligence than a worm," said Josephine.

He blinked, noticing her for the first time. Gratien was good friends with Josephine's brother Robert. He was one of the many boys who loved to challenge Josephine to wrestling matches when they were younger. He never won against Josephine. Gratien blushed and shrugged. Josephine shook her head.

"Your life. But I think you could do better."

"If you say so. But she is bright and a daughter of the mayor. Doubt she'd be serious about a blacksmith's son," Gratien frowned.

Josephine frowned. "I doubt that from the looks she was giving you. You are a kind soul, Gratien."

"Thanks, Josephine."

Gratien picked up his bucket, returning to the forge.

Josephine shook her head. "I suppose if all people had dreams of adventure and grandeur, there would be no one left to be saved by the heroes or to grow crops, make supplies for the heroes," Josephine mused, speaking to herself.

Starlette turned her head to Josephine with a bright yellow eye.

"Sound theory," she said with a tinge of mockery. Josephine chuckled, not bothering to reply.

For a moment, Josephine felt her vision go strange, it went black.

She shook her head, and it corrected itself.

Jake walked out at that moment, confused.

"What was that racket?"

"Josephine playing matchmaker," said Starlette in a solemn voice.

Jake frowned as he mounted Willy.

"Ignore her. Where to now?" asked Josephine, flicking the back of Starlette's head with her fingers.

"He's not done fixing the gear part, so want to race to the rock pile to pass the time?" asked Jake.

"To the rock pile sounds good!" laughed Josephine, taking Starlette's reins into her hands and, with light pressure to her sides, to urge her forward.

As quick as lightning, the two imposing horses galloped through the town towards the pile of old foundation stones on the west side on the outskirts of town.

"Looks as we have outstripped them again, Starlette!" Josephine laughed. Jake and Willy were only a speck of dust in the distance. Starlette laughed as the wind tickled her shimmering white mane.

"You doubt my amazing skills?"

"Never!" Josephine laughed back.

The sweet smell of the early morning swept over her as Starlette galloped along the path; pine trees lined up on either side of the road. They were reminiscent of the walls of a cathedral, the sunlight streaking through their branches with newborn leaves like stain glass windows, shining on Starlette's silver tinted fur.

The melodies of various song birds rang out as they ran through the forest, the unicorn's diamond hard hooves stomping through the quiet din.

Once in a while a few rabbits ran by or a little fillylon, the little green lizards flicking their tails, slipping around in the grass, searching for a warm rock to sleep on.

Josephine and Starlette loved doing this, running through the forest, the two of them working together as one entity, weightless and without worries. As the path spread out, the grass became thicker and wild, with large boulders and damaged, rotting logs lying abandoned in a clearing. The remnants of an ancient barn burned down long before Josephine's birth. At the sight of the barn's old broken skeleton, Josephine pulled back on Starlette's reigns.

"Six minutes," thought Josephine to herself happily.

"He's got six minutes to break his old record."

While she waited for Jake, she climbed on top of the stones and pulled out her hair to let it shine in the sunlight. Josephine loved spring mornings. Though the sun was warming the still air, a slight nip to the wind lingering from winter. Starlette walked over and stared, sniffing the budding clover.

She heard Willy's hooves galloping towards them as they walked into the clearing.

"Not bad, Jake!" laughed Josephine. "Only three minutes after me! That has to be a record for you!"

She waited on the rock with her hands behind her back as Jake rode up, coming to a halt.

He gave her his crooked smile and said, "You never know, maybe I'll be able to keep up with you one of these days!"

She rolled her eyes before jumping down off the rock and mounting Starlette.

"Only if you stop taking so many naps."

Jake didn't answer, but played with Willy's reins. Josephine raised an eyebrow at him.

"Jake, what's bothering you?"

"Huh? Oh nothing."

Josephine sighed, turning Starlette's head to stop her from eating the young clover.

"Jacob Maxwell Ford, I know you got something on your mind because you're playing with Willy's reins. Whenever something is on your mind, you play with the nearest thing and don't look at anyone straight in the face."

Jake stopped and looked up at Josephine with a slight frown. He sighed then said in a slow tone, "Josephine..."

"What is it, Jake? Dragon got your tongue?" she smiled, tugging on Starlette's bridle, which earned her a glare from the young unicorn.

Jake took a deep breath, readying himself to say something serious.

"We're sixteen now, right?"

"Last time I checked," Josephine answered, wondering what was worrying Jake. Sweat was building up on his forehead. His eyes focused on a nearby bush. She became confused. They had an easy friendship, able to tell each other any mistake or secret.

"Yeah well... I was wondering if you... I mean, I'll understand if you don't want to, but if you do..." Jake stammered.

"For King Nicolas's sake, Jake!" she laughed. She jumped up on Starlette, then tapped her so the two stood side by side. Jake developed a small blush on his cheeks as their legs touched.

"What's wrong?"

"Well, nothing's wrong. It's more like I wanted to ask you something. I..."

Josephine blinked. Jake was talking, but she couldn't hear him, the sound of birds, the wind or anything. A vacuum formed around her; she was deaf. She almost screamed out from the sensation when her vision went black. Josephine saw not the surrounding forest, but a large cave. A hammer hitting against the wall of the cave, then an echoing of a glass object falling to the ground. The sounds of men cheering. A rush of icy darkness spread through her body, and then releasing her from the vacuum.

"Josephine, are you okay?" asked a worried Jake who within that second noticed that Josephine had spaced out.

"You look pale and that's saying something."

"Yes, I'm... fine..."

"JOSEPHINE DRAGEON!" barked a voice that reached to the sky.

"Not anymore you aren't," snickered Starlette, turning to see the woman that went with the loud booming voice.

Josephine jumped. Aunt Shelia was on her brown mare, Brownie. The stoutly built woman had an expression of utter fury. She was wearing a deep blue riding dress, her light brown hair pulled back into a bun. Her hazel eyes were full of anger. Now Josephine had seen her Aunt Shelia furious before (almost every time she wore pants), but not like this. She appeared not only livid, but a bit scared.

"What's wrong, Aunt Shelia?" asked Starlette, also noting the mixed emotions.

She did not answer Starlette's question but barked, "Come now, child. Jake, come too if you wish. We need to return home now."

The two shared a look of unease before urging their rides to move. As they galloped at a brisk pace to home, Josephine tried to get answers from Aunt Shelia, but to no avail.

But under her breath as they hurried home, Aunt Shelia muttered things like,

"While my brother is away, to bring this up!" and "Total Rubbish!"

When she muttered something about Dejen, Josephine blinked in surprise. He was a wizard and a good friend to her family. Why would something that Dejen said make Aunt Shelia mad like this? It made no sense.

When they reached the Drageon's large home, the formidable woman ordered the two teenagers into the house while she tied up the horses. Josephine and Jake walked into the two-story gray-blue house.

They entered through the side door into the kitchen, where they found Dejen sitting at the table, drinking a cup of tea. Dejen was tall with dark brown skin. She exchanged a smile with her adoptive uncle/teacher.

Josephine noticed he was wearing his traveling leather coat and holding in his hand his wide brim hat. As he stood up, Aunt Shelia appeared hastily behind Jake, who jumped, then moved out of the way.

Josephine stared from Aunt Shelia's furious face to Dejen's calm one, not getting a single clue about what was going on.

Aunt Shelia barked at Dejen in a panicked voice that shocked Josephine.

"Dejen, this is utter nonsense! With Walter and Kitty with the boys in Francia... to come here and...!"

He sighed, shaking his head. "We knew this was coming, we talked about this, you know of what we planned," he said with narrow eyes, "Josephine is what she is and the forces have been gathering and they are reaching their peak. You know the king has been setting embargos on shipping from Francia, causing discord between the kingdoms. The increase in tensions in recent years, the earth is getting more nervous by the day."

"The last few now are living simple lives. Why Josephine? Aren't there any others...?"

Dejen looked at Aunt Sheila with pity. "She is it, Sheila. There are others but..." Dejen waved his hand in the air, "Besides, Sheila, you know your niece, your family history, and how magic is."

He moved to be eye to eye with Josephine. "Josephine, do you know why your eyes are the way they are?"

"I have a suspicion," she answered.

Dejen smiled a sad smile, making his wrinkles more pronounced. "Luck has smiled upon you, dear Josephine, for few are alive to remember what your eyes mean, for it has been two generations now. Of course, you must be told now what they mean so that you will continue to be safe."

"HUH?" Jake voiced exactly what Josephine was thinking.

She shifted her weight then said, "I don't understand, Dejen; what do my eyes mean?"

Aunt Shelia glared at Dejen. Josephine saw a flash like before and instead of her home, a cave appeared. This time the stone laid on a rock was on display. A spotted hand as though the person it belonged to was diseased, touched the black stone, and it glowed. This time, the doomed feeling she had was overwhelming. Josephine felt as though her spirit had been crushed into nothing.

Josephine grabbed Jake's broad shoulder to stop from falling over completely when the kitchen came back to her sight.

"Are you okay?!" asked Jake for a second time, while helping her stand straight again. Josephine wiped her forehead to find to her surprise that she was sweating.

"You're seeing it, aren't you? It's happening sooner than we thought," Dejen asked in a soft tone, the strain leaking through, "He's found something, hasn't he? Understandable that you are having visions, since many had them before a crisis of this size happened; James and Jewelvana were famous for it..."

Josephine stared at Dejen. He had mentioned two. Josephine's mind was racing. Was he saying that she was a Dragon heart?!

"Oh, for the love of the kingdom, she's only sixteen! Can't any of the old ones that are still around...?" Aunt Shelia was breathing heavily and near tears.

The wizard placed a hand on her shoulder, then said, "You know better, Shelia. Their powers are not what they once were. That is why this new generation has come forth. Her destiny is awaking inside her and the others."

Jake ruffled his hair in frustration and said, "All right, I am now totally and completely confused!"

"I'll say you're not even talking straight," Josephine giggled, now standing on her own.

Jake glared at her, then turned to the two adults, begging, "Would one of you PLEASE tell us what is going on?!"

"So, does this mean that us new Dragon hearts are coming into their power? Are we being hunted?" asked Josephine.

Silence fell over in the Drageon's kitchen. Aunt Shelia's face was half-angry and half-scared, while Jake was dumbfounded.

"What? I have dragon-shaped eyes and I read. I just would like to know why we never talk about it," she grumbled at Aunt Shelia.

"Yes... it's just..." she took a deep breath before saying, "We don't talk about it because of what happened at the last battle. The current king is not fond of magic, it.... was to keep you safe."

Josephine turned to Dejen.

"That is true. Plus, your powers did not awaken when you were six. I believe that is because the time was not right..."

Aunt Shelia glared, snipping at him in a hard-raspy voice. "Dejen, the battle of the betrayed was over sixty years ago! Even without the Dragon Knight Alliance, the land has been peaceful. Yes, there are problems here and there, but you can't get rid of criminals completely. Most of those traitors have long since died! There will *always* be evil..."

"And when there is a great evil, there will always be a greater good to fight it. Yes, some traitors are dead, but not all of them, and they are *returning to finish what they started*," Dejen retorted.

Josephine stared with astonishment at her teacher. She had never seen Dejen so angry with anyone. Even when she had broken one of his pottery projects and hidden the evidence in the bottom of his mattress. He had not even frowned at her. This was a side of Dejen that she found unnerving.

"Josephine... A DRAGON HEART?!" gawked Jake, still trying to absorb it.

"YES, a Dragon heart," sighed Aunt Sheila with a small smile. "And keep your voice down, Jake; the entire world does not need to know."

"Not yet at least," added Dejen with a smirk.

"But..." started Jake, but Dejen cut him off with a wave of his hand.

"Jake, her eyes are Dragon eyes, not cat's eyes; she is unarguably stronger than all the men in this village and," he chuckled, "she cannot stand to be inside for more than thirty seconds. This is understandable, for dragons are known for roaming around."

"Not to mention," sighed Aunt Sheila, accepting the inevitable, "she can see, hear, smell, and even feel things before anyone else."

"Give it up, Jake, I'm a Dragon heart. Move on," Josephine smiled, glancing at her aunt, who nodded.

"Though I don't understand something, if I am a Dragon Heart," said Josephine, confused, looking from Dejen to her aunt, "as you said, why hasn't any of my magic come about?"

From what Josephine understood, Dragon Knights conjure dragon fire at will, make themselves more animal-like, and speak any language spoken to them. She had even heard once that a Dragon Knight could turn themselves into small lizards to move about without their enemy's notice, not to mention the Dragon companions.

"Because m'dear, your power has yet to be awakened. As the same for the other young ones that have come about. None of their magic has awakened," answered Dejen, in an amused tone. Josephine smiled back.

Whenever she had a problem and the answer to it was right in front of her, she would see the look on his face that he currently had. He even folded his arms and leaned back on the sink. The sunlight streaming through the window highlighted the gray hairs in his shaggy black hair. His old white shirt with three-fourth sleeves showed off his scarred, toned arms. When Josephine had said nothing more, Dejen explained.

"After birth, Dragon Hearts' eyes would show that they had Dragon souls. At four they would begin training, and then at the age of about six or seven their powers would "awaken" or spark, as well as their dragons would hatch.

However, you did not receive that training nor have been around hardly any magic. It's my belief that is why your powers haven't acted up till now."

Josephine looked at Dejen, still a little confused.

"A Dragon Knight's strength and such is natural. As for your ability to control whatever element you are and speak any language, it takes the hatching of your Dragon to do that."

"Okay, but then why now, all of the sudden? Why wait till now to tell me? Has something major happened?" Josephine questioned, folding her arms, frustrated.

Dejen sighed, rubbing his left shoulder. Josephine knew it was the shoulder where he had taken an arrow when he was a soldier in the Red Rose army.

"That reason is, my dear, because of the unrest. An old friend of mine has learned of late that a takeover is going to take place in the Red Rose Kingdom. The prince, whom we all know is a Dragon heart, is going on the run because of the fears of his father, our majesty, King Justin. Rumors are also spreading that a great evil is returning, the evil that destroyed the Dragon hearts in the first place," Dejen explained in a tired voice.

"Huh? But I thought they killed that guy? That Dragon heart who betrayed them?" inquired Jake.

"Yes, that's what I thought," said Josephine, frowning.

Josephine had read a few stories about the last major battle the Dragon Knights had fought, known as the Battle of the Betrayed, due to all the Dragon hearts who had broken their knightly oaths. The accounts she had studied said the last leader of the Dragon Hearts had killed the major betrayer and leader of the group known as the Shadow Dragon Alliance.

"That story I cannot tell, for I do not know the entire story myself. However, I know someone who does, and I promised her I would get you to her in Red Rose the moment that something ominous happened. The King's grip on the lords of the cities and control even within his own chambers has been slipping and changing as of late."

"Like what? Can't you be a little more precise?" Jake demanded of Dejen, tired of the wizard's lack of information.

Dejen's brown eyes became dark with anger. "Jake, I cannot tell you everything, for it's not safe, and even I am not aware of all the particulars. My friend just got word that the King has been making moves to secure a dark magical object made of shadow magic. Supposedly, he wants to use it to secure his control of the throne, for it is weakening. She wishes to move now before the king can get a hold of it. This shows that the Kingdom, the whole of Anglii truly, is about to become a dangerous place. You, the prince, and the others need to move to safety before it's too late."

Jake continued to glare at the wizard. "It's just it would be nice if we knew more before you take Josephine away!"

"Indeed. Josephine, are you going to go on this crazy journey or stay home where it is safe?" Aunt Sheila said, trying to keep her voice neutral.

Josephine took one look at Dejen's eyes and said without hesitation, "When do we leave?"

Dejen nodded and Aunt Shelia shook her head, but she smiled. Jake couldn't believe what he had heard.

"You're crazy, Josephine. You just found out that you are some kind of Dragon... thing...."

Josephine glared at him. She had a feeling she already knew what Jake was trying to get at, and she wasn't too pleased with the implication.

Jake shook his head at her glare. He glanced at Aunt Shelia as though pleading, "Come on, Josephine is a girl for the love of the land!"

"What, you think I can't be a Dragon knight because I'm a girl?" Josephine snarled, her eyes becoming nothing more than slits.

Jake backed up a little. He tried to talk back, but his words were sticking in his throat. Josephine waited another second to make sure her message had gotten across and then relaxed her face into a tiny smirk.

"You know, some of the toughest, strongest Dragon Knights were girls," laughed Dejen, watching the two. "Sandra Heartwell with her Dragon partner, Storm, and Akane with her Dragon partner, Crystal, to name two."

Jake found his voice yelling, "That's not what I'm saying! Honestly, I'm just thinking she's rushing into this!"

Worry was all over his face. "You haven't thought this through enough; you need time to think about this, Josephine. You don't even know where you are going or why!"

She sighed and placed a hand on her friend's shoulder. "Jake, you don't understand. The last word out of Drake City was that Shadow creatures were returning and that the royal guard has been gathering up for something. Something big is going to happen. I've read the history of the

Dragon Knights, and things are heating up. I know I should be mad that no one told me, but there seems to be more here than meets the eye."

Jake gaped at her. Dejen laughed again. "I see you learned very well indeed, Josephine. Not to brag or anything about my teaching skills." he smiled.

"Who cares about the past?" asked Jake.

Dejen shook his head, disappointed that Jake had not listened as well to his lessons as Josephine had. "You should care about it, Jake, for it is about to come back and haunt us. But come, Josephine, we must leave right now."

She rushed towards the stairs without looking at Jake or Aunt Shelia. She jumped over the old oak banister and up the stairs, past her parent's and brothers' rooms to the end of the hall into her small room. It was square shaped and in one corner was her four-poster oak bed. All over the room stood organized stacks of books she had inherited from her Grandfather Drageon. She pulled out her clothes from her dresser, rolled them, and stuffed as much as she could into her camping pack. She pulled out her sleeping roll and blanket, along with her small medicine kit that she always took on her camping trips with her brothers.

Josephine took a steady breath. She wiped the tears away, stood up straight, set her jaw in resolve, then walked out of the room with her pack, closing her door without looking back.

She spied Dejen through the window, bringing his black horse Wind Drum to the front to stand with Starlette. As she opened the door and stepped out onto the porch, Jake grabbed her and dragged her to the far side of the house, out of hearing range for Aunt Sheila and Dejen. Jake's jaw moving as though he was grinding his teeth, trying not to lose his temper.

"Jake, what is wrong with you?!" she demanded, shaking herself from his grip and folding her arms.

Jake placed his hands on her shoulders and whispered, "Can't a friend be scared about what his best friend is getting herself into? Why are you leaving? Let someone else fight; Dejen said that there are others. Prince Jonathan is rumored..."

Josephine shook her head slightly, never breaking eyes with Jake. She said in a kind but firm tone, "You know me better than that; I will not let someone else do my work for me just because I am a girl or for any other reason. Besides... I don't belong here. I don't fit in with this town's views of what a lady is."

Jake blinked, then shook his head.

Josephine sighed. "Jake, besides you, Starlette, and my brothers, you are the only one my age who is close to me. The people here tolerate me when it is in their best interests, but they do not care for me. Nor I them. Some do care, but they don't understand me and treat me differently. The wind is calling me to my dream. To see the world and make new friends; it's in my blood, Jake. There are bad things coming and if I can make... if I can help stop something from destroying our home..."

"I don't understand," he said at once.

Josephine placed a hand on his shoulder. "Jake, you have never wanted or imagined what could be over the horizon. Ever since I was little, I envied the Caminantes because they could go wherever their whims wished. To fly away with the birds, to see the world from above, below, and every view in between. I now will make my mark on the world."

Jake shook his head; a small tear and a crooked smile came to his round face.

"You realize that what you are about to do will not be a picnic. You'll probably have to fight trolls, and be in constant fear of death," he said, trying to speak reason to her.

"Oh, I know. Electrifying, isn't it? I'll be making new friends, learning how to fight with a sword..."

"Only you could make it sound like a sociable walk instead of a run to stay alive."

Jake took his hands off her shoulders, letting them drop to his sides, his shoulders sagging in defeat. He gave her a weary smile.

Josephine walked away a little, then turned to him and said, "It's one of my specialties. It's a wonderful talent to have when one is going on such a task. Whatever that will be, and I know I shall find out soon enough."

"You know the old saying about getting what you wish for?" said Jake, in one last effort, trying to plead, but his voice was small.

She rubbed his shoulder.

"I know. It might be too much for me to handle. But Jake... how am I ever going to know unless I go? Think about it this way: I am neither a warrior nor a simple village girl. I won't know which one I am until I walk down the road. You know what I'm like, Jake. You grew up with me."

She walked towards Starlette, looking at Jake with solemn eyes. She saw him glance at the tall maple where a half-made tree house sat tied to its branches, weathered and a little forlorn from lack of use. Jake took a deep breath and closed his eyes. Once he had done that, Jake walked up to Josephine and helped her with tying up her packs.

"Well, if I can't get you to stay, then how's about I go with you?"

Josephine closed her eyes and smiled. "Jake, you hate camping, are utterly petrified of snakes, not to mention you cannot stand being more than three feet off the ground."

Jake chuckled. "I guess I wouldn't be much help, would I?" He peered at her from under his long lashes.

"Jake, you will be a great help by looking after everyone here. Promise?" she said with a cheerless smile.

From afar, Dejen and Aunt Sheila watched the two. Aunt Sheila seemed as though she was hoping for something. Dejen shook his head at Aunt Sheila; his weather-beaten face was full of pity.

"Of course, Josephine, need not ask."

He smiled with authentic happiness this time, but the smile did not reach his eyes.

Josephine nodded, mounting Starlette.

"Don't worry, Jake. I will make sure I am only half as reckless as usual, if that makes you feel any better."

Starlette gave out a snort. Josephine tapped her on the head to reproach her.

Jake gave Josephine a dagger that he normally carried around to deal with poisonous snakes. He asked in a small voice, "Just don't get your head chopped off, promise?"

"Promise," she said back.

Dejen came over and then mounted his horse.

"Where are we going exactly?" Josephine asked nonchalantly as Aunt Sheila looked through Josephine's things one
more time.

"To Red Rose," answered Dejen, tightening Wind Drum's
reins.

"City?" frowned Josephine.

"No, forest."

Josephine and Jake both blinked in surprise.

"But that's right on the Royal castle grounds," said Jake.

Dejen taped Aunt Sheila on the shoulder, who glowered
but tied off Josephine's bags. She then stood beside Jake,
away from the horses.

"Yes, it is. An old friend of mine that I mentioned earlier,
named Gazelda lives there. We are going to meet her there
at Red Rose Forest. She will answer all of those questions
that you have, no doubt," Dejen said with a wistful grin.

"Wait, how can she live in the royal forest? It is part of the
castle grounds, and no one may be there unless given special
permission," Josephine challenged. Dejen's information totally threw her off, already wishing to meet this Gazelda,
whoever she was.

"You'll see," was all Dejen would say, the grin on his face
becoming a full-fledged smile. As he turned Wind Drum
around, a sharp loud roar ripped through the village, shaking the glass windows of the house and stables.

"What in the name of Red Rose..." gasped Aunt Shelia.

Another roar came to their ears, the sound of a large
animal crying in pain. Not long after, the earth shook as it
crashed to the ground. Without thinking, without knowing
why, Josephine snapped Starlette's reins and ran towards

the noise. Aunt Shelia yelled after her, but she did not stop or glance back.

⋈⋈⋈

"What was that awful sound, Dejen?" asked Aunt Sheila, placing her hand over her heart.

"Her destiny calling her," Dejen muttered.

Jake stared at the wizard, lost in his annoyingly cryptic response.

"Come, Jake, let's see if we can help." Dejen said, slapping Windrum's reins.

⋈⋈⋈

Starlette's hooves flew over the ground as she rushed to the noise. As they went around a curve in the road, Josephine's eyes went wide. She yanked hard on the unicorn's reins. Starlette let out a gasp. Lying on the northern path out of Wind Sage, covered in bite marks, was a red dragon.

Chapter Two
Destiny Calling in the Wind

Prince Jonathan Nicholas Falcon stared out into the garden, the wind tickling the spring blooms. He took a deep breath, enjoying the scents. Red Rose castle's shadow giving his hiding spot in the tree a little more camouflage.

Jonathan glanced at the castle, his home, and his family's legacy. It was both a home and a prison. From birth, the eldest Falcon son was designed to inherit and govern the castle and its lands after his father either step downed or died. Not that his father would give up his rule in any way shape or form less it was on pains of death and even then...

A wayward seed landed on his white shirt. He picked it up with the tips of his fingers, letting it fly away again on the wind.

A giggle came to his ears. He tilted his head to smile.

His younger sister whipped around the tree he was sitting in, waiting for one of her other brothers to appear, he assumed. Jonathan leaned back on the rough bark of the old oak tree, placing his hands behind his head.

Jonathan stifled a chuckle as Jordan appeared, frowning and walking slowly towards Jonathan's tree, trying to figure out where their sister had vanished. The gangly four-teen-year-old boy glanced up to see his eldest brother and glared. Jonathan chuckled and gave an unhelpful wave of the hand.

Jordan turned around to go back to the west side of the gardens.

"*Never leave your back exposed, you know better than that,*" thought Jonathan, as his little sister bounced on her brother and sent his weapon right into the budding bushes. Jordan jumped, yelped, and then glared.

"HEY!" he protested.

"HA! Come on Jordan, you can do better than that! Oh, that's right, you're a boy!" said Jenn, laughing cockily at him, her brown hair swaying in the wind. Jenn twirled her long, pointed-end tree branch in her right hand.

Jordan's brown eyes became inflamed by old-fashioned sibling rivalry.

"Okay, that's it!" yelled Jordan as he picked up his tree branch sword.

Jonathan had shaped it for him as he had Jenn's, not that Jordan couldn't do it himself. He had told him yesterday it was that Jonathan was better at it.

He charged into Jenn's guard.

"Jenn, watch it. You're going to pay for that," chuckled Jonathan.

A blissful peace came over the prince as he watched his siblings. Both had come far in their weapon studies. While their father neglected them, their mother trained her children to defend themselves, each other, and their kingdom.

Jonathan sighed at the thought as Jenn blocked Jordan's attack and went to counter. But as Jordan raised his stick, a deep voice not dissimilar to a squealing toad's came crashing through the garden courtyard.

"PRINCESS JENNIFER!"

"*Oh no*," groaned Jenn.

Jonathan tilted his head to see Lord Wilson stomping from the castle, shaking his finger and walking right past Jonathan's resting spot.

Jonathan could only wonder how Lord Wicked, a nickname that the royal children had christened him with, could move so fast being so fat. His lavish robes stretched over a vast stomach, which jiggled as he came to a halt.

"What do you think you are doing?! Young Princesses do not sword fight! I have told you this a thousand times!"

Jenn rolled her eyes.

"Don't you roll your eyes at me, young lady!"

"AND you should remember your place, Lord Wilson. I am the one and only princess of Red Rose Castle, and so I can do what I wish," she said in her huffy voice, flicking her hair back.

"Not sword fighting you cannot, young lady! You are but a twelve-year-old little girl, while I am your father's trusted advisor! He has reprimanded you before about being disrespectful to me," he said, narrowing his horrible green eyes.

Jenn looked over Lord Wilson's shoulder at Jonathan, pleading.

He smirked and nodded.

The prince called out to the fat Lord, "Perhaps the princess would rather fight for her land than send others to do it for her."

Lord Wilson turned on his heel to glare at him for the first time that day.

Jonathan leaned forward with his elbow resting on his knee, letting the other leg swing free from the tree branch.

"THERE YOU ARE!" he barked at Jonathan.

"Where else would I be?" chuckled Jonathan, ready to put to use the quick wit he had inherited from his mother.

"I will pretend I did not hear that!"

"Oh, so you do hear what I say?" Jonathan's dark brown eyes glared back at the Lord with contempt that had begun in early childhood.

Jenn and Jordan silently snickered behind him.

Lord Wilson fumed at the eldest prince. "Mind your tongue, Prince Jonathan! Come now, your father awaits you in the royal study."

He puffed himself up and walked away, doing a marvelous impersonation of a fat turkey.

Jonathan sighed. He jumped down out of the comfortable tree to follow Sir Serious, another nickname that Jenn came up for him, into the castle.

The two of them entered through a passageway that led from the gardens into the back hallways. Jonathan smelled the food for tonight's dinner wafting down from the west wing of the first floor. The sunlight was reflecting off the cool marble and stone floors, making the cavernous room seem a little brighter despite the shades of gray and browns.

They walked down the long hallway, passing the coronation oil paintings of past Kings of Red Rose Kingdom, including his grandfather, Rupert Falcon and his father, the current ruler, Justin Falcon. Jonathan stole a glance at his grandfather's painting, taking comfort in the brown eyes of the man whom he had regarded as a hero during his childhood.

Lord Wilson led the way to the northwest tower, stomping up the long staircase, grasping onto the solid oak banister as he galumphed up to the second floor. He stopped short at the curved wall, a part of the renovated tower to recover his breath.

The lord then pulled the oak doors wide to lead Jonathan into the King's private study. Private, as in only the king and Lord Wilson are permitted in the room. The study was a newer addition that his grandfather Rupert had built not long after he became king; circular to go with the natural curve of the tower with bookcases lining the room. A magnificent red oak desk was in the middle of the chamber's marble floor.

King Justin Falcon was engrossed in a letter as the two walked in. His blue-grey eyes focused on the parchment, his dark eyebrows arched in concentration, and his mouth wrinkled in a small smirk.

Jonathan noted how different he was from the king in just appearance.

In the opinions of various princesses and ladies-in-waiting, he was the living "prince charming". His charcoal black hair and chocolate brown eyes that were always either somber or full of trickster's glint. His physique was muscular, broad shouldered, and tall. Jonathan's nickname throughout the Kingdom was "Noble Dragon Eyes," for his eyes were Dragon eyes, and the people loved them, seeing him as the new hope for them.

Jonathan was donning a plain and wrinkled white cotton shirt, a tiny dragon charm on a simple silver chain was hanging from his neck, black leather pants, and matching boots. He was a sharp contrast to the traditional prince look and temperament. Jonathan did not see himself as the "prince charming" type, as many shallow lord's daughters discovered. And that was the way he liked it.

Unlike his father, whom he noticed was wearing fine, crushed, blood red velvet robes, his gold rings with his "small" jewel encrusted crown upon his brow. Once his father was almost as tall as Jonathan, but nowadays his shoulders were stooped with the weight of his greed. King Justin's graying black hair with matching beard completed in turning him from noble king to sour old ruler.

Jonathan came to a stop in front of his father. Lord Wicked stood beside him. Though Lord Wilson was of average height, he seemed much shorter than normal when he took a stand beside Jonathan's long and broad form. Lord Wilson, like his king, wore blood red robes of the finest velvet and wore many rings to show off his high status. Not only was he graying, but balding.

"Where were you?" the king asked, frowning at his son as he placed the letter into a pile.

"Watching Jenn and Jordan," he answered. Most days he would have lessons, but his tutor for military history, Captain Lance, was away on an assignment by his father, leaving his morning free. It had left him a prickly feeling, however. His father had been sending troops around the kingdom to obscure places without much hint on why. His childhood friends, serving together in Rose Red's military, warned him they were told to be ready to leave this morning on short notice.

The King glimpsed over his son for a minute, his look severe, then turned to his round advisor.

"We just received word from the mines; they found the black crystal of Cetus; well, it probably isn't the exact one he used, but it still is one."

"That is wonderful, your majesty!"

"Wait, what are you two talking about?" glared Jonathan, a sense of dread sweeping into his stomach from hearing the words "Cetus" and "black crystal".

"Remember the legend of Cetus the Dragon heart?" his father asked with an amused and smug face, folding his hands. A muscle in Jonathan's jaw twitched in annoyance. It was an important piece of history that every child in Anglii knew.

"It isn't legend, it is a fact. Sixty years ago, Cetus the Dragon Knight betrayed the Alliance, before James Dracolus used a powerful spell to defeat him. Cetus swore he would never surrender to them, and in one last effort he used a shadow magic crystal that..."

"Was thought to have been the last Shadow Stone, however," Lord Wilson spoke, adding to Jonathan's annoyance,

"There had been rumors that one was somewhere deep in the mines of the Mayani Mountains. A generous lord came forward about the stone and so we..."

"Decided to just take a gander, and if it was there, you would use it to gain more power?" snapped Jonathan at his father.

He stared right back at Jonathan, who did not falter at his father's gaze.

The king looked away, sighing, "It has been sixty years since that battle, and the Dragon Knights are gone save for you. This stone, if used right, will ensure that our kingdom will be always safe."

"Safe?! Father, that is crazy. Sheppard says shadow magic is pure evil, and even when used for noble reasons can still cause unwanted death and destruction! If the stone is real, it must be destroyed!" Jonathan stressed as he leaned forward on his father's desk so that the king had to look at him in the face.

He could not believe that his father was going this far to keep his power. Not only that, but how he kept this information secret. Jonathan, his mother, and brothers tried hard to keep their noses in whatever their father was doing so they could, if need be, stop whatever plan he had cooked up. In the past few years, they had interrupted several shadowy plans that involved snatching up Francian territory or causing issues with the Viken, but this one came as a low blow. His stomach jumped to his throat at the thought. The king shook his head.

"Sheppard is an old dragon that has gone irrational..." muttered Lord Wilson.

Jonathan turned his head and glared at the lord. "Sheppard has been the guardian dragon of this castle for the whole of his life, which was after the Battle of the Betrayed. There is magic to keep Shadow magic out, if you have forgotten, which he is a key part of. He knows much better than at least the two of you," he spat.

Jonathan knew he'd gone over the line, but he didn't care; he was well aware of what evil the two were conjuring up.

Lord Wilson snorted. He reprimanded Jonathan, waving his arm in the air, "Honestly, Jonathan, I do not know what that dragon has told you, but this Shadow crystal will help keep the other kingdoms in line..."

Jonathan snapped back, "What? Do you mean the War-Wink Kingdom? Last time I checked, you married off Holly in an arranged marriage so you could keep ties with War-Wink and earn a little extra income from those trading taxes you passed."

That injustice still left a bitter metallic taste in Jonathan's mouth. His loving cousin Holly did not deserve a cruel and unloving marriage. Of course, for royals, politics always came before family and love. The taxes were more unfair ones that his father had been adding a little at a time for the last several years, leaching from not only their own tradesmen but the Francian's traders as well.

"I would watch your accusations, young prince. Your cousin Holly married the prince of her own wish. I think you should get your facts straight before you go saying such hog wash," Lord Wilson said, inflating like a fat toad.

Jonathan snarled as he lowered his face to Lord Wilson's. "You cannot fool me. This is my kingdom, not yours. You would do well to remember that for your own good health. I am no mere five-year-old you can order around anymore, swiping at him with a walking stick."

"Enough," King Justin said in a tired voice, removing his glasses.

Jonathan straightened up, stood at attention.

"I understand your concern, I am not a fan of magic as you well know, as it was the reason my grandfather was slain, but," King Justin chuckled in a self-important voice as though talking to a young child scared of a spider, "This is truly for the good of everyone. I was going to give you the honor of going to Grand Mill town and retrieve the crystal, but obviously you do not see what it could…"

"Oh, I can see exactly what the crystal will do. It will bring death and despair to our kingdom and the entire land!" he shouted at him, still standing as though a soldier.

King Justin leaned back, shaking his head.

Jonathan then said, "And as you just said, you hate magic. Why would you want such a vile object like a shadow stone?"

Wilson barked, "That is enough, Prince Jonathan! If you wish to keep your birthright to the throne, I suggest…"

"If losing my right to rule my kingdom is the only way to save it, then so be it," Jonathan said, making eye contact with his father.

He shifted a little in his seat.

"I may hate magic, but this may truly be the best way to defend ourselves. As it is there have been mutters from the lords about the fact you are a Dragon heart that could cause issues…"

Jonathan turned to leave the room, and before he did, he turned to the two men.

"The only enemy we have is you and your hunger for power that will destroy us from the inside."

He stormed out of the room, almost running over someone. The someone being his mother, Queen Adriana.

"Mother, I-" She held up her hand to silence him.

"I know."

She glanced around behind him into her husband's study and then beckoned him to follow her. They walked in silence until she paused a moment to poke her head into the small study library to call out to her second-born son, "Jeremiah, please go get your sister and tell her to pack up, then find Jordan. Make sure no one realizes what you are doing except Mary and Sheppard."

Jeremiah walked out, pushing his black frame oval glasses up on his nose, nodded and headed off without a word. Queen Adriana said nothing to Jonathan until they were in her study. She closed the door and sat down behind her desk, interlocking her fingers and then staring right at Jonathan.

With a sigh, she said, "I see that your dear father and Lord Wilson tested you to see where your loyalties lie or to see how well they could control you."

"Should I have played along?" asked Jonathan, smiling at his mother, who chuckled.

"Well, we probably would have been able to find out what they were up to more easily, but what is done is done, nor do I think they would have trusted you, anyway. You are too much like..."

"You?" he grinned.

"True." she grinned back.

Jonathan's smile, though, faded at the thought of his father. "Mother, what is going on? Father has been gathering up the troops, readying them for something, and he was talking about them finding a shadow crystal. Is he plotting to go to war? Is that way he sent Nathaniel's father away to Francia?"

Queen Adriana sighed. "Your father and Lord Wicked," –Jonathan smiled–, "have been doing secret digs around the kingdom. Apparently, someone approached them and asked for help in finding a crystal. I only found that out from a spy of mine this morning."

"Yes, Lord Wilson mentioned some Lord. Who is it?"

Queen Adriana leaned back in her chair and shrugged. "No idea. From what I know from old friends of your grandfather's and Sheppard's, he may live in Drake City.... no surprises, really, since Drake is a crime-ridden city and plenty of shady characters come from there. Among them is the city's own dear Lord Vanell," she muttered with a slight scowl.

"Yeah, but how many are looking for a shadow crystal? I doubt it's Lord Vanell, for he is an underling for Lord Wicked," Jonathan pointed out.

"Indeed. Sir Etheve said Jamard is in the troop that is digging for that stone. Hopefully, he will send you some more information. I think your father has been doing this with smaller battalions so that we wouldn't find out, which is what has happened."

"Jamard is as loyal as Nathaniel. I am sure he will try if he can. He is level-headed enough," Jonathan said.

Jamard and Nathaniel were his childhood friends, childish ne'er-do-wells in his father's eyes. The three of them tended to get into lots of trouble, mostly for pranking Lord Wilson.

The queen sat up straight. She stared at her son for a moment, then sighed, "Jonathan, with this new plan of your father's, there is something we need to discuss."

Jonathan saw her brown eyes become somber, making his heart contract with worry.

"What is it, mother?"

She stood up and walked up to her window, her arms behind her back. Jonathan held his breath. She only did that when she had something important to tell. His mother, as long as Jonathan could remember, looked dignified and beautiful, even now, with the gray streaks that were showing in her bright brown hair. She, unlike her husband, was more inclined to dress in modest attire. Today she was in a simple linen dress, a short gold and pearl necklace around her long and noble throat.

"You were born with a destiny, my son. One beyond your heritage of this kingdom. Your blood is more than just royal, as you well know," his mother whispered.

She then reached into her desk to pull out a large silver ring adored with a large opal colored stone. She handed it to him.

Jonathan inspected it closely to see that engraved on either side of the stone were Dragon heads. He smiled at her, and a small smile appeared on her face. "In your blood, or I should say your soul, runs the power of a Dragon Heart, my Jonathan."

He smiled again. He and all the kingdom knew he was a Dragon Heart, mostly because Grandfather Rupert, before he died, hinted to him he was one. Both Grandfather and Queen Adriana had made sure that he had training beyond what a normal heir would receive. To top it all off, his eyes were the shape of a dragon's, so it wasn't too hard to figure out. It was also the reason, he knew, why Lord Wilson was always monitoring him, trying to take control of his life. He knew too that was why his father was nervous around him.

"Gee, I never knew," he teased, putting the ring on his left pointer finger. He noticed that the ring somehow fit perfectly, but thought little of it. His mother walked over to him, and with a soft hand, touched his cheek. He could smell her scent of lavender and lilac.

"I am proud of you, Jonathan. You have done things that most couldn't have done at such a young age," she said in a tender tone.

"Helps when you have a great mum," he whispered back. Jonathan felt he could never fully express to his mother how much he loved and respected her.

She smiled then walked back to the small window and said, "All these problems that are now arising, Grandfather Rupert claimed, would be from mistakes of their generation. He said that he and others felt so bad, for they were the ones who have caused the mess, but it will be the responsibility of the new generation to clean it up. Do you think that is true, Jonathan?"

He half shrugged and said, "From what I've learned, they did what they could do. The past is the past, and there is nothing else to do but to learn and move on. Fight in the present for the future."

It was something that he had learned from his readings of his forebears, including the Falcon who had built Red Rose Castle all those centuries ago.

She gave a slight nod and said, "Indeed, we must never forget the past, but not be stuck on it. We must learn from it and move on, and with the help of the past, we help our present and protect the future. That's what Maynu Foxglove used to say, well, in one form or another. You are not bitter about having to fight?" the Queen asked of him, moving to stand in front of him.

"No. Why should I be? Regardless of when or how it began, if something threatens my kingdom, then I must stop it."

The queen laughed, making his eyebrows go up a little. She placed her hand on his shoulder and said, "You are truly a Falcon, my dear little birdie."

"Mum, please don't call me that, huh?" said Jonathan with a slight twitch of his eyebrow.

His mother rolled her eyes. "You used to love it when I called you that."

Jonathan rolled his eyes, then smirked. "When I was five, Mum."

Mary, the Queen's lady-in-waiting, slipped through the door into the room holding Jonathan's leather back pack. She was in a simple brown frock and her yellow-gold hair was pulled into a braided bun. This surprised Jonathan because Mary always dressed befitting of her title.

"I packed for you as soon as Prince Jeremiah told me to help Princess Jenn," she whispered, handing it to him.

He took it and pulled it on as his mother gave him instructions.

"You and Jenn are to meet up with a friend of mine named Gazelda, in the Red Rose Forest. She will tell you everything that you need to know about what's going on in more detail. She will also be your teacher from this day forward, so treat her with utmost respect, for she could turn as nasty as your old archery teacher, Miss Mallory."

Jonathan moaned, "Just great. I still have a scar on the back of my neck from her bow when I missed that one time and it hit Lord Wilson's carriage. Which went what, for four miles? Honestly, it wasn't *that* bad. He finally got over the poison ivy and started to sit again without a terrible itch. She must have had a crush on him, that old... yeah," sighed Jonathan, stopping in mid-sentence from the look on his mother's face.

She chuckled and added in an amused tone, "If I remember correctly, you did that on purpose, for when you did that you could hit a bull's eye from seven yards."

Mary giggled with a hand over her mouth. Jonathan said nothing, but the corner of his mouth twitched a little.

"Anyway, keep a sharp eye on your sister. I don't want her here if Lord Wilson causes a coup. Your brothers and I will keep after things here and see what else your foolish father and Lord Wicked are up to for as long as we dare. If things become dangerous, we'll leave for Remile City to stay with cousin Kalie. Your father, or whoever is pulling his strings, is going to make a move soon, and I don't want any of us nearby for whatever plans he has cooked up."

Jonathan nodded, now understanding Mary's attire. It would make sense that if they, the children, left, so would she and Mary.

"Everything is ready, your highness. The horses are in the stables so Lord Wilson sees nothing," whispered Mary, rushing out with her petticoats swishing.

As Jonathan grabbed the door handle, his mother tapped on his shoulder to whisper in his ear. He had to lean over to hear her while she got on her tiptoes. "Just in case, we will really head through the forest and go to Tuatha Dé Danann kingdom for safe haven. Though I trust Mary, neither we nor you can take any chances."

"Wait, you know the Tuatha Dé Danann king and queen?" blinked Jonathan in shock.

"Yes, as a matter of fact, I do. Didn't know your mum had such high connections, did you?" she chuckled.

"I should have realized just because father did not bother to keep up the friendship, did not mean you would not," said Jonathan.

She smiled, then patted his arm, adopting a somber tone.

"Take the hidden passage through the kitchen into the stables, and take the long way around the castle to that old oak tree you lot love to climb so much."

"Right," Jonathan whispered, giving his mother a quick kiss on the cheek before running down the hallway.

The queen let out a long breath, then walked back to the window. She jumped when she realized a tear was rolling down her cheek. She brushed it away and whispered, looking out to the blue, almost white, sky, "Well dear Grandfather Rupert, it's starting. My eyas is spreading his wings and becoming a fully fledged falcon. Please bless him and the others who will fight with him."

The eldest and youngest Falcon children ran through the damp passage, then crawled up the ladder and into the massive stables. Jonathan helped his sister up, who was now wearing a simple green linen dress and riding boots. She pulled her curls into a ponytail while Jonathan swung his pack onto his large male unicorn, Ulysses.

He had been a gift from a foreign man for Jonathan's eighth birthday. Ulysses never knew his parents; he'd been captured as a small foal. He and Jonathan were close friends.

Jenn jumped up on her cream-colored mare, Sweet Rose.

Jonathan mounted Ulysses, who snorted in a low voice, "Yo, Jonathan, what's going on? Old twisted foot Egbert mounted me. He was so scared he almost put my saddle backwards and didn't even complain when I pointed it out. He never, *not* complains, the old rooster."

"I'll tell you when we get out of here and are in the woods."

As they left by the back doors, Jenn asked, "Why did you call Egbert an old rooster for?"

Ulysses snorted and said, "Cause like an old rooster, he pecks all the time and not to mention crows, too."

"Huh?" said Jenn, but Jonathan hit his unicorn on his head behind his horn and muttered,

"Shut it, Ulysses. Not now, not to Jenn. Better yet, never bring that up again. I'm going to kill Jamard for that one."

Jenn scratched her head, then shrugged as they moved around the garden with its flower patches that were budding, and the sleeping water fountains. Jonathan nearly froze when he saw troops walking up to the castle when they reached the side in front of the castle. But Ulysses kept creeping along, not taking notice of the troops.

"What is the guard doing?" muttered Jenn, watching them with a frown.

"Something in my gut tells me a coup d'état," said Jonathan darkly.

The two exchanged no more words until they were deep in the west side of Red Rose Forest. They stopped right in front of an old oak tree that had marks from arrows and the carved initials of all four Falcon children. The oak tree, like the maple and white oak trees around it, was budding, its leaves almost ready to bloom. Jonathan glanced up at the tops of the trees while Jenn pulled on her horse's reins.

"Okay, we're in the woods, so what is up with everything? Mary didn't tell me squat. She helped me pack, then shoved me into the passage and made me wait there till you came," whispered Jenn in a nervous tone.

"Someone enlisted father's help to find a shadow crystal, you know, something that's had Shadow magic channeled through it so it can store the power?"

Jenn nodded.

"Let me guess, they found one and, oh, let me guess, Lord Wicked is really behind everything. Such a shocker that is NOT," said Jenn, her voice echoing under the trees.

"According to father, yes, they have, and no doubt Lord Wicked is behind this, but he isn't the one who wants the stone. Somebody else does. Remember, father hates magic."

Jenn frowned, confused.

"I have no idea who it is, Jenn. Only that they are working for someone that is not for themselves. Anyway, for now, we have to wait for a friend of Mum's named Gazelda here. Hopefully she can tell us what's going on in full," explained Jonathan, glancing around the woods.

"Alright. Whatever you say, Dragon eyes," said Jenn, not too sure what was going on but was willing to follow wherever her eldest brother went.

Jonathan appreciated his sister's trust, but it felt like a heavy weight on his shoulders.

She gracefully dismounted her horse to climb the tree, while her brother took a seat underneath it, folding his arms and listening hard for a sign.

Chapter Three
Fair Lady: Teachers and Students

O n that fateful day when the Alliance was forever changed, I Fair Lady, along with Dragon Knight Master James Dracolus and young Knight Sandra Heartwell, were traveling back to Red Rose castle after delivering supplies to a nearby village.

At the time of my story, the Dragon Heart Alliance had found themselves up against a new dark influence not seen for centuries since the time of Taranis. An evil group was stirring up turmoil throughout Anglii, robbing caravans, attacking small villages, and they had murdered two high-ranking royalty using Shadow magic. The problem was that no one knew who was committing the atrocities. There was no reason given by them for their acts or clues to who they were. The only information that the Alliance had to go on was a rumor that they called themselves "The Shadow Dragon Alliance". Whenever an attack happened, by the time any of our knights got to where the incidents were occurring, the attackers were gone. The Shadow Dragon Alliance took care to leave no witnesses. We did not know if they were Shadow magicians organizing themselves or if an enemy kingdom was involved or truly what their intentions were, except maybe to cause havoc and discord within the alliance.

As we made our way back home on horseback, Hamlet and Storm flew above us in the sky; their blue and yellow scales glittering in the spring sun with their long leather wings making soft thumping noises as they flew, keeping a steady beat. The earth was uncommonly quiet that day. Hardly any birds were singing. The wind was brisk and stiff on our faces. The only other sound was that of a small spring's rushing water.

We were riding along in silence, the land under us shifted in a violent lunge. The horses tried to rear, and birds flew to get away from the trees. The quake stopped as suddenly as it had begun. Sandra cooed to her horse. James and I shared dark looks.

"Uh, Master James, any ideas on why the earth is shaking so much?" asked Sandra.

"It has to be another omen," I muttered.

James nodded. Hamlet, the ice dragon and Storm, the lightning dragon landed in front of us.

Hamlet folded his massive blue wings. He said, "That is the fifth quake we have had in this past week. There is something sinister going on, and it's getting stronger."

"Did you see anything as you were flying?" inquired James.

Hamlet shook his scaly head. "No. But I dare say the earth has sensed something... There's something in the wind, a foul smell, like blood and smoke."

"*It is*," I muttered under my breath.

"Do you think it has anything to do with this 'Shadow Dragon' Alliance, Sandra?" asked Storm warily.

"Who else has been causing problems? Master James, I... can smell the blood and smoke on the wind, too; do you think something has happened?" asked Sandra, pulling back her long curly blonde hair, her worried brown eyes on James.

He scratched his left ear, an old habit of his when he was pondering something.

"Smells fresh, and it's coming on the wind from the northwest. Storm, Hamlet, go fly on ahead and see if anything has happened."

Hamlet and Strom nodded, then with pronounced leaps the two flew up high and forward to the castle of Red Rose at a faster speed than they had been before the quake.

"James, I do not like this," I said at once as the two dragons disappeared out of sight.

"You're not the only one," muttered James as we started forward again, urging our horses to trot a little faster than before.

"What is there to worry about? We'll pound this dark Shadow Alliance or whatever into the ground, just like all the others before. They are just another group of misfits who want to take over," said Sandra with confidence.

"Never overestimate your powers, or underestimate your enemies," said James in a kind but commanding voice, "Because you are now a full-fledged Dragon Knight, you must be extra alert. Think before you act. Act your age instead of being like an overly curious hatchling."

I laughed, then said, "You're one to talk, James! I remember when a certain someone went and battled Zu before he became an ally—somebody bragged his head off, then went and got a nice big scar right on his..."

"NO need to remind me of that Fair Lady, as I was simply telling Sandra that because I... don't want her to make the same costly mistake I did," said James as he stiffened, sitting a little straighter in his saddle.

I laughed again. James was getting quite wise in his old age of forty-two, but he was still in certain respects a boy at heart.

Sandra glanced at her teacher with a cheeky smile. "I remember Zu mentioning that fight once; didn't he get you with a dagger right in your...?"

"Shush, Sandra," growled James, under my laughter.

"Besides, you have bigger things to worry about other than where my old battle scars are," he said, trying to get back a little of his dignity.

Sandra stared.

"Like what? All the trouble with the Shadow Dragons?"

"Other than that. The powers of the Dragon Knights are weakening," said James.

"I don't understand. What do you mean?" asked Sandra in a whisper, glancing between the two of us.

"Come on now, Sandra, haven't you noticed that there have been no new Dragon hearts born since you, Cetus, and the others?" I demanded of her.

Sandra half shrugged. "Sort of. Cetus and Rook both noted it the other day, but I wasn't paying much attention to them," she admitted.

"Watching Mark playing ball with Zu and the gang again?" I asked cheekily, raising an eyebrow at her.

Sandra's cheeks got pink, and she said with indignity, "I was not watching Mark!"

"No, she wasn't. It was someone older, wasn't it?" smirked James before I could say anything.

"Someone else older, wasn't it?" he said again. I looked back and forth from between the two, but neither looked at me nor gave me the slightest hint.

Sandra was glaring slightly at James, a little flushed. James had an enormous grin on his face.

"Anyway, there have been no new Dragon hearts, which means something big is going to happen, and it's probably not good," sighed James as we rode closer to home.

"Since when has anything good happened lately?" I muttered.

James looked at me with a sad face. "Fair Lady, do not lose hope yet."

I sighed as I watched Sandra's horse go ahead of us. "It's not like I have lost hope, it just... eludes me. Even with that prophecy..."

"I know. Mango isn't too happy, but even she admits it's a true prophecy," he said with a bitter tone of voice.

I stared at James. "Of course it is! You made it! And it means that we will have a chance! It..."

James smiled at me. I noticed his eyes, once a shocking white-blue, now seemed grey. "Prophecy is hardly clear and can be false. How do we know that my vision of a bright future for fighters is not one of those? As much as I appreciate your faith in me, Fair Lady, you know better than to trust it. For who am I to say what will be?"

"I know, I know, because nothing is absolute, and you write your own destiny no matter what, live your own life as best you can, and placing complete faith in a prophecy or a seer can be a deadly mistake. The future is never certain," I muttered, repeating what so many of the teachers of magic taught the young Dragon Knights in training.

"Exactly. Oh, Fair Lady, do you think we will fully ever follow the wise teachings that we give our own students?" James asked of me.

I sighed as we reached the crest of Red Rose hill. "Sadly, I don't think so, James."

"That's what I thought."

We rode on for a little bit longer, and then I said with a slight grin on my face, unable to help myself,

"Hey... James, is the scar still there?"

"Down, Fair Lady," James cautioned.

"Just asking. Maybe I should ask Kelly," I smirked.

He gave me a death glare, but I ignored it, laughing.

As we reached the top, the whole of Red Rose castle came into view. The castle, made of stone, was built on a large peak. The many wonderful and beautiful towers stood tall, the rose vines growing all over them, showing age. Below and around the castle's hill sat the city of Red Rose, protected by the winding wall, the large drawbridge and moat full of fresh water creatures that were not friendly to anyone save the people who fed them. That was just the inner wall.

The outer wall was about three feet away from the inner wall and had two large oak doors, which were enchanted by the residential wizard of Red Rose to do many different things. Uninvited guests would fly backwards into the woods if they tried to force themselves in. Those who were part of the Alliance had no worries; they were recognized by the spell, so if in a hurry they could continue without worry of being thrown twenty feet.

As the three of us rode down the path to the doors of Red Rose, Zu came rushing towards us. He was wearing brown pants and a rust-colored tunic. The worry in his eyes told me that indeed, something horrible had happened.

"James! There's been another attack!" he yelled.

"Where, Zu?" demanded James, jumping off his horse.

"Drake Town! Everyone is gathering in the main room."

Without hesitation, Sandra and James rushed forward, as I whirled around, turning southwest towards Drake. On the horizon, small clouds of smoke floating over the tree-tops. I knew the moment that I entered the castle, nothing would ever be the same again. I didn't know how I knew; it was just a feeling of dread in the pit of my stomach.

Chapter Four
The Guardian Named Gazelda

Josephine rushed forward and squatted beside the dragon, which had to be at least four yards longer than Starlette and weighed twice as much. Its dusty scales were a deep red, though not quite maroon, and its claws were as long as Josephine's leg. He was carrying a bag that was over his shoulders. The dragon's vast wings were only half folded to his side; the thin bat–wing– like–skin was covered in shallow scratches, and blood was slowly flowing out of them in little streams. There was a gash from the tip of his nose on the left side to just before his small, cat–like ears. His eyes were closed and his breathing was labored.

When Josephine placed her hand gently on his nose, the dragon opened his yellow eyes and said in a raspy voice, "Careful, young Mademoiselle, there's a gargoyle flying around. That's what attacked me."

"Shush, let me worry about your wounds. What is your name?" she said, looking around in her pack for cleansing ointment that she had. She couldn't cover all of his wounds, but she knew she had to at least disinfect them. She poured some water from her water pouch over his wounds to clean them.

"It is Ark."

Dejen and Jake came riding up.

"Dejen!" gasped the dragon, jumping up so fast that Josephine got water on her pants and shirt.

"NO, don't move, you'll only make your injuries worse!" pleaded Josephine, pushing down on his snout, only to feel as though her shoulder was almost pulled out of its socket.

"Dejen, Mandara said you were an ally. Friend of Gazelda, Fa..."

"Yes, I am. Ark, was it? I am guessing that you were delivering a certain item to Gazelda?" he said, placing a hand on Ark's chin, which made him calm down enough to make him lay his head back down on the ground. Jake and Josephine exchanged confused glances.

"Y–yes. It's in my bag. A gargoyle attacked me, and it may be back at any time. You must get it to Gazelda right away. The princess..." Ark choked.

"Is right here." Dejen smiled, and with that he picked up Ark's bag and handed it to Josephine.

She stared at the bag, unsure what do to with it.

"Well, well, I can't wait to get back to WarWink and brag that I delivered it right to.... ouch, Zut!" growled Ark as Dejen tried to exam his wound.

"Uh, what do I do with the bag?" asked Josephine, eyebrow arched.

"Go on, Josephine, in that bag is the key to your destiny. A symbol of what you are. Open it and wear it and whatever you do, don't give it up to anyone — wear it at all times." Dejen ordered at her before turning to Ark's other wounds.

Josephine gaped at Jake, who shrugged. She opened it to find inside a necklace. She pulled it out by its long silver chain to see it was a heart–shaped locket with an opaque stone in the middle. An elegant knot design bordered the stone, and at the top where the two sides met, two dragon heads with their snouts touching.

Josephine gazed at it, almost feeling a pull towards it. For a moment, she could hear a low humming coming from it. Without thinking, she touched the center stone.

It flashed, blinding Josephine for a second. It glowed a light blue, and then it flashed red, yellow, white, deep-sea blue, and dark orange before it stopped on the light blue color.

Jonathan was broken out of his concentration waiting for Gazelda to see to his amazement, the stone in the ring his mother gave him flash six different colors then stop on a diamond clarity.

Somewhere a few miles from Red Rose City, a young girl with red hair in a field smiled as the dagger she was holding flashed the same colors, but stopped back on red.

Not too far from where the red-haired girl was, in a large old house, five eggs were crackling, and then with a snap, they hatched and five small dragons emerged from them. A middle-aged woman smiled with approval. She patted the light blue Dragon hatchling on the head.

"Hello, young dragons."

Josephine was frozen in place, bile building up in her stomach. She realized several things at once. She could hear not only Jake breathing beside her, but his heartbeat, to his hair rustling from being tickled from the wind, the smell of Wally's hair on his shirt. As she stared at the necklace, she could see every line, every imperfection, on the surface. As sick to the stomach as she felt, taking in her super senses, she could not take her eyes off the necklace, it felt almost like the stone was alive, and she was waiting for it to tell her something.

"Josephine, are you okay?" asked Jake, kneeling beside her. Her face was like she was in a trance.

"Josephine?"

"I–I don't know. I feel different..." she said, not taking her eyes off the necklace.

"What..."

"I can't describe it."

She brought her hand up to her face and opened and closed her fist. She felt a little off center and found the cool spring breeze comforting.

"It's like liquid ice is flowing through my veins along my blood... I feel stronger...yet so dizzy."

Dejen stood up, wiping the dirt off his hands onto his pants.

"Dejen, what just happened?" she said, shaking her head, trying to clear her head of all the new sounds that were enveloping her.

"Your powers, Josephine."

He smiled, bending down and placing a hand on her shoulder, a joint cracking as he did. Josephine felt dizzy again, trying hard to not focus all at once on the wrinkles on Dejen's face.

Josephine went to say something when a horrible shrieking noise rang out. A large grey creature with yellow eyes, horns, bat wings, and a demon face was coming right for them. It seemed to be covered by a black slimy film.

Ark stood up on all fours, baring his fangs at the creature. "Not this time, you rotten demon! I don't know how you can be flying around during the daytime! But this time I will rip you apart!"

With an almighty roar that vibrated Josephine and Jake to their bones, Ark jumped into the sky and ripped after the gargoyle.

The gargoyle unleashed an unholy scream. Josephine, Jake, and Dejen covered their ears from the clash.

Dejen pulled Starlette forward and pushed Josephine to mount her.

"Josephine, GO! We'll be fine; you have to go and meet Gazelda!" he commanded, grabbing a long sword from Wind Drum's back while Jake ducked under Dejen's arm to get hold of Wind Drum and Willy. Dejen rushed forward to Ark and the gargoyle.

Josephine hesitated; she did not want to leave them.

"Josephine, go! It's probably after you! Get out of here!" yelled Jake, pulling the ruffled horses away.

"JOSEPHINE GET OUT OF HERE NOW!" yelled Dejen again.

"Josephine, the gentleman said to move it!" said Starlette, grabbing her sleeve.

She jumped up on Starlette, finding she had no choice. As Starlette went to gallop, she felt a blast of wind against her back. In one swinging moment, without looking, she pulled the short sword and drove it into the monster's mouth. It went through and through. The gargoyle shook its head vigorously, unable to yell out. Seizing the chance, Ark bit its tail. Its blood sprayed across Ark's face.

Starlette didn't wait for Josephine's nudge; she galloped off with Ark's roar still echoing in both of their ears. Josephine's stomach was still churning from the smell of the dragon's blood and the gargoyle's. She prayed with all her life that everyone was all right as Starlette galloped north, straight to Red Rose.

Jenn sighed with frustration.

"Remind me again how we are supposed to know this Gazelda person?" asked Jenn, hanging upside down by her legs from the limbs of the oak tree. Jonathan sighed and looked up at his sister. He focused on her voice, trying to ignore the enormous headache that had hit him after his ring had stopped flashing.

"Well, seeing how not many people live or travel through the royal forest, I don't think it'll be that hard to find her. And I would get down if I were you before your blood goes all to your head and it explodes."

Jenn stuck her tongue out at him and jumped down from the branch.

"It will not explode," she muttered.

"But you'll get dizzy," he muttered, staring hard into the waning light.

Jenn rolled her eyes before climbing back up the tree. They waited a little while longer until they heard something or someone walking towards them from the bush on their left. Jonathan sprang to his feet as he heard a woman's voice sighing in relief.

"Oh, thank all the Dragon spirits above!"

The two siblings did a double take when the person who the voice belonged to came out of the bushes. Instead of a woman standing in front of them, it was a large female unicorn. She was donning an elegant gold and crystal choker necklace around her neck; her mane was a pearly color, a rainbow shine to her coat, and fairly muscular legs. Upon her forehead sat a large gold horn. She turned her head to stare at them with bright yellow eyes. She walked a little closer to them and dipped her head slightly in a bow.

"Prince Jonathan, Princess Jennifer, I am Gazelda, guardian of the Red Rose Forest."

The two siblings exchanged "okay, this is different" glances.

"No offense, but how do I know that you really are who you say?" said Jonathan, taking his mother's words to heart.

The unicorn nodded her head and with a smile said, "Your mother told me that her nickname for you was birdie, and I knew your grandfather Rupert. His favorite time of day was twilight, when, as a kid, he used to sneak out his room window and climb down the vines and would sit on his horse Captain to enjoy it."

Jenn giggled, and Jonathan smirked.

"Okay, only someone who knew my mother would know that."

Gazelda smiled warmly. "I had the pleasure of knowing both your mother and grandfather."

Jonathan shook his head slightly with a confused face.

"You knew my grandfather?"

"I knew him as a young teenager," said Gazelda.

"You grew up with him?" asked Jenn.

"Yes, you could say that, Princess Jennifer," she said with a smirk on her face, making a coughing noise.

Jenn frowned. "You can just call me Jenn."

"All right then, Jenn," she nodded seriously, her mane tickling her long face.

"Okay, Lady Gazelda, now that we've established that we can trust you, what is happening?" asked Jonathan, folding his arms.

"You can call me Gazelda," she said, moving forward, "And you might as well get comfortable because this is going to be awhile."

Starlette ran at breakneck speed towards the Red Rose Forest. Josephine's heart was pounding hard in her chest and her stomach was in her throat. She could taste her fried eggs threatening to come back up, but she swallowed it back.

It was a clear run from Wind Sage village, but the pair worried about being followed. Josephine pulled out a map. Once they were sure they wouldn't be attacked, Starlette could rest.

"There are a few other roads that lead to Red Rose. I think we may want to take them. It'll be almost dark by the time we get there, but at least we know the chances of someone noticing us will be small."

"Yes, a very tall girl in pants riding a unicorn does stand out," remarked Starlette. Pursing her lips, Josephine let the comment pass.

Josephine pulled her hair back into a bun, then took out her black cloak, hoping the hood would conceal her. The leather jerkin she'd grabbed from her brother Rupert's room was bulky on her, helping her disguise.

With that two forged ahead, resting only once to eat and drink before rushing along.

The was sun was sitting on the horizon when the girl and unicorn reached the outskirts of Red Rose City. On either side of the road were the budding branches of Red Rose Forest, and at the path that split to the right was the long road to Red Rose City; further up on a hill on the left side path was Red Rose castle. There was a tall, proud stone wall that surrounded the front of the castle, which had two main towers in the most southern part of it. On either side of the building, more towers behind it stuck out, the tips being the only things visible. The two framing towers to Josephine appeared to be the oldest, as the vines were layered on thick like a green blanket.

"Okay, now what are we supposed to do?" asked Starlette, slowing down to a full stop.

Josephine turned around in her saddle to see that they were alone. The only living things around besides them were birds and a ginger cat. Twisting back the right way, she fiddled with the reins, thinking about what to do.

"Well, Dejen did say she lived in the woods, not the city or castle..."

Josephine glanced into the forest to see the trees in sharp relief from the setting sun. It was beautiful, but it didn't help them find where they should go.

"Pssst!"

"Starlette, was that you?"

"No," she answered, turning her ears for the source of the sound.

"Here, over here!" came the small voice again.

Josephine almost fell off Starlette when she saw what was talking to her. At first glance, she swore it was a firefly. A blue bell colored pixie. It was no larger than Josephine's hand. It glowed in the dim light, donning a simple one-piece dress. Its wings were light blue and as transparent as tracing paper.

"Come, come, are you Josephine Drageon of Wind Sage Village?" she asked, landing light-footed on a branch of a tree.

"Yes, I am," she said, unsure of this little creature that knew her name. It seemed trustworthy, but after the gargoyle she wasn't going to let her guard down.

"Lady Gazelda is going to be so happy!" she declared, clapping her hands together.

"Wait, you know this Gazelda person?"

The little pixie giggled, covering her face with her tiny hands. "Of course! She saved me once from almost getting caught by a nasty troll. Tried to rip my wings off, the putrid creature...Anyway, it doesn't matter! I must take you to Gazelda, young princess!"

She took to the air, her wings like a hummingbird's beating; they flapped rapidly, and in a blink, she raced off yelling to Josephine, "Come! Come! No time to waste!"

"You're telling me we are going to follow some pixie into those woods, that if we enter without permission, we could get thrown in jail?"

"Great way to start an already intriguing adventure, eh?" smirked Josephine, nudging Starlette to run after the pixie.

"Sure, not like this adventure hasn't already been intriguing, being told you're a Dragon Knight, almost becoming a snack for a gargoyle, which I might add fly normally at night but was flying instead in broad daylight not anywhere near an abandoned church, graveyard or mountain area but in *Wind Sage*. Really, Josephine, if this is your idea of fun..."

"I thought you said proper people aren't sarcastic," Josephine said, leading Starlette to where the pixie was going.

"I'm tired and I grew up with you," mumbled Starlette, her ears back in annoyance.

Josephine chuckled.

"Sooo...what are we waiting for again?" asked Jenn as she was hanging once more, upside down, from the old tree. Gazelda chuckled (which sounded like a horse snorting).

"A friend of mine is bringing a special girl here to come with us. She is for sure a Dragon heart, perhaps even the chosen one."

"Chosen one, as in the princess of the Dragon hearts in, like the prophecy?" asked Jenn enthusiastically.

"Well, yes. From what I can tell, your brother is most likely the prince."

Jonathan laughed, shaking his head.

"Figures," muttered Jenn.

"Anyway, we'll know if a certain magical item reacts to her. Speaking of, I wonder where Ark is with it?" she said, more to herself, tilting her head up and back to search the sky.

"Ark? Isn't he a famous dragon?" Jenn questioned, jumping down from the tree.

"He was a young dragon warrior during the Last Battle. You know, a dragon that doesn't have a special connection with a human."

As fascinating as that was, Jonathan found that his interest was to find out more about this girl...

"Pray tell Gazelda, who is this girl we are going to meet?" he asked nonchalantly.

Gazelda held back a smile and said, "An exceptional girl from what my friend Dejen has told me. She is adventurous and enjoys being outdoors a great deal. Doesn't like sitting still for long."

"Gee, I wonder who that sounds like," mocked Jenn, sticking her tongue out at her brother as she walked around the tree.

Jonathan ignored her.

"Yes, well, I only hope she can get here in one piece," sighed Gazelda.

At that instant, Josephine was ducking the low branches and trying to keep up with the pixie.

"Um, excuse me, but what is your name?" asked Josephine as politely as she could without getting branches in her mouth.

"My name is Jessie Bell!" she called back, totally intent on reaching their destination. Josephine let out a breath of slight frustration, her bangs going up and falling back down on her face.

"Honestly, that creature is like a raging stallion," panted Starlette. When they finally caught up with Jessie Bell, she was standing in midair with a large goofy grin plastered on her face.

"Here she is, Lady Gazelda!" she said, twirling around in the air to face her.

"Finally!" Starlette gasped under her breath.

"Oh, thank goodness! Thank you so much, dear Jessie Bell!"

When Starlette stopped at the small clearing, Josephine's jaw almost dropped when she was at last face to face with Gazelda. She was a unicorn, only she was much more muscular and older than Starlette, with a longer horn.

The unicorn nodded to Jessie Bell, who tilted her head, then flew up to sit down in a tree.

Gazelda was not only beautiful, but held herself with an air of authority. She stood straight (for a unicorn). With a hint of humor in her voice, she addressed Josephine, "You must be Josephine Drageon. You look just as Dejen told me."

Josephine did not know what to say, so she nodded her head with a nervous smile. "And you must be Gazelda, the guardian of the Red Rose Forest. Sadly, Dejen never gave the impression of what you would be like."

Gazelda laughed. Josephine found it was like a neighing sound but yet not; she was not too sure what it was like.

"Pretty and quick-witted. But need not be formal, Josephine, please just Gazelda. Now that you have finally arrived, we can get moving. Oh yes, here, I need to first introduce you to someone..."

Josephine's jaw dropped when Gazelda turned.

Chapter Five
Josephine, meet Jonathan

When Gazelda turned, Josephine wanted to half laugh, half drool. The boy that she saw was not like any of the boys that she knew back home. They were stocky farmers, and he was anything but those things. This boy was tall and muscular, but not over the top with muscles; his Dragon eyes were a dark chocolate brown, showing deep warmth. His midnight-colored hair was tossed like he'd been in a windstorm. He wore simple attire and around his neck was a silver chain with a silver Dragon-shaped charm. When she noticed it, a sudden realization came to her.

"Jonathan Falcon, meet Josephine Drageon, Josephine, Jonathan."

Josephine quickly curtsied to him. For, after all, he was the prince and future king of the kingdom. When she looked up at him, she was surprised to see a disgruntled look on his face.

"Please do not bow to me, Josephine."

He walked over to her and took her hand, then lightly kissed it. "Besides, you are too strong looking of a young woman to bow to anyone; please, just call me Jonathan."

Josephine felt quite flattered. She felt he wasn't trying to flirt with her or anything like that. His face seemed exceptionally serious and his eyes—there was a type of depth there she couldn't explain, but she knew she was willing to stare into them.

She had been told by several people in the village that Jonathan was a kind and modest prince who did not take to the thought of anyone being under him. She noticed behind him that the young brunette that she figured was Princess Jennifer rolled her eyes at her brother. Meanwhile, Josephine did not notice that her necklace had changed to a lavender color.

"Why thank you, Jonathan. You live up to your reputation of being modest."

She smirked, which Jonathan matched.

"MODEST HA! Only when there's a pretty girl. Though that's not very often..." snorted Jenn.

"And that is my sister Jennifer, if you didn't already know," sighed Jonathan.

"Just call me Jenn!" she smiled.

"All right, Jenn," grinned Josephine.

Gazelda cleared her throat. "Now that the formalities are done, we need to get down to business. Josephine, where is Dejen? Please don't tell me you came by yourself?" she sighed, turning to her.

"I had to. Dejen was going to come, but just as we were about to leave, a gargoyle attacked this red dragon named Ark and..."

"Wait, a gargoyle attacked Ark?" asked Gazelda, her eyes narrowing.

"Yes, he is fine; at least, he was when I was ordered by Dejen to run. Ark made me take this–" Josephine pulled out the heart necklace to show it to Gazelda.

"As Starlette and I were about to bolt, the gargoyle came after us, and I had to use my dagger, and I pierced it through its mouth. Last thing I saw was Ark tearing after it."

Gazelda made a weird noise from her throat, resembling a growl and a snort. "So, he somehow was able to do a shadow spell on a gargoyle. Not only that, figured out that I didn't have the necklace, but Mandara did...it seems that somebody is onto us."

Out of the corner of her eye, Josephine noticed Jonathan raise his eyebrow at her. She took a breath to keep her smirk off her face.

"I don't get it. Gargoyles can only fly at night," said Jenn with a raised eyebrow and a pout.

"You are correct, Jenn, but there is a Shadow magic spell that can fix that to a point. When you touched the necklace, Josephine, did it glow?"

"Yes! And when it stopped, I felt...different." Josephine could feel things but she didn't know what, like she could feel emotions other than her own. She also was finding the warm sun not as pleasant as she usually did.

"Hm. I am guessing that your ring glowed, too, did it not, Jonathan?" smirked Gazelda.

He blinked in surprise, then nodded.

"Yeah, it did, and like Josephine said, I felt a bit different too... it's like cotton has been taken out of my ears, it's giving me a headache..." he said, rubbing his temple.

Josephine felt her own head in sympathy at the remark. It was disconcerting to hear everyone's heartbeats, from Gazelda's large heart to Jessie bell's tiny one.

Gazelda smiled. "That's great. Means everything is in order. Now we can head on out and answer some of those questions that I am sure you have. First things first, though. Jessie Bell, I need you to send out two messages: first to Dejen, let him know that Josephine made it to us in one piece. The other to Mandara, letting her know what has happened and that the necklace made it to its rightful owner."

"Should I send one to Mango?" she asked, standing up.

"No, she'll already know what has happened. Come along everyone, we need to get to Rave Town as soon as we possibly can. This means you'll have to doze in your saddles on the way, for we have no time to waste."

Jenn grumbled, but mounted anyway. Josephine's eyes widen again when she saw what Prince Jonathan had. His mount was a sturdy looking male unicorn with a creamy coat and muscles that even made Gazelda look a little small.

"Maybe this won't be so bad..." said Starlette in a hushed voice as Jonathan mounted his unicorn.

He chuckled at the admiring look on Josephine's and Starlette's faces.

"This is Ulysses."

"Hello." Ulysses smiled, dipping his head.

"Hello, my name is Starlette," she answered, trying to keep from giggling.

Josephine rolled her eyes, which Jonathan noticed, making him smirk.

"Let's go now, let's move," barked Gazelda, galloping forward. The others followed suit, with Jessie Bell waving them off.

As the group reached the end of the old path, (Jonathan had a few red marks for not ducking in time to evade the branches) Gazelda stopped. Josephine opened her mouth to ask why, when they heard a man's hard voice in the quiet of the night:

"Now listen well. Prince Jonathan and Princess Jennifer have escaped. They are traitors to the crown. If seen, you are to arrest them at once. I have already had the Queen and the two other princes detained to be safe. They are believed to be trying to overthrow our king."

"But Lord Wilson..." piped up a younger male's voice, but the older man snapped at him.

"No buts! Prince Jonathan practically threatened the king! Therefore, they must be treated like criminals. No exception."

"Yes, Lord Wilson."

"*Lord Wilson?*" thought Josephine. She shifted in her saddle and found that even though it was fairly dark, she could see extremely well. She saw through the forest brush to see a short, fat man in deep wine-red robes and a short beard on his face with a receding hairline. Lord Wilson yelled at the group of royal guards to get moving and walked off.

Josephine was ready to move when Jonathan suddenly dismounted Ulysses, snuck up behind the royal archer who had spoken up, then yanked him into the bushes away from the other troops.

"HEY!" the young man yelled, but Jonathan covered his mouth and pressed his finger to his own mouth.

"Shush, Nathaniel! Do you want us to get caught?"

The young archer's eyes went wide. He knocked away Jonathan's hand before ruffling his brown hair in bewilderment. "Jumping Fairy Lights Jonathan! Are you crazy?! Did you not hear what Lord Wilson said? If he catches us, we are in deep crap!" he whispered.

"Yeah, I kinda figured that out by the way Lord Wicked was talking as though if he could, he would hang us up by our toes. Are mum and my brothers alright?"

Nathaniel sighed and nodded. "If you consider being confined to your own rooms like a prisoner, being okay. Your mother was going to use one of the secret passages to escape, but I convinced her to wait till we had heard from you. Sheppard is being watched, too; he's stuck in the courtyard."

"Where's Jamard and Mary? Your father?"

"Jamard is heading for Grand Mill. He said there was mentioned of going into the mines or something was all he could tell me before he had to leave. Mary is locked up with your mother. As for my father, he's with the rest of the troops at the ready, but no idea why as far as I know. I was training with the rest of the archers when a messenger for Wilson came to tell us to assemble."

Jonathan let out a breath of relief.

Gazelda said, "Nathaniel, can you give the queen a message? Tell her Gazelda said that the hatchlings have flown. Wandering off towards a loyal family member would be a good suggestion, and that Sheppard should fly to high hills."

Nathaniel looked at her confused but shook his head that he understood he was to give her the message, even if he didn't understand it.

"Keep an eye on Lord Wicked, too, if you can. Send a message if you hear anything major, and make sure you're not caught," Jonathan added.

"Aye, whatever you say, but don't get caught, you," said Nathaniel.

He and Jonathan shook hands before Nathaniel snuck off to rejoin his fellow archers.

"I assume that we'll have to go the long way around?" asked Josephine.

"Yes, we'll have to go straight forward to take the old thorn path to Rave Town. It takes longer, but it is probably safer."

The group waited till the road was clear and then crossed into the other side of Red Rose Forest to race towards Rave Town.

As they did, Josephine glanced at Jonathan and asked, "Are you sure we can trust Nathaniel?"

"Yes. He has been my best friend besides Jamard, Ulysses, and Sheppard, the old guardian dragon of Red Rose. We grew up together. No worries, they are loyal to a fault."

They went on in silence, the sharp and cold wind blowing in their faces.

Chapter Six
Fair Lady: The Approaching Conflict

I ran to the castle, my skirts gathered tight in my fists. I cut my stride short in the foyer as King Nicholas Falcon was standing in the main entrance hall talking to James. King Nicholas muttered to him in a low voice. James nodded to him in understanding. He dashed into the meeting room through the side doorway from the main hall.

I took a moment to take in the appearance of the King of Red Rose. He was standing tall in black robes, the very definition of pride. On his chest was a pin with the crest of the Dragon Knight Alliance—two gold dragons twisted around a sword, behind a shield with a color to represent each element. On his robes themselves was the Red Rose Kingdom crest—a falcon and a Dragon on either side of a shield with a red rose in the Dragon's mouth and a white rose in the Falcon's claw. Settled atop his head, King Nicholas was wearing a simple gold crown on his black and gray-peppered hair. I sucked in a deep breath as I walked up to him.

"Fair Lady," the king greeted in a solemn voice with a nod.

"Your Majesty, what has happened?"

His brown eyes were filled with a heart wrenching level of sorrow that I had never seen before.

The King pulled back his bangs and said, "I was going to announce it to everyone but you being a teacher, you deserve to hear it first..."

"Oh, King Nicholas...," I whispered, scared of what he was going to say, my heart pounding hard in my chest.

He looked right into my eyes. "It was the Shadow Dragon Alliance. They... slaughtered almost all of Drake, killing Rook, Catalina, and their dragons in the process when they tried to stop them."

I placed a hand over my heart, and a tear came down my cheek. I had taught them all. They were part of the newest group of Dragon heart masters. Rook had been a strong wind knight, as was his Dragon Lenore. Catalina was kind and capable of great water magic, as was her Dragon, Mar.

"No... they were so young!" I cried.

"I know. But that is not the worse part."

I gaped with shock. "What? There is more?"

"It seems the enemy has taken Reed, Razor, Maruko, and Cain," said King Nicholas bitterly, placing a gentle hand on my shoulder.

"Why would they take them but kill the others?" I muttered, my voice a hoarse whisper.

King Nicholas shook his head. "I do not know, Fair Lady. Maybe the others will know something. Come, everyone is waiting for us in the meeting room. I'm... I'm afraid that we may not all survive the battle this time."

"It's total war, isn't it?" I asked as we walked in.

"I'm afraid so. After all the other attacks over the past year, there can be no question of the Shadow's intentions."

The cavernous room echoed with the urgent whispers of everyone around. Once inside the room, I followed King Nicholas to the front of the long, red oak table. He took his spot at the head.

As I sat down beside Queen Maria, who looked at me with a face of worry, I nodded to her, then turned my head to see who else was there. I noted that the two seats at the top of the table on my left side were empty. Sydney, the resident wizard of Red Rose castle, and Jewelvana, one of our only two Dragon Knight seers. James's seat, too, was empty.

Zu sat down along with many other royal people, including King Kingdor of the Tuatha Dé Danann. I shared a nod with King Kingdor, then turned my head in time to see James sit down between Dragon Masters Shoney McHale and Manyu Foxglove.

The king of Red Rose stood, causing a hush to fall over the council. Sandra, I noticed, sat down near the end of the table, beside Cetus and Matt, two other apprentice knights who had only become official Dragon Knights three months ago.

The King glanced around solemnly before he announced to everyone the horrible news:

"My dear Alliance members, the Shadow Dragons have hit again; they have destroyed Drake town and killed all the youngest Dragon hearts except Rachel and her Dragon Viper, in what must have been an ambush. Not only was she the only Dragon heart alive, some of the other dead dragons and Dragon knights... their bodies are missing. Reed, Razor, Maruko, and Cain."

There was an outcry from everyone before he continued,

"Rook died trying to save Rachel and a little girl—I'm sorry, Mina."

I glanced down at Rook's cousin, Mina. She was staring at the table with a terrified expression. Sandra placed a trembling hand on Mina's hand from across the table. The youngest of the Dragon Knights, they were a close-knit group.

"Did Rachel or any of the survivors tell you who or what attacked them? Was it really this Dark Dragon Alliance?" asked Cetus, leaning forward as well to place a gentle hand on Mina's. Cetus was one of the smartest of the Dragon Knights I had ever taught. His skill with the sword and his control of ice magic were almost as great as James's. So, of course, he was on the same page as the rest of us.

"No, unfortunately, Rachel lost a substantial amount of blood and is unconscious. She is with the faeries and Diana now. We hope she recovers enough to speak to us, but it is touch and go. As for your other question, there is no doubt. The murderers left their mark of a Black Rose with a thorn vine wrapped around it," he said, throwing the evidence down on the table. Another round of whispers went around the table, then stopped again.

"The few that survived that were conscious said all they saw were Shadow creatures rushing around, killing anything that moved."

Sandra took her eyes away from Mina to ask in a crackly voice, "Your Majesty, is the army that is coming... are they the ones who...?"

"No. This army came just after Turku and the others rescued Rachel and the survivors from Drake. The army just... seemed to come from thin air. It's marching from the area of the village of Wind Sage and the Mountains of Clocha Móra," grumbled Mango.

She was the resident witch of the Mango's desert and a warrior of Dragon heart Alliance who did many things for us, one of which being a magic expert.

"An all-out surrounding battle," sighed James.

"I wonder why they took the bodies of some but left the rest..." muttered Manyu.

King Maxus Castel of WarWink stood from his seat, his shadow spreading out across the table. He was an ugly man, with a bit of a twisted face, like a sneer was permanently affixed.

"Who cares? It probably is just some necromancers. There is a large army coming towards us! It was just luck that I came to visit with some of our troops! It would have, of course, been more helpful if we had found out something more about these Shadow Dragons..."

King Maxus glared at James, who said nothing, keeping his face blank. I, however, curled my lip. It was not like James and the others had not been searching desperately for any information about the Shadow Dragons. There was just no information to be had.

"Yes, we are very aware of this, King Maxus," said Dragon Heart Master Michael Grace admitted calmly, only a slight look of disgust in his green eyes.

King Maxus glared at him. Nobody thought much of the King of WarWink Kingdom from the Land of Francia. He flaunted his wealth around by wearing many rings and a diamond incrusted crown. No one really liked the Francians for their arrogance, but WarWink was a key ally for Red Rose and the Dragon Knight Alliance.

Michael's twin sister, Dragon heart master Nina Grace, glared at King Maxus, her temper overflowing as she ripped into the king.

"Of course, it is important! If it is necromancers, we need to warn everyone to look out for them! Those were our young charges! Those twisted magicians may use their bodies to get under our skin; to make us hesitate in battle so they can slaughter us! And if you are trying to imply that James hasn't been doing everything in his power to find..."

"Nina!" James barked.

She glanced at him, then folded her arms and said nothing more. King Maxus glanced at Nina, the smug look wiped from his face, replaced by one of intimidation as he sat cowering in his chair. I suppressed the urge to laugh at his chubby face.

"What can you tell from all this, dearest Lady Mango?" asked Cetus, calmly and firmly.

She sighed, ruffled up her extra curly brown hair, and then stated, "That there is a traitor in our midst."

"What?!" yelled King Kingdor, glancing at James, then back to Mango.

Others, too, around the room stared at Mango with aghast faces, muttering.

I shushed them as Cetus asked,

"What makes you say this, Lady Mango?"

"Simple logic shows it, if a person has the brains to see it. Only someone who knew exactly what our movements are could guide an army of this magnitude without so much as giving an arrow to hint it. Not to mention keeping the information about this Dark Alliance out of our range of hearing."

"There is more than that, my dear Lady Mango," came a voice from the side door.

Sydney the wizard and Jewelvana, a Dragon heart with her dragonling, Eclipse, walked in to the Alliance council meeting. Jewelvana, in her usual flamboyant attire, flopped down in her chair, her over-sized jewelry clinking as she crossed her legs, then glanced out at the group of people. The black, miniature dragon took a seat on her left shoulder, wrapping his long tail along her upper-arm.

Sydney was wearing his formal black robes adorned with the bright crest of the Red Rose across the chest. He stood stoically, then folded his arms into the large sleeves of his robes, his piercing blue eyes moving from face to face, illuminated further by his silvery hair.

I frowned and said to Sydney, "Pray tell, Sydney, what in the name of the Dragon spirits are you talking about?"

"That there is more than one — there are, in fact, several traitors."

"Well, who the bloody heck is it?" demanded Nina.

"It doesn't matter now. What matters is the fight we are about to fight." Sydney's eyes flashed down the table and back.

I glimpsed at him, confused. It almost sounded like he knew or suspected who the traitors were.

"What do you mean, it does not matter?!" barked Nina, her fiery green dragon eyes blazing with anger.

"Nina..." muttered Dragon heart master Jessica Williams, speaking for the first time, but Nina ignored her best friend.

"Of course it matters! We must catch them before they get away and make them tell us all that they know!"

"No," said Manyu, looking at Nina before giving Sydney a side-glanced.

"Even if they join the Shadow Dragons during the fight, it probably wouldn't make much of a difference. Anyway, if they do, they will be dead before they could do anything. Of this, I am sure. We must concentrate on protecting this castle. Red Rose Kingdom must not fall, for if it does the whole of Anglii will fall, then WarWink, after that the rest of the world. If they get hold of the shrine..."

"Too right," muttered James.

"What does your power of future sight show you, James?" I asked in a low tone.

Everyone stopped muttering, and all turned to look at him.

"That we have many traitors, two to be certain, though I cannot say who."

He closed his somber eyes and then continued,

"This fight will depend on us to stop the Shadow dragons, but we will not be the ones that will defeat this evil. The next generation of Dragon hearts to come will be the ones to stop them, not us. Our powers are no longer strong enough. All we can do now is save Red Rose to help and hopefully save the future."

Jewelvana snorted, "Foolish wishing. We are going to fail; there is no hope. These Shadow dragons have powers we do not! They can choke out one's soul, cut one's throat without a sound, take over a person's body... I saw it all in my crystal ball that we will fall to the shadows."

"With an attitude like that, we will," muttered Hamlet from behind James, sitting with the other dragons.

"Stuff your foolish hog slop, Jewelvana! You have never been good at future seeing in the first place, secondly the future is never one hundred percent certain, and lastly, no amount of it will help us win! Only our will, magic, and swords will do that now!" yelled Mango at Jewelvana.

Eclipse growled at Mango, showing his tiny sharp teeth, scales raised like a cat's fur when angry. Mango hissed at the black dragonling, which scared it enough to make it retreat behind Jewelvana.

I sighed at the two. Mango and Jewelvana had never liked each other, and it was not unusual for them to fight like this. Once they had gotten so bad, Mango made Eclipse flash several shades of pink for a month straight.

"Now, now, Mango," said Sydney with a chuckle.

"Yes, well, anyway," said King Nicholas with a tired voice, looking warily at Jewelvana and Mango, "We have mostly all the main parts of the Alliance army here, so we stand a good chance."

"Personally, I'd feel better if the Xian clan were here. Mei, have you heard anything from your clan leader?" asked Sydney.

The tall, slender acrobat fighter closed her eyes and shook her head, her long, silky hair moving back and forth.

"No, sire, nothing, and it is not like my people to not come to the aid of our allies."

"It's fine, Mei. We'll just have to make do," said James, though he had the same curious look that I had.

"Come, Dragon Knights," sighed King Nicholas. "Let us go fight for what may be our last time together. But remember this, we are not just fighting for ourselves — we are fighting for the future generation."

As everyone moved and got mobilized, Nina, Mike, and Jessica rushed up to join us up at the front. They were the other Dragon Masters from James's generation.

"James, if you don't…"

James simply held up his hand to shush Nina. The two shared a flame- igniting stare.

"I know exactly what you are thinking, but I don't know who the traitors are, anyway. Look," he said, lowering his voice that only we could hear, "Right now the important thing is to protect the shrine. I want you and Jessica to do that. Michael and the rest of us will be on the front line. No arguments, all right?"

"Yes, oh fearless leader," muttered Nina as she swung her skirt, her auburn ponytail swinging with it.

"And stop calling me that!" he yelled as she disappeared around the corner.

Jessica shook her head, then kissed Shoney on the cheek and whispered something indecipherable. She then nodded and said to James in her calm voice,

"Later, oh fearless leader," before she, too, disappeared.

Hamlet chuckled and said, "What do you want us to do?"

"Organize the Dragons," sighed James.

As Hamlet and the other Dragons left, Shoney chuckled and said as we left the hall, "Ah, some nicknames just won't die, don't they, James?"

"Yeah, like Jessica's nickname for you, ah what was it...?" James pulled a mocking face of concentration.

"Cuddle bunny, if I remember rightly," I snickered.

Shoney got a little red in the cheeks. "Figures you would bring that up just before an enormous battle," he complained. But then he smiled and said,

"Well, at least Nina's nickname for me is more flattering, same with Manyu's."

"Yeah, yeah," muttered James.

"Honestly, what is it with Nina and nicknames? It's not like she doesn't know our names," laughed Maynu in his deep exotic voice.

"It's just Nina's thing, like Fair Lady chugging down an entire bottle of mead in one sitting after losing another bet," said Shoney.

I glared as we reached the armory to gather our gear. "I only did that once, and we were celebrating his appointment as fearless leader, not because I lost that bloody bet," I grumbled as James and the others laughed.

"But you admit you are a sore loser," pointed out Manyu.

"Ech, whatever Desert Lightning."

We grabbed our gear and moved out to the front courtyard to see their dragon companions sitting and waiting.

"Hurry up! Don't have all day, ya know!" complained Ken, the water dragon, flapping his wings.

"You know, it's the human who is supposed to be impatient, not the dragon," I muttered as they mounted their partners.

"We'll be back soon," said Spark in a gentle tone as the three Dragons of bright yellow, ice blue, and green blue jumped off into the darkening sky. As they flew off to scout out the army, all those splendid memories flowed through my mind. Instead of happiness, sadness filled me, for I knew it was all gone.

It was time to fight.

Chapter Seven
The Dragon Knights of Fire, Water, and Lightning

I t was almost dawn when they reached the edge of Red Rose Forest where the Vanora Prairie started, with the Mayani Mountains sitting on its horizon. On the edge of the Vanora Prairie was the large town of Rave. Josephine was asleep, leaning on Starlette until someone shook her with a gentle hand to wake her. She blinked to see it was Jenn.

"We're almost there, I think. We are almost clear of the forest."

Jenn yawned wide enough to show all her teeth, which made Josephine giggle.

"Sorry about that," Jenn grinned, rubbing the sleep from her eyes.

"Jenn isn't much of a morning person. Be careful, her breath can be really rank," teased Jonathan.

Jenn stuck her tongue out at him.

"You surprise me. You don't talk like royalty," said Josephine with a smile.

Jonathan smiled back. "I may have been taught to be a prince, but I choose to be myself, which irked my father and Lord Wilson to no end. It also did not help when, instead of spending time with other high-born member of court, I played with Jamard and Nathaniel, both sons of high-ranking royal soldiers, with rebellious streaks."

"And your mother?" smiled Josephine.

"She found it amusing, especially during the large royal feasts when I and my older cousin Holly would start food fights." He chuckled, pausing Ulysses to let Jenn and Josephine catch up with them.

"Truly? I had heard that the queen was beautiful and kind, but I never heard a tale of her sense of humor," smiled Josephine, imaging a younger Jonathan and Princess Holly covering a hall of royalty in food.

Jonathan smiled at her. His eyes were bright and warm in the rising sun.

"Your mother must be as well, to let you wear pants and all."

Josephine threw her head back in laughter. "Yes, to beauty, kindness, and humor, no to the pants. Neither she nor my aunt approves of my un-lady like dress, but they just gave up. I remember fondly once telling my mother I could not wear a dress, for I couldn't then wrestle with my brothers, for obvious reasons."

"Cute. How old were you?"

"Twelve, and to this day hold Wind Sage Village's best body and arm-wrestling spot," chuckled Josephine.

Jonathan gawked after her, a grin plastered on his face.

"She's a keeper," muttered Ulysses.

Jonathan tapped him on the head as Starlette snorted in displeasure.

"Well, you have me beat; the only thing I was great at was sword fighting and spit wads," remarked Jonathan.

"Ah, something in common we both are good at—spit wads."

Josephine grinned at him, raising her shoulder a little, then turning back forward. Jonathan's eyebrows went up, and Ulysses snickered.

Jenn leaned over to whisper to Josephine, keeping her voice low. "So, what do you think of my brother so far? Do you like him?"

"He is different from any boy I've ever met. Not exactly what I would picture as a prince, but still interesting. He is braver than my dear friend Jake; he wants to avoid trouble at all costs. And he also wasn't very good at making spit wads."

"For good reason. He thinks before he goes and does something," noted Starlette.

"So, you like him?" pressed Jenn.

"Yeah, I think so."

Though Josephine couldn't see his face, she knew he was smiling.

The group went quiet after that, following Gazelda as she navigated them through the forest. It amazed Josephine how the tall trees that made up the roof of the woods. The trees were like all the trees in Anglii, budding for spring, the early rays of the morning sun streaking down. Josephine was caught up in the beauty of the ancient trees when suddenly she felt the hair on the back of her neck stand up.

Josephine glanced around again, but saw nothing. But her hair was still prickly; she knew they were being watched. She went to say something when the wind changed direction. Josephine could smell strawberries...

Wait, it was barely spring yet, too early for strawberries! Josephine went to yell when a tree branch as thick as Starlette's back leg fell near them. Sweet Rose tried to rear, and then Josephine heard someone yelling,

"*Subsisto!*"

She didn't understand it, though, at first. Then she felt something behind her. Josephine reached for her hunting knife when she felt the icy blade of a sword in the front of her nose.

"Declare thy name if you are truly a Dragon heart, or else I shall cut your throat!"

Josephine's instincts kicked in. She dug her heels into Starlette, who reared; Josephine whipped her arm around, dagger in hand, at the creature behind her. A flash of red hair jumped out of the way of her dagger.

Starlette turned to face the sword- brandishing figure. Josephine stared into intense green eyes. They were like hers and Jonathan's: dragon shaped. And they stared un-waveringly back at her, glaring. It was as though the red head was sizing her up.

Gazelda walked forward and said, "EVE! It's all right! It's me with the new Dragon nights! For Nicholas's sake Eve, put that away... jumping the fence as always..."

The girl named Eve glanced back at Gazelda, then placed her sword in a scabbard on her belt. She stepped back a little, but kept her eyes locked on Josephine. Josephine shivered a little. This was an ally?

Eve turned and said, "Sorry Gazelda, royal guards have been sifting through Rave Town and the main roads since last night. Word got out that the queen and the royal kids were arrested for treason but then escaped. When the royal troops rolled in, Grandpa sent us into the old wood so that they wouldn't find us."

"Why wouldn't they follow you into here?" asked Jenn.

Eve smirked. Josephine concluded this girl had a dark sense of humor.

"They think that nymphs that live here like to draw in young men and kill them because some stupid soldiers a few years back got lost in the woods and died. Which, of course, is false. Only a few nymphs live here and they are all gentle. The most dangerous things in this forest are the weather, rotting branches, me and Flash."

"Flash?"

Eve grinned, then let out a high whistle. A lizard about a foot and a half long from head to tail crawled with amazing speed onto Eve's shoulder. It had the face of an iguana and the body shape of a chameleon. It changed color like one too; Eve was wearing a deep red tunic, and the creature called Flash changed from bark brown to the red color. Jenn let out a "aw".

"This is an..."

"An Iguacharmon," Josephine smiled.

Eve's eyebrow went up a little, a small smirk on her face, folding her arms. "Indeed. You have seen one before?"

"Only in books that my teacher owned," answered Josephine, matching Eve's look.

The red head nodded, as though approving her. Josephine wasn't sure if that was a good thing or not. Yet.

"Eve! What is going on? What's with all the yelling in Dragon language? Please don't tell me you were so hot-headed and eager to fight that you've hurt Gazelda or someone else?!"

The girl that went with the frustrated voice emerged from the woods. She had brown hair with blue streaks and sea-blue eyes. Beside her was a girl just as tall as Josephine. She had dark skin, braided midnight black hair, and bright yellow eyes. Both had swords at their hips and had dragon eyes. The shorter girl jumped forward to wrap her arms around Gazelda.

"Oh, yeah, like there are sooo many evil unicorns in Anglii that I could mistake Gazelda for," mocked Eve, rolling her eyes.

"Oh, Gazelda, we were so worried with the troops searching for us..." muttered the blue-eyed Dragon heart girl.

Gazelda pulled away from the girl, eyes wide. "You, as in you three?"

She nodded. "Either somebody in town tipped off the king that we were here..." started Eve.

"Which I doubt," mumbled the dark-skinned girl.

"*Or,*" Eve growled, "The soldiers are under someone else's orders besides the king's, which I admit," said Eve, glaring at her friends, "is possible seeing how they came to Wave's and my house first. The families with the old names."

Gazelda nodded. "In that case, we have someone who is smart, which means we must be ten times that. Come, let's sit for a bit and then develop our next plan."

"And some explanations," muttered Jenn.

Eve waved her arm to follow her. She and the other two, without a sound, ran right into the woods off the path. Three yards in, the group came to a pile of fallen trees. Eve jumped up and over what had to be at least six feet off the ground. The girl with blue streaks in her hair muttered something like "show off" and led them around the trees to their little camp.

It impressed Josephine. With all the thick trees, thorn plants, and the fallen debris, no one would be willing to come far into the forest to search. Beyond the fallen trees was the girls' camp. The trees made it like a natural fort. They had made a small campfire, and their gear was spread out around it. The girls moved their things aside to make room as they went to sit on a few falling logs. Gazelda ordered everyone, including herself, she joked, to rest for a bit and then they would talk. Josephine could only nod as she laid down on a blanket, only dimly aware that someone placed a blanket over her.

Josephine woke up to see the camp shrouded in firelight. The sun had set and everyone else was awake. Jonathan smiled and offered her some warm soup, which she gladly took.

"We never introduced ourselves, did we?" smiled Eve as Josephine ate. She was standing against a tree. She seemed to have warmed up a little to her, Josephine guessed, for she was more than willing to talk to her without glaring.

"I'm Eve Nina Grace," she smirked. Her eyes, though green, seemed to have a fire within them, as Josephine had observed the first time.

Josephine politely nodded. Eve, Josephine noted, was wearing a deep red tunic and long leather pants, a sword on her side and high black boots.

"Josephine Drageon."

"I'm Wave Katherine Kelly Williams," said the girl who was sitting in front of Eve and across from Josephine, smiling widely. She observed she was taller than Eve but shorter than the dark-skinned girl. Her light brown hair with blue streaks was up in a ponytail, showing her heart-shaped face. Wave was wearing a blue cotton shirt with a long black skirt with a high cut and under it were black stockings and black boots. She, too, had a sword.

"And I'm Marie Ann Nikki ThunderFly, Marie for short," smiled the last Dragon Heart.

She was about as tall as Josephine was. Marie was donning a brown tunic and brown leather pants, a sword, and buckled boots. Her speech was Angliian, but Josephine could hear another accent, a rich one, like an islander's, underneath. Her Dragon eyes were a shocking pale yellow that glowed against her skin.

"Now that we are all introduced and fed—Eve full report," Gazelda said, sitting at the head of the circle.

Eve sighed and shifted her weight. "After the morning's deliveries were made, rumors came from the Innkeeper that a whole slew of royal troops were heading right for us in Rave Town, destination: the Mayni mines. They were looking for anyone with strange looking eyes, and if found, to be taken right into custody."

"Dragon eyes, in other words," mumbled Marie.

Eve smirked without humor and continued. "Yeah, the troops arrived about three hours later with reports that the queen and royal children were under arrest by our oh so wonderful king for treason," Eve grumbled sarcastically. "Also, that Prince Jonathan and Princess Jenn had escaped, and there is a hefty reward for their capture."

"Alive or dead?" snorted Jonathan, who Josephine noticed had taken a seat right beside her.

"Princess Jenn alive. You dead is a welcomed option," Eve laughed hollowly. "Saves them from having to do the deed themselves. Loyal subjects may be less likely to resist whatever they are doing if an enthusiastic bounty hunter kills the prince."

Josephine looked at Jonathan, worried, but saw he was relaxed in his posture. He noticed Josephine's worried expression and shrugged. "It's not the primary concern right now."

Gazelda nodded. "No, it is not. But before we get to the problem with the mines..." She tilted her head at Jonathan and Josephine. "I have a feeling that you have a thousand questions, especially you, Josephine."

Josephine nodded her head, placing her bowl aside. She took a deep breath, then said, "I am at a loss here. Not only have I found out I'm a Dragon heart of legend, but the princess? What does that even mean, and how do you know I'm this princess? Why me and not Eve, Wave, or Marie? I had no ties to the Dragon hearts as far as I know, not in my immediate family, at least."

Gazelda's eyes seemed to laugh as Josephine spoke. Gazelda replied, saying, "The Vanora necklace. The Vanora Crystal has not flashed for half a century plus ten. Only when a Dragon Heart touches it will flash, and only the princess could make it do so. Eve, Wave, and Marie have all tried to activate it with no success. You are the young girl in the prophecy. There is a bit more to it, but that can wait till later when we go visit a friend more experience with magic."

"You mean this necklace?" asked Josephine, pulling it out from under her shirt.

"Yes, it is a symbol of your title. And from the looks of the color of the necklace, your powers have awakened as well as everyone else's."

Marie, Eve, and Wave all nodded their heads, but Jonathan shrugged.

Gazelda smirked. "Do you have the ring that your mother gave you?"

Jonathan nodded. "Yeah, and I noticed it flashed earlier. And I can hear everything in a three-mile radius. I assume that means they have?"

"Yes. Good. That means that we can move to the next step."

"What do you mean by our 'powers have awakened'?" asked Josephine.

"Well, what do you know of the Dragon knights, Josephine?"

"From what Dejen told me, Dragon knights were humans with the souls and abilities of dragons. Their eyes normally reflect their dragons' souls and even element. They could control the element which they were, and they shared a special connection with a dragon that would hatch the same time their powers would surface."

Gazelda nodded. "I see Dejen taught you fine. A Dragon heart is born with powers, but they are quiescent. Usually, a Dragon heart's power would awaken at the age of five or six, then they would be trained, but due to the fact that you all have been around little to no magic, it's no surprise they've only just appeared."

"What kind of powers do we have?" asked Josephine, sweeping her hair back.

"Dragon Elemental magic. That is one misconception about the Dragon hearts that they are like witches or wizards. They have the will and strength of whatever type of dragon they are, but they perform nothing else like that." Gazelda shifted her weight then turned to Eve.

"For instance, Eve has green eyes, so that doesn't give away her element, but her vivid red hair does. There is almost always one physical trait that stands out, whether it is the eyes or hair that reflects the element that the Dragon heart is. She is a Grace, and most of the time people will follow the family element, and the Grace family members are usually fire dragons. She is also a master swords woman."

"Not to mention a hothead," smirked Marie, who earned herself a glare from Eve.

"Also, I cannot be burned by fire," said Eve, turning to Josephine.

She picked up a blazing stick from the fire and placed it against her skin. Josephine and Jenn gasped. When Eve lifted the stick away, her skin was burn free. She threw the stick back into the fire and snickered at the looks on Josephine, Jenn, and Jonathan's faces.

"Wow, not a single mark," said Jenn, in awe.

"When you are a Dragon heart, you are completely immune to the effects of your element. Just like a dragon," said Wave.

"Right. In my case, my yellow eyes tell all. Lightning hitting me won't faze me," said Marie.

"So, okay, let me guess, water?" asked Jenn, catching on.

Wave smiled and nodded. "Water. I can't drown due to this fact."

Josephine stared at Jonathan with sparkling eyes. His eyes were brown and his hair black. That really didn't give her much to go on. But then the wind tickled him as it went around him and not through him.

"Wind," said Josephine quietly.

"Huh?" Jonathan looked curiously at her.

"You must be a wind element dragon. The wind goes around you instead of hitting you straight on." He looked surprised at her but then smiled.

"You got me. I figured out a long time ago that I was a wind type. When I was young, I could be outside in storm winds, but they wouldn't knock me off my feet. The wind would... sort of go around me. I was always a sucker for watching the birds and wishing I could fly with them."

Gazelda looked at Josephine with renewed hope. "Very good, Josephine."

"Well, that only leaves two elements," chuckled Jonathan, looking at Josephine's icy-blue eyes.

"I'm guessing I'm the ice dragon." She smiled, thinking of earlier when the air had become cooler and she had found it so pleasant.

Gazelda nodded. "Right. Anyway, your powers. You, of course, have great strength, hearing, seeing, feeling, and even sensing. Dragon hearts, like dragons, have the gift of language. Dragons and Dragon hearts are empaths. Emotions are something you can sense and decipher which comes in handy when negotiating with diplomats. You can understand and speak any language as long as you listen. Last, do things with your respective elements, helped along with your dragons."

"That's it?" pouted Jenn.

"That's it?! Jenn, that's something right there! It depends on one's skills and training, whether they can cut it," said Gazelda.

Josephine smiled and asked, "What about turning into a lizard?"

Gazelda laughed. "I will never know how that rumor started... No, you can't change into a lizard."

"We, however, become more dragon–like if we tap into that part of us that is harsh and wild," said Eve. "Our eyes will become slits, nails long like claws, and our teeth will become more like fangs. But the power of shifting is not one of our powers. I am guessing because of those things, is where the rumor came from."

"Your powers, however, won't be great, nor can you start training using elemental magic until we introduce you to your dragons. Even then, it would be best to not experiment until we can find proper teachers for you. Elemental magic is hard to master, and many Dragon hearts didn't even bother with it. Eve, this means watch your temper," she said sternly at Eve, who had a sour look.

"Yeah, yeah, I know."

"So, what kind of bond do we have with our dragons?" asked Josephine.

"That will have to wait till we go to get them," replied Gazelda.

"How will learn how use our empath powers?" asked Jonathan. Josephine glanced at Gazelda. Josephine felt as though she was already getting a hand on those. She could match the feelings that were coming off the others to their facial expressions easily, and when she focused on other things, she could ignore it.

"With time. For now, it's all about focusing on thing at a time, like your enhanced sight and so forth. Being older, I can imagine it's more overwhelming," said Gazelda. Josephine felt a wave of sympathy come from off her.

"Very. My headache at least has finally gone away..." sighed Jonathan.

"It will take time. As Gazelda said, us being older, it'll take a bit to get adjusted vs those like my aunt who powers awoke when they were younger. If it makes you feel better, I had a colossal headache too for a bit..." sighed Eve, scratching her temple.

"I got a bit nauseated from everyone's emotions," sighed Wave.

"But wait, you said that Josephine is the princess, but what makes you think Jonathan is the prince?" demanded Jenn, back tracking.

Gazelda smiled. "It's just a theory. Jonathan is of royal blood and is a Dragon Heart, so it fits."

"That and he's the only guy here," smirked Eve.

Jonathan laughed. "So, I'm just the prince because I'm the only guy to show, eh?"

Eve gave a cheeky smile. "Not as special as you thought you were, Mr. Wind Prince?"

Josephine giggled. Ulysses chuckled behind him. Jonathan raised his eyebrow at the two of them.

"Yes, well... it really doesn't matter right now because regardless, we have bigger problems on our hands," smirked Gazelda.

"Yeah, the mines," muttered Jenn.

"Right. I've been tracking the activities of the kingdom for a while now, and from what I have gathered, the king," Gazelda glanced over at Jonathan, "... was asked by someone to locate a shadow crystal, and my source tipped me off, saying that they found one."

"Is it the same one that Cetus used?" asked Jonathan.

Gazelda shrugged. "Probably not. No one knows what happened to that one after the last battle of the Dragon hearts. Though I suspect it probably got destroyed."

"So what exactly is a shadow crystal? I know Zankeno created them, but besides that, I do not know," asked Josephine, shifting her weight on her log.

"Pure darkness," answered Marie, a grim look on her face. "As you know, long ago in the beginning, before the founding of the Light Dragons of the Crystal Alliance, a terrible wizard known as Zankeno or the 'Shadow King' created these crystals. Shadow crystals were rare magical stones that the legendary dark wizard used; a person who uses it can gain unholy power. He took shadows and with his magic compressed them into stones that stored power. They were meant to assist one during a difficult or long battle. Shadow magic is pure hate, and all the emotions related to it. The reason for its name is that creatures named Shadows were born through this magic and react to ones who do it. They are said to be the souls of the dead who died horribly or who had evil in their hearts and could not move on to the next life, becoming nothing more than parasitic black shapes."

Eve jumped in to add, "Zankeno had some kind of magic he used to summon them and let the spirits wander the land, taking the life that they once had. Part of what makes them so dangerous is that they excrete a venom that if someone is bitten, came consume a person and kill them within hours, unless you are treated with Phoenix magic or Unicorn magic."

"What about Dragon hearts?" asked Starlette, glancing at Josephine.

"Dragon hearts can survive a Shadow creature attack as well, if they are not too weak or have a Vanora Crystal object to help purify them," answered Marie.

"That's what we will be fighting..." muttered Josephine.

Starlette nudged her. She smiled in return.

"Who would want a Shadow crystal?" asked Jenn. "I mean, the art of the Shadow magicians died out, didn't it? And Cetus is dead, right?"

"We wish. Just because we haven't heard of any for a long while does not mean there aren't any, and Cetus is alive. He is the one searching for it, most likely. And why does anyone turn to evil? Power," shrugged Gazelda.

"But I thought Cetus died!" said Jenn in a shocked voice.

Gazelda shook her head. "No. He fled that day after James defeated him, swearing revenge."

"I don't get it really... who was he, anyway?" Jenn asked, looking at Gazelda's long face.

Gazelda sighed sadly. "Cetus was a traitor.... he fought alongside everyone with a mask that not even James Dracolus could see through."

"He used a Shadow crystal to enhance and gain his shadow powers. Cetus then tried to use it with another crystal to combine with his dragon powers to fight, didn't he? My grandfather mentioned it once," said Jonathan. Josephine noticed he was playing with his necklace charm as he said this.

"Yes, Cetus used two crystals. He had a Shadow crystal and the mythical dragon crystal known as the Vanora Crystal, which you three are wearing."

Josephine touched the necklace with her hand. The crystal was icy cold.

"There are six total Vanora objects that were forged after the battle. The necklace, ring, dagger, rod, crown, and the bracelet," explained Gazelda.

"How did he gain this Shadow crystal and the Vanora Crystal?" asked Josephine.

Gazelda shrugged her shoulders. "No idea. He probably found it during his solo missions for the alliance. As for the Vanora Crystal... it was being guarded by an ally clan of

Jinzhou named the Xian. Cetus raided the temple that was protecting it."

"How many of these dark crystals are there?" asked Jenn.

"Precious few are still around. They destroyed many of them during some of the most epic battles of the two Shadow Wars. But rumors say that Zankeno's followers stored a few away in a mountainside, but which one, no one knew."

"Why would he want one now?" asked Jenn. She played with Sweet Rose's bridle for something to do with her hands.

"Shadow magic is like a drinking problem. Once you start doing it, it is hard, or in most cases, impossible, to stop. He needs this crystal to restore his shadow magic. It was drained during his fight with Dragon Master James," explained Marie.

"His Dragon powers, too?" asked Josephine with a frown.

Gazelda again shook her head. "Dragon and Shadow magic are totally different. Dragon magic cannot be totally drained to where you can't use it anymore, unlike shadow magic. James's Dragon magic was weakened, but not drained. He still could use a small amount of his ice powers, and his other natural abilities stayed the same. Cetus was.... somewhat purified, for lack of a better word. He needs the Shadow crystal to help him channel and maintain his Shadow powers, which he had to learn through horrible training. I am sure that all he had has long been taken out of his system by his dragon powers. Though the memories and want for that magic were not," she added grimly.

"Indeed. Shadow and Dragon magic are like oil and water. No matter what they say, when the term 'Shadow dragon' is used, it only means that they are Dragon hearts that use Shadow magic. Nothing more," said Marie, waving her hands in a gesture to finalize the topic.

"Except for the fact that they can do both," pointed out Jenn.

"Yes, but just because they can doesn't mean much to a true Dragon heart," said Gazelda with a crooked smile.

"We have some amount of protection from these creatures, right?" asked Josephine. She touched the necklace around her neck again, feeling the magic hidden within it.

Marie nodded. "If you have a strong will and/or heart, the Shadows cannot take over your body and mind. Shadows naturally will retract once they get close enough to you."

"That's how you fight them. When they flinch, you stab them until they are no more," said Eve.

Gazelda sighed. "The creatures themselves are no problem; however, the magician controlling them is a matter in of itself. But anyway...."

"Yeah, so what is the plan?" asked Jonathan.

Josephine wanted to ask what sort of training a magician goes through to control Shadows, but she got the feeling that Gazelda did not want to go into details. As though she could read Josephine's mind, Gazelda looked at her, shaking her head.

"We need to figure out a way to get to Grand Mill," said Wave.

Eve walked forward to her pack, then pulled out a scroll that turned out to be a map of Vanora Prairie and Grand Mill Town.

"From what little I could get before we left; this entire area is covered in soldiers with more coming in the next two days escorting a Lord representing, I'm guessing, Cetus. The mines are about here..." She pointed to the land that lay in front of where the Mayni Mountains start.

"I can confirm that from what my father told me. There is a shadow stone," said Jonathan.

"The only problem we're going to have, assuming, of course, that we can sneak in and get back out again, is trying to find where the Shadow stone is. It's a large network those mines..." sighed Marie.

Josephine gazed at the map. The vision from before in the front of her mind. She knelt down without thinking and laid her hand on the map, aware of every bump under her hand. She let her hand move on its own. Stopping to hover over the northwestern mines. Eve raised an eyebrow. Marie kneeled beside Josephine to see where she had stopped.

"The northwestern mines... those are the oldest mines. No one has dug there in many, many years," Marie whispered, unsure of what had just happened.

"I think it's there. I don't know how, but I think that's where the shadow stone is. I... I saw something earlier before that gargoyle attacked me ..." stammered Josephine, aware of everyone's shocked glazes.

Gazelda's eyes widened. "You mean... you had a vision, Josephine?"

"I guess so."

Jonathan was gazing at her with curiosity.

"Is that bad or something?" asked Jenn.

Marie shook her head. "No, it's not unheard of, just rare. There are few Dragon hearts with the gift of foresight."

"Indeed.... have you had any other visions, Josephine?" asked Gazelda.

"No...," said Josephine.

Gazelda nodded her head, then narrowed her eyes. "Most of them are believed to be guidance from the dragon spirits of old. Many of the past Dragon leaders were picked due to having that future vision. Just be careful, Josephine. The art of seeing what may come is not exact. Don't depend on it. It's not very... consistent. There can be tremendous gaps between visions on top of it being inaccurate."

"Good, that can be rule number seven... never depend on the powers of fortunetelling or foresight. For you can almost always change it," said Eve.

Josephine blinked. "Rules?"

Wave laughed. "The Dragon Heart Alliance's rules of life. Some invention of Eve's," she said, waving her hand in the air.

Eve growled. "Is not. My great- aunt and great-grandfather were working on them. It's just a bunch of things that they learned while training or fighting. They never finished them or wrote them down, sadly, so I'm going to make our own list. Dragons spirits only know we'll need them."

"So, I'm guessing you're only up to rule number seven?" smirked Jonathan.

"Yeah. So far, I've got only seven," she said.

"Well, what are they?" asked Jenn, sitting up straight, eyes bright.

Eve smiled and said, "Well, one is 'Love is the most important thing of all,' two is 'Never let Wave cook.'"

Marie laughed and Wave "humphed".

"Why dare I ask?" asked Jonathan.

"Duh, she can't cook. The Dragon heart of water could burn water and did once," chuckled Eve.

Wave glared at Eve, who ignored it. "Anyway... rule number three is 'Trust your gut when it says something is wrong,' four is..."

"Rule number four is never calling Eve 'Shorty' or anything that mocks her height," laughed Marie.

Eve hissed then said through clenched teeth, "Rule number five, 'Never EVER say 'you and what army?' or worse, and most especially of all never say 'things couldn't possibly get any worse'.'"

"Why?" asked Jenn.

"Because fate always finds a way," sighed Marie.

"You'd know that rule better than anybody, eh, Brainy?" smirked Eve, who then coughed from the look on Marie's face.

"And rule six is to be always alert for danger or deception when around ones you don't know," finished Eve.

Josephine shifted a little as she sat back beside Jonathan. She knew that was true, but... she couldn't help but trust everyone, even sarcastic Eve. Even though she had scared the wits out of her, she had... purpose. There was just something about their eyes that told her gut that she could trust them. She smiled to herself as Gazelda made them focus back to the mines.

"Right, if Josephine's second sight is telling the truth, then that means we will have to split up. Once we meet up at the mine where it is, we'll have to make it up from there."

"Eh?" asked Jenn.

"We won't know how many soldiers will be stationed to guard it. And when we take the thing, we have to get back out," Gazelda elaborated.

"That's going to be interesting," muttered Wave, putting her chin in her hand.

"Yes, and speaking of the stone, under no circumstances do ANY of you touch it with bare hands. It is dark magic and your Dragon heart powers will make it impossible to touch it without getting burned or repelling it. Me being a unicorn, its darkness will not affect me, understood?" Gazelda barked her last statement as an order.

Everyone nodded.

"That includes me?" asked Jenn.

Gazelda grumbled something under her breath, then said, "You are going to stay here. You will not be coming with us."

Jenn whined, "Why can't I come and help fight?"

Jonathan jumped in at once. "Because Jenn, you do not have enough training, and Mum wouldn't approve, not to mention that there are too many of us as it is. It'll be hard enough trying to sneak around with you trailing behind. You'd never keep up, sis; you're human while the rest of us are Dragon hearts and a unicorn. The reason you came with me was because Mum didn't want to risk your safety. Jeremiah and Jordan are better able to fight than you."

Jenn sighed and nodded at her brother's reasoning.

"Still better than Jordan."

Josephine patted Jenn on the shoulder, and Jenn smiled back at her.

"Not to be fussy or anything, but should we even bother to try? We don't have the experience..." said Wave, biting her lip. Gazelda sighed.

"You are not wrong. I would prefer more experienced knights to try to keep you lot hidden but we don't have any, yet. Even those who I know would come at my request, it would take them far too long to get to the mines. It may be fully fruitless to try to stop him from getting that stone..."

"But we need to at least try," said Eve.

Gazelda nodded.

"Before we go, Eve needs to teach Josephine how to use a sword. Eve, if you would, please."

Eve nodded and reached for something behind Gazelda. When she straightened out, Josephine gasped at the beauty of the sword. It looked to be a claymore, a long sword similar to those made and used in Ériu. It was long and appeared heavy. Josephine was sure if Eve hadn't been a Dragon heart, she would not been able to hold it. The sword had to be at least forty-five inches long, hilt and all. It was in a simple black sheath, but the hilt was anything but simple. The hilt was fashioned with a dragon wrapped around it, a white topaz in the sword's pommel which was rose shaped.

She took it from Eve with great care, scared that with her newly awoken strength she would break it. Even so, the sword felt a little heavy in her hands.

Gazelda smirked at the sight. "It's all right, Josephine. That is not a common sword. It was made to be used by a Dragon Heart and, in fact, was used by one. A good friend gave it to me to take care of it, and now I give it to you to use. Do take good care of it. Its name is, funny enough—Ice Thorn."

"Yes, I will," Josephine nodded, taking in the sword's beauty. The work was amazingly detailed. The Dragon looked as though it would come alive at any second. Josephine heard Gazelda say something and tore her focus away from the sword.

"The last thing we must take care of is the leadership of this Alliance. I am temporarily its head...."

"Who exactly gave you that, anyway?" asked Eve, folding her arms.

"The last person who was in care of it," said Gazelda.

"Come on, Gazelda..." complained Wave, but Josephine could tell Gazelda would not spill. Josephine also got the feeling that they had this conversation before, with the same results.

"That conversation will have to wait. Anyway, I appointed Eve as my first commander, Marie as the tactical officer, and Wave is our head healer. Of course, if you wish to change that, you may, Josephine. But first I must ask if you are even willing to take the leadership," explained Gazelda.

Josephine straightened her back at once.

Gazelda nodded her approval at the gesture. "Being a knight is not all romance and chivalry like the stories claim. Being a Dragon knight is about putting one's safety above all others, especially in the leader's case. It will be a bloody road you will take if you accept this task, Josephine."

Gazelda gave her a stern look. Josephine slowly nodded her head. She thought about the gargoyle that had attacked her. It was terrifying and gory, but she knew in her gut that there was no way for Josephine to turn back now, that her fate was sealed the moment she touched the Vanora necklace. She clenched her jaw, determined not to show her worry in front of the others.

"I understand."

Gazelda nodded her approval.

"Good. I was hoping you would take it. You have a fire in you like the others, Josephine. Now, Josephine, if you would please, repeat after me. We sadly do not have time for fan-fair and a banquet. Speak the leadership oath, as I say it."

Josephine nodded.

"I, Josephine Drageon, accept the heavy, humbling burden of being the leader of the Light Dragons of the Crystal Alliance. As a knight, I will carry the duties placed forth, and forsake everything, even my own life, to protect those who need my help. I swear my sword, myself, and my dragon partner's honor, if he or she agrees to uphold the law and peace."

As Josephine repeated the oath, she felt more confident, and her heart swelled. When she finished, she felt a mixture of dread and excitement that she could not explain. Josephine glanced over at Jonathan, who was smiling widely, and he gave her a nod.

"Now, you have two options, take over as head right now, or let me continue to be the leader with the provision that I show you how to lead, and you still have final say in everything we do from here on in."

"I think I like option two, and I approve of the officer choices," smiled Josephine. The other three grinned.

"If things go bad, Eve would be next in charge," said Josephine.

"Yes, she would be."

"I almost forgot..." suddenly said Eve, and she drew her sword. Wave and Marie glanced curiously at Eve, but when she kneeled down in front of Josephine, they, too, drew their swords and did the same. Josephine stood up, guessing what they were about to do, which made her stomach tighten from uneasiness.

Eve began talking, and at first, she didn't understand but then... "I, Eve Grace, here and now swear my sword FireRose to you, and my dragon if he/she approves, and total alliance to you, Josephine Drageon, and I will fight by your side with unwavering loyalty, and to my fellow Dragon Knight Alliance warriors. I will fight for within my earthly powers to protect."

"I, Wave Williams, too here and now swear my sword Whirlpool to you, and my dragon if he/she approves, and total alliance to you, Josephine Drageon, and I will fight by your side with unwavering loyalty, and to my fellow Dragon Knight Alliance warriors. I will fight for within my earthly powers to protect."

"And I, last but not least, Marie ThunderFly, swear my sword Thunder Break to you, and my dragon if he/she approves, and total alliance to you, Josephine Drageon, and I will fight by your side with unwavering loyalty, and to my fellow Dragon knight Alliance warriors. I will fight for within my earthly powers to protect."

Josephine drew her new sword and touched each of their swords with her own and said, "I accepted with humble honor your loyalty, and I thank you."

The three bowed, then placed their swords back into their scabbards.

Josephine was confused, wondering why the three didn't swear in alliance to Jonathan. Gazelda noticed the confused look on her face.

"Jonathan, though a Dragon heart, is a prince of his own kingdom, and that is why they swear loyalty to you and not to him. Red Rose is a member of the Alliance, but not a part of the leadership."

Jonathan smiled and stood up to face Josephine, never taking his eyes off hers.

"Therefore, I am the one who is going to swear loyalty to you, Josephine."

Josephine felt her heart skip a couple of beats as Jonathan drew his sword and kneeled.

"I, Prince Jonathan Nicholas Falcon, as the heir of the Kingdom Red Rose, swear Alliance to you, Josephine Drageon, and as a warrior, I give you my total alliance of myself and my loyal troops, as well as my dragon if they approve. I promise to fight by your side with an unwavering loyalty that is worthy of my kingdom, my family, and myself."

Josephine touched Jonathan's sword with her hand. She took a few deep breaths. She understood what this meant to Jonathan, to fight and die for his kingdom.

"I humbly accept your alliance. Thank you, Prince Jonathan," she whispered, staring back into those warm brown eyes.

"All right, Ice Princess, time for you to learn how to handle a sword. Any ideas how?"

Josephine shook her head, and Eve smirked. The two walked off some little ways to Eve's training grounds. It was clear of brush, three wood posts covered in slash marks standing in the middle.

"I am not surprised. No worries, Josephine, I am your second in command, and I have sworn to protect you; therefore, it is my duty to teach you. Wanna join us, Jonathan?" chuckled Eve, glancing behind her.

Jonathan strolled into the clearing, Flash right behind him. The small lizard crawled onto a branch of a tree, wrapping his tail lazily around him for a nap.

"If you don't mind," He shrugged.

Eve contemplated him, glancing at the long sword at his hip. Josephine glimpsed at it as well. It lived up to its name; Josephine had never seen a sword at such length save the one she was now holding. The hilt was simple, with a leather grip and a silver crossguard, with an engraved pommel shaped as a falcon's head.

"You have been trained, right?" inquired Eve.

"Yes, more than most would consider necessary..." Jonathan smirked, as though remembering something.

"Nothing wrong with that. Our enemy was trained in our techniques, was the head of the class, and has got at least eighty years more experience than us. Rule number eight: 'Do what you can to know your enemy'. This leads to the lesson."

Eve smiled in a way that made Josephine a little nervous. Though a girl, Josephine was never afraid of wrestling with any of the boys in town and beat them often. Not even Gawain, at two hundred and -something -pounds, had ever scared her, but instead of an unruly teenage boy that tripped over his own feet, she was facing a girl much shorter and skinnier, who's appearance was intimating, even without the dragon eyes.

"Josephine, what can you ascertain about me from what you have seen?" Eve asked.

"That you're a big mouthed show-off," muttered Marie, appearing beside Jonathan.

"Shut it, Brainy. And if you don't mind, Marie, I am, last time I checked, the smart-mouthed one, so shush, will you?" said Eve. She folded her arms and waited for Josephine's answer.

Josephine frowned. Even with the simple movement of folding her arms, Josephine could see that she moved with, well... grace. She stood straight and proud, currently having a calm look on her faerie-shaped face, green eyes watching with the air of a teacher. She knew from the small scene in the woods that she was an excellent warrior, probably even before her powers awoke. Her last name spoke for herself; the Graces were the strongest and most famous of the Dragon heart families, being direct descendants of two of the original six Dragon hearts.

Josephine stared at Eve for a few more seconds, then said, "You are well trained in the sword from just watching you in the path and the way you stand. You are a little rash in your judgments–"

"That's putting it mildly," chuckled Marie.

"–And you're well-adjusted to your powers already and were testing me to see if I was. You wanted to make sure I had the courage to fight. You do not give oaths of loyalty to anyone who does not have a backbone to hold their sword."

Eve lifted her elegant eyebrow and gave Josephine a crooked smile. "You are right. I do not give oaths of loyalty to just anyone. You're no dummy; I'll give you that, Ice Princess."

"You also like to give nicknames," Josephine smiled. Eve laughed.

"Old habit I picked up from my great-aunt. Anyway, you know how to watch your enemy, so now it's time to teach you how to fight them."

Josephine gave an involuntary gulp as she watched Eve pull out her sword. It had a silver hilt, the pommel round and engraved with a weaving design, diamond chips, and one large ruby. On the blade was an engraving.

Josephine blinked when she realized she could read the strange letters and spoke them aloud.

"Courage is only truly courage when you face your fear head on."

Eve grinned. "It's Dragon script. That's why you can read it. It is a replica of my family's sword, passed down for many generations, and the phrase is the motto of the Dragon Knight Alliance. This is only a thirty-two-inch blade, for the full-sized sword is about forty-five inches long and I could never pull it from its sheath. We've lucked out with you; the sword is the right length for your height and weight. With that said..."

Eve placed herself into a simple stance. Legs spread, knees bended, toes turned, hands above one another on the hilt.

Marie smiled and spoke up, "In the style of the Dragon hearts, is a mix of all different sword styles from Tuatha Dé Danann to the clans of Jinzhou and modified them for our strengths and weaknesses. Taranis himself began this style, and generations from then on have added and flushed out all the problems to make one of the deadliest sword styles known to the earth. Actually, the Graces were really the ones who took it on themselves to work on it, next to the Cyrus family."

Jonathan blinked and so did Josephine at the surname.

"You mean....?" started Jonathan but Eve jumped ahead and answered him.

"Oh yes, Cetus was part of one of the most prestige families of the Dragon Knights. Therefore, this makes this especially important; he knows all that we know and more, so we must match it," Eve said, eyes narrowing at Josephine.

"Sword fighting is like an elegant dance. It demands precision." Eve circled Josephine.

"You need sure footing and sharp instincts... for this dance..." Eve made a quick move, shifting to behind Josephine, and before she could even blink, Eve's icy blade was under her chin. "Is deadly."

Josephine let out a gasp. Eve moved back to her spot in front of her.

"Normally I'd have you use wooden swords to start out with, but we don't have time to do that, so make sure you don't cut yourself up with useless flashy moves," Eve half muttered to herself as she made Josephine move her feet to a better fighting position.

"For all the good this will do, I'll get slaughtered the moment they see me."

"Don't worry, the rest of us are well trained. We'll cover you," said Marie.

"You know how to fist fight and shoot an arrow, so rely on them first," said Eve as she forced Josephine's leg back into the right position that it'd slipped from.

Jonathan watched with amusement as Eve tried to teach Josephine the finer points of sword fighting. But Josephine got her amusement, too, as Jonathan tried his hand at fighting Eve, only to kiss the ground.

"Not so cocky now, eh, Mr. Wind Prince?" chuckled Eve, helping him up. Jonathan shook his head in amazement.

"I have never seen someone move so fast in all my seventeen years... not even Lord Wilson, when that hornet's nest fell on his head, the idiot..."

Eve laughed. "Just because your sword has a better reach does not always guarantee victory, remember that."

Josephine glanced at her reflection in the blade of her sword.

"Wouldn't it be wiser if we let them be for now instead of risking them seeing us and/or killing us?" she asked as she faced Eve.

Eve sighed.

"No, but at least we can get information on numbers and so forth. See what condition Cetus is even in if he shows up, if he IS the one behind all of this."

"Seems risky to go in without real training against Shadow magic or in our own magical powers, running a risk of getting killed," said Jonathan in a not unkind voice.

Marie and Eve both shrugged.

"Risk is what we do. Odds are against us. We have to do what we can and be smart in our recklessness."

"Can you be smart when you are being reckless? I thought that corresponded with stupid?" smirked Jonathan.

"Look Mr. Wind Prince, if you got a better idea for four sixteen-year-olds and a unicorn to stop an evil Dragon heart getting his shadow magic, feel free to share. Otherwise-"

Eve side stepped Josephine's wild swing and feinted, pretending to strike her through her chest.

"-Go with the flow."

Rodger Grace, Eve's grandfather, came after a while and helped Josephine understand some of the finer points of her footwork. Once that was all set and done, (and Josephine had gained some impressive bruises) they all went to bed, so they would be ready to rush off in the morning to Grand Mill.

Chapter Eight
Away in the Mines of Mayani

A s the tiniest rays of sun snuck through the clouds, the small group headed off. But before they did, Eve showed them a little Dragon heart magic.

"Okay, if all goes smoothly," Eve said, to which Marie muttered, "The likelihood of being zero."

"No one will see us; however, as Miss Brainy Pessimist over there said," she glanced towards Marie, who rolled her eyes and continued to pack her horse, "That may not happen, so we need to do a little magic to keep ourselves safe," Eve said.

Josephine blinked. "But I thought...."

"No, not that kind of magic, the natural magic and defense mechanisms that dragons, Dragon hearts, and all animals have. Like Flash," Eve nodded to the little lizard that was now turning to a brown color same as Wave's mare, "we can change our eyes so that they look, well, normal which helps to hinder our trackers if they can't find anyone with Dragon eyes that stand out like a black eye."

Wave and Marie came over to join them.

"It's kind of hard to do at first, but you can't force it; it must come naturally. I've never been told exactly how to do it, just the purpose and theory behind it, but all the same..."

Eve closed her eyes, and they all mimicked her. Josephine could feel her ice magic in her veins, making her colder than normal, but that was natural now. She wondered how the other's veins felt now, when Eve said,

"Let yourself go. Think about the danger we are throwing ourselves into; focus your thoughts on your eyes. That may do it."

"And if it doesn't?" chuckled Jonathan.

"Then we're dead, so shush and concentrate," mumbled Eve, half hardily swatting Jonathan's arm to silence him.

Josephine swallowed her giggle and took a deep breath. "*I need my eyes to disguise themselves... it's not safe for my dragon eyes...*"

"Anybody else feel realllly stupid right now besides me?" asked Eve after a few seconds.

"Eve!" growled Wave.

"Right, sorry."

They stood there for a few more seconds when Josephine suddenly felt something with her eyes, like she had placed a glass lens on them. When she opened them, Jenn was looking at her in shock.

"Your eyes look normal!"

Josephine glanced at Marie to see her yellow eyes looked like someone had taken a brush and rounded out her pupil, the same as the other three.

"Interesting," muttered Marie, staring at Wave's eyes.

"How long will that last?" asked Jenn, mounting her horse.

"Until we lose our tempers, more or less." Eve smirked. "If we feel a little ominous and lose our temper, our eyes will return to normal, or if we feel safe. Though I have a feeling it'll be awhile before anyone of us feels safe," sighed Eve, who went and mounted her horse with the others following behind.

Jenn snuck off with Rodger Grace to hide out with the Nymphs for the time being, until they got a message from Gazelda. From there, they took a wide path around Rave town to avoid the soldiers. It was a hard day and a half, but they were able to get through to Grand Mill town by the night of the second day. They arrived in the east part of town. It would not be easy to get in. Near almost every building was a trio of royal soldiers. Jonathan couldn't see his friend Jamard, so they kept their distance. The streets were narrow, covered in dust from the mines. In the far north of the town, Josephine could see, even without her new sight, the two large windmills that were creaking in the wind.

They left Ulysses, Starlette, and the horses in an abandoned stable, then snuck through town. Once they had gotten to near the mine, Gazelda stopped at the entrance.

"The plan is simple. If you get an opening, grab the stone but DO NOT–" She glared at Eve, "–risk your life for it. As bad as it will be if he returns to full strength, it would be devastating if one of you got killed and he also got his powers back. This is a slim chance we are taking."

They all nodded in understanding.

"I need to go around for obvious reasons. If I even can squeeze into the narrow ways. Go straight and keep your heads down. Don't worry about me," Gazelda smiled at the concern on Josephine's face, "I can take care of myself." She glanced at Eve, nodding.

"Eve, you're in charge, go."

They watched Gazelda somehow noiselessly leave in the dark, and when she disappeared, Eve urged them forward. There were no guards at the entrance, which everyone found weird, but they had no time to stop. Once inside, they saw the tunnel split into two paths.

"Wave, Marie, Jonathan, go left, Josephine and I will go right."

Even though Eve whispered, it seemed awfully loud in the grubby silence of the town. The only other thing Josephine heard besides the wind blowing dust around was the windmills creaking and groaning.

"The town is a military outpost, yet there is almost no one around here," mumbled Eve.

"Didn't take long... I wonder if they found a Shadow crystal and they don't want the soldiers to see and start talking," muttered Josephine back.

Eve frowned in the torchlight. "You just might have hit it on the head, Ice Princess."

She nodded toward a large room at the end of their tunnel.

"It's tight in here..." muttered Josephine.

"I'll say. Hope we don't get caught up in too big of a fight or the whole mine could come down our heads..." Josephine wiped her nose off, trying to clear away the metallic smell.

"What is even mined here?" Josephine whispered, trying not to hit her head on the low ceiling. She also had to keep adjusting her quiver on her back from smacking the walls and her as they slipped through.

"Silver and copper, mostly. I know there are some precious stones mined here more recently if I remember rightly..."

At that second, Jonathan and the other two came in, and the five of them slipped behind a large stack of crates and mounds of dirt and gravel.

"Really cheery place, isn't it?" muttered Eve sarcastically to the others.

"This is one of the original mines," explained Jonathan quietly. "The trolls made most of this old tunnel system, but humans killed them and chased out about a century or two ago. From the looks of it, it's gone dry." Jonathan wiped his hand along the cave wall to see only dust on his long fingers.

"Makes sense that a shadow crystal would be here. Legend holds that Zankeno came from somewhere in the Mayni Mountains. But still a slim chance of a Shadow stone..." muttered Wave, slipping her sword just ever so slightly from its sheath.

"And they got that chance," muttered Josephine as she nodded to the middle of the room. In the center of the cave, there was a large box with a sinister glow coming from inside. In front of it were two men. The first one was a man with a yellow sash draped across his chest, and he was wearing a black army uniform with a bird and rose symbol on his collar.

"Hey, isn't that Sir 'Horseman' Lance?" muttered Marie, looking at Jonathan.

He nodded. "He taught me how to ride. Still a strong fighter after all this time. I wonder why he was sent?"

"Doesn't look too happy, does he?" smirked Marie.

Josephine nodded in agreement. His lips were pressed together like a straight line. The other person was a head taller than Sir Lance and was wearing a large cloak, his face in complete shadow. His hand was resting on the box. There were black scars, like old burns, on otherwise pale skin on what she could see of his hand. The cloaked figure turned, and they saw he had a long face and long brown hair that obscured his eyes. His black cloak made his already colossal frame more imposing.

"I must thank your men for finding me this, Sir Lance. They have done me a great service."

The knight glared at him and said, "If you say so. Any word from the king about the prince and princess?"

The man acted as though he hadn't heard the question. He turned back to the box and with great care took the top off, smiling at the contents. "From what Lord Wilson told me, the rogue prince and his sister are still at large. They are to be charged with treason when caught."

Lance said nothing, but Josephine felt what she'd akin to disapproval. He glared at the Lord. "Pray tell... Lord Martin, I believe? What is it you are planning to do with that stone?"

Lord Martin grinned. "What do you know about shadow magic?"

He frowned at the question.

"I know that it's all-consuming magic," he finally said, shifting his feet.

Jonathan, in one smooth movement, pulled out his bow and set an arrow. Eve placed her hand up to tell him to wait. Sir Lance seemed uneasy as the lord took the black-green stone from the box. He stroked it with long, pale fingers. The knight took a few steps back. Out of the shadows, a young soldier jumped out and grabbed at Lance from behind.

"Jamard?!" whispered Jonathan in disbelief, "what is he doing?!"

Eve grabbed Jonathan's arm to keep him from getting up.

"That smell...is that rotting flesh?" muttered Marie.

"You are Cetus Cyprus, aren't you?" demanded Lance.

The man pulled back his hair and hood, showing his piercing ice blue dragon eyes. "I see you are not stupid, Sir Lance... but then again, maybe you are..."

Chapter Nine
Fair Lady: The Last Battle

Near sunset, the Dragon Knights were ready for an all-out bloody assault. Many of the allies had come to the call of the war drums and horns. James and the others had not returned from scouting.

As I was checking my arrows and my sword, King Nicholas rode up to me on his mighty black stallion. He wore silver armor, on his hip a sword with a falcon head pommel, looking like a king should.

I sighed and smiled at him. He smiled back and then stared out over the battlefield. What had been a few hours earlier, the "front yard" of the city of Red Rose was now a large battle field covered in torches and traps. The dimming sunlight shined off the armor, flashing across the field, and the wind was now blowing from the east. King Nicholas shook his head and said to me,

"Fair Lady, what do you think our chances are of defeating this dark army of so called 'Shadow Dragons' or whatever they are?"

"Fair—we have better fighters."

"Yes, but from what I've heard, they have more fighters."

I shook my head and said, "You know better. Having more men doesn't always guarantee victory. It helps, but not a foolproof way to winning. You also need to remember to stop listening to the rumors that Braonán and Eimhir say. Annoying little pixies…"

King Nicholas chuckled, and then he sighed.

"You know, lately I noticed that we're sighing constantly."

King Nicholas smirked. "You know, Fair Lady, you don't have to fight. You can go with my wife and the rest of the women of the court."

I rolled my eyes. We went through this conversation every time there was a major battle. Despite being old friends, he still felt it was best for me not to fight.

I placed my sword in my sheath and then said, "Do we really have to go through this?"

The king smiled a somber smile before saying, "My dear old friend, this is serious."

"When is the battle against evil not serious?" Before he could say anything, I added, "As a member of this Alliance, it is my duty to fight. Besides, you know I am the most unique fighter you have."

"Yes, I know that," he said in a careful tone.

"Not to mention the fact that I can only take orders officially from Zu and James," I reminded him, folding my arms.

"Yes, I know that, too…" He glanced at me.

I smiled, for I had already won and he knew it.

I said with great flourish, "Also, I have saved your butt so many times that I practically own you. I've known you since you were fourteen with pimples. I saved you from that snake that was only about ten inches long…"

"All right! All right! I give in! You win as always," laughed King Nicholas, shaking his head. "I hope you remember what you are getting yourself into."

"Your majesty, I don't think any of us really truly know what we are getting into this time."

The sun set a blood red. It was somewhat quiet; the soft sounds of swords being sharpened, bows being tested, horses neighing, and dragons flapping their wings. I nervously walked around, giving my students pep talks that were more for me than for them.

As I finished helping place a few extra traps, Zu walked over to me and said, "Feels terrible this time, doesn't it?"

I nodded and watched as he dumped some water over his dark brown hair. Zu Carnelian was one of the few individual warriors we had that was human and part of the Dragon Knight Alliance, known as Dragon warriors. His skills matched only by Nina and James, though he wouldn't admit it.

He sighed. "Just remember our motto; True courage is facing..."

"... Your fear head on." I pouted.

Three dots on the horizon appeared over the treetops, then three almighty roars echoed across the way. Zu and I rushed forward to see the three land.

"They're coming!" yelled Hamlet.

"How many?" asked Sydney, riding on his horse.

"Hundred thousand at least!" yelled Spark with despair.

My heart sank to my stomach. *"Even with the main part of the Alliance here, it still might not be enough. How are we going to last through this?"* I thought, shaking my head.

King Nicholas nudged his horse to beside me. "What is it made up of?"

"Mostly Trolls, some Viken, and if you can believe it, a few Dananns and Dragons," said Manyu as he pulled his dark hair into a ponytail.

"And a few Shadow magicians, I have no doubt," muttered Zu.

James nodded and said, "Most likely. I think one of them is our old friend's Shadow magician, Mitch the moron."

Hamlet snorted at the name. Mitch Begot was a Shadow magician that we had fought many times. He was Francian and, though evil had little in brains; once while fighting me, he tripped on his ridiculously large black cloak, and almost got eaten by a hoard of goblins. I shook my head.

"How are we going to fight them all?" I said, with hope-lessness.

"Only way we can—with all our strength," said James, getting back on Hamlet and yelling out orders.

After the sun hid behind the horizon completely, a thunderous roar echoed through the valley to our ears, and then another one came, becoming loader each second.

As one, everyone moved to their fighting positions. As the Alliance did so, massive shadows darkened the field, distorted from the light of our torches. Six hundred or more soldiers came marching towards Red Rose Castle. I watched

Hamlet, Ken, and Sparks take to the sky. Shoney raised his sword in the air, and as he did the archers, their arrows. The army, mostly made up of trolls and men, raced across the forest and field towards the gates.

As they approached, several fell prey to the hidden pit traps filled with spears; however, many dodged the pits.

"They know where the traps are? That's impossible..." gasped Sandra.

"Not when a traitor has told you," growled Mango, pulling out a long dagger.

When the army had gotten within a few yards from the main gates, Shoney slashed his sword down as the signal to the archers to open fire.

Fire arrows and regular arrows took flight with a uniformed twang, taking down most of the charging force. However, as most of us older fighters knew, that large volley of men was the first wave. As those fell, a much larger force came charging from the southwest. Then many trolls and other dark creatures came from the southeast, and even more men flanked by dragons came straight from the south.

James yelled out to our troops, "They're trying to overrun us! Don't let them get the better of you, no epic-worthy heroics—just strike hard and fast! The fate of us all rides on this! Come now, my friends; let's show them what being a real Dragon heart means!"

Everyone yelled and roared in agreement, slashing their swords into the air. The rest of the Dragon hearts flew into the air behind the Dragon Knight Masters. I saw Turku,

Sandra, Mina, and a few of the young Dragon Hearts that were left, but one was missing.

"Where's Cetus?" I asked, looking over at Zu, who shrugged.

Three dragons, brown, yellow, and black, came rushing towards the main line. When the light from the full moon hit them, I suddenly realized who it was.

"I don't believe it," I whispered.

Zu swore and glanced up to Sandra, then back to the three Dragon knights coming towards the other three. Hamlet roared a battle cry as James urged him forward. The two dragons met in midair, sparks flying from the riders and the Dragons. Hamlet gave another almighty roar, tearing at the black dragon. At that, Shoney and Manyu took that as their cue, as did everyone else. I noted bitterly that we knew now what happened to the three young Dragon Knights and their dragons. They had turned over to the enemy.

Battle cries rang out across the field as the defenders of Red Rose advanced on the dark army. More arrows came down on the army, and then the Dananns and Centaurs advanced on them when they had braced for impact. It did not take long for the smell of blood and burned flesh to penetrate the air. It was total chaos. I fought and watched my fellow fighters fight like I had never seen before. Mei's gymnastic fighting-style was like nothing I had ever seen her perform: splits, cartwheels and other moves, doing them combined with her razor-sharp Kanata and Bo staff. All the Dragon Knights were fighting to the death. I spied even the Kings taking part in the fighting, such as King Kingdor, using his Tuatha Dé Danann magic to take down all enemies in his path. Blood was soaking into the ground, the bloody mud caking onto shoes, vision blurred by the darkness, relying on hearing and other senses to battle.

At one point, the trolls broke through and were trying to take down the wall. I, with Sandra, who had battled and defeated Missy and her wind Dragon, fought them back, and soon we were joined by Zu and King Nicholas. As I slew a troll, I turned to see where James and the other two were. Just ten feet in front of me, King Nicholas fighting. James fighting with one of our former charges in the air. Manyu was on the ground with Sparks using their super speed to take down everything in their path. Close to him were Shoney and Ken with their water overcoming anyone or thing that dared to challenge them.

"AHHH!"

I whipped around to see a large Fylgja tying to overtake Sandra. It had already injured her leg, and Storm was in the air fighting a gargoyle. In one great leap, I jumped to her side, and then in one sweep of my sword I beheaded the horrible red-eyed dog creature.

"Thanks, I guess I'm getting careless," muttered Sandra, trying to get up on her left leg that was still bleeding. d

"I think it's fine, it's just a..."

A booming, thunderous roar ripped through the field. I looked up to the sky to see James and Hamlet toss down Reed in time to see another black colored dragon fly forward; the rider cloaked in the dark of night. I rushed forward, a dozen feet behind King Nicholas. James seemed to have recognized the Dragon knight for he glared and yelled something at him, but the sounds of the battle droned out his voice to my ears. James urged Hamlet forward to meet the new arrival, but he blasted from his hand a gust of ice-fire and blew Hamlet off course. The dragon then flew past James, and the rider jumped down onto the field, broad sword drawn...

"NICHOLAS NO! LOOK OUT!" I screamed, but it was too late.

Before I could even move, the King turned quick enough to just see his attacker. He fell with a surprised look on his face, his eyes cold and empty.

"NO NICHOLAS!" I cried.

The King's killer, who was cloaked in black robes that hid his face, turned from Nicolas's body and lunged at me, and he said in a voice that I had known so well, "Now for the fairest of ladies!"

I brought up my sword in time to block the murderer's sword. I held him off long enough for James to catch up to us. James shot from his hand a blast of ice so that I could jump clear.

Nicholas's killer turned to stare down James.

"Well, well, well, now it's getting interesting, isn't it, Master James?" he said, gathering energy and channeling it to his sword. James narrowed his eyes at him and then said,

"What kind of power...?"

"Oh yes, let me introduce you to the power of the Vanora crystal that you gave to the *former* Xian clan to guard," he said with a sinister laugh. James looked at him with a surprised face that quickly turned to hatred. The traitor swung his sword. James met it in midair as Hamlet and the other Dragon raged in a bloody fight above. I went to go help him, only to have Kingdor grab my arm.

"No Fair Lady, let James fight this. None of us can interfere. If anyone should, it will be Manyu or Shoney. Come, the trolls are overtaking the wall."

I hesitated, taking half a step towards the two.

"Come, my friend, there is nothing we can do. This is James's fight," repeated the King.

I looked hopelessly at the two, sparks flying from their swords. I snorted in frustration, then followed Kingdor to the outer wall.

The battle carried on and on through the entire night; it was as though time had slowed down enough for us to see blood fly and bodies fall. We all fought, yelling our war cries, slashing swords, doing magic, with no proper end in sight, our strength weakening from exhaustion. Just as Sandra and I had just stopped the last few trolls from reaching the castle wall, a flash of light blazed through the battlefield.

"AH! What?!" yelled Mei from behind us.

We all shielded our eyes from the blinding blue light, then looked to see that the Shadows had retreated. James was crouched on the ground, blood tricking down his face, his sword in the ground helping him stay upright. On the ground in front of him was some sort of jewel.

"I will return! You will pay one day!"

I heard Cetus's voice, but I could not see him anywhere.

It was over, and we had won, but at a terrible cost.

The time was an hour or two past sunrise. The field in front of the castle was burned and soaked in blood, with bodies of the enemy and allies alike scattered all over. Sunrise was dull and gray from the smoke that filled the air. We had won, but many of our allies had been killed, including many Dragon hearts. Dragon Master Michael and his dragon Ember had died while they fought bravely against Reed and his dragon from killing King Kingdor, who in turned injured Reed and killed his dragon partner, Aello. Reed, however, in the confusion of the bright light, had disappeared. As I helped the injured, Sandra limped over to me.

"Master James wants everyone in the great room now," she hissed through her clenched teeth.

"Sandra, rest your leg. You and Storm need to rest." I sighed, starting for the castle.

"I'll be fine!" she said stubbornly.

"If James can keep going after what he just did, then I can handle a little pain from a minor scratch."

"If you say so," I sighed again as I helped her along.

Chapter Ten
Cetus's Return

Josephine's heart stopped. Eve cursed, while Wave let out a small gasped.

"Oh, come on, it's not like we didn't know he was alive," growled Eve, shifting her weight so she could get a better grip on her sword.

"But it poses a slight problem, Eve," muttered Marie darkly.

"I don't think any of us, even Gazelda, really counted on him coming in person, but..." hissed Jonathan.

Josephine had to agree with him. Cetus would have made the trip himself to ensure that the stone wouldn't be stolen en route to Drake City and to gain his powers that much sooner.

As Sir Lance went to pull his sword, but a young soldier grabbed him from behind, binding his arms.

"Jamard! What is he...?!" growled Jonathan.

Jamard had dark skin like Marie's, and appeared to be several inches taller than Lance. He was wearing a Red Rose uniform.

"Jonathan, look at his eyes," whispered Marie. "He's under a spell; his eyes have gazed over!"

Jonathan cursed again, then pulled on his bow. Eve put her hand out to him to wait. He paused and watched the scene in front of them.

"Cetus Cyprus," Sir Lance muttered, "Only you would have the ambition to dig up something so foul."

"Not really, there are a few others... but none of them have my skills...I am relieved no one else found this..." muttered Cetus, flipping the stone over and over in his hands.

Eve tip toed across Marie and Jonathan so she could see better. She pulled out her bow and set an arrow.

Cetus' cloak slipped away, exposing his injured frame. There were large black scabs with a red rim rash across his body that she could see from under his dark clothes. His face was untouched, save for the blackness within his eyes.

As he spun the stone, the room became colder.

"He's attracting shadows!" muttered Wave. Lance struggled against Jamard, but to no avail.

"Hm, need some blood to..."

"Sir Lance!" A soldier appeared, running past Josephine and company's hiding spot.

"NO! GET...!"

The young soldier fell flat on the ground as tentacles came in and impaled him, blood gush out on to the ground.

A large mass with glowing eyes came down on the soldier. It then sat up, taking a somewhat reptilian shape. It hissed, blood dripping down.

It slithered up to Cetus. He held up the stone, and the creature hissed, flattening itself to the ground.

The torches were flickering, threatening to go out from the unseen creatures running around in the corners.

Wave slapped her hands to her mouth as Josephine swallowed back the bile that had gone up her throat.

Josephine took her hands off her bow to try to keep the Vanora Crystal from flashing, but she could feel the cold building up. Eve took her hand to cover the dagger as Jonathan left the ring on, not wanting to take his hands off his bow.

"Finally, I can use it again. Let's see if this stone can return what Master James took from me..."

"That's our cue!" hissed Eve. Josephine's fingers snagged as she pulled to release her arrow. The Vanora objects all flashing in the wake of the arrows releasing, the shadows screaming at the light.

The arrows whistled through the air, only to be shattered by the swirling black–blue energy that was engulfing Cetus. It crackled like lightning.

Marie shivered beside Josephine as they drew their swords. Eve jumped up and ran right for Cetus, sword swinging at the shadows in her way.

"EVE!" yelled Marie, chasing after her, but Eve had already reached Cetus.

Josephine felt a chill go down her spine at the same time she saw Eve's body shake. Cetus's eyes were blacker than the darkest pits, the swirling energy flowing up his arms healing the scabs on his body. Cetus flinched, then with one blink, Eve flew backwards into Marie. Josephine jumped forward to see that Cetus had not sent Eve flying, but a figure cloaked in black. He was as tall as Jonathan, but what he looked like Josephine didn't have time to find out, as a loud ear drum busting sound echoed through the cave. Josephine looked up in time to see Cetus staring right at her with curious eyes before disappearing into a mass of swirling shadows with the other cloaked figure.

Cetus Cyprus had gained his powers and gotten away.

Chapter Eleven
The Utter Bitter Taste of that First Failure

"What, that's it?! No fight? No 'I am back, beware I will rule the earth' or, 'You will never win, you young fools, be ready to meet your doom!'?! I feel bloody cheated!" snarled Eve as she kicked a rock as Jonathan helped Sir Lance up from off the ground.

"Eve!" snapped Wave. She glanced at Wave, then the dead solider that the shadow had eaten.

Eve muttered a sorry. Several soldiers appeared to help move the dead young man.

"I'll make sure to tell his family myself. It was partly my fault," said Sir Lance. Josephine could feel the frustration and heart-break coming from him.

"Following the orders of your king, what else could you do?" muttered Jonathan.

Josephine had to bite down on her tongue as they took the dead man out. She could see that he had almost no blood in him, his skin pale as milk.

"At least his soul was probably safe, being already killed before the shadow came on him…" said Marie, wiping a tear away.

Sir Lance stood at attention in front of Jonathan.

Jonathan forced a smile and said, "Are you going to take orders from a traitor now, Sir Lance?"

Lance's upper lip twitched as he said, "No, your highness, I do not plan to. Lord Wilson gave me no choice. What is your first order?"

Jonathan chuckled, then said, "I'm not too sure myself at this point. I think it would be best to see where Gazelda disappeared to and find out what we are going to do now that Cetus has returned to power."

"Find him, kick his butt, and then fry him until not even the trolls would wanna eat him," snarled Eve, throwing herself on the ground.

"It's going to be a little more complicated than that, Eve," smiled Gazelda, walking into the room, her diamond hard hooves echoing on the walls with each step.

"He got away, Gazelda," muttered Wave.

"I know, Wave. I didn't really think it would work, but it was, as they say, worth a try. Even though it did nothing but cause more problems for us." She frowned.

"How so?" asked Wave.

Josephine glanced over at Eve, who gave her a frown in return.

"He saw us. He knows now that there are young Dragon Knights again walking around, their powers most likely awakened if he didn't already sense that with whatever young knights he probably has under his thumb. Once he is rested, he will probably gather or hire a few people to take us out before we are a serious threat to him. We aren't now, he knows, but we will be. Cetus knows we will get training."

"Right, Josephine. Of course, we knew that risk in coming... but... never mind now. I think the best thing for us to do now is get out of sight. Cetus's power will probably return within the fortnight; Lord Wilson has taken over Red Rose castle. We need to focus ourselves on training."

Gazelda glanced over at Josephine. "Do you agree, Josephine?"

"Um, yes, I do. Jonathan?"

He agreed.

Jonathan turned to the knight. "Sir Lance, I need you to go to Rave Town and pick up my sister. Once you get there, escort her to our aunt's house in Remile City. Avoid a fight if you can, but if you must, use force. If you can get a hold of the Queen with Sir Etheve and Sir Andrew to see what the three of you can do to regain control. And...break the news of his son to Sir Etheve..." Jonathan rolled his lips in.

Lance nodded. "Yes, your highness."

Gazelda sighed. "I'm sorry, you lot... I should have realized that he would come here himself to gain the power that much sooner."

"Well, destiny was against us, Gazelda," muttered Marie.

"Destiny... oh, how I hate prophecies. People thinking they need tea leaves to live their lives and all that garbage... never mind, let us get out of here before more problems reach out to grab us."

"Gazelda, what happened to you, anyway? Could have used your magic," said Eve, not glaring but slightly annoyed. Gazelda matched it.

"Had to take the long way around to fit through and as I got close, shadows started attacking me. I do not know if that was of Cetus or another Shadow magician was hidden as I was being attacked. I know not, but there was not much

I could do. One moment I was fighting a hoard, the next second, they dissipated..."

Josephine put her hand on Gazelda's side. She smiled at her.

"Once Mother takes control over the kingdom from Father, all heck is going to break loose. When crooks and nut cases and other kingdoms get wind that Red Rose is in dissension, they are going to jump all over it," said Jonathan.

"At least they will be contained and we won't have to worry about them running off. Meanwhile, we'll slip away into the desert."

"Your Highness, you are not returning with us?" asked the senior knight with a raised eyebrow.

"My mother will take care of everything. She is more than able."

"Indeed."

Sir Lance bowed to Jonathan, then left.

"Right now, it's time for us to disappear into the dark, too," said Gazelda.

She walked out and the rest of them followed, their steps echoing against the walls. Josephine stopped to study the area. The ground was scorched from the shadow magic, leaving an awful smell of something rotting. She shivered, though she was far from cold. Josephine walked out, a feeling of being watched following her out.

Chapter Twelve
Irene's Desert Hotel

Josephine felt as though she had gotten off a bucking stallion. Her legs were burning, as were her back and her eyes. Josephine wasn't too sure that her back would ever recover. Even Eve was showing her fatigue, with red-rimmed eyes and an occasional yawn.

They departed as Sir Lance left for Red Rose City. Nobody had bothered asking Gazelda where they were going. By the late afternoon, they cleared the forest and met with the Swift Way River. The line of trade towns that reached all the way down the length of the Clocha Móra Mountains was on the other side. Gazelda stopped at the bridge. Marie jolted awake and let out a large yawn, making Wave and Josephine giggle.

"Listen up, Dragon Knights. We're about to head into Duke Town. It's the least... rowdy of these towns, but that doesn't mean much. And..." Gazelda shifted her weight.

"What's wrong, Gazelda, you got a rep here or something?" chuckled Jonathan.

"Rep?" asked Josephine, raising her eyebrow at him.

"A reputation. Is it really bad, Gazelda?" chuckled Eve.

Gazelda snorted. "No, that's not it. Stop that. It's that they know me with a... different appearance here, that's all."

Gazelda smirked, then walked back into the woods before anyone could say anything. Josephine glanced into the woods, trying to see what she was doing. For a minute she was gone and when she reappeared Josephine let out a gasp, as did Starlette.

At first, Josephine would have thought it was someone else, but the woman's long silver white hair left her no doubt. She was as tall as she was when she was a unicorn. Her ears were pointed like a Tuatha Dé Danann or a faerie, her eyes their bright yellow color. Where her horn was supposed to be was a headpiece with a large gold center, with plain gold bands that wrapped around her head. She was wearing a simple blue silk dress and black boots that hugged her thighs. She pulled her hair back and buttoned up her blue cloak.

"Now we can go on into town." She smirked at the looks on everyone's faces.

".... How long have you been able to do THAT?!" demanded Eve.

Gazelda smirked. "Come on, if you don't want to sleep in the woods again, let's go."

She walked across the bridge, leaving them behind in disbelief.

Eve glared at her. "You think you know a unicorn..." she muttered, nudging her horse.

They walked into the surprisingly quiet town. Gazelda headed into a building with a big blue sign overhead, saying,

"Irene's Desert Hotel"

She walked right in. The group tied their horses up and followed. Josephine and Jonathan had Ulysses and Starlette in the middle of the others to make sure that their horns wouldn't be too noticeable. Starlette wasn't happy, but she said nothing as Josephine patted her and went into the hotel.

The hotel was warm and roomy. There were ten round tables spread around the room, and a bar in the middle of the back wall, a spiral staircase beside it. At one table was a large, red-haired woman. She seemed kind with her brown eyes and a sky's worth of freckles across her face. She wore a green patchwork dress with her sleeves rolled up to her elbows. She straightened up and gasped.

"Bless my soul! GAZELDA!"

She rushed forward to give Gazelda a bone-crushing hug.

"Irene McCarthy, it's been too long," she gasped back.

The woman smiled, then stepped back to look at the rest of them. "What in the name of the Ériu Moors have you been up too!?" she gaped.

"Grand Mill Town, my dear."

The two exchanged a meaningful look. Irene then went over to a table and slapped her hand on it, waking a sleeping man.

"Move it, Roscoe! You've been dozin' all morning. Time to get your butt home!"

As Roscoe staggered out the door, Irene placed a close sign on the door window.

"All right girlie, what is going on? Rumors have just reached me from Marianne that some kind of rebellion is going on. The king is still in charge, but the army is all over the place. Word is that the prince tried to kill the king and is now on the run." her eyes flickered at Jonathan.

"I can assure you, Irene, that not all that is true. Prince Jonathan did not try to kill the king. It is more like the other way around. But first thing first, Irene, we just saw Cetus Cyprus' return, and we've been sleeping in saddles all night. I know I could use some of your famous coffee right now."

Irene's eyes went even wider, and her mouth dropped. "Cetus... he... it... he's back?"

Gazelda sighed and nodded, but Irene had already gone behind the bar to pull out a coffee pot and grounds. She shook her head and muttered, "Cetus Cyprus.... I'd thought I'd die before he came back..."

Gazelda sat at the table nearest the bar. The others right behind her. Josephine smiled as Jonathan pulled out her chair for her. She smiled and flopped down, instantly regretting it, for it made her butt hurt more.

"Do all of ya want coffee?" Irene asked.

"Hot chocolate for me, thanks, if you have any," requested Eve in a low tone.

As Irene pulled out another pot, she gave Gazelda a run-down of all the local stories.

"It's been crazy around here since you last left, Gazelda; gang fights have been gettin' worse amongst the miners of rival companies. Callaghan being the head of it, not only is he making the mining jobs hard to keep, but he's also gettin' on the Dragons' cases to let them mine deeper into their territory. They are gettin' to the end of their ropes. I swear by the end of the spring, if Callaghan keeps up, these towns will be nothin' but ashes."

"No surprise there. Callaghan is so arrogant. But I can't understand why he would encourage all the gang fighting...

if the mining business goes belly up, then so does Callaghan, being the richest of the lot. Unless he's trying to scare everyone else out then scoop up their claims..." muttered Gazelda, "Even so, picking a fight with the Dragons isn't smart. Even if he got all the claims; the Dragons could easily get rid of him." She shook her head.

"Aye, just one snap of the jaw, and it'd be all over," chuckled Irene darkly.

She left the beans to filter, disappeared through a door behind the bar, left to the spiral staircase.

"I'll cook up some of my eggs and bacon for ya all. After all that fightin' and runnin' you have to be starving," she called.

"Yes, please, Irene, but make mine apple pancakes if you can," Gazelda called back.

Josephine smiled and looked over to see Jonathan staring into space. "What's wrong, Jonathan?"

He blinked and looked over at her, a frown on his face. "It's... just I think Callaghan may have other ideas then just the claims in mind..."

"How so?" asked Marie, joining in.

"I don't know, I've heard that name before, but I'm not sure..."

"Maybe your father did some dealings with him," Marie suggested.

"Probably..." Jonathan stared into space again with a puzzled frown.

Josephine glanced over to see Eve with her eyes closed and head back. Marie, too, was staring into space, and Wave was pulling her fingers through her hair.

Josephine took the moment to listen with her heighten hearing. She listened as a few people were walking on the street outside. A lighted-footed person was walking straight for the inn. Josephine figured the person would stop and walk away once they saw the sign, but to her surprise the person did not pause but came right in. Her head snapped up to look.

She saw sandy colored hair, and bright hazel eyes under the brim of a wide hat. He looked no older than them. He was wearing a dusty, cracked leather long jacket, a simple long sword at his hip.

He took his hat off and left it on the coat rack with his coat, showing his tan tunic with a few patches, as well as a patch on his trousers. He walked up to the counter and placed a bulging pack on it. The teen was about to grab a coffee cup when Irene's voice came from the back:

"Indiana! Is that you?"

"Yeah, Irene, it's me."

"Then get your pack off the counter and leave the coffee alone! That's for Gazelda and her friends!"

Indiana went wide-eyed and, with a scowl, moved his pack to behind the counter. Then he turned to see them sitting at the table. Josephine could see out the corner of her eye Eve's eyebrow upturned a little at the new arrival.

"Gazelda, what brings you here to this forsaken part of Anglii?" He smiled.

"Indiana, it's good to see you. I have to say you have grown so much since I last saw you. At least a good five inches! Of course, the last time I saw you, you were what, thirteen?"

He chuckled. "Something like that. What's with the guard?" He smirked, nodding towards the rest of them.

"Oh, just some friends of mine... actually, Indiana, it's good you're here. What is the quickest way to get to the Dragons' home?"

Indiana did a double take. "Why, for the love of life, do you wanna go there for? Haven't you heard about the trouble going on?"

Gazelda's eyes narrowed.

"No, but I have a feeling I know what is going on," she groaned.

"Yeah, Dragons are getting really territorial again, fighting over the Phoenix Springs with the Tuatha Dé Danann Kingdom. It's bad enough Callaghan is trying to rule these towns with his gangs, but if the Dragons and Dananns fight, then the east coast of Anglii won't exist," He sighed, putting his hand through his hair. It stood up in funny angles.

Irene came in at that moment with a coffeepot in one hand and a large plate of various styles of cooked eggs in her other hand.

"Hi ya, Indie, did you introduce yourself?"

He rolled his eyes. "Gazelda knows me," He muttered, pulling out some more mugs. Irene sighed and shook her head.

"Silly... Everyone, this is Indiana Mar..."

"They don't need to know my full name," he growled, slapping down a mug a little too hard.

"I'm Indiana Phoenix; ya can call me Indie if you want," he muttered, picking up his pack and heading up the spiral case without looking at any of them. Irene clicked her tongue.

"That boy... Is it any wonder that he kept anything I taught him about manners..." She shook her head.

"Is that your son?" asked Eve.

"Oh, heavens no! Not by blood, at least. I took Indiana in when he was eight; his parents died in a fire. They were the only family the poor lad had. So, I took him under my wings. He is a good lad, but I don't think he's ever gotten over his parents' deaths. Indie is a bit of an adventurer; I think is what you would call him. For the last five years, he's traveled all over the place, finding things and what not. Does odd things here and there. I think he even does street fighting on the side, but I've never been one hundred percent sure. But he is always here when I need him. He may be a little rough around the edges, but he's a good lad."

She poured coffee and hot chocolate for everyone. Indiana came back down and helped Irene clean up.

"Indie, could you get the rooms ready for them, please?" Irene asked. He went to do that while the others went outside to get their packs.

But Gazelda asked Josephine to stay for a minute. When Irene disappeared upstairs behind Indiana, Gazelda sighed and finished her coffee.

"I'm sorry to put more into your mind when you need to rest, but I need to teach you about your role as leader of the Alliance." She glanced at Josephine, who nodded. On the inside, though, Josephine wanted to cry because her back ached so much, but she didn't say anything.

"You probably would have not gotten the leadership if not for that prophecy. Leadership of the Dragon Knight Alliance is through skills and an election of the members of the council. Well, if there was one. It is not an inherited role as like the throne of a kingdom. As the temporary head, I probably would have made Eve or Marie the leader."

Josephine nodded again and clarified, "Because they understand the role of Dragon Knights and the laws better than I do."

Gazelda sighed. "Yes, but... you are no dummy, and more even-headed than either of them. Wave is too timid for the job."

"I see. So what is exactly this prophecy that says I am the new leader of this Alliance? You never clarified why it was me that had to be the leader. Just because the necklace lit up for me, I'm the leader?" Josephine said, turning her mug in circles. She looked through her bangs to see Gazelda frowning into space.

"It was made just before the Dragon Knight Alliance fell. It said that the one that made the Vanora Crystal necklace to light again with magic, making the dormant powers of fellow Dragon Knights awake, is to fight the one who betrayed and destroyed the Alliance. Though... it probably could have been any of the objects... it just happened that you touched the necklace. Here I kept a copy written down ..."

Gazelda pulled out a small book from her pocket and flipped through the pages until she found what she was looking for. She read aloud:

"*So will come again,*

Through Love's Strength,

The Dragon Hearts, once again, will be called,

Six with partners beyond the powers of the Dragon Knights who came first.

The one who can make the Crystal of love shine again,
Will be the princess of brilliant light,
She will stand with her love, the prince, against the might
Of the Dark's fight.
And the prophecy of the forgotten magic will finally come
to pass,
Shall rise to help the great Dragon Hearts.
So again, will be the golden age of the free and just dissolv-
ing the corrupt magic of old."

Gazelda closed the book and passed it back to Josephine. She took it, staring at the cover, absorbing it all.

"Do you really think I am that Dragon Knight?"

Gazelda took a deep breath. "Well... you made the necklace glow. But also... you have the signs of being a good leader, even more so than Eve. But rule-of-thumb Josephine, don't trust in prophecies. No matter who makes them, you write your own future, your own choices. Don't let them rule your judgment. Just as rule number seven says never depend on the powers of fortune-telling or foresight," she smiled.

Josephine smiled back.

"Anyway, as the leader you decide, but Eve and the others, being the top Dragon Knights, have a say as well. If something happened or you made an order that they see is against the Dragon Knight Code or any laws, they can overrule you. But that rarely happens, and unless a spell or something similar is placed on you, then I doubt we'll have to worry about that."

Gazelda took another sip of her drink.

"What about Jonathan, though?"

"Good question. As the heir to Red Rose, he is part of the council automatically, but he has limited duties as such. In certain things that deal with the Alliance, he could not do anything, for what is he first? King or Dragon Knight? So that is why he can't be second in command. Unfortunately, I think that will case issues for him with the Lord's council but we'll deal with that when need be."

"Yes. I understand."

"Right. Now the Dragon Heart Alliance is in permanent war mode. You are not only a leader, but a general. If need be, you can make decisions without the others, but be careful about that. A few leaders have come under fire and cause problems in the past with doing that."

Josephine nodded. "I understand."

"Right, well, I think that's all for now. You look like you're about to fall over, so go on to bed, Josephine. I probably look like a gargoyle myself, so we'll let the rest wait for morning with clear minds, eh?" She stood up and stretched.

"What is that like? Going from unicorn to human?" Josephine asked, placing her cup on the counter.

"Very different. I'll tell you sometime later when we're not on the run. Come, let's sleep."

Josephine walked groggily towards the stairs. She paused a moment and turned to Gazelda, who was finishing her meal.

"Gazelda?"

"Hum? Yes, dear?"

Josephine rolled her lip for a second then said, "That line... 'She will stand with her love and Prince against the might'... Is it saying that the prince is my love or that with my love

combined with the prince's power they'll defeat the darkness?"

Gazelda grinned widely and chuckled.

"That, my dear, is what we call an ambiguous line. It's all
up to you on how you want it to be. I wouldn't worry about
it. Love comes on its own. It needs not a prophecy to grow.
At least, from what I've seen so far."

She winked, then gestured for Josephine to head up to bed.

Josephine walked into the first room she found, seeing
Wave was there by herself. She dropped on the other bed,
draping her arm over her eyes.

It was funny how almost three days ago she was riding with Jake and now she was all the way up the coast
of Anglii, with fellow Dragon Knights. No. Dragon hearts.
Josephine didn't feel like a knight, not yet at least, and she
liked the sound of heart instead. Maybe that would be the
title of the new Alliance. It wasn't what it once was, and
they were a new generation. The Dragon Heart Alliance.
That had a nice ring to it. Josephine slipped under the clean
sheets, falling asleep listening to Wave's slow, rhythmic
breathing.

Chapter Thirteen
Mango's Oasis

The next morning, Josephine soaked herself in a warm bath, trying to detangle her hair and relax her stiff muscles. Once she was dressed, Josephine wandered down the stairs to see Jonathan eating. Flash on his shoulder, taking the small bites. Jonathan smiled at her. Josephine could feel her heart skip a beat. Maybe it was his warm brown eyes that made it do that...

She sat beside him and saw at another table Irene and Gazelda were studying a large map of the surrounding region.

"Well... we have to go to Mango's, no doubt about that... but would it be better to get to the Dragon's lair via the towns or the desert? Either way, it is kind of nasty..."

"Eh, you'll more likely be able to talk civilized to viper fang dragons than the slime balls in these parts," snorted Irene.

"True... but... ah..." Gazelda mumbled something incoherent and stared at the map. At that, Indiana came down the stairs, his hair wet, wearing an old wool tunic and trousers, with leather bracers on his wrists.

"Hey Indie, know any other way to get to the Dragons' home in the mountains?"

Indie didn't even bother to look at the map. He poured some coffee instead.

"Nope. Either Mango's Desert or the trade towns. viper fangs or thieves. Trust me, I've traveled around those parts enough times to know."

"What are viper fangs exactly?" asked Wave, with Marie and Eve behind her walking down the spiral case.

"Little lizards that spit poison... one bite and you're done like a fluffy sheep in a shearing shed," answered Irene.

"Remember, Wave, I use that stuff in my potions sometimes, and it burns holes in my table?" smirked Marie, grabbing a biscuit and bacon.

"Oh, right," Wave mumbled, sitting down and pouring herself some juice.

"What kinds of potions need viper fang venom?" asked Josephine, raising an eyebrow.

"Eh, not many, I tend to, um... experiment..." Marie sheepishly muttered, her face becoming strawberry tinted.

"Yeah, Marie is an amateur alchemist, loves to blow up her lab and anything in a ten-meter radius of it. After that last time, Teek made her 'relocate' in the backwoods of town. She took out her sister-in-law's garden..."

"It wasn't that bad, and I only burned her one flower bush..." Marie muttered, looking at the table.

"We're going into the desert, then?" Wave asked, saving Marie from more of Eve's jokes.

"What, you little girls aren't going into the desert by yourselves?" laughed Indiana, looking up from his eggs and biscuits.

"We are more than capable of looking after ourselves, thank you. Flash is more than a match for a viper fang," Eve said coolly.

Indiana's eyebrow went up and an enormous grin graced his face. Eve's eyes narrowed. Before he could make another joke, Gazelda said,

"It would be better to go to the desert anyway, because Jonathan could easily be spotted, so..."

The door at that moment opened. Josephine closed her eyes, feeling them change from her heart jumping. She opened them to see a man on the threshold of the hotel. His chestnut hair laid over deep, piercing eyes. He was wearing a leather jacket and a silver mining helmet, with a rope on his belt and a small pick.

"Good morning, Irene; how are you on this beautiful morning?"

"Fine, until you walked in, Callaghan," muttered Indiana, walking back up to the second floor.

"I'm doing all right," Irene grunted, going to the bar. She began putting together a bag of food for Callaghan. Josephine assumed for it was for Callaghan, anyway.

"Good. Good. Ah, Gazelda, my dear Lady! Long time no see! My, you've hardly changed! What brings you here?" He smiled, walking forward.

Josephine studied him to see scars all over his skin that weren't covered by dusty clothes. No surprise, of course. Mining was a dangerous line of work. Beyond that, something about how he talked and walked made Josephine's skin prickle.

She glanced at the others to see that Eve, too, was suspicious of him. Marie and Wave were trying to be more nonchalant. Jonathan was not looking at him, his hand to his temple. Josephine realized he was trying not to let

Callaghan see his face. She watched him from the corner of her eye, trying not to draw his attention, shifting a little to block Jonathan from view. The miner didn't seem to notice them as he was still talking to Gazelda.

"Hey, I heard that you, the Dananns, and the Dragons were arguing again over the Phoenix Springs," he chirped up, leaning against the bar.

Josephine couldn't understand why he was talking to Gazelda like that, when she realized that she probably posed as a Tuatha Dé Danann and even Irene probably did not know her true form.

"So, I've been told. I have not been home for a while, Callaghan, you know more than I do."

He chuckled.

"I'll never understand women who travel instead of getting married... Dragons have been getting really snippy about anyone coming into their territory, even friends, and now they want the Phoenix Springs back for who knows what reasons. And you know your kind; it's all theirs. Nobody else is allowed..."

"It is sacred ground, Callaghan. They will let anyone use it as long as they talk to them, er, us first," said Gazelda.

He shrugged. Indie returned with boots on this time.

"Hey, Indiana! Dragon boy, do you think you could talk to your dragon friends about—"

"Even if I could, Callaghan, I wouldn't. You don't need nor deserve any more mining ground. "

"Oh no, it's not about mining ground! Heavens no, no need for that anymore." He chuckled.

Josephine could see out of the corner of her eye Eve and Marie share a glare.

"No, just wondering if they could lighten up their protocols. I don't see the need to keep four Dragon sentries around..."

"Yeah, well, Callaghan," Indiana chuckled back, "you are a cheating scum bag, and they are making sure you pull nothing funny."

Callaghan didn't seem the least abashed at the comment. He shrugged, taking his food and coffee from Irene.

"Whatever, Indiana. Doesn't matter, anyway. An old friend of mine has come back, and he'll sort out those dragons, anyway."

He tipped his head to Gazelda and Irene and left, taking a peek at Josephine and the others before leaving. Jonathan got up at once, as did the others. Flash made an angry noise and ran off towards the back.

"He has to work for Cetus. He wanted more mining ground to find a Shadow crystal!" growled Marie.

"I wonder if Cetus is going to threaten the Dragons to make them join him," said Wave.

"Don't worry; I don't know why he'd think that. Dragons are too smart and powerful to be intimated... well... at least the ones I used to know," sighed Gazelda, standing up, too, rolling up the map.

"We need to leave. The sooner the better," said Eve.

"Not till the cover of night. Best to be lost in the dark. That way we can slip into the desert without worrying about them following. Anyone but us would get easily lost."

"And how are we not going to get lost?" asked Wave.

Gazelda grinned at Indiana. "We'll have the best guide around — how about it, Indiana?"

He frowned.

"I don't know, Gazelda. What's this about Cetus being back? I thought he died years ago. What is going on?"

"Cetus Cyprus has come back. He isn't dead. He's been biding his time and is about to make a great, evil comeback. Don't worry, we will pay you," snapped Eve.

Josephine glared at her, but Indiana didn't seem insulted.

"Oh, that's all." He shook his head. "Well, if you need help, I'll get one of my buddies to do it. I'm not leaving..."

"Don't worry about me, Indie. I am more than able to take care of myself," said Irene, patting him roughly on the shoulder. "I want you to go with Gazelda; at least I'll know you're all safe. I'll go to stay with Sister Janet at Little Hilltone if I need to leave."

Indiana nodded.

"Lady Irene..."

"Just Irene, love. Yes, Josephine?"

Josephine blushed, "While you're going that way, could you stop at WindSage and let my aunt know that I'm okay? And my mother, if the rest of my family has come back?"

"Of course, dear. No worries, it'd be my honor."

Eve slipped back in from mounting the horses.

"All done," she whispered, pulling back her midnight black cloak. Flash came out of nowhere and slipped under her cloak, popping his head out from under it on her shoulder.

"Nobody saw you?" asked Josephine as she pulled her hood on.

"Nope. Not only am I small, Josephine, I am as silent as a cat stalking her prey."

"Good to know," smiled Josephine, a little unnerved.

"When she wants to scare the crap out of you," muttered Marie as she walked toward them.

Eve stuck her tongue out at her friend.

"What I lack in height I make up for in personality."

Gazelda walked out with the others to the back steps and said,

"Thanks to Irene, we have enough supplies to get us well to the Dragons'..."

The sounds of breaking glass and loud popping noises exploded out in the street. They ran back in to see some of the Inn's windows broken, the torch light throwing the mess in sharp relief, rocks the size of small plates on the floor.

"Quick, run for it! Callaghan is coming!" yelled Irene, running through the front door.

"They did recognize us!" whispered Wave.

"I don't know, lass, but don't linger! Indie, I'll be fine, just get them to Mango's!" snapped the Ériu woman as she pushed Indie out the back door with the rest of them.

He glared as he placed his sword on his hip and mounted his horse.

"Irene..."

"If I can live through clan wars, I can deal with Callaghan! Just go!" Irene pulled a small dagger from her skirt and waved them off.

Gazelda hugged Irene and whispered something, then jumped on with Eve, who stuffed an angry Flash into her pack. It was then that Josephine heard the singing:

"Away, away, the Dragon Alliance fell. So shall the head of the prince and king of Red Rose, our leader shall come again! No more royal rule for us!"

The rest was drowned out by a bunch of "Yahooing" and sounds of breaking windows, along with more popping.

"GO!" yelled Irene.

Indiana snapped his reins, and the rest followed. Josephine glanced back for a split second to see Irene pulling out her own horse. She glanced back at Indiana, who was focused straight ahead. The surroundings were rocky with little bush. They went forward, trusting Indiana to guide them to the desert. Before they took a hidden path in the trees, Josephine saw a tall cloud of smoke, a light glow in the dark.

Indiana kept going, either unable or unwilling to look back. Indiana did not trust himself. To do so would bring back too many memories he had sworn to lock away and never think of again. This group had better be worth it to risk thinking of that night. But somehow, though he had never been one who believed blindly, there was something about the sympathy in the girl with ice-blue eyes that made him think: Yes, they were worth it.

The small group of three unicorns and six teenagers ran right through into the dawn of the new day.

"How much farther is it, Indiana?" whispered Josephine as the rest were asleep. They were on the edge of Mango's desert. They had traveled at least twelve miles. It was a miracle that the horses could keep up the pace. Indiana smiled at Josephine.

"Not too far. Mango, the resident witch of this place, is not far in. And you can just call me Indie." He ruffled his hair and glanced back over the barren wasteland.

"Indie." She smiled, and then it slipped away.

"I'm sorry about what happened. You were dragged into this..." He didn't look at her, but waved his hand.

"Don't worry about it, Josephine, was it? Trouble has followed me for a long time. It's nothing new."

Josephine was going to ask what sort of trouble, but at that moment Gazelda stood up and he said nothing more, walking over to check the horses.

They continued to ride towards the home of the mysterious Mango on the edge of the desert.

"Who is this Mango, anyway?" asked Jonathan.

Indiana answered with a snort.

"A crazy old bat of a witch, that's who."

"Hey now, she isn't crazy... just a little on the intimidating side," Gazelda laughed. "Scares even death away..."

"What was that?" smirked Eve. Gazelda waved a hand.

"Oh, just the way an old friend described her once…"

"Heh, sounds about right," muttered Indie.

"Hey, Mango is a kind, smart lady," reprimanded Eve.

"Yeah, I bet you two get along seeing how you two are so alike, eh, babe?"

Josephine blinked as Eve whipped around, jumped off her horse, walking straight up to Indie, who was guiding his horse to give it a break. It was laughable at how tall Indie appeared compared to Eve standing in front of him. She glared at him.

"BABE? Now you look here, you jerk. My name is Eve Grace. You may have gotten us out of harm's reach, but that is no reason to be insulting."

Indie cocked an eyebrow and grinned.

"Okay, I'm guessing you don't like being called a babe. Okay then, sweet cheeks…"

Eve's eyes became slits. Marie sighed and so did Gazelda, who didn't bother to turn around. She kept walking.

"Listen and listen good, you male chauvinist pig…"

"Hey now, I was just kidding around. I have the utmost respect for women. With Irene and Gazelda around, how could I not? So, if you don't mind, darling, we might wanna get to Mango's before the sun gets up so high that we fry."

"Fine with me. Since I am a fire dragon, I like the heat. But remember this, you twit, I am not any man's 'babe' or 'darling'. Don't keep calling me such stupid pet names if you wish to keep your tongue. Either call me Eve or nothing at all." With that, Eve took her horse's reins and led it forward, not missing a step.

Flash stayed on the saddle, his head up high, enjoying the warm weather. Indie watched her storm off with a shrug. Josephine glanced at Jonathan, who was trying not to laugh. Wave was shaking her head with despair, but Marie was grinning with a glint in her eyes. The group continued on.

Josephine was going to ask how much further it was when she noticed something. She did a double take. Palm trees?

"Am I seeing things or...?"

"Yes, Josephine, those are palm trees," giggled Wave.

"Mango is a master of plants. She can make anything grow, even here in the desert," smiled Indiana.

"Oh," said Josephine.

Mango's home came into view. It was a three-story house, a glass dome in the middle with a large telescope visible under the dome. Her door was blue. The ivy all over the house made it appear old. It was on stumps, surrounded by not only palm trees but mango, peach, and kiwi trees; trees Josephine knew could not normally grow in the desert. At least, not this far north with the weather blazing hot in the summers and bitter cold in the winter. There was a small oasis in the back of the house covered in flowers that were bright, names that Josephine did not know. She smiled and looked over at Jonathan, who smiled back.

"Amazing, right?" she asked, dismounting.

"Very," he answered, following suit.

"Now where is she...?"

No sooner had Gazelda said that, the door opened and closed. Standing on the doormat was a woman looking to be in her late forties, a few inches taller than Eve. She had piercing green eyes, skin the color of light sand, and black hair pulled into a braided bun. She stomped up to them.

"THERE YOU ARE!! HALF WORRIED ABOUT YOU FOOLS...!" She stopped just in front of Gazelda and did a double take. "Gazelda! Human form?! If I were you, I'd rather be in my proper form!"

Eve glared at Gazelda's back.

"Hello, my dear Mango. I would, but your house isn't built for unicorns."

Mango half-laughed, then turned to Indie. "Well, well, look what fate dragged in! Indiana Marilyn Phoenix!"

Eve coughed to cover up her laughter. Indiana glared at Eve, then Mango.

"You old hag, you know better than to use my...!"

"Gazelda!"

Mango ignored Indie, which made the vein in his forehead pulse even more.

"So, you're here to get the book and everything. Am I in the right to say my job is finished?"

"Yes, that part of your job is over now, Mango," smiled Gazelda.

"Okay then, I QUIT!" And with a twirl of her skirt, she stomped back to her house. Everyone blinked and stared after the woman.

Gazelda, instead of being taken aback by the small woman, started to laugh. Her laugh was cut off by the woman in the house yelling, "Well, are you all going to stand there like gaping idiots or what? Come on in, unless ya want to become burned piles of flesh!"

Gazelda laughed again as she followed Mango in; Indie, Eve, Wave, and Marie close behind. Josephine and Jonathan exchanged a glance with their unicorns, then with each other. Jonathan shrugged and went forward, Josephine close behind.

Mango called out again, "Stable in the back for the horses."

Starlette and Ulysses nodded and guided the horses to the back. Josephine was the last one to cross the threshold of the house.

Inside was as amazing as the outside. Josephine met a dozen distinct smells; old books that covered almost the entire house, different plants/herbs. Some she recognized, some she didn't. She could smell jasmine, basil, garlic, catnip, and much more. There were candles all over as well, all different colors, shapes, and sizes. The room was smaller than what Josephine thought it would be, but she put that down to the clutter. She turned to follow the others down a hallway leading off the main room. They passed a door that led up to the telescope. There was another door that she was not sure what was behind it, but she heard scratching noises like a cat was locked in the room. She felt something, too... like someone was bored and frustrated, but it wasn't Josephine herself. She frowned, wondering what was going on.

Once they had reached the end of the hallway, there was another door. The room was much larger, with one small window. In the middle was a rectangular table with six mismatched wood chairs. Indiana walked over and sat on the windowsill while the rest sat at the table. Josephine marveled at all the books. The shelves were built into the wall, covering all the sides except the fireplace and the window. There were all sorts of different books, some so old that the lettering was gone on the spines and newer books that looked as though they had yet to be read.

Josephine saw Jonathan was glancing at the books, too. Eve and the other two weren't, so Josephine guessed from that and the way Eve had been talking that they knew this Mango as well.

She walked in at that moment, pulling in a chair for herself. Josephine glanced at her overall appearance. She was wearing a long purple tunic with a matching skirt, and around her neck was a gold hand pendant. She chuckled and yelled out to Gazelda as she left the room again.

"You know, Gazelda, it was bad enough looking after little lizards and this..." She reappeared with a large leather-bound book and slammed it down on the table. Mango placed her hands on her hips. "Well, are you going to say anything, or are ya just going to sit there with a stupid smile?"

Gazelda sighed. "I've heard you say that before, Mango, you know."

Mango snorted. "But this time I mean it."

Gazelda shrugged. Mango glanced at the rest of them.

"Well, well, this is the rest of the Dragon Hearts. Jonathan Falcon and Josephine Drageon."

Josephine blinked. "You know my name?"

Mango waved a hand. "Of course. I know many things, my dear. It's part of my job to know things. You're a little skinnier than I would prefer for a Dragon heart, but after a little training, your muscles will help fix that. You seem like a smart lass..."

"Sorry, what was that, Mango?" mocked Indie.

Mango glared at him, picking up an ornate walking stick as a silent threat, then continued,

"... but I've said that about others and been wrong. The world you are going to enter, well, have entered, young Josephine, is dangerous. Evil shows no mercy to their enemies, and you will have to do the same. I will not sugarcoat it. No glory in war, like some people," Mango glared over at Eve, "would like to fool you into thinking. You will have to kill. No getting around it. For a Dragon Knight, you must do what you have to protect the innocent and keep your humanity. Some have good intentions going in and then end up becoming what they hate the most. Never become numb to the waste of life, you lot. For when you do, you are on the first step of losing yourself to the dark."

She took a breath then went on, "Evil, too, will try to twist your words and convince you to join them. They will say pretty words, but never take them at face value. Evil will fool you into thinking that you can negotiate, but that is all a lie. Evil cannot be reasoned with or allowed to go on. That is the story of history. Evil and good shall always be fighting. But it is not foolish to fight, for it is right that the innocent should not suffer. Good does always win. It takes its punches, and evil may out-trick but will never out-smart good. Power, too, is something you must watch, because if you have too much, you will become overconfident. Many, including Cetus, thought with their great powers they were superior and let it all go to their heads! Do not let power over-take you, lest you become what you fight. Do you understand this, Josephine, Jonathan, Eve, Wave, and Marie?"

They all nodded. Indiana watched them, trying to understand why Mango was giving such a speech. Gazelda obviously understood. She watched with approval in her eyes.

Jonathan spoke. "I have seen it already in my father. I shall not become what he has become." He clenched his fist under the table.

Mango nodded. "Good. You all understand. That is partly the speech that they give young Dragon Knights during their first lesson and the ceremony of naming."

"Ceremony of naming?" asked Indie.

"When the Dragon Knights name their dragons," answered Gazelda.

Josephine held her breath. This was what she was looking forward to, meeting her dragon companion. When a Dragon Heart's power awakens, a young Dragon would hatch at the same time. Naming the Dragon was the way a bond would form between the Dragon heart and the dragon. As long as the two wished, they would fight together and be together. But if the dragon or Dragon heart found a time where they no longer need or wish to be together, the bond can be broken; however, it was rare for that to happen.

Mango saw the excitement in Josephine's eyes and gave a bona fide smile.

"Your Dragons are your partners. They are as smart as you are. They are not pretty pets; they are powerful creatures that can easily kill you. Understand that and respect that and you will have no problems. They are the same element as you and together you shall master it. But before we get to that, let's get this book out of the way."

She picked it up by the corner and dropped it.

"This is the record of the history of the world and the Dragon Knight Alliance, which is intertwined. From when Taranis formed it and when James disbanded it. Every leader and their seconds-in-command have written in this book to record what they saw or at least what they thought they saw during their time as leader. Any fool can learn from their own mistakes, but a truly wise person can learn from others."

Josephine nodded, taking the book from Mango.

"You are the keeper now, or if you wish, you can give it to one of the others to care for. Read it well and keep it close at hand. Many a lesson is in that from the beginning to now. You can wait until the end of your leadership or write presently, which I suggest. Sometimes I find when figuring out a puzzle rewriting it comes in handy to solve it," Mango suggested, taking a seat in her large oak chair.

"I understand and will guard it with my life," Josephine said, taking the book, treating it with great care.

Mango laughed. "It's not that important to die for it, maybe a leg or something, but not your life. At least I know you're taking this seriously..."

At that moment, out of the corner of her eye, Josephine saw a little snout poking around the door. She turned around in her chair to see a small creature run into the room, across the table, before jumping into Eve's lap. It was a red lizard sniffing Eve's face. Eve smiled and began patting it.

Mango folded her hands. Josephine heard a cooing noise Four other little lizards wandered in, the colors of bright yellow, deep-sea blue, icy white-blue, and midnight black. The black one walked right up to the other side of Josephine, jumping into Jonathan's lap. He smiled and patted the lizard. With amazing speed, the yellow one flew into Marie's embrace. Wave scooped up the sea blue creature with webbed claws when it walked timidly up to her. The icy blue one waddled over to Josephine and blinked at her.

It seemed to say, "Hello, who are you?" in its yellow eyes. Josephine, with her two fingers, patted its head. It purred in response. Josephine smiled, but was a little shocked at the purr. The lizard jumped up into Josephine's lap. It gave Josephine a chance to admire what she could guess was a girl dragon. Her light blue bat wings had thin skin that was attached to strong, thick bones that looked like icicles. The scales were small and covered her whole body except a small patch on her belly. The scales reflected the many colors of the rainbow. Her icicle spikes ran the full length of her, ending at the tip of her tail. The Dragon could have been carved from ice itself; she was so beautiful. She felt cold to the touch, but in a pleasant way.

When the lizard let out a squeak, Josephine saw tiny but razor-sharp teeth, two fangs on both the top and bottom standing out as the longest. Her tail was equal in length to her upper body.

A baby ice dragon.

"Hello there," Josephine smiled.

"Hello!" it chirped back. Josephine blinked in shock.

"It talked," said Indie, also a little shocked.

"Well, of course it talked. What did you think it would do? Chirp like a bird or babble like a dumb monkey?" mocked Mango.

Indie glared, but didn't say anything about the monkey jab.

"I dare say that you and your dragons will get along just fine," smiled Gazelda.

"If this was the Alliance of old, there would be a large ceremony where you meet your dragon, then name them and become official students of the Dragon Knights. But of course, we don't have any of that..." smirked Mango.

"What do we do?" asked Jonathan, giving his dragon a thorough scratching. It was purring like mad and rubbing against Jonathan like a cat.

"Oh yeah! Loving this!" he laughed, rolling on his back. Jonathan laughed.

"You..." Gazelda laughed at Jonathan's dragon, "simply name them and it makes a bond. For them, letting you name them begins the bond of trust. Sometimes you get the name right away or it takes a few guesses, but once they accept the name you give, the bond is complete. You become one in essence, not to sound corny," she laughed.

Eve smiled.

"May I go first then and show them?"

Gazelda waved her hand to go on.

"Do you like the name FireWind and will take me, Eve Grace, as your partner?" she asked her red dragon.

The red dragon was a hard, deep red, and her scales flowed in a patterned that reminded Josephine of molten lava. It stood straight on its five clawed paws and said in a clear, ringing voice,

"Yes, I accept."

Eve smiled, and the newly named FireWind smiled back, nudging her.

"That's how it's done," smiled Gazelda.

Wave looked at everyone as though asking, and they nodded to her to go ahead.

"May I name you after the mighty storm Hurricane, and will you be my partner, I, Wave Williams?"

The Water Dragon smiled a toothy smile and said, "Yes, I would be honored to be your dragon, Hurricane."

She smiled and gave Hurricane a hug. Hurricane wrapped her long, almost kelp like, finned tail around Wave's arm.

Marie cleared her throat and then frowned at her bright yellow, almost white, dragon. Out of the five dragons, it was the second smallest next to Jonathan's. It took Marie a moment, then she grinned.

"You know that all but one match the gender of their partner?" smiled Mango, and Gazelda chuckled back.

"Rare."

"Well, so am I," said Marie, holding her head up.

"May I, Marie ThunderFly, name you Perun, my grand-father's name, and will you do me the honor of being my Dragon?"

He grinned and licked her cheek.

"You have to say it, dummy," barked FireWind.

"I accept," Perun said, and then he stuck his tongue out at FireWind, who replied the same way.

Josephine glanced at Jonathan and gave a nod to him. He frowned, then smiled.

"May I, Jonathan Falcon, call you Aeolus, and be your partner?"

"Yes, you may."

The small, slick, black wind dragon smiled back at Jonathan.

Josephine looked back at her dragon, who stared back with cute, patient eyes. She wasn't too sure what to name her. She was beautiful, so she needed a name that matched. She thought for another moment when the thin spring sunlight floated into the room. It bounced off her scales and showed different colors. It reminded her of something she had wanted to see since she was little.

"I, Josephine Drageon, ask if you would like the name Aurora, and if I may, be your partner?" asked Josephine.

She nodded.

"I would be honored," the ice dragon smiled.

"Very good indeed." Gazelda smiled.

Josephine began to cuddle Aurora; she could feel happiness as though it was water coming off her in waves.

"I can feel her emotions...?" she asked at the two older women.

Mango explained,

"It is your bond. You can feel each other's emotions and communicate through that. Not as fancy as, oh... maybe mind reading, but it gets the job done. I find reading each other's minds myself overrated," she smiled.

Josephine thought of happiness, staring at Aurora. She replied the same back. They smiled at each other. They could also faintly feel everyone else's happiness.

"How well can we will be able to feel other emotions?" asked Jonathan, staring over at Josephine, who couldn't quite understand why her blood was pooling in her cheeks.

"Once you are attuned to your own dragon's emotions, you will find over time it will be easy enough to be fully attuned to others. Very handy if you are talking to someone who has a bad habit of lying," said Gazelda, who leaned forward to pat FireWind.

They all sat there for a moment, trying out the power of their emotions, when suddenly she heard something crash in another room.

"CRAWWW!!!"

"Hmmm, wonder what he's done this time," chuckled Indie under his breath.

Mango went to say something, but the door flew open. A fat tiger cat with white paws ran at neck-breaking speed, running around the room; right behind the cat was a black raven, screaming a rough bird call at it.

It took a moment, but Josephine was able to make out what they were yelling:

"ALAN, YOU'RE GOING TO GET IT! THIS IS THE FINAL STRAW!"

"DON'T YOU MEAN WORM!?"

"JERK!"

"COME ON, I'M SORRY, I DIDN'T REALIZE IT WAS YOU, SIS..."

"YOU KNEW PERFECTLY WELL IT WAS ME!"

"ALL YOU BIRDS LOOK THE SAME TO ME!"

"OH, SO WHAT, YOUR BIG NOSE IS BROKEN, YOU FAT...!"

"I AM NOT FAT, I'M JUST BIG BONED, YOU BIG MOUTHED..."

Mango grabbed the bird, shoving it on her shoulder, then grabbed the cat's tail and swung it on Josephine's lap, forcing Aurora to perch on Josephine's shoulder. The cat was heavy compared to the house cats Josephine had at home.

"Okay, I'll bite. What did Alan do this time? Not that we can't already guess from what Mirage was screeching...," laughed Indie.

"He tried to eat me!" the bird yelled from Mango's shoulder.

"Did not," muttered Alan the cat, glaring at the bird. "I was just fooling around. You pick around so much, no wonder I can't tell you apart from actual birds."

"HEY!"

"ENOUGH!" bellowed Mango, glaring at both animals. "Mirage, you have my permission to nettle pick him as long as he lives."

"Thank you," Mirage the raven said, fixing her feathers and standing straight.

"Ha, but what if she dies before me?!" Alan said, sitting up and pointing a paw.

"I'll haunt you," snapped Mirage.

He opened his mouth for a second, but thought better of it. So instead, he curled up in Josephine's lap and stuck his tongue out.

He glanced around, then said, "Gazelda, are these your new students? Not bad looking, if I do say so myself." He gave Josephine a big grin, which Josephine returned with a raised eyebrow.

"Glad you approve," said Gazelda with a smirk. "Everyone, this is..."

"Alan Marvel, the wizard extraordinaire," said the cat happily, "And the raven is my twin sister Mirage Marvel, the witch."

The raven glared at the lack of extraordinaire at the end of her name but said, "Former resident witch and wizard of Red Rose Castle." She stared at Jonathan when she said it.

"Nice to see you again, young prince. Last time we saw you, you were only a newborn, I believe..." said Alan, standing up on his back paws and placing his front ones on Josephine's shoulders to look at Jonathan.

The prince's eyes went wide. "Really... now that you mention it, until my father became king, we've always had a witch or wizard to help with any magical issues that may arise, especially after the Dragon Heart Alliance fell... but Father didn't trust magic users..."

"Uh huh, being one who does not study or is not born with any special skills of magic, Dragon heart or otherwise, no surprise," said Gazelda.

"Right. Hmm, I think I do remember Mum mentioning you two once, but I thought you were human."

Alan coughed. "We were but, uh... we had a slight accident," Alan chuckled nervously, sitting back in Josephine's lap.

"We were until a certain someone messed up!"

Alan groaned and buried his nose in his paws. "Do we have to go through the whole story?" he whimpered.

Mango's eyes became narrowed. "Don't start. You made a stupid mistake; you pay the price."

Mirage puffed out her feathers then said in a stiff tone, "We were the students of Sydney Alcove, his last, before he died. He made us his replacements due to the fact that, as twins, we were powerful. And because of that, the king was not... too happy about us. Sydney was a good man, but in his old age he became easy to push around by the king, but we were not. We were too smart to fall for his games. He wanted to use our gifts of magic to gain some things that should be left buried, like shadow stones."

Josephine could feel Jonathan grow angry; he stiffened in his chair. Aeolus looked up at him, his eyes sad. Jonathan patted him to let him know it was okay.

"Right. That's when you two contacted me through Mango to inform me that was what he was doing," said Gazelda.

"Yes, it was. The king, after we refused to find a Shadow stone, told us he no longer required us and..."

"Threw us out in the cold," grumbled Alan.

If Mirage had eyebrows, Josephine was sure they would have gone straight up.

"Yes, well anyway, we came here to Mango's and..." Mirage turned to her brother. "Would you like to finish the rest, or shall I, oh great klutz?"

Alan growled at her, "*Wasn't my fault.* You feathery... you were the one who tripped and you know it..."

"They were doing a location potion, which, funnily enough, is similar to a transformation potion. Alan was not watching what he was doing and tripped and threw in raven feathers and cat fur, therefore...," laughed Marie.

"Turning them into a fat cat and a loud raven," laughed Indiana.

"I AM NOT FAT, JUST BIG BONED!"

"LOUD-MOUTHED, WHY YOU...!"

Mango snapped Mirage's beak shut and glared at Alan, making him stop as well.

"Enough you two, I can only take so much of your stupid fighting," yawned Eve.

"Same here," growled Mango, getting up and making Mirage fly over to Indiana's shoulder. She poked him with her beak. He rolled his eyes and ignored her.

"Now last few things, your dragons are small now but they will grow and grow fast. Dragon Heart Dragons grow to reflect the magical strength of their partners and to help their partners fight. I won't be surprised if they are nearly full grown by the time you reach the Centaurs. If they aren't fried by the Dananns and Dragons going to war..."

Gazelda moaned, "How bad is it getting down there?"

Mango sighed, sitting down. "I don't know what is going on with the Dragons, but they are getting stupid. Leo was really the last good dragon left. His daughter was one of the many in the past years to question the bond between Humans and Dragons, saying that Dragons are too great a creature to bond with worthless bags of flesh — that was whose words... ah yes, wasn't its Marco the earth-dragon's?"

Gazelda shrugged. "I don't know, maybe. Never met the lizard. He left the main colony in the mountains and went to Ériu, so beats me. Though I remember hearing stories about him."

"The Dragons hate us?" asked Wave.

Eve let out a breath of frustration and placed her chin on her hands, elbows on the table.

"Great Aunt Nina was afraid of this…"

"Yes, she would have known. Not only are the Dragons declaring that humans are useless, but they are also saying to stay away from them just like the Trolls and the Unicorns."

Gazelda stiffened at the mention. Josephine could feel tension coming from her. It made Josephine wonder why Gazelda had left her home in Francia and had come here to Anglii, but Mango talked again. "Not only that, but King Kingdor is fighting with them over the Phoenix Springs. The Dragons claim the Dananns have sent dragon slayers after them and other means of upset and underhanded warfare. Also, the same old claim that it is theirs by all rights, so says the current leader of the Dragons, Beacon the Lightning Dragon. The Dananns and Dragons have had a long history of fighting over the springs…"

"But why? What makes the Dragons think so?" asked Indiana.

Marie spoke this time, "During the first Shadow war of the eleventh century, the Dragons found the power of the Springs. Of course, the Dananns had put a claim on it because of their personal history and the fact they have lived in that area since the ninth century. But the Dragons saw the power in it, and even though the Dananns are more powerful than humans, they looked too similar for the taste of Bres, the Dragon leader of the time. He wanted the powers, and they are on the edge of the mountains. That began the first real war between the two magical power houses. In the end, both kings were killed. Their sons, Cadman the Tuatha Dé Danann and the dragon of ice, Amergin, took over the leaderships. The Dragon Heart Alliance was formed not long after. They fought verbally, for they didn't dare incur the safety traps the Alliance had for such things. It's been an on and off issue for years. Some dragon leaders did not care while others grumbled. When Leo the ice dragon over, he said if anyone even thought about taking it, they would find themselves without their tails."

Perun shivered. Marie patted him on the head.

"So, you can see that your diplomatic skills are going to need to be the sharpest, Josephine," said Gazelda, turning to her.

"They will twist everything, so pick your words wisely. I will do some of the talking, but they know the prophecy, so they will expect you to lead."

"Beacon is going to be a hard egg to crack," sighed Indiana.

"Last time I was down there a few months back, he was talking about starting a war. But why bother after all this time? From what I've heard, King Kingdor is willing to let the Dragons come over to share, but..."

"Ah, King Kingdor, good man..." smiled Gazelda, "And just because they can start something. I don't think Cetus is involved, not directly, at least, to their knowledge. Some use Cetus as an excuse to withdraw and become arrogant. This will hurt them in the end..." She shook her head.

They all sat there for a few minutes, mulling things over in their minds. Josephine thought about the Dragons and

the Dananns. Both had been in the old Alliance, but if neither were possibly willing to help, Josephine wouldn't be
able to count on them. If so, they the Dragon Heart Alliance
would be in trouble with only the Centaurs, Faeries, and
what little of the Red Rose army loyal to Jonathan for support if they had a huge fight with Cetus. The trolls would
never help, the masters of the sea, the Viken, wouldn't probably be too willing to help either due to their pirate natures,
at least not without a payment of some kind. There would
be no guarantee that they'd be reliable...

"Well," Mango sighed, interrupting Josephine's thoughts,
"while you lot are here for the next week, we will start training you more in fighting. Eve will, of course, train Josephine,
and also in this time you must bond with your dragons,
understanding each other's personalities and whatnot. I'll
school you in whatever I may think will come in handy, and
Gazelda as well."

"Will you be staying on with us, Indie?" asked Gazelda,
turning to look at him. He gave a half shrug.

"Irene wanted me to stay here for her message and besides
that, I got nowhere better to be."

Josephine blinked, confused. "But I thought you said you
were quitting, Lady Mango?"

Gazelda laughed.

"The old Alliance, dear, no point staying a part of what's
dead! Please don't call me lady or anything, just Mango.
As such, I, Mango, would like to swear my alliance to you,
Josephine Drageon, if I may as a Dragon warrior. I think
this new one needs a little more of old blood to help it along."

"Yes, I thank you, Mango," smiled Josephine.

"Crazy old bat," muttered Indie.

Chapter Fourteen

Fair Lady: Broken Alliances and Sad Farewells

I entered the castle again; the smell and sight of blood from the wounded overwhelmed me. I walked straight into the great room. They had removed the grand table along with the long velvet rug. Almost everyone was there. Sandra dragged herself over to the left side of the room and sat down upon Storm's good leg, with Zu helping her. King Kingdor, Mango, and several of the colony dragons. These were dragons who did not have human companions and lived in the Clocha Móra Mountains in a Dragon colony, and a few others here and there. The atmosphere in the room was solemn.

As I went to stand next to Mango, The King's eldest son, along with James, Shoney, Manyu, and Sydney came into the room.

"My friends, until we sort things out... I am still only the prince, so I cannot..."

"It is all right, Rupert," said Sydney quietly. "We will honor any decisions that you make."

"Yes, I will as well," said Queen Maria as she into walked into the room. Her eyes were red-rimmed. She placed a hand on her son's arm. Rupert squeezed it tight.

Rupert nodded and then turned to James.

"Dear Master James, what news do you have to give us?"

James leaned against Hamlet for support, then said, "Jew-elvana, along with Maruko and his Dragon Cain, have fled. Whether they fled together or separately, I do not know."

"I trusted Maruko, that worthless pile of dung," growled Mango.

"As for Jewelvana, she was a..."

"Yes, Mango, we all know perfectly well what you thought of her," King Kingdor smiled sadly.

"This is unbelievable. To have Dragon Knights turn on us, and so many of them of being our youngest students," said Zu, shaking his head.

Sandra hung her head in shame. Zu noticed and placed a hand on her shoulder.

"But why? Why would Cetus do this?" whispered Jessica. "Reed, my own..." Jessica's water Dragonling Wave nudged her snout at Jessica. Jessica smiled and patted her nose.

"From what I could feel, it was the thirst of power. It's shocking how many wanted it," muttered Ken.

"Yes, the number of traitors that have penetrated our ranks has left us no choice to do but one thing," sighed James as he looked over at Shoney and Maynu, who nodded with somber expressions.

"And what would that be, James?" I asked, raising my eyebrows.

"To dissolve the Dragon Knight Alliance."

"WHAT?" yelled Sandra and Storm in disbelief.

"But why..." asked Zu.

Mango shook her head and said, "James is right. It is the only way. The Alliance cannot do what it once did. With this much evil in our ranks as well with what we've lost... We just cannot cope anymore."

"What about the traitors?" asked Queen Maria.

"That is why we will disband in three months. We must, in that time, find as many as we can. From that point on, it will be up to the individual kingdoms to deal with them as best as they can. We must also establish guardians to look after the crystal."

"What crystal?" asked Jessica, walking over to stand beside Shoney.

"Mango, if you would, please."

Mango pulled out an extraordinary crystal. It was roughly four inches long, shaped like an oval, and as clear as the ocean. It shimmered and gleamed in the dull sunlight. I could feel its power, bright and warm.

"What is that, James?" asked King Kingdor, taking it from Mango to get a better look at it.

"It's the legendary Vanora Crystal. It is said that Dragon Knight Master Taranis and QuickStrike used this to channel their powers better. I do not know if that was true, but there is no denying it has power. When James, Shoney, and I went to train in Fu Sang, we found this crystal, and it has been kept at the Xian home temple. Cetus must have gone and raided the temple..." said Manyu, his voice trailing off.

"Has Mei been told yet?" asked Mina, her eyes faded from all the fighting. I felt like she felt empty and too numb from the shock to come to terms with the pain.

"Yes, she has already left to go to Jiǔzhōu," answered Hamlet, his voice full of remorse.

"How is Nina?" I asked quietly.

The three men looked at me with wretched eyes, then turned their heads. A few tears fell from my eyes, but I quickly wiped them away.

"She's not letting on how much she's hurting. She's helping with the wounded, as is Tyson," said Jessica, wiping away her own tears.

"What are we going to do with that thing?" asked Ken warily, trying to change the subject.

Shoney took it back from Kingdor and sighed, giving it to Sydney.

"Well, first we will have to do a special spell on it for a start," said Sydney, staring into the depths of the crystal.

"I know of a spell that would make it so only a Dragon Heart with a pure heart could wield it. It takes a large amount of energy, but it can be done. I do not wish to do it, however, until we break it up into separate pieces. That way, it cannot ever be used like the way it was used today."

"Who was the leader of this Alliance? The one who killed the King?" asked Noble Leo the wind Dragon, the leader of the Dragons.

I closed my eyes and said bitterly, "It was Cetus. He killed the king," I said, clenching my fists.

"The is nothing we can do about him now. And it is not your fault, so don't go mentally beating yourself up about it. There are more pressing matters we have to deal with. We need to figure out who is going to forge the pieces of the crystals into something," said Mango, glaring at me then looking around the room expectedly.

"We the Dananns will take a piece and forge something," said King Kingdor.

"Aye, us too," said Cyllarus of the centaurs, stepping forward.

"We will have the smiths here at Red Rose, make an object," offered King Rupert.

"We the Faeries, too, would like to help," spoke their queen.

"We the Dragons, of course," added Leo.

"I speak for our queen. I know she would wish for us the Unicorns to make one of these objects," finished the heir to the leadership of the Unicorns, Cahan.

Sydney agreed.

"The Phoenix fire and Unicorn magic will help for something forged from those cannot be touched by a shadow or someone who is a Shadow magician," Mango said.

"There is one other issue that must be dealt with at this moment, and that is the last five Dragon eggs in the hatchery," said Shoney.

"What, you mean those five eggs that haven't hatched?" asked Cinder as Mina jumped down from her head.

"Yes. Those eggs will have to be moved and cared for until their human partners' powers awaken, which will probably be a long while from now," said James, a sly smile on his face. He stared right at Mango.

"OH NO YOU DON'T JAMES! I've had a gutful of those blasted hatchlings! I swore the last group I would look after was Thunder Rose's kin, and that bunch nearly tore my whole place apart! Storm here almost took my right hand off!" yelled Mango.

Storm lowered his head shyly with a sheepish grin on his face.

"Now, now Mango," sighed Manyu. "You are the only person whom we can trust. No one else has your experience with hatchlings."

"Will you please do this one last favor for us, Mango?" asked Shoney with a pout that made me want to laugh.

"Come on now, Mango, are you saying you're getting old?" asked James cheekily, "You have taken one-on-one battles with Shadow magicians, fought with trolls, even made full grown dragons quiver in fear, but you're not willing to take five little dragon eggs? Your old joints starting to get to you?"

"I am not that old!" growled Mango as a warning. Most men would have quivered at just that, but James kept his amused look.

"Then there is no reason that you can't take them," said Manyu, waving his hand in the air as though brushing aside her protest.

"Please, Mango?" Shoney asked in a childish, pleading sort of voice.

I snickered. James, Shoney, and Manyu were the only ones that could sucker the tough old witch into something. They had it down to an art form.

"ALL RIGHT! Fine! I'll take the rotten things! If only to get you three to stop begging!" complained Mango, throwing her hands up in the air.

"That's our dear sweet old Mango! We knew you wouldn't let us down," James smiled.

"Keep calling me things like that as though I'm your sweet old grandmother and I'll slug you," muttered Mango.

"Sir James, may I ask why the Dragons may not take the unhatched dragon eggs into their care? One of those eggs is my sibling," inquired Korah, Leo's daughter.

"Because these dragons will be Dragon heart dragons, that's why!" growled Mango. "They will need to be around a human until they are joined by their Dragon Knight, as is the tradition. Do you have a problem with that?" she snapped.

Leo growled at his daughter, then said, "No, we have no problem with it. Go right on ahead, Lady Mango. My mate and I are glad our last hatchling will be in your care," he said, glaring at Korah.

"Thank you very much," muttered Mango.

"For someone who didn't want the job..." chuckled Zu.

"Can it or I'll make you taste nothing but snot for a month," muttered Mango, who then disappeared, no doubt to collect the eggs.

I shook my head, but with a small smile.

Once everyone went to do separate tasks, James pulled me and four others aside and said, "I need to ask something of all of you."

"Does it have something to do with the prophecy?" I asked.

James said, "In a way. I need you all to do me one last important duty."

I nodded my head and said, "I am here, James. Whatever you need, I am at your service."

Then, three months after the battle of the betrayed, the Dragon Knight Alliance was no more. Everyone was scattered like seeds into the wind, to the far reaches of the earth.

What the future held for the earth was unknown. I grew wary of what was to come.

As I finish writing this, I give what I learned from my experience. Our student took our teachings and tore it apart. My heart weeps for with hindsight I know of what he did not see, and it was from his blindness we lost our Alliance. Peace is what we earn from sacrifice. If the generations to come do not appreciate the legacy that gave them their freedom, that freedom shall be doomed.

Chapter Fifteen
Debating the Future

For the rest of their stay, all of them were being trained by Mango, Gazelda, and each other. Early in the morning, Mango would teach them the ins and outs of how magic worked, with some help from Alan and Mirage, mostly Mirage; Gazelda in the early afternoon would teach them the rules of the Dragon Heart Alliance; and then in the afternoon to the late evening, Eve and the others would help Josephine learn the way of the sword.

Josephine found that watching two other people do a few movements then doing them herself was the best way for her. Most of the time, Eve and Marie would demonstrate, then Jonathan would be Josephine's partner. She found she was getting much better; by the end of the third day, she beat Wave with a straight one-on-one duel. Eve said that was good, but Wave was the weakest when it came to the sword, and Josephine still had a way to go. But it was nice not to have so many bruises on her backside from falling on it.

At every chance the group got, they bonded with their dragons. All the dragons were already the size of a bulky dog. Aurora was much like Josephine. They both were the bookworm type, as Aurora enjoyed looking over Josephine's shoulder as they read the *Dragon Heart Chronicles*. It did not take much for Josephine to teach Aurora how to read, for dragons are fast learners and the Chronicles were written in Dragon script. She instead of talking, observed. Aurora helped Eve point out what Josephine was doing wrong with her sword, or how people act during different situations. Aurora and Josephine had both noticed that Jonathan enjoyed being near Josephine, whether it was at the dinner table or training. Josephine found it humorous, but she also found it a little worrisome. She knew she liked Jonathan, but they didn't have the time to worry about romance when they needed to train.

But they weren't the only ones. Eve and Indie's arguing increased, but there was something about the way they contended that made Marie want to burst out laughing. She said that Eve found Indie as challenging as he does her, and that was obvious because of the way they trained. This attraction became obvious to Josephine during one of her and Eve's one-on-one training sessions.

"Watch your footing, Josephine!" squeaked Aurora, watching Josephine and Eve training yet again that day. They had been at the small oasis for going on five days. In that time Josephine found her brain a little stretched between Eve's sword lessons, reading over the history of the Dragons and how their society worked, and Mango's lessons about understanding magic. So, it was no surprise to Josephine that she was having problems keeping focus.

"Oh look... out," sighed her dragon as once again she found herself on the ground, her butt protesting in pain.

"You're not watching how I'm moving," chuckled Eve, helping her up.

"I think it's because there's so much to remember..." said Josephine, trying to ignore the headache that was coming on.

FireWind was chopping on a small mouse. She said, "Glaud," FireWind gulped, "that we dragons don't have to mess around with metal sticks. We've got our claws, jaws, flame, wings, and tail to destroy our enemies."

"Oh, you don't have it that easy," smirked Josephine, "You'll have to train to know how to use your claws, jaws, flame, wings, and tail, just as we must learn how to fight with you on your back, in flight..."

"Drat," said FireWind, swinging her tail in distaste.

"And just how are you going to learn all of this?" asked a male voice.

Josephine glanced up above FireWind's tree branch to see Indiana sitting watching them.

Eve glared up at him. She said, "There are a few Dragon Knights left from the old Alliance, they can at least train us to work with our dragons and/or elemental magic, though we'll be hard pressed to find one that's trained in elemental magic."

"Why?" asked Indie, cocking an eyebrow.

Eve let out a frustrated breath. "Because Elemental magic is hard. Only about a third was trained and good at it. It also depends on whatever element that Dragon Knight is. The ones who were best at it were mostly wind, water, ice, and earth. Those who were fire or lightning had a hard time controlling their elements. My Great-Grandfather Michael was not mastered in fire like his twin sister Nina. But Great-Aunt Nina died, so I have no one right now to teach me how to fully control my Dragon Fire. If I do ever find one."

Indie snorted. "Well, I guess elemental magic is not that great if that many didn't bother with it."

Eve's eyes narrowed. "It is the best thing in a Dragon heart's attacks. However, the elements, especially lightning and fire, are hard to control as I said. The elements are dangerous in their own right but fire and lighting can be slightly more destructive with less force whereas wind and water require more force to be that dangerous. If you make a mistake with wind or water, you'll just fall down or get soaking wet. But when it comes to fire or lightning, you could easily kill yourself or others."

"From getting too mad?" he chuckled.

Eve glared at him, then turned back to Josephine. "Why don't you try practicing by yourself for a while? It's getting a little annoying out here..." she muttered the last part, nodding to FireWind, who jumped over to walk with Eve. Flash jumped up on Eve's shoulder as they walked into the house. Indie watched her go and Josephine could feel a little bit of admiration coming from Indiana as Eve left.

"Would you like me to teach you for a bit?" asked Indie, jumping down from the tree.

"I guess it's okay," smiled Josephine.

She got the feeling that the two enjoyed arguing with each other, and that was apparent when they dueled. Indie was good; he was on par and even once beat Jonathan and only narrowly lost to Eve. Josephine bet that if Eve wasn't a Dragon heart that they would be equals.

"Equals, ha!" Eve scoffed at Josephine when she had suggested it to her. "He's good, but not that great, Josephine. He uses tricks more than skill to win his fights. Just out wit him and he's out, which doesn't take much," she muttered the last part.

Josephine wasn't so sure Eve believed that, for when they worked together later that night, Josephine and Aurora both saw a look of admiration as they fought, which seemed more of a dance than a duel. If it wasn't for Indie's smart comments and Eve's temper, Marie figured they would already be courting. Marie even started a bet with Wave on how long it would take for them to get together. Gazelda and Alan even joined in. But Jonathan, like Josephine, thought it was best to not take part.

"What if they find out about it? Won't Eve try to, like, rip your heads off?" asked Jonathan, watching Marie take down Alan's bet.

Marie shrugged. "If a certain prince and princess keep their mouths shut, I don't see how they could." She gave a wicked grin, then turned to Perun to get his input.

On top of everything else, to build up Josephine's diplomatic skills, the girls would have debates with Josephine as the neutral party. They would debate (or argue, as Indie put it) over everything from who cooked the best (it was a tie between Eve and Marie, Wave lost with just one sentence from the other two), to more serious things as in certain laws that the king had passed. Jonathan would join in on those debates, too, and would help to be an enforcer when Eve got a little long on her ranting. Eve was a passionate person and would go on about things. One item being what

Josephine hadn't thought about but knew she had to: killing. The group, minus Gazelda, Mango, Mirage (who flew in and out every other day for news), and Alan was outside under the trees beside the water hole.

"In the end, Cetus and whoever kills in his name will have to die," Eve sighed. "No getting around it. If we don't, he'll escape and keep killing until we are dead and even after that. He shows no mercy to us, so why should we show mercy to him?"

This time, Wave sighed. She had been playing with Hurricane in the water. "Because we have hearts, Eve. We are better than him."

Eve snorted, making the butterfly that Flash was stalking take off. "Exactly. We don't kill for ourselves, for power, or for revenge. We do it for justice. He kills for evil, and there is but one way to make him pay."

"I agree with Eve," chimed in Indie. It was the first time he had said anything during their talks. He never ever spoke, and Eve blinked to make sure it was Indie who had spoken and raised an eyebrow. "He has to pay for his crimes. There is no doubt of his guilt. He took lives, therefore, he has to forfeit his own."

Eve raised an eyebrow and nodded her head. "Well put, Indie."

He shrugged, carving a piece of wood on his perch in the Mango tree. Wave didn't look too impressed.

"Come on, Wave, the punishment should fit the crime," added Jonathan from beside Josephine.

Josephine frowned.

"Not too sure you agree, Josey?" asked Indie.

"I... don't know. If I fight him during a battle, then fine. But if we captured him... well, I guess really in the end the answer really is only trial, then death. The law says so."

Marie nodded in approval.

"Wise response, Josephine," Eve said, lying back on the sand, FireWind at her elbow, Flash at her head.

"What do you think, Aurora, Aeolus?" asked Josephine, turning to look at the two dragons.

"I agree with you and Eve," said Aeolus.

"I agree with you Josephine," said Aurora, laying her head in Josephine's lap.

Josephine smiled, then tickled Aurora's stomach. "You'd better be truly saying that! Not just because you're my dragon!"

"NO! Stop!" Aurora laughed.

"I don't know why you don't just let Eve do all the diplomatic talking," smirked Indie. "One look from the wicked midget, and they'd sign right up from fright and for life."

Eve jumped up and hit the tree, bringing Indie down right on his back, taking some hard, unripe mangos to his head. Once sure that Indie had gotten a fitting punishment, Eve stomped back into the house.

"... because they'd want someone that intimidating on their side, grouch," muttered Indiana, dusting himself off.

Marie was laughing, while Wave was looking after Eve with a sour look. Jonathan looked over at Josephine; they both shared a grin.

"Ah, will that boy and girl ever learn?" chuckled Gazelda, sitting down at the library table, sipping mango juice.

Mango came into the room with a spell book, chuckling. She said, "Give them time, they'll grow up. They'll have to consider what's just over the horizon."

She sat down as Eve stomped upstairs to her room and slammed the door.

"What am I doing, Mango? Condemning these children to this?" muttered Gazelda, rubbing her temples.

"It's not your fault; it's just the way it is. Cursed future sight," Mango sighed, slamming the book.

"What?" Gazelda asked, warily looking over at Mango.

"Oh, forgot to tell you last night; the Dragons aren't going to join up."

Gazelda spoke a few of her favorite curse words in her favorite languages.

"Don't sound so mad. We knew it was a long shot," Mango muttered, stealing a sip from Gazelda's drink. The Metamorphia glared at the witch.

"Should we skip them all together?" Mango shook her head.

"Nah, still go. Maybe Josephine could still convince them to join, or at least some of them. Josephine needs the practice, so don't tell her or she might not try as hard as she needs to. Not to mention she needs to practice being diplomatic in life and death situations. Helps give you thick skin."

Gazelda stopped mid-sip to look at Mango, who waved her hand.

"Not that it would be like that, not in that way. But still..."

Mango went to pull another book. Gazelda looked out the back window to see Jonathan tossing some of the fallen Mangos to Aeolus, the others getting up to do the same. FireWind jumped up and hovered at the second-floor window to coax Eve to come back down.

Mango followed her stare, then sighed. "I know what you're thinking and don't. The Alliance did what they could. Do you think even if they weren't the Royal Dragons, do you think any of them would let Cetus *take away* their homes? Especially Jonathan?"

Gazelda shook her head. "They are so young. They should be worried over their clothes, who they should/shouldn't court, going to festivals, traveling, going to schools... not fighting the darkest evil since the Second Shadow War."

Mango gave Gazelda a stern look, which she ignored.

"Gazelda F-"

Eve stomped down the stairs and went back to the lake to join the others, making sure to not look at Indie as though he was not alive. It reminded Gazelda fondly of two old friends, which made her sigh, for she felt the glare coming from Mango.

"I know, no point worrying about the what ifs."

"Exactly. Give them time; they will make it."

Gazelda sighed as she watched Eve throw a rotten mango at Indie for a joke he made about her acting just like a nasty fay he had run into once.

She turned to Mango and said, "Did you foresee it?"

"My dear," Mango said, watching Indie rush inside to escape Eve; Wave, Marie, and FireWind grabbing her from chasing him; Josephine and Jonathan wisely watching and did not get involved.

"I don't bother looking into the future unless I have to. I find faith a bit more comforting and more helpful, even if it doesn't work out the way we wanted."

Gazelda chuckled. She couldn't argue with that.

Josephine stared out the window with a thousand things whirling in her head. Aurora was asleep beside Hurricane on the floor, and Wave was in the other bed with an arm over her eyes. Josephine sighed and slipped on her slippers, deciding that a cup of warm milk would help her brain. With a pang of sadness, she remembered that her mother was the on who told her warm milk was the best cure for a restless mind. Josephine went down the stairs and was going to turn towards the kitchen when she spied the door to the telescope open. She slipped up the curving steps to see Mango at the top of the third floor, looking out over the dome.

"Mango? Are you okay?" Josephine whispered, stopping at the last step.

Mango jumped, then sighed, "Oh, Josephine, you gave me a fright!"

"Sorry," whispered Josephine, a little red-cheeked. Josephine liked the witch but found her intimidating. She was like a tough teacher that you would love for one instant, then when she called on you for a tough question, hated the next instant.

"It must be something about short women," Josephine thought in her mind as Mango urged her to sit beside her at the telescope's eyepiece. The raven-haired girl did as Mango asked and sat on the rug.

"Ah, Josephine, have you not seen a more beautiful sight than the night sky?" Mango asked, sitting down on a three-legged stool. Josephine stared through the dome. She could see some constellations that she couldn't see down south. The Dragon star that pointed north was at the edge of the dome behind her.

"Yes, it is very pretty, I guess. But it's so dark. I like when it's dawn the best, when the sky is clear and the air has a bite to it."

Mango smiled. "To each woman her own. You think that is beautiful, then wait to see the Aurora Borealis, my dear. As an ice dragon, you will truly love that light show." Mango smiled as Aurora poked her head up the stairs.

"Josephine?"

"Yes, Aurora, I couldn't sleep."

Aurora just was able to squeeze into the room and curl up beside Josephine. Mango lit another candle, a white one. A blue one was already aflame.

"Too much on your mind, young Dragon Knight?"

Josephine sighed and nodded.

"Yes, as the leader, get use to losing sleep over things. Most leaders over-think things, so get used to it." She smirked and Josephine shrugged her shoulders.

"It's not that... or maybe it is..."

Mango leaned back and waved her hand. "Go ahead. Aurora and I are all ears." She smiled and waited.

Josephine took a deep breath. "Mirage hasn't been back yet. From her last report, riots are spreading through the major cities, and Red Rose City is in lockdown. The Alliance's strength depends on Red Rose Kingdom's troops, which we may only have a few dozen at best. Without the Dragons, we have little hope of making it." Josephine looked up to see Mango with a thoughtful stare.

"I see. So, how do you plan to deal with this?"

Josephine shook her head.

"I do not know. Even with the Dananns and the Centaurs, we'll be short. The Trolls will sign on with Cetus, and so could some of the Red Rose troops and Lords. And the Viken, too, most likely."

Mango smirked. "All I can say is deal with what you have control over. Only until after the Dragons should you start to make plans on where to go. Getting the Alliance together is only part of the problem."

"Yes, I know. We have no idea what Cetus is really up to. The mostly logical thing is, of course, he is building up his troops. But we have no true number of what that is, nor how strong Cetus himself has become with his powers restored."

"Right again."

"I... just am not sure what to do."

Mango looked at her thoughtfully. Josephine pondered over what she just said, and it hit her.

"Trust Gazelda and whoever joins to help, right?"

Mango smiled. "Good girl. A leader is just the brain; it needs the rest of the body to tell it what is going on. You may just live through this yet, Josephine." Mango placed a hand on Josephine's cheek and the other hand on Aurora's head.

"You two will go far, that I can see without the need for future seeing. Look after each other and the ones who follow you. The Alliance has always been more than just a way to keep peace; it is a family. I saw it fall apart, and I pray I die before this one does."

"You... You were alive when it disbanded?" blinked Josephine, giving Mango a closer inspection. Mango to her eyes looked no more than forty. "But I thought..."

A bang came echoing into the room from the outside. Mirage was tapping frantically on the glass dome. Mango opened one of the bottom panels.

"Big trouble!" gasped the raven, landing on Mango's shoulder.

"Wake everyone up. The sooner you get to the Dragons, the better!"

Chapter Sixteen
The Safety of the Desert

"What' g... onz?" muttered Marie, scratching her head. The others were groggy, too, except Eve, who seemed to be wide awake. The Dragons were at the window, for they were too big to all fit in the library. Josephine went to explain, but then Gazelda and Mango came in. Gazelda was in her riding gear. Mirage flew in and sat on the chair at the head of the table.

"The king is sending troops to the trade towns. No one except the troops is allowed in or out of Red Rose City. There have already been some... incidents."

Jonathan squeezed the back of his chair.

"How many people?" asked Eve, her voice thick with anger.

"I don't know, a few, but it could have been worse, I guess," the raven said, shrugging.

"I found Sheppard; he is safe in the Phoenix Mountains. Your mother and brothers are safe, too. They were able to escape from the castle with Sheppard. They are gone to stay with a loyal member of the court."

Indie looked up. "Did you find...?"

"I got a hold of Irene through Jessie Bell; she flies faster than me. She is with her sister. Also, Josephine's family is back home safe."

Josephine let out a breath of relief. But how long would her brothers, father, and Jake be safe from the troops?

"Are they recruiting anyone yet for the army?" Josephine asked.

"No. They have more than enough troops to patrol the castle and keep Anglii in check. You have to get to the Dragon's lair as soon as possible. It is one of the few places you'll be able to be without worrying about the army. Take back roads to anywhere else you go."

"Well, there goes the rest of our week and sleep," grumbled Marie. Gazelda nodded.

"Afraid so. At least we'll get the dragons trained a little if they'll let us..." Gazelda's sigh gave Josephine the impression that may not happen.

"Mango, what are you going to do?" asked Eve, sadness coming off her in waves.

"Move out. I need to catch up with a few old friends..."

"Diana being one of them?" questioned Gazelda with a smug smile.

"I said friends, not annoying, arrogant enemies."

Gazelda rolled her eyes, and Mango slapped her on the arm.

"Don't give me that. Now, let's get you all packed up and to the Dragons. Nowhere is safe; remember that and you'll keep your heads."

"But what about your books?" Marie asked, looking around.

"Don't worry, Alan and Mirage will look after them for a while. Don't worry, Eve and Marie. I'll make sure to take your favorites to Rave Town for safekeeping." Eve nodded and whispered a thank you, as did Marie.

The group disappeared into the glaring sun; Mango was too busy packing to see them off. Alan purred and meowed as they went; Mirage let out a few cries then flew with them overhead for a while with the dragons, then when they were halfway through the desert, she turned off to the East.

Indiana was in the lead with his horse. They would have to stop every so often for a brief sand storm. Wave wasn't too happy about those; it was too dry for her, and Josephine, too, felt it was too hot and too dry. The others didn't mind; Eve was very much enjoying the sun and even took off her scarf to take in the sun's rays.

"How long is it from here to the Dragons' den?" asked Marie when it was cooling down to sunset.

"A half a day more. We've made good time, and the sandstorms haven't been too bad." Indie went to say something but then cursed, looking right past Josephine. He grabbed her and pulled out a small dagger and threw it. Josephine then heard the rushed footsteps of a creature running from the dagger. It hissed, taking refuge behind a small dune.

"Bloody Viper dragons," Indie muttered.

The creature had an orange-colored mane of skin around its neck with dull purple spots. Its jaw was like a dragon's, and the same size as Flash. It hissed, showing off its venom covered teeth. Aeolus came up behind the Viper Dragon and roared at it, making it turn and hiss at him like a cat. Aeolus snarled at it and swiped it with his tail, sending it flying a good twenty feet away.

"Aeolus, that wasn't nice, and be more careful! That venom is dangerous!" Wave frowned.

"Viper dragon venom isn't strong enough to get through dragon scales," Gazelda smirked.

"Nice one, brother, twenty feet. Bet though I could beat that," laughed FireWind, landing next to Aeolus.

"Tsh, just you try," chortled the Wind Dragon.

"Won't that hurt it?" asked Wave, frowning.

"Nah, sand gives them a nice soft landing as long as they don't go too high in the air," said Marie, grabbing a drink.

Starlette sighed and shook her head in annoyance, sending sand out of her mane. Josephine smirked and patted her neck.

Jonathan tossed back Indie's dagger, and he stuck it back in his boot.

"Nice throwing dagger; where'd you get that?" asked Eve.

"It's Tuatha Dé Danann made. Got it in a trade a few years ago from a Caminante."

"Was she pretty?" taunted Marie.

Indiana glared. "It was a man."

"Ha, doubt you've had many girls court you," mumbled Eve.

Indie went to say something, but then a tremendous roar came echoing over the sand. It made Josephine's hair stand on end.

"What was that?!" asked Starlette.

"A warning," said Gazelda, narrowing her eyes.

"Let's go. Sounds like something has happened."

"Gazelda, the horses are too tired..." started Indie, but Gazelda was already off.

"Did you understand that roar?" asked Ulysses, turning to look at the Dragons.

"Not really. It was too far away. But it sounded like a warning to me," said Aeolus.

The dragons jumped back into the sky, and the rest of them nudged their tired horses and unicorns further into the unnerving mountains.

The third day after leaving Mango's, they reached the edge of the Clocha Móra Mountains. Then it took another good day and a half to where the Dragon's lair was. By this time, everyone was sore, dirty, and a little on the grouchy side. Three times Josephine and Jonathan had to yell at Indie and Eve to stop arguing. The dragons were in better tempers than their partners, at least. They were now the size of the horses, which made them a tad jumpy. Ulysses and Starlette were able to keep them calm as they went.

Ulysses was probably the only one in the group who was in a fair mood. Starlette was getting twitchy and kept asking Josephine to dust the dirt from her mane. It annoyed Josephine a little bit but considering the circumstances; she kept her temper in check and dusted her off each time she asked without complaint.

The group took a rest in the mountain path so the horses could catch their breaths because of the altitude.

"You know, we aren't having any problems breathing at all," mused Wave.

"Speak for yourself," muttered Indie.

"I'm guessing because we are Dragon hearts, that's why," answered Josephine, ignoring Indie. "What good would a knight be if they fainted off their dragons?"

"True," giggled Wave.

"How far are we to the Dragons' den?" asked Jonathan.

"We've been in Dragon territory since early yesterday morning. They claim pretty much the whole mountain range expect the very edges of the mountains," answered Indie.

"Mmmm, just a few miles and we'll be right at the caves that they call home..." sighed Gazelda, staring into the distance.

"What kind of reception do you think we'll get?" asked Eve, pulling the horses back towards them.

"Not a cheery hello, that's for sure," muttered Indie.

"Do you have to comment on everything?" sighed Eve.

"Not now you two," ordered Gazelda, "And to answer that... not a happy hello," said Gazelda. "They will not like seeing Dragon Knights again, so be on your best behavior, you lot." Gazelda glanced at Indie and Eve before saying, "Leave all the talking to me or Josephine unless one of the dragons asks you a question directly. This is dangerous waters we are treading, and nor will it be the last."

It was almost dark when they reached it. They had climbed up then across a winding path through the mountains, only thing around was sparse vegetation. Indie jumped down onto a hidden ledge, leading his horse to do the same. Josephine glanced at Marie, who was beside her. She shrugged, and they followed Indie's lead. They found themselves under the mountain, in a large what–looked like carved out room that reached to the top of the mountain itself. Josephine felt Starlette shudder with fear and placed a hand on her side to comfort her. Aurora nudged Josephine from behind.

"I guess I shouldn't be surprised. Dragons are large; they need their space," Josephine chuckled.

"Still... it's amazing, isn't it?" Aurora giggled.

Starlette snorted, "Intimidating is more like it."

Josephine nodded. "Both, I think, are true."

Gazelda took over the lead in her unicorn form. On the other side of the cave were tall stone doors. They were about a half a mile long and tall. Gazelda stopped short of the doors and stomped her hoof three times. The sounds echoed portentously through the mountainside.

An orange-red dragon only a bit bigger than FireWind came down from the shadows of the ceiling.

"Well, well, well! Lookie who's here! Gazelda!" he snickered.

"Not now Blaze, I–... we need to see Beacon."

"Oh, Beacon isn't the leader anymore," said Blaze, eyes going wide.

"What?" glared Gazelda.

"Oh... I'm guessing you didn't... well... a dragon challenged him to his leadership and, well... Beacon lost."

"Who challenged him?" asked Indiana, glaring.

"Oh, hey Indie, long time no see, too. Well, um... You wouldn't know her but Gazelda..."

Gazelda made a whimper. "It wasn't, it couldn't..."

Josephine glanced at the others, and they all shared the same uneasy feeling of serious trouble as Gazelda's face reflected.

"I couldn't believe it myself..."

Whoever it was, Blaze was looking at Josephine, and she knew it was somebody who wouldn't like them being there.

"Is it Marco or Korah?" Gazelda asked in a level voice.

"No, he died in a freak accident a few years ago...and she left with Leo for Ériu...it was, well..." He glanced at Gazelda with a wary look.

"I'm not going to kill the messenger, Blaze, who the blood–please tell me who it is."

Blaze took a deep breath and said in a dead tone, "Sasha... The Ice Maiden of Red Rose..."

Josephine heard a gasp and turned to see that it came from Eve's mouth.

"You're telling me that... *Cetus's Dragon is now the head of the Dragons*!?"

Chapter Seventeen
Compilations of the Darkest Kind

The statement hung in the cool air for a moment while everyone tried to comprehend it.

Blaze shifted his clawed feet then said, "Yeah... well, don't take it too bad, I mean... She broke the bond with him... she didn't fight in the battle..."

Gazelda's eyes were now slits. "But she failed to come to the Alliance and tell them of his treachery. She is as guilty as Jewelvana or Maruko." She stomped her foot and scrapped it along the ground.

Blaze looked down. "I know that... but tell the elders that. The Alliance did not formerly charge her and it disbanded. Neither did Leo nor any of the other dragons ever officially ban her, so... she had full right to challenge for leadership."

"What a load of..." Eve started, but Marie cut her off.

"Yeah, we know, Eve. But it doesn't change the situation. At least in one way, we still have to try. She was a former Dragon Knight dragon... maybe..."

"But her knight betrayed the trust, and she broke the bond... there's little chance that she would be warm to the idea of us," sighed Jonathan. "From what I got from Mango, breaking a bond is one of the most painful things that one could ever deal with."

"Yes, it is," said Gazelda quietly.

Blaze stood, waiting to see what they wanted to do.

Gazelda looked at Josephine, who squared her shoulders and nodded.

"Blaze... please take us to Sasha the Ice Maiden."

Blaze nodded and tapped on the door, and on the other side, they heard pounding. Then Blaze let out a light roar and two more dragons, much bigger than any the other dragons present, easily the size of the whole of Red Rose Castle, came from where Blaze had and pushed the doors open. The stone doors scraped the floor and unwillingly moved to the strength of the two sandstone-colored dragons.

Josephine and Aurora shivered in anticipation. Gazelda asked Ulysses and Starlette to go with the horses; Blaze showed them where to go. They kept going, Starlette and Ulysses, both wishing them luck. The caves were large and seemed endless. Josephine felt small as she kept glancing around the walls of the tunnels. The smell of dragon musk was so heavy it was almost too much at times.

She noticed that there were markings on the walls but then realized some of them were claw marks, as though remnants of some long-ago battle. The group went for a good mile before meeting a large arch way; when they reached it, they saw what resembled a large throne room. In the middle of the room was a raised platform made of stone, with large pillows of red silk. Sitting there was a blue-almost-white dragon.

She was an ice dragon, like Aurora. She was, however, massive, the size of a small barn. The female dragon lifted her head to look at them. The room was covered in gold draperies and what looked like animal skeletons that had been picked clean. Two dragons, one red, one deep forest green, sat on either side of the ice dragon, and a line of four dragons were behind the ice dragon, partly in shadow. All around the room there were other dragons, all different sizes, shapes, and colors. But none held the air of authority like the white-blue dragon. Josephine knew that had to be Sasha.

"Well, welcome back, Gazelda. It has been a while since you have graced the halls of my ancestors."

Sasha jumped down from her perch to stand in front of them. Gazelda bowed to Sasha, and the others did as well, even Indiana. Once they had straightened out, Sasha stared at them. She stared at them as though she was sizing them up. There was a tang to the air, like a tight wire ready to break. Josephine glanced at the dragons behind Sasha to release the feeling was coming mostly from them.

"I must say, it is an honor to meet the new generation of Dragon Knights. I welcome you to the Dragons' Lair of Clocha Móra. Lady Mango sent us a message that the eggs from the last dragon companions had hatched and the new knights had awakened."

Sasha paused at Josephine and Aurora. They met her gaze, jaws set. Sasha, they could slightly feel, seemed almost... envious. That was the closest thing Josephine could name it to. Sasha saw they could taste her emotions and turned to Gazelda; the feeling gone.

"I am guessing you are here to renew the Dragon Knight Alliance?" asked Sasha.

"Yes, well, now it is called the Dragon Heart Alliance, but yes, I, and Josephine Drageon," Gazelda nodded her head in Josephine's direction, "wish to ask the Dragons if they would like to swear allegiance again with the Knights, as you did so long ago."

Josephine took a step forward. Sasha turned her head back to her.

"I, Josephine Drageon, the new leader of the Dragon Heart Alliance, would like to extend an invitation to the Dragons. Cetus Cyprus, as you yourself all too well know, betrayed one and all, and we must stop him from taking over. He has gained back his Shadow powers. We need ones such as you to help this new Alliance to survive and fulfill what the old could not do and make Cetus pay for his crimes and return law and order to Anglii and all the lands of Past and Present."

Jonathan's mouth twitched, as did Eve and Marie's. The Dragons, of course, would not answer right away. Her statement reminded Sasha that would have just as much to gain from imprisoning Cetus, and mentioning it in an undertone to let Sasha know that Josephine at least had a general grasp on what had happened. More so than most. Sasha blinked once. The feeling of surprise rolled off her for a second, then dissipated.

Sasha stiffened her neck, then said, "I see. I must say, you are a well-rounded speaker. A good quality in a leader."

"My Lady Sasha, we will not join!" demanded a sea-green dragon, who came to stand beside her. "These are humans who wish to take the secrets of the Dragons. They are not anymore trust-worthy than the last leader. He, too, if I remember, gave pretty speeches, and look what happened!"

"I am well aware of the events of the Battle of the Betrayed Atlantic. But we will discuss this before making any hasty decisions like hatchlings," Sasha said calmly. She turned her blue eyes back to Josephine. Aurora twitched her tail, but Josephine placed her hand on her neck to warn her and gave her a wave of calming emotion.

Sasha nodded to the two yellow dragons that had appeared behind them. "Snaptooth and Pike will lead you to your rooms. Gazelda, if you wish, we may talk now in my private chamber while your students rest."

Josephine glanced at Gazelda, who shook her head, then nodded to go with the others. Gazelda walked forward and followed Sasha. Atlantic glared at her. Josephine could feel the unease and hatred coming from him. Josephine shared a glance with Jonathan, then followed the others. They were all wary of Atlantic's intentions and the meeting that Gazelda was going to have with Sasha, knowing full well it was going to determine their fates.

Josephine agreed with Eve when she muttered, "No offence to Gazelda, but I would like to be part of an important talk that involves my life."

"Welcome to my world," muttered Jonathan.

"Do you think they'll join?" asked Wave, jumping in.

Eve glanced at the two dragons they were following and muttered, "It's a fifty/fifty shot. Sasha seems to like us, but her pain from Cetus hasn't gone away. I could feel that when Josephine said his name. Sasha is no fool, but of course..."

Eve sighed as Snaptooth stopped in front of a large room with curtains for doors. "I have been wrong before."

Josephine felt a longing, sad, yet guilty wave from Eve, but she did not know what to make of it. She looked at the girls and FireWind, and all three had uneasy faces.

"What did she mean by that?" asked Aurora, watching them, too.

"Give her time, she'll explain," sighed Wave, going in after Eve.

The room they entered was smaller than the throne room, but still spacious. It was covered in red silk drapes, and there were two separate rooms on either side of the large one.

"One side for the girls, one for the boys. For you dragons, there are rooms down the way," smiled Pike, the smaller of the two lightning dragons, and then they left.

"Wow..." gaped Wave.

"This must have been the rooms that Dragon Knights stayed in when they trained," said Marie, glancing over the small collection of books on the oak shelves near the door to their room. The dust on the spines was at least an inch thick.

Indiana chuckled, going to his and Jonathan's room, and called out,

"Yeah, this area of the mountain is younger than the other parts. They were made after the third Dragon Knight Leader took over."

Eve blinked. "For a scruffy treasure hunter, you sure know your history."

Indie poked his head back out and said, "Scruffy?! Hey, I'll make you a deal; I won't call you babe if you don't call me scruffy. How's that?"

Eve chuckled and nodded.

"Anyway, I know a bit. I've come here a couple of times. I got lost in the mountains and lost my pack. Blaze, that dragon you met, found me while he was hunting. Not long after, a Tyger attacked him. I saved him from with a once-in-a-lifetime-shot. I've been welcome here ever since. For once you save a dragon's life, you are always welcome. At least, it used to be like that, but I doubt that will last much longer."

Jonathan agreed. "The tension was high in that room. Half of the dragons in the room were glad, almost ready to cry with joy at the sight of us."

"The other half, however, would probably like no more than to eat us for dinner," sighed Eve, flopping down in a slightly moth-eaten velvet chair.

"Yes, especially Atlantic," growled Perun.

"I must say he is most definitely not an ally," sighed Marie, putting a book back and sitting beside Eve.

"Ya think? He came right out and told her not to join the Alliance. By the way," Eve smiled, "when did our name change?"

Josephine blushed. "Oh, I'm sorry; I meant to ask you all about it, but it slipped my mind. I had asked Gazelda about it and thought it was fitting to make it a simpler, friendlier name for everyone."

"And not a mouthful, I like it," smiled FireWind.

"Do you all approve?" asked Josephine.

"You're the leader. You make the choice, but if you are asking for our opinions, then I say yes," smiled Marie. The others all nodded.

"Well, that's it, then. Dragon Heart Alliance we are," smiled Josephine.

"Just whether it lasts..." muttered Aeolus, glancing back out to the hall,

"Is another story all together."

Chapter Eighteen
Dragon's Whispers

"**S**tupid, foolish, overgrown lizards!" snapped Gazelda, stomping into their room in human form.

"Hey!" complained Aeolus, looking up from his dinner of a small mountain boar.

"Sorry, not you lot, the... well, *informed, wise, old Dragon leaders*," Gazelda sneered, while speaking with malice that made Josephine cringed.

Starlette flickered her tail in distaste.

"Let me guess, they're saying no," said Eve, reaching to pick up her sword.

"No, they are in a meeting right now, but that is going to be the outcome, for Sasha is clever. It will be easy for her to make it go in her favor."

Gazelda sat down beside Wave and Hurricane. The Dragon and Dragon Heart frowned. Wave placed a hand on Gazelda's shoulder, while Hurricane placed her nose on Gazelda's head.

"I'm fine. Well, I guess that can be debated."

"If Sasha has already decided, then why were you talking with her for almost two hours?" asked Aurora.

"She has been informing me of matters that we need to be aware of," snorted Gazelda. "The Dananns shall keep the springs for the moment, but if the Dragons find that they are 'overstepping' their use of the mountains, then they will take over the springs."

"Either hand over the springs or lose those trade routes," said Indie.

"Yes... which will bring pressure from not only the Dananns' tradesmen but the human traders will also be banned from those routes; killing off the Dananns' trades. At least from certain goods that come from the mountains. Some of it can come from other places, but it'll take much longer and cost more."

"Clever, she hits them in their purses," muttered Jonathan, leaning against Ulysses, whose ears were turned down in displeasure.

"Indeed. Even though it only affects those who travel from the ocean ports of Tailltiu City and all the trade towns in the mountains, it is still a problem. Also, rumors have been spreading that Dragon slayers have been sneaking around, plotting to take out Sasha and some of the o. Though at this point, the assassination plots are just rumors. Oh, and last but not least, Sasha will not let your dragons be trained here."

"What, but...!" Eve started.

"I know. When it comes to teaching, nobody does it better than the fierce Dragon warriors. However, Sasha says to do so would mean they would declare an alliance with us, which they will not do. So, I will just simply call up a few old friends to teach you five what you need to learn," Gazelda said. "Way things are that may be the best path, anyway. Most likely, they would try to fill your brains with false information and try to get you to break your bonds. The less time we're here, the better."

"Anything else?" asked Hurricane, bowing her head in trepidation.

"Yes, we are not to come here unless invited," said Gazelda. "That applies to you, too, apparently, Indie. I am sorry about that."

"Eh, not your fault, Gazelda. Sasha would have asked me to not come back, anyway. She doesn't trust humans."

"Right. So now what is the plan?" asked Marie.

"Well, there are a few loyal dragons here, and they will come to our aid if the need arises, and a few who will keep tabs for us on the goings on here." Gazelda stood up and stretched.

"When will they make their decision known?"

"Tomorrow morning."

"So, we should be ready to leave by tomorrow?" asked Aurora in a defeated tone of voice.

Gazelda nodded her head.

Jonathan shook his head. "To come all this way for naught."

"Not really. We may have a few allies here," said Josephine, placing a hand on his shoulder.

"True, the whole of the Dragons would have been nice, but we'll take what we can."

"Right. We are going to go straight to the Dananns after the meeting. I'll have Blaze and Snap tooth take us to the border of the springs. That way, we'll be there in less than three days."

At first, all Josephine saw was comfortable blackness, and then she felt herself wander into a dream. Josephine found herself in the middle of a drenched moor. In front of her was Aurora, at least three times bigger than currently in real life. Her teeth were showing; growls were coming from deep in her throat. Across from her was another dragon. It could have been her twin, but it was a darker blue. It was equal to the dream-Aurora's size. She, too, had her fangs bared. Just behind the other dragon was a teenage girl with bronze blonde hair that was to her waist. Josephine could feel pain coming from her and worry from her dragon. She also had this feeling of being trapped. The girl had shackled wrists, which were bloody from trying to get the chains off. Josephine yelled when Aurora and the ice dragon lunged at each other, roaring. The girl said nothing and cried in silence.

Josephine woke up gasping for breath, feeling as though she'd fallen in ice water. She glanced around the room. Eve, Wave, Marie, and Gazelda were asleep. She slowed her breathing to match Wave's. The room was dark, but Josephine had no problem seeing. She took a moment to get a grip on her dream. Who was the girl and her dragon? She was obviously a Dragon heart, but why was she in her dreams? Was it a vision? Was she even real? Josephine was pondering her dream when she heard something outside of the room. She slowed her breathing to listen.

"I don't like this, Árdal..." whispered the voice in the dead of the night. Another dragon's voice answered in a loud hiss.

"Do you think *I* like this? Use your brains, Bertie!"

Josephine, in a quick heartbeat, reached the door and peered out. She saw the two massive dragons turn a corner. Josephine looked around, debating with herself. Should she follow them? If caught, they could be in serious trouble. She couldn't imagine the Dragons taking eavesdroppers too well. But if there was something else going on that Gazelda didn't even know... Josephine ran back and grabbed her knife. It wouldn't do any good against a Dragon, but she still liked having it.

"Rule number nine, better safe than sorry: always carry a knife."

She followed them around four corners while trying not to be heard or seen, listening to the two dragons' conversation. From the back of them, she recognized them as dragons from the guard. One was brown, the other blue; both were wearing purple silk sashes. The two dragons disappeared, still talking, into a room with a curtain over the opening like theirs but much bigger.

"Do you want to be branded as cowards?" demanded Bertie.

"Do you wish to be food for Fylgjas or Wyrads?" snapped back Árdal.

Bertie said something more, but they turned into a room and she couldn't catch it. She tiptoed right to the edge of the doorway, holding her breath, trying to keep her heart beat rate from going up. She hadn't noticed someone was behind her until their hand was over her mouth.

Josephine reached for her knife, then realized in the same second it had to be one of her friends; no one else around had hands. She blinked to see it was Jonathan's brown eyes that were in front of her. He mouthed to her,

"Sorry. I heard you get up then them; let's listen, shall we?"

She nodded, and he dropped his hand.

"Look, it's not that I don't like these young ones or anything, but Bertie, they're young hatchlings! They don't know what they are getting into, and I don't want to stay here and be a big bull's eye for Cetus OR the Dananns! I think Sasha is making a big mistake ticking them off..."

"I know! But we're part of the guard; if we leave, what rumors will be left behind? I don't want to make more trouble for Sasha."

Josephine heard Bertie shift his feet, nervous at whatever look that was on Árdal's face.

"She is to bring the wrath of the Dananns on us! I do not care one bit about her or her leadership! I did not agree when she wished to challenge the leadership, nor did I like it when she won over Beacon. She was Cetus's Dragon, and she sat back and let Cetus destroy everything! From the slaughtering of the young Dragon Knights and the whole of the Xian Clan... I hope she runs into more problems and someone finally gets the guts to challenge her. But I'm not going to stick around for it. First chance I get, I'm leaving for my brother in Hispania." Árdal snorted and waves of impatience were coming from him, while Bertie had an uneasy feeling.

"Well, if you want to, go ahead, but... I'm not sure yet. I might come with you, but I fear Sasha's wrath. The dishonor it will bring out as though I am a coward or something would cause problems..."

"Honor or life, Bertie, it's up to you, but I dare say the age of the Dragons of Clocha Móra is over."

The two went into another room, and Jonathan looked at Josephine, curious if she wanted to follow. Josephine shook her head no and grabbed his hand to leave. He smirked, and the two said nothing as they returned to their rooms. Josephine sat down and rubbed her temples. Jonathan sat across from her. They gathered their thoughts for a minute, then Jonathan spoke.

"So not all the dragons are pleased with Sasha's actions. No surprise really, they don't even like her. We already knew that."

"I wonder about what Árdal said, about Sasha letting Cetus destroy everything..."

Jonathan nodded. "Hm. Me as well. Does James talk about Sasha?"

Josephine shrugged and pulled the Chronicles from her pack, then sat back in her seat, flipping to the last chunk of the text while Jonathan read pieces of it sideways from his spot.

Josephine had only finished reading the first two Leader's stories, Taranis and his predecessor, his first officer Arlen Grace, one of Eve's ancestors. She found it fascinating to read Taranis's accounts of the dark ages because the real

story was much different from what most knew. The first
water Dragon Knight Kegan Sullivan had betrayed his fellow Dragon Knights. Taranis had picked Arlen, the first
Knight of fire, over Kegan for second-in-command, and
he didn't take it too well. From what Taranis had written, Kegan thought that Taranis was scared or jealous of
Kegan's power. When the second Shadow War broke out,
Kegan's brother was found to be a Shadow magician and
was killed by Taranis and Selma. Kegan saw this as taking
away his glory and destroying his honor. He slowly picked
up Shadow magic, plotting to kill Taranis, and began a
following, which was easy, for it was a huge war revolving
around the Shadow magicians of the east. Arlen discovered
the assassination plot and confronted him. There was a
tremendous battle between Kegan, Arlen, Leon, and Nia. It
wasn't until Taranis and Selma joined the fray that they
won. With his dying breath, Kegan revealed that he loved
Selma, that the Dragon Knight Alliance was pointless, and
that the Dragon Knights should all die. Therefore, he cursed
his family with the darkest of curses. His descendants, if
born Dragon Knights, would become one with the shadows
and would be mad with anger beyond the realms of sanity.

According to Arlen, just before he gave the leadership to
Matthew Williams, the last of Kegan's family, a man named
Wilhelm was killed in the massive battle of Fusang, and
along with him, the last great force of Shadow magicians.

Josephine found so much irony in this tale; the way she
had grown up, the first six Dragon Knights were seen as
saints. To read the true tale of them was a little sad, but that
was the way it was sometimes when it came to people's he-

roes. Not to mention similar to what had gone wrong with Cetus. The story confirmed rule number ten to Josephine. History repeats itself, so beware and learn from it.

She glanced over James's account of the Battle of the Betrayed but did not see Sasha's name anywhere. She flipped back to double check, but James's story recounted, as most did, from the writer's point of view. Helpful, but yet not, for they could only give so much of what they knew to be true.

"Hey, I see it, right there." Jonathan pointed just as Josephine turned the page.

"Later, I discovered the location of Cetus's original Dragon partner Sasha, the Ice Maiden. She had apparently broken her ties with Cetus when he started to plan his takeover of the Alliance. She did not help him."

"Hmm, did not help, but I see she did nothing to stop him," muttered Jonathan.

Josephine peeked at his face to see a scowl. "Sounds like it, does it not?" she agreed.

"How could she just stand by and let Cetus do all that?" he growled.

"I do not know. James says that there was a court held for her and they found her innocent. James does not seem to deem her as important as Cetus himself. Though he says here..."

"Nina is right about Sasha. She is as guilty as Cetus. She did not stop him. Her punishment of guilt that will haunt her for the rest of her life will have to be enough. The council found her innocent of all the deaths of all those victims of the battle. Sasha is not who we want. She is merely an unfortunate dragon with an evil partner. I do not know

what to truly say about Sasha. Cetus is who we all truly want. Him and Reed."

Jonathan sighed. "I see the council's point. She did not take part in the murders or the battle. Morally, she is guilty, but lawfully not."

Josephine sadly nodded. She saw the logic but still felt anger at Sasha.

"She should have at least been banned by the Dragons," said Josephine, rubbing her temples again.

Jonathan smirked at her.

"Don't worry, Ice Queen, she will pay for her actions just never when we think it should be paid."

Josephine smiled back at him, pondering the admiring look in his warm eyes. She glanced back at the book and started flipping through the pages. It seemed that all but four of the traitors were killed or tried and executed. She read the end of James's story, which ended with a quote:

"We fight for the next generation, but what do we leave for them?"

Josephine frowned, wondering James's reason behind the quote, when Jonathan flipped the page on her.

"Hey!"

"Sorry, but there's a story after his!" he said, stunned.

"Fair Lady of Francia?"

Josephine blinked and frowned. "Who is Fair Lady, and why is she here after James?"

The two read the first page and then paused.

"She doesn't seem to be a Dragon Heart, not the way she talks."

"Yeah... you're right..."

Josephine and Jonathan were so absorbed with Fair Lady's narrative that they did not notice that the others were behind them until Eve said,

"Sorry, are we interrupting a romantic moment?"

Both of them jumped, suddenly painfully aware that they were really close because they hit their heads together.

"Gah! Eve, no!" whispered Josephine, blushing. Was that what they looked like? For the briefest of seconds, the prophecy line popped into Josephine's head, but she shook her head to clear it from her mind.

"What are you two doing up?" asked Indie, walking in. Josephine smirked at his bed hair.

"Oh, nothing, just following members of the Dragon Guard and eavesdropping on them," smirked Jonathan. The two told the rest of their little adventure.

"You two, the Leader of the Dragon Heart Alliance and the Prince of Red Rose, sneaking around the Lair of the Dragons? Great way to set an example, you two," snickered Eve.

"Which leads to rules nine and ten, — better safe than sorry: always carry a knife, and history repeats itself, so beware, respectively." Josephine said, ignoring Eve's jab.

"And rule eleven, sometimes it pays to bend the rules," giggled Marie.

"But weren't you two reading in the Chronicles when we came in?" asked Indie, who nodded towards the book in Josephine's lap.

"We were pondering over this mysterious Fair Lady," answered Jonathan.

"Fair Lady who?" asked Wave, tilting her head to the side.

"That is the question. I was reading up on Sasha from James's notes when Jonathan noticed her story after his. She also talks about the Battle of the Betrayed from her view."

"Well, it's not Mango, seeing how she is mentioned in here," Josephine said nonchalantly.

"WHAT!?" hissed the other five.

Josephine handed the book over to Marie, who became flanked by the others.

"Huh, apparently Mango and Jewelvana did not get along," Marie smirked.

"How old is that old bat?!" demanded Indie, looking at Eve.

"Heck, I don't know! Mango is like an aunt to us! A witch that lived in the middle of the desert. Never imagined she was any older than like... thirty-nine."

"I don't think that is the right person for us to be questioning her age," said Marie, speed reading the book with Wave, who gasped,

"How old is *Gazelda*?"

"What?" said Indie in utter annoyance and disbelief. "What makes you think...?"

"It fits! Look..." Wave pointed to a passage, "Sandra Heartwell! Gazelda and Mango were talking about her the other day!"

"Not you, too, Wave! Of all people!" chuckled Eve.

Wave blushed. "I was getting a drink of water!" sniffed Wave. Eve snorted, but Wave chose to not answer her and continued, "Look, she talked about Sandra like they were best friends!"

"That means nothing. They could have met some years ago and became close..." started Jonathan.

"No! She was talking to Mango about Sandra and the warrior Zu! Things that I doubt Sandra would have told her unless she was a part of the Alliance!"

"..."

Everyone blinked and stared. Eve then took the book from Wave and began reading it herself. Josephine added up the missing pieces.

"Did anyone ever wonder why or how Gazelda became Leader Pro Temp?"

"Oh, my..." gasped Wave, and Eve frowned, sharing a look with Marie.

"How old is Gazelda?" Indie gaped again.

"Hey, that is a question you never ask a lady!"

Eve dropped the book on Indie's foot. He muttered a few words under his breath as Gazelda came into the room.

"Well, are you lot ready to go?" asked Gazelda, braiding her silver hair.

"What, is it time to go already?" blinked Josephine.

"It's almost dawn." Gazelda smiled and said, "Get your things all packed up and ready. But what were you all talking about when I came in?"

"Josephine and Jonathan overheard some intriguing information," answered Eve.

"Indeed? Well, then save it until we're clear of certain ears," advised Gazelda.

They nodded.

"Though I do not understand what that has to do with my age," she chuckled.

"Uh, we kinda got off subject," muttered Wave, picking up her pack. Gazelda shrugged and went to leave the room when Indie asked,

"Gazelda, exactly how old...?"

Gazelda turned and gave Indie a glare that would have made a dragon run.

As she left the room, all of them thought at the same time,

"Rule number twelve: never ask Gazelda how old she is."

Chapter Nineteen
Phoenix Springs

They left as the sun peeked over the horizon. Josephine did not have time to talk to Sasha face to face. When Josephine asked Gazelda about this, along with what she and Jonathan had overheard last night, Gazelda clicked her tongue.

"Sasha really does not trust humans or any creature that looks like humans, like the Dananns and Fairies. She made me stay in my unicorn form to talk. Cetus left scars on her heart. She would not talk to you because she's wary of you and... jealous."

Josephine raised her eyebrow and blinked.

"Jealous?"

"She can see that you and Aurora, though young in this, trust each other. Something that she and Cetus never had; not to mention she wishes to have nothing to do with Cetus, against or with him. That's why she would only talk to me. No trust."

"None whatsoever?" glared Wave. "That's not fair!"

"I said that's the reason, not that it was rational," chuckled Gazelda darkly.

As Gazelda walked off, Marie thought out loud.

"I wonder why Sasha trusts Gazelda so. I mean..."

Eve and Indie stopped bickering with each other to listen.

"Yes, she is a unicorn, and yes, we call her our temporary leader, but how does that make any difference? Sasha acted as though she's known Gazelda, almost as like a..."

"Teacher? Yeah, I noticed that, too," muttered Eve. "Gazelda knows so much more than she lets on; she has a past and I'm starting to wonder exactly what that is. I've never questioned her, because Grandpa and Great-Aunt Nina always loved her and what not, so I never stopped to think about what her life has been. But now..."

Wave glared at Marie and Eve. "What her life was before all of this is her business, Eve. It has nothing to do with—"

"Oh no, Wave, I think it has everything to do with Cetus," interjected Jonathan.

"I trust Gazelda, but it would be nice to know some more about her. Rule thirteen; question those who you give authority to."

He looked at Josephine. She shrugged.

"I think so, too. The way she and Mango talked, as though they had known each other longer than a few years, did make me wonder, but I haven't gotten far into the Chronicles. So far, I haven't found anything."

"I doubt she'd be in that far back. I'd try either Master Léi or Master James Dracolas," said Marie, reaching for the book in Josephine's opened pack. She flipped it open to the last half of the book, searching for Gazelda's name. She frowned.

"What, can't you find her anywhere?" asked Eve, walking over to help look.

Indie placed his pack down and frowned. "I think it would be better, you know, if you just ask her? If you read something that someone else wrote, you'll get the wrong impression, and that'll just tick off Gazelda..."

"What will tick me off?"

Marie slammed the book shut on Eve's finger when Gazelda walked into the room, curiosity in her eyes and a smile on her face. Eve cursed and sucked her index finger, glaring at Marie. Wave busied herself with tying up her pack, Josephine and Jonathan exchanged nervous glances. Indie folded his arms, not the least bit worried.

"Well? Really, you lot, what is making you wary to ask me something?" chuckled Gazelda when nobody answered.

Josephine went to say something when Snaptooth came and said it was time to get moving. Gazelda did not ask again, which made everybody relax. Josephine was on Indiana's side this time; if she wanted to tell them something about her past that was important to do with Cetus, she would tell them in due time. Right now, she was more concerned with them getting to the Dananns in one piece. Riots had been breaking out up and down the trading towns, and the king had sent troops, so it was important for the Dragon Knights to stay as far as possible from the towns. Fortunately, only a few abandoned towns lay near their path to the Phoenix Springs, and they would not have to go through them. It made all of them feel better because it probably was crawling with outlaws.

"Hmmm, it must have rained here last night..." smiled Wave, her eyes closed as she took in the smell. Josephine copied her; it was refreshing to smell the wet grass again after all the metallic smells of the mountains.

They stopped a half mile from the springs to eat. The Dragons had flown off a little way to hunt some Achlis that were nearby. The elk-creatures were grazing by walking backwards, for they have such large lips. Josephine smirked when the Achlis ran for it. They were fast, but not fast enough to outrun Perun.

"Hey, whose turn is it to scout ahead?" asked Indie, finishing his coffee.

"Mine, I think," said Jonathan, getting up.

"I'll come with you."

Josephine smiled, getting up as well.

Eve chuckled and Josephine glared at her as she picked up her arrows. Eve just smiled as the two walked on ahead.

"Don't get lost, you two... or distracted!" Eve laughed as the two disappeared into the tall grass and felt Wave slap her shoulder.

"What was that all about?" Wave demanded.

"Oh, come on, Wave! They like each other. As in lovey-dovey. It's so cute that I can't help myself."

"Of course, I've noticed! I have an eye for love," Wave said with her chin up a little.

"Right, that's why I am going to win that bet," smirked Marie, dumping the dregs of the coffee on their fire.

"What bet?" asked Eve.

Marie blushed and coughed. "Nothing, never mind!" She quickly went over to check the horses.

"Nice one," muttered Gazelda to Marie. She glared at Gazelda.

"Anyway, leave them alone, Eve. They have enough against them without being embarrassed by you," commanded Wave.

The dragons landed full from their hunt.

Eve said nothing more as Wave moved to Hurricane but thought to herself, "*Yes, they do have something against them... time.*"

Josephine and Jonathan were silent as they slipped through the tall grass. The landscape did not have many hills, a few small patches of trees and meadows. Josephine was a little mad at the comment Eve made. She tried to concentrate on the surroundings but caught herself once or twice watching Jonathan and thinking again about the prophecy. But Josephine's thoughts were shoved away when she smelled something extraordinary.

"Is that... the Phoenix Springs I smell?" asked Josephine.

Jonathan smelled the air and smiled.

"I think so. It's amazing, isn't it? I don't think I've ever smelled water so clean. It almost doesn't have a scent, it's so pure. The minerals give it that slight smell, I bet."

"It's said that it is because a Phoenix died here, and its last act was to bless the water, for the Dananns had tried their best to save its life," smiled Josephine. It was a favorite story of both her mother and herself.

Jonathan nodded and leaned his head back to enjoy the breeze. Josephine couldn't help but admire Jonathan at that moment. His black hair, those warm brown eyes, the way his hair moved in the wind... Josephine blushed and averted her gaze when Jonathan had turned. He smiled as he walked over to her. Jonathan was a dash taller than Josephine, so she could stare right into his eyes without having to tilt her head.

They stood there for a few minutes, both trying to figure out what to say. Josephine was the first to gather her thoughts.

"Jonathan... I think we need to talk," she smiled.

He matched her grin. "I think so, too. Would you like to start?" he asked.

Josephine nodded and continued, "We've known each other for such a short time but... I don't know... it seems so natural to talk to each other." She glanced at him, and he grinned to encourage her to keep going. "I think we are falling for each other... but everything is so chaotic that it's hard to ever to be sure. Not to mention we know so little about each other... and I don't wish to think it's just because of the Dragon heart prophecy..."

"I agree. We should change that. Every chance we get from now on, we should talk about ourselves more. We all should. It's been such a whirlwind of action that it's been hard. But I agree. I think we may have something growing between us. Prophecy or not. And frankly, I had a crush on you before I heard the prophecy," he said, smiling wide.

Josephine felt a little shocked, yet silly at the same time. She hated the fact that her cheeks blushed without her permission.

"Well... okay, that was easy. And... same goes for me," she chuckled.

"I doubt it will be, but yeah, that part was."

He glanced over the area and said, "Well, maybe we should start on our way back..."

SNAP!

Josephine and Jonathan whipped around, pulling their swords in the same movement. They glanced around, but they couldn't see anything. But they could feel some tension, and it wasn't coming from them.

"I hear lots of heartbeats," said Jonathan in a low tone.

"Hello? Who's there?" called out Josephine. No answer.

"Maybe it's a pack of animals," muttered Jonathan.

"No, I don't think so, doesn't feel like it, plus too many...," said Josephine.

Animal emotions were less complex than humans or dragon. This did not feel like simple fright. A second after she spoke, an arrow hissed past them and hit a tree almost five feet away from them.

"Who are you and what are you doing on these sacred lands?!" called another voice.

Josephine glared into the dense forest, and she heard the twang of another arrow being readied.

Jonathan called back, "We are the new Knights of the Dragon Heart Alliance. I, Prince Jonathan Falcon, and this is the Leader of the Alliance, Josephine Drageon. We are here to renew the ties with you, the Tuatha Dé Danann."

For a moment nothing happened, then rushed footsteps came towards them.

"No, my lady, it's not...!"

A young woman crashed out of the dark greenery. She was as tall as Josephine, with apple green eyes and shoulder length ruby hair. She also had pointed ears, an angular face, with full cheeks. She glared at them, then relaxed.

The teenager smiled and asked, "If I may, if you really are who you say you are, who is your teacher?"

"Gazelda, the unicorn," answered Josephine, smiling in relief.

The Tuatha Dé Danann girl nodded. She raised her hand and lowered it, signaling to the others to lower their weapons. She flipped back her long green cloak to replace her own arrow and bow to their quiver. She smiled at them as she fixed the cuffs on her green tunic.

"I am Princess Ticka Walsh, Leader Josephine and Prince Jonathan. Welcome to my father's kingdom of Tailltiu City."

She bowed, and they bowed back. When they looked up, they heard the others rushing toward them.

"Hey, what's going on?" asked Starlette, eyeing Princess Ticka with a frown. Gazelda sighed and walked past Starlette in human form, a huge smile on her face.

"Ticka!"

"Gazelda!" laughed Ticka, rushing forward to hug her.

The others looked on as they did. Eve smirked at Josephine and Jonathan.

"Didn't take long for you two to find yourselves in a pickle."

Josephine went to retort when Gazelda said, "Ticka, how are your father and your mother? I can't imagine too well, due to the dragon's grumbles and Cetus returning."

"Yes. We got word the moment Cetus regained his powers from Lady Mango. Father was relieved when Mirage came here and told us you were safe, but worried again due to you going to the Dragons. I imagine they said no?"

"And much more. But let's save the rest for your parents."

Ticka nodded. "Of course."

Ticka led them right past the springs on a small bridge as they headed to the city. The smell was stronger, but not by much. Josephine marveled at the diamond clarity that the water had. No dirt or anything. It was perfect glass-smooth water. It almost seemed to have a silver shine to it. Josephine wondered if it had anything to do with the phoenix tears.

They walked into a forested area and went for a good two miles. Indie looked ready to kill something when Ticka stopped. She smiled and turned to her guard.

"Toru, go on ahead and tell King Kingdor that Gazelda and her charges have arrived, please."

The Tuatha Dé Danann, with long black locks, nodded. Without a sound, he dashed off.

Ticka walked forward and spoke to the trees in front of them, "*Open, please, the forest to the seas.*"

Wave let out a small "wow" as the trees shimmered and disappeared into large log doors. As they opened, there was creaking of the ropes and pulleys dragging the doors open to welcome them in. They followed Ticka through the doorway.

"Welcome, friends, to Tailltiu City!" Ticka smiled.

The city reached all the way to the coast. The buildings were a white that glistened in the afternoon sun, making the city's appearance brighter. There was a castle that was high on a hill on the north side of the city. All over, the town was covered in flowering vines and brightly colored ribbons. Ticka led them to the castle through the city by the main road.

"Princess Ticka, how are you able to keep attackers out when your protection is an enormous set of enchanted gates by a forest?" asked Indie.

Ticka smirked, giving her a faery-like quality to her face.

"The forest is dense. Not even the skinniest snake can go through. Our people grew the trees to prevent large armies sneak their way in."

"Clever."

Tailltiu City was clean and crowded; Jonathan knew that once Red Rose City had been like this; full of cheerful people going along in their lives, trading, eating.

Josephine saw sadness in Jonathan's eyes. She gave him a questioning look. When he saw her face, he shook his head, smiling, but it was forced. Josephine made a mental note to ask him about it later. People in the streets paused to watch them with Ticka. Many clapped and cheered as they walked along the streets.

"Looks like at least the Dananns are glad we're alive," smirked Marie.

Josephine nodded in agreement. Children gasped and giggled when they saw the Dragons; all five of them were flying overhead. Aeolus looked to be showing off a little with FireWind, doing cartwheels.

"Show offs," chuckled Wave.

"Um, Princess Ticka...?"

The Danann princess smiled at Josephine.

"You may just call me Ticka. We are of equal status."

Josephine smiled shyly back.

"Okay, Ticka, is there a celebration going on?"

"Oh yes, we have a week-long celebration for the beginning of spring," she smiled as a group of young children ran past them, their eyes focused on the sky.

There were no moats or anything around the castle. Its protection was a thick wall covered in ivy that had places perfect for archers and men with enormous cauldrons of burning oil. The doors opened, and the group walked into a large entrance hall. There were a few paintings of landscapes and large vases and a drapery here and there, but it was not as lavishly decorated as Red Rose Castle. But to Jonathan, that made more of a statement. The Dananns enjoyed the earth more than gold or jewels. They walked down the hall, then through a doorway into the throne room. It was circular, the stone floor covered with red velvet. There were garlands of flowers hanging from the high ceiling. At the head of the room stood two gold chairs, both equally grand. The dragons did what they could not to let their tails drag on the floor to prevent damage, as the unicorn's hooves echoed along the way.

Ticka stopped to bow to the couple standing in front of the chairs. They had to be Ticka's parents. The man was tall and well built; he had a simple gold crown and short, black-brown hair. He seemed to have a glow, a glow that reflected in Ticka. Not just the glow, but Ticka shared his full face and height. The woman was a few inches shorter than her husband and daughter. She had the same-colored hair, sparkling eyes, and full figure Ticka had. Josephine could feel the underlining magic that was clearing in them, and it was powerful.

"King Kingdor and Queen Andromeda, the Royal Dragon Knights and their teacher Gazelda 'Fair Lady' have arrived."

King Kingdor nodded once, then Ticka waved to her guards to leave. She then stood behind her parents with her arms behind her back. The king smiled, and the queen rushed forward to Gazelda and hugged her.

"Oh, Gazelda, how long has it been?!"

"Too long, my dear," Gazelda said, hugging her back.

Josephine glanced over at the others. Their faces echoed the shock that Josephine felt. Gazelda was Fair Lady! Well, now they had a good idea of Gazelda's age... sort of.

The king smiled at Gazelda, but then turned to Josephine. She felt his emotions, and they were curious about her. It was of joy, but also sadness and maybe, wistful?

"Hello. You must be Lady Josephine Drageon," The king's voice was as kind and deep as Josephine had imagined it.

"Yes, I am, your majesty."

"You remind me of someone I once knew," he said with a sad smile. Josephine went to ask who, but Gazelda turned to look at everyone's astonished faces save Eve. She was furious.

"I am guessing from the looks on your faces that you all have now read or know of James and my story. Come on, it's time for a history lesson."

Chapter Twenty
A History Unfolded

They moved into the dining hall of the castle for a late lunch. The dragons stood along the side to wait while Starlette and Ulyssess had been led to a special pavilion for them to eat and rest.

While they ate at the large oak table, Eve kept shooting dirty looks at Gazelda, who was either aware of Eve's looks and was choosing to ignore her or was too involved with talking to the queen to see. Josephine caught Eve's gaze and narrowed her eyes back at her, sending the message of "Don't start". Eve shrugged and went back to her food. Indie was glaring, but for different reasons.

Josephine had to stop herself from giggling at him. The many forks and spoons were annoying Indiana. He obviously had never dined at this level of formality. He had to keep glancing over at Jonathan, who, of course, was an old hand at the royal dining tables. Jonathan had noticed and was trying not to smirk. He had been dining like this since he was old enough to sit above the edge of a table. Again, he admired the simple décor of the Dananns. Their plates and goblets had gold, but it was a simple intertwined knot design with leaves. However, to Jonathan, it was much more impressive than the golden, jeweled goblets of Red Rose. Once they had finished, everyone stared expectantly at Gazelda.

She sighed, finally, either from noticing or acknowledging Eve's angry face. The king dismissed the servants.

There was a slight pause after the doors closed, and then Eve said, "You were a member of the Alliance and YOU NEVER TOLD US?!"

"Eve!" yelled Wave, but Eve ignored her. Firewind wagged her tail in annoyance.

"Of course I'm a member; I'm the pro temp," smiled Gazelda. Eve's eyes, if it were possible, became even more livid.

Gazelda sighed, and the smile was gone. "I did not tell you girls because it was not important." Gazelda raised a finger to stop Eve's next sentence. "You were only children and also, it was for your safety. I have been traveling around these last fifty years digging up information, and in the last ten scaring up old contacts and getting information on old enemies. It was my duty as a guardian to not only find the next generation of Dragon Hearts, but to protect the Vanora object I was given. And the other that I ended up with." Gazelda nodded to Josephine's necklace and the dagger on Eve's hip. "Also, as pro temp, and a warrior, it was my duty to find all the traitors that slipped through the Alliance's fingers. Though that was a task I was unable to fully do."

Josephine saw and felt the pain and anger her teacher carried.

Wave, in a small voice, asked, "Did you find them?"

"Maruko and his Dragon I found a year ago, dead. Maruko was killed in his bed. His Dragon looked as though he put up a fight before his head was removed."

The dragons all shuttered at that image.

"That was my first sign that Cetus was coming back. Jewelvana, as far as I know, is a drunk back home in her land of Hispania. Reed is now a hired assassin. Reed and his new Dragon are probably the ones who took out Maruko and Cain."

"Have you seen Reed?" asked Jonathan.

"No. Even if I had, I wouldn't have been able to approach him. I am skilled but not skilled enough to take on a Dragon Knight with assassin skills on top of his knight training. If he saw me and didn't think he could take me on, he would have run anyway. He knows both of my forms, seeing how I had taught the snot, and we did several missions together, needing both my Tuatha Dé Danann and unicorn sides."

"You taught...?" began Marie.

"Yes, I taught all the traitors. I have been with the Alliance since James became the leader. After some time, when I was trained and skilled enough, James asked me if I would like to help teach, which I did as a member of the Dragon Warriors. They are a group under the Dragon Knight Alliance who tend to be either normal humans with great battle skills or those like me who wanted to fight for the greater good and not just for their own people."

Josephine's mind took a minute to absorb everything. So only Cetus, Reed, and Jewelvana were still alive out of all the traitors. Maruko must not have wanted to help his old traitor friends, so to make sure that Maruko wouldn't try to help those he betrayed, Cetus had Reed kill him. Reed must have signed back up with Cetus and was doing dirty work for him. Josephine returned to listening to the conversation when she heard Gazelda's voice.

"Yes, I taught all of them. And no, none of us saw the warning signs in Cetus," Gazelda said, anticipating Eve's next question.

"Any idea why he did it or how?" asked Indie.

"Like I said before: power. He wanted it, and he felt he would be better to take it than earn it. How is what I have been trying to sort out these past sixty years..." Gazelda paused, then went on to say, "He started slowly, using his status and teachings to get a following. He did it so well that it wasn't until his army was at Red Rose Castle's door did we know about it."

"Indeed, he was much more skilled than even James in magic and Nina when it came to swords," said King King-dor. "I, myself, trained a little with Cetus, and in a match of swords I lost."

"Is that why you wrote 'Peace is what is earned from sacrifice. If the generation does not appreciate the legacy in which gave them their freedoms, then those freedoms shall be doomed' as the end line of your entry, Gazelda?" asked Josephine.

Gazelda shared a long look with Josephine. Gazelda gave her a wave of admiration.

"I thought long and hard about what Cetus did. I, for the longest time, was full of too much anger at his arrogance to even stop to think about why he did what he did. After mediating on it for a time, I wrote in the Chronicles on James's request. His thought was if anyone else had earned the honor of writing in the book, it was me, due to my taking on charge of the next generation. I came to think about it at length about how Cetus went down the path he did. His upbringing combined with questioning the peace we had, not realizing where the peace had come from, made him self-righteous. But it is only a theory. I cannot completely say it with certainty without talking to him myself."

Josephine mulled over it all while Ticka asked another, not completely unrelated, question.

"I do not understand something; if he was a Shadow magician, how was he able to cover up that? When you do Shadow magic, even regular human beings can feel the aurora you give off. Dragon Knights are especially attuned to such power, for they are the light to that dark," asked Ticka.

"We have yet to figure that out. Though I have a theory; his Dragon magic masked it," said King Kingdor.

"How? Dragon heart powers purify the Shadow magic," frowned Eve.

"Okay, I'm lost," complained Indie.

Ticka answered, "Dragon heart magic and Shadow magic have been at odds with each other since the beginning of the earth. Dragon heart magic is the antidote to the poison of Shadow magic. If a Dragon heart uses Shadow magic, it goes into one's system and flows through the veins. Dragon Heart magic constantly tries to get rid of the Shadow Magic the moment it enters the user's body. If they stop using Shadow magic, then the poison is purified. A Dragon heart has to stop even more quickly than a normal person, for it destroys their body from all the strain. Shadow Dragon hearts have shorter lives because their magic is fighting the Shadow magic and, over time, it breaks down the body."

"I hate magic," muttered Indie.

"You know much about magic," smiled Josephine, looking at Ticka.

"My father is one of the few Dananns who can do our type of magic. I, too, as an heir, have been taught the ways of magic. However, I am not very good at it," she grimaced.

"Don't believe her; Ticka is quite good at it. She is extremely modest," came another voice.

They turned to see a young Tuatha Dé Danann man standing in the doorway. He was a double for the king, except for his eyes; he, like Ticka, had the queen's eyes. He walked in and kissed the queen on the cheek.

"Everyone, this is my son, Riagán Walsh."

"Pleasure to meet you, Dragon hearts. I apologize for not being here when you arrived. I was away on the coast for a few days. I returned an hour ago." Riagán inclined his body into a slight bow, smiling right at Josephine. Riagán was donning a leather jerkin over a black tunic with a long sword at his hip. It was narrow, like a type of sword that would get through chain mail. It had a simple silver pommel and a cross hilt with detailed engraving.

They all nodded and introduced themselves to him. When Josephine told him her name, he smiled wider and winked at her before looking back at Gazelda. Eve noticed that Wave, Marie, and Josephine seemed to like the young Tuatha Dé Danann prince, but Jonathan and Indie were frowning just a little at Riagán. Eve caught their eyes, and Indie just mouthed "later". She shrugged. She thought Riagán was a little pompous and seemed to eye Josephine in a too friendly way, but she didn't see what the big deal was.

"So, if your theory is right about Cetus, could that mean even with his powers back, he won't be full strength as he once was?" asked Marie.

Josephine could feel careful optimism from Gazelda.

"I think so. He has at least one helper, that is obvious. He's holed up somewhere, training new magicians that I have no doubt. But, in the end, he wants the power all for himself. Cetus must now have confidence in his new underlings to seek a shadow stone to recover..." Gazelda sighed, rubbing her forehead.

King Kingdor smiled at her.

"Well, I know you have been traveling for quite a few days, so let's rest for now. The servants will take you to your rooms, and then I am sure that Ticka and Riagán would be delighted to give you a full tour of the city and to help you enjoy some of the festivities," the king said, standing up.

Josephine smiled at Ticka, who grinned back. But before they left, Josephine remembered...

"Before we go, King Kingdor, will you or will you not join the Dragon Heart Alliance?" she asked in a firm voice.

"An excellent question," smirked Gazelda, turning to look at Kingdor. The king smiled and straightened his posture.

"As the king of this kingdom, I can say yes. As High King, it is up to the other two kings of the Tuatha Dé Danann race to decide, though seeing how I am High King and have joined, I doubt the others will decline. Especially the King of New Tara. Their island is isolated. Joining the Alliance would put his people at better ease." He paused, then added, "The Dananns, ever since the end of the last war, have kept to themselves. We protect our own people and lands.

However, as before, it will not take long for Cetus's shadow to reach us. Yes, as before, the Dananns of Anglii shall be a part of the Alliance of the Dragon Knights. As King of Tailltiu and as High King, I swear our lives and land to help the new Dragon hearts and those who are a part of the Alliance. We shall help them as well as they help us." King Kingdor put out his hand. Josephine took it.

"Thank you," was all Josephine could say.

Behind the king, Jonathan noticed that the queen and Tic-ka were smiling, but Riagán had almost a bored look on his face. Riagán smiled slightly when he saw Jonathan looking at him, but Jonathan did not feel any warmth in that smile until Josephine turned to him. Jonathan glanced over at Eve. She had a frown as well. Jonathan decided that there was something not right about Riagán and that he would find out what it was.

Chapter Twenty-One
The Spring Festival

T he rooms were big enough for the dragons to join them. Ulysses and Starlette even got special accommodations. Ticka explained that in the days of the Alliance, Unicorns and Centaurs would visit and stay in special gazebos and huts, so they set the two unicorns up in there. Josephine smiled, seeing the happy and flattered look on Starlette's face.

Josephine was pulling out her nicest tunic when Aurora peaked behind a curtain and let out a gasp.

"Oh, Josephine! Look at this!" Josephine smiled and walked over to see Aurora's find. Hanging up on a small hook was a pale blue silk dress. It had a square neckline and long bellow sleeves that were split up to the elbow, and around the waist was a blue rope belt. The bottom of the dressed flowed out into a narrow skirt. A knock came at the door, and the two turned to see a smiling Ticka.

"I thought that at least for one night you could dress to match your title. I've brought some of my hair decorations and make-up as well."

It flattered Josephine. Silk was something that only the upper middle-and upper-class owned, and same with make-up, for they are hard to make. Though she didn't care for dresses, she was willing to make an exception for this kindness.

"Thank you so very much, Princess Ticka. I am honored."

Ticka chuckled. "Need not call me Princess, Josephine. We are of equal ranking. Come, let's see what we can do with each other's hair."

She smiled, walking over and placing her things on the vanity. The two young women and the dragon sat talking and making up each other. Somehow, during that time, they became best friends. It came so naturally that they didn't even notice, and unbeknownst to them, they would forever be.

Josephine and Ticka came out of the room, looking much different from when they came in. Josephine smiled at the thought of how glad her aunt and her mother (especially her aunt) would be to see her in a gown. A regal gown, no less. Though Josephine wasn't too thrilled, she had to admit to herself that it felt nice to be dressed up. Josephine's silken hair was in a braid, then pulled into a bun. She was donning the lightest of pink lip color that complemented the baby blue shadow that drew out the light color in her eyes. She wore a small circlet that was done in an elaborate knot with a blue stone in the center, and the Vanora crystal necklace was around her neck.

Ticka was wearing a dress that was a little more elaborate than Josephine's. It was scarlet, with delicate gold embroidery and lace in the large skirt. A royal insignia pin kept a purple sash in place across her chest. Her crown, like the insignia, had oak leaves, but it also had two phoenixes. Even Aurora was dressed up; she wore a blue silk sash around her neck with a bouquet of white crocuses pinned to it.

Jonathan and Riagán were waiting for them out at the end of the hall. Jonathan wore a black silk doublet and leather pants, his tiny dragon charm around his neck and the Vanora ring on his left hand. Riagán looked a little more sinister with a blood red silk tunic. He was donning a sash that matched his sister's. Jonathan gave the Tuatha Dé Danann prince a distasteful glance before smiling at her. He handed her a bouquet of white daffodils while Riagán gave his sister yellow daffodils. The siblings walked on ahead when Jonathan offered his arm to Josephine. She smiled widely and placed her arm through his, her heart running a thousand miles a second.

"You know, an angel would be jealous," he loudly whispered.

"Flatterer," she whispered back, shoving him a little.

"Thanks," he chuckled.

"Why were you glaring at Riagán?" Josephine asked as they headed down the steps. Jonathan's eyes tightened.

"I just don't know about him," he said, being honest.

"What are you worried about, a little competition?" laughed Josephine, elbowing Jonathan's side.

"*That* I am not worried about." He smirked, then frowned. "He just... has this nasty feeling about him, but it's faint... I can't place it..."

Josephine shrugged, unperturbed. "I wouldn't be too worried. He's nice, even if he is a little... different."

"Not the word I was thinking of," muttered Jonathan as they walked to the front door.

Once outside, Eve, Indie and the other two girls were standing at the bottom of the entryway steps. Wave was wearing a sky-blue dress with three-fourths sleeves; Marie was wearing a periwinkle dress with a ruffled-lace skirt. Eve was not wearing a dress but black pants and a deep red silk shirt with cuffed sleeves, the Vanora dagger at her hip, and a small diamond necklace around her neck, and a miniature rose behind her right ear. Indie was sporting a black shirt like Jonathan's but tan colored pants and a leather necklace, his sword at his hip. They all smiled when they came into view. Indie let out a low whistle when Josephine and Jonathan came down.

"Lookin' good, Josey." He winked. Eve rolled her eyes.

"Thanks, Indie," laughed Josephine.

The group walked into the front courtyard that led into the town. There was a large, white marble fountain in the shape of a phoenix. It glittered in the fading sunlight, and it was full of flowers and draped in garlands. There were paper lanterns hanging through the city's streets, ready for when the sun set. The four other dragons were waiting for them and well as Starlette and Ulysses.

"Oh, Josephine! So lovely!" gushed Starlette. Josephine laughed and even twirled around to make Starlette giggle. She smiled at the joy coming from her friend.

"Don't get use to it," she joked. Starlette rolled her eyes.

"Is anyone else feeling a little overwhelmed by all the flowers?" gagged Perun.

Jonathan wrinkled his nose.

"A little. The Dananns are not as great of gardeners as the Faeries, but still..."

"For us, spring is extra important, for it is said that it was the first day of spring when the great Phoenix fell to the earth," explained Ticka. "Our ancestors tried to help the fallen Phoenix, but it was to no avail; it was beyond even its own special magic. So they prayed and used their magic to help its spirit free itself. It cried tears of gratitude and purified the spring, blessing our kind with a long life and the gift of being able to understand animals. The flowers that grow here always return regardless of drought or flood, in an endless cycle, just like Phoenixes. It is the celebration of rebirth of the earth, and a time to remember our past and to... rediscover ourselves."

"Therefore, we decorate with thousands of flowers and the color of scarlet," added Riagán.

Jonathan noticed when Riagán turned forward, his smile became a frown. Jonathan glanced over at Eve. She was frowning — she had noticed it, too. Josephine hadn't.

"Wow. I knew the legend of the Phoenix Spring, but only half of it," remarked Josephine.

Riagán turned again to smile at Josephine. "It is an intricate part of our culture. Few outside of our city know the full story."

They crossed the courtyard and walked into the beginning of downtown. There were over several hundred vendors and at least half the city was in the streets. Different smells came to them, some familiar, others exotic.

"Just be careful, guys. Don't step on anyone," joked Marie.

Aeolus rolled his eyes and Hurricane said, "We'll stick around here for a while." Hurricane grinned as several young Tuatha Dé Danann children were peaking around things to stare at the dragons and the two unicorns. All with curiosity and wonder in their eyes. Josephine frowned. She wanted to bond more with Aurora and felt like she'd been neglecting Starlette. Aurora felt her disappointment.

"It's okay. Bring back something nice for us."

Starlette nodded.

Josephine nodded and hugged the pair of them.

"I promise, I will," she said, gently stroking Aurora with a finger down her nose. As the teenagers headed out, they split up. Eve grabbed Indie and looked pointedly at her soul sisters. They invited Riagán and Ticka to come with them. Riagán looked as though he wanted to go with Josephine, but with one slight glare from Eve, he wisely did not protest. Indie went to protest when Eve said,

"Can it. Don't start. We want to give Josephine and Jonathan some time alone."

"That I get, but why did you have to drag me along with you?" Indie snapped.

Eve glowered. "Simple. I lost the coin toss."

For a bit, the festival was overwhelming, but she began to just focus on certain smells or people to help her sensitive senses. She and Jonathan made their way through all the stands. Josephine picked another sash for Aurora in pale blue to match her eyes, then a small hair comb that was a gold flower for Starlette.

Once they had finished exploring the main street, they returned to the main courtyard. Marie, Ticka and Wave joined them soon after, claiming to have lost Riagán in the massive crowd.

Eve and Indie walked slowly through the side streets on the left side of the celebration, heading back to the castle. Indie insisted on having Eve's arm through his; he did not like the looks that some nobles were giving Eve. Eve found it silly. She was more than capable of caring for herself. No man could match her strength, Dragon heart, or otherwise. Eve let him, though, to keep him quiet. He had a rather pleasant voice, but it was annoying when all it did was nag, so the silence was golden. Eve had found a hair band that was made with silken red roses, and also was donning a red silk scarf around her hip for her sword's scabbard.

"Really, Eve, pride yourself on being the lady in red?" smirked Indie as she was tying it to her belt.

"Matter of fact, I do. It is my favorite color and my element."

"Ever try wearing other colors?" he joked as they continued walking to the northeastern part of town.

Eve went to answer when she smelled musk. She turned to where the wind was blowing it from when she felt an electrical shock through her spine, raising the hair on her body. Something foul was near, and her instincts were going crazy. She wanted to rip apart whatever had given her that shock. She ran towards it, hissing.

"EVE!" yelled Indie, racing after her.

"EVE! What the heck?"

But she did not turn or stop. She turned a few corners, then froze. She felt cold, so cold. Like when they were in the mines. Eve froze as her fire power flared in her veins. When she came to a large white church, she took a crouch behind a corner. Indie caught up with Eve, gasping.

"Curse it, Eve! You run like a man!"

Eve snapped her hand over his mouth. "Shut it! I felt something cold," she hissed.

Indie shook his mouth free. "Sure it wasn't that barrel of chilled wine?"

"No. This is a dark cold, the cold that is my enemy," she said, staring at him with a face that seemed of a more ancient being than of a sixteen year-old girl. Indie rubbed goosebumps on his skin. He nodded and pulled his small dagger.

"I don't dare use the Vanora dagger. If it is Shadow magic, the stone might set off my fire powers."

"You really think it's Shadow magic?"

Eve shrugged. "It's the only thing that would make my senses go crazy like this."

"But in the middle of Tailltiu City...?"

"Yes. More like someone who has used it. Their 'aura' is saturated in it if you can even feel it, according to your goosebumps. Unless you are always a scaredy-cat."

Indie sneered, but otherwise ignored the comment. "So where is this Shadow person if there is one?" he muttered.

Eve peeked around the corner, like a cat spying on its prey. "Sneaking around."

She saw a man in a long dark cloak, the hood up to cover his face. There was one other man, and it was Prince

Riagán. Indie peeked, too, and cursed in such a soft voice that Eve almost missed it. Riagán was talking in a soft voice as well. His lips were moving too fast for Eve to read. The prince paused and the other man, who was just an inch taller than him, spoke louder.

"I understand. But do you, Riagán? What needs to be done?" His voice was harsh, and a chill shook Eve's body. Indie grabbed her shoulders to calm her. Eve's gut told her he was the Shadow user.

"I understand perfectly well, thank you," Riagán snapped back.

The cloaked man turned on his heel, turning towards where Eve and Indie were hiding. Riagán glared at the man, then left the other way.

Eve shoved Indie, then pulled him into the arched doorway of the church. Eve shuddered and Indie grabbed her shoulders again. He wasn't too confident he could keep her from jumping out and attacking the man. Eve could keep herself in line against her better judgments as the man walked towards the southern end of town, giving the church a wide berth.

"My gut tells me that Jonathan's gut was right; Riagán is not good, far worse, downright evil!"

Eve opened her bag to let out Flash. He was still nibbling on a sausage that Indie had given him.

"Flash, go follow Riagán, and watch him; make sure he doesn't leave. Let me know if he does," Eve whispered in Dragon tongue. Flash snapped the last of the sausage, then nodded to Eve. He licked her, then disappeared, living up to his name.

Josephine and Jonathan, while waiting for Eve, Indiana, and Riagán, chatted with Ticka. The princess went to greater detail about the history of the Phoenix Springs and the Dragons.

"The situation with the Dragons is nothing new," explained Ticka. "It first started after the last of the original six dragons died. Because the Dragons were born from the mountains, they, the first dragons' descendants, thought that their territory should reach to the springs. Many of the Dragons saw the power in the healing springs, but Glen and the others saw it was us, the Dananns, who at the time were much weaker, if you would, and needed it. With Glen's death, the debate came up again, and they argued. They fought for several years until Taranis, Arlen, and Kegan, with their dragons, stopped the battling. The only reason it did not come to war with us and stopped it from becoming so again was because of the Dragon Knight Alliance."

Josephine nodded. "Right, if you are a part of the Alliance, you cannot declare war on a fellow ally. If you do, you lose the support of other kingdoms, and they could turn on you and protect the ally you are trying to pick a fight with."

Ticka nodded and smiled.

"Yes, you understand the treaty well. If the Dragons had gone to war with us again, then Red Rose would have come to our aid, including many of the Dragon Knight warriors who are from Red Rose or here. A few humans have come and lived here to heal or to find spiritual peace. Also, many clans from Jinzhou would have come to our aid, for we have many trading agreements with them. You see, the mess that the Dragons would have faced. Of course, Taranis and Quickstrike stopped the first war themselves, and they created the first peace treaty. It was later on when Taranis founded the Alliance did this all come into play."

Josephine stroked Aurora for a few seconds, then asked, "When did the fighting completely stop?"

Ticka chuckled. "It never has. It has gone into lulls when the Dragon leader did not think it was the Dragons' place to control the springs, but that did not mean that the ones in the guard didn't believe it. You see, as much as I especially hate to admit it, some wars or fights will never end, silly or pointless as they may be. Some thoughts will never go away or will ever change, like the never-ending clan wars that go on in Jinzhou or the fighting between Francia and Anglii over the Solie Islands, who want to be ruled by no one. Deep-seated hate may never die. Even with all the treaties that have been made between my ancestors and the Dragons, once a new leader comes and still believes the old ways, there is no stopping it."

Josephine gazed at the city as she pondered Ticka's words. Riagán walked up and bowed to Josephine, then to his sister. Was what she said true? Are there really wars that will never die just because of the hate? Josephine filed the thoughts away for another time when the queen, king, and Gazelda appeared. The sun was setting, and the last glow of twilight was evaporating into black.

"It's almost time. Everyone ready?" smiled Queen Andromeda, her eyes sparkling with excitement.

"For what?" asked Josephine, glancing at Ticka, who was grinning widely like her mother.

"For the beginning of spring," King Kingdor said, smiling as well, "we celebrate by having a special performance. I won't tell you what it is, but I know you will enjoy it."

Jonathan chuckled and Josephine glared at him. "You know what he's talking about!"

He laughed. "Yes. My cousin Holly Falcon was here once and saw the performance. She told me all about it. Trust me, Josephine, you will enjoy it extremely." Jonathan chuckled as Josephine pouted at him, and so did Aurora.

The two walked after the queen and king when he saw Eve and Indie running up the stairs. He frowned, wondering what was wrong of the emotions that were coming off them. Eve went to say something when her eyes became large. She slammed her mouth shut. Jonathan turned his head a little to see Riagán walking after the others, eyeing Eve. There was a look of smugness on his face. Indie saw this and glared, his face getting a tinge of red in it. He walked on without looking back. Jonathan didn't bother looking back at Eve; he saw all he needed to know. There was something wrong with the prince of the Dananns.

Eve and Indie didn't dare say a thing as the group walked down to the largest park of the city that lay right in the middle. Riagán was just too close, but from the look on Jonathan's face, Eve figured that Jonathan had figured out that something was amiss. Eve watched Riagán, but she did not feel any shadows of any kind. Just excitement radiating from him and the rest of the town, like with Josephine. She did not notice the unease of Eve, Indie, and Jonathan as they walked through to the park. Not until Jonathan took her arm. Josephine frowned at him, and he just shook his head.

"Later," he whispered, staring at Riagán. Josephine wondered what it was now that had made Jonathan so uneasy about the other prince. But she was so overwhelmed by the high emotions that she felt nauseous. When they stopped at the park, Riagán noticed her chalky face and whispered,

"Just breathe and concentrate on your and Aurora's emotions; it helps block out everyone else's."

Josephine glanced over at Aurora and took a deep breath. She could feel Aurora's happiness and focused on that, along with her own happiness. The hurricane in her stomach subsided. She opened her eyes and said thank you to Riagán.

"You are welcome, m' lady."

Jonathan felt his fist close tight. He let out a breath and glanced over at Eve, who looked as though she wished to do nothing less than rip his teeth out. But she, too, took a calming then turned her attention to King Kingdor. He, like his wife and children, was wearing a purple sash. He was wearing robes made of velvet of the deepest gold and a small but impressive gold crown with three small diamonds set in it.

"Welcome, my friends, to welcoming the new spring! This spring, as you all may know by now, is going to be filled with light and dark. Cetus Cyprus has returned from his dark retreat to plague this world once more, but when there is a great evil, there is always a great good to fight it."

"*Rule number fourteen,*" thought Eve, stealing a quick glance at Riagán's blank face.

"Here with us is the new generation of the Dragon Hearts! I have renewed our loyalty with their leader, Josephine Drageon." He gave a small bow to Josephine, who bowed back. "Through combined efforts, let us all hope this will bring peace and justice back to this land."

The queen smiled, then walked forward with her arms wide and said,

"And now let's celebrate the first day of spring with the firefly dance!"

Cheers answered Queen Andromeda, and she smiled even wider.

"Let the dance of the fireflies begin!"

Josephine blinked, then gaped at Jonathan, who was grinning widely. Josephine turned back to see that a small band of musicians were at the center of the park. There were seven of them, all with an instrument. There were four young women, all wearing long white gowns with lace trimming and circlets with moonstones and silver wrapped into phoenixes. The three young male Dananns were wearing all white as well and had simple circlets made of silver. The young black-haired Tuatha Dé Danann woman with the reed began the song, then the man with the lute, then the one blonde woman with the . Once she played, the others joined in, a harp, a psaltery (an instrument similar to a hurdy gurdy), and the flute.

The melody started out melancholy, and then slowly picked up. The harp became the loudest, humming right down to a person's soul. Josephine glanced at the others to see various expressions of awe, even on Eve's face. The three wind instruments fluttered as though trying to sound like a bird flying. It was then that Josephine noticed the fireflies. She had been so entranced by the minstrels that she had missed seeing fireflies flying in and around the park. They were flashing to the beat of the song. Josephine also noticed that some of them were touching the flowers, and they would open as the flute continued to play.

The song went on, playing a story in which the fireflies were the actors playing around in a circle around the minstrels. When the melody slowed, Ticka walked forward slowly and ducked under the wide circle of fireflies to stand in front of the players. She stood straight and still, then just as the flute hit a certain note, she opened her eyes, which were a blazing blue color. Everyone watched in amazement as Ticka raised her arms, slowly closing her eyes. A small wave of energy the same color that Ticka's eyes had turned whipped around her. It slowly twisted around her like water, then with a flash the energy became a distinctive shape of a bird, not just any bird, Josephine realized, but a phoenix. It let out a cry, and Ticka opened her eyes again, which were shining from the magic. The white phoenix shape let out another cry that was in tune with the music. It then flapped its wings with the harp's playing, then flew towards the sky and evaporated, adding a little more shimmer to the sky for a moment.

The song ended, the melody sounding happy yet sad. Josephine then realized that it was a story, the story of the phoenix of the springs. The fireflies represented the Dananns and Ticka had made a phoenix out of what must have been their brand of magic. A few seconds of silence, and then the entire city began cheering and clapping. The seven minstrels and Ticka all bowed to the crowd, then to the queen, the king, and the rest of them. They followed the king's lead and bowed back. Gazelda smiled and walked over to hug Ticka.

"Oh dearest, that was amazing; you have come so far in your magic!" she praised.

"Thank you, Gazelda," Ticka said, hugging her back.

Jonathan took Josephine's hand and whispered into her ear, "Glad I didn't tell you?"

Josephine laughed and nodded.

"That was amazing, Ticka," praised Wave.

"Thank you, Wave. It's taken me almost a year to master it, but it was worth it." Ticka smiled.

King Kingdor placed a hand on his daughter's shoulder.

"I couldn't agree more."

After that, the group headed back into the castle.

"Eh, here is a new rule for you: Rule number fourteen: when there is a great darkness, there will always be a great light to fight it, though in this case I am going with rule three and rule six," muttered Eve with biting anger to Indie, watching Riagán laughing with Josephine.

"Good night, Josephine, everyone," the prince smiled, and bowed his head before parting them. Ticka did the same, and once she was out of ear shot, Eve grabbed Josephine and the others and pulled them into the empty dining hall.

"Eve, what is going on, and why are you glaring at Riagán like he's Cetus?" demanded Wave.

Eve rolled her eyes. "Maybe because he might be working with the scumbag," she answered.

Josephine felt her eyebrow rise. "Say what?"

Eve and Indie glanced at each other, then she spoke. "We saw Riagán on the west side of the city having a shady meeting with a shady guy,"

"As in a Shadow magician kind of shady," said Indie.

Josephine did a double take.

"Come again? Are you sure it was a Shadow... yeah..." sighed Marie, stopping mid-sentence at the look on Eve's face.

Eve turned to Josephine. "The prince is not on the up and up, Josephine. We can't trust him."

Josephine looked at Jonathan, who shrugged. She looked over at Aurora, then at Eve's narrowed green eyes. "Well, I don't know if there is much we can do. We could go to Ticka, but I don't know if she'd believe us. It's her brother. We'll just have to keep an eye on him until we know for sure and can go to the king. I dunno what else to do unless somebody else has an idea."

Eve did not look happy, but she didn't seem to have a better idea, for she said nothing, nor did anyone else. They left in an uneasy silence.

With a little help from a kind chamber maid named Kelly-Anne, Josephine got out of the dress (with a breath of relief) and climbed into bed. Once Kelly-Anne had left the room, Josephine turned to Aurora.

"What do you think, Aurora?"

Aurora flapped her wings, then folded them, and she sat down on her bed before answering, "Riagán? I dunno. I think we should at least monitor him. Shadow magician or not, I believe Eve when she said the one man was, but I don't know about Riagán himself."

"At the very least, he is a charming person."

Aurora frowned. "How about this, Rule number...What is it, fifteen? Eve said we are on? A charming person can just be as dangerous as a rude person and twice as cruel."

Chapter Twenty-Two
Darkest Love

Josephine, at first, wasn't sure what was going on. She felt like something was dragging her; it was dark, whatever it was. She could not move her body, no matter how hard she tried. Josephine's mind was in a hazy, dream-like place, like someone had scared her out of a deep sleep. Her heart was racing in fear, trying to escape whatever had its grasp on her. She fought against the black hands wrapped around her, but she remained immobilized. Was this a nightmare?

Josephine heard what she thought was Aurora's voice echoing in her mind, "Josephine!"

"Aurora?"

A second later, a bright flash blinded Josephine. She sat up straight to find herself eye to eye with Riagán. His eyes were ink-black and cold. Josephine reached for her sword, but Riagán shoved her against the wall, placing his hand over her mouth. Aurora was tied up in a binding that was made of shifting shadows. She was pulling as hard as she could, but the binding would not break. With her jaw restrained, all Aurora could do was let out growls.

"I am truly sorry, Lady Josephine..." he whispered, a shadow creeping over Josephine's mouth to gag it. "I have no wish to kill you... quite the opposite."

She kicked at him, but he swiped her legs to give the shadows a change to restrain her. The shadows crawled around, making her skin crawl, and bile run up her throat. They hissed at Josephine.

Riagán caressed Josephine's face with his forefinger and index finger, a strange longing in his eyes, like a forlorn lover. He leaned in and whispered into Josephine's ear. His breath was extremely cold, but not like the cold she could take.

"If I was not bonded to Cetus, I would never do this. But I must kill at least you, Jonathan, and my sister. Rest assured, dear Josephine, your beauty captivated my shadowed heart."

Josephine closed her eyes and prayed.

"Please, Jonathan... Eve, wake up, somebody hear Aurora...!"

Riagán kissed Josephine on the cheek, and with a face clear of any sort of emotion, he raised a dagger covered in shadow.

"And so ends the shining hope of the earth," he said, taking a deep breath.

Josephine tried to scream when another bright flash of light blinded her. She fell to the floor and gasped. Riagán was screaming, holding his face. Josephine grabbed her necklace. It was fading back from the flash.

Riagán's face and hands were scratched, burned, and bleeding. Josephine grabbed her sword, but Riagán ran from the room.

Josephine focused on the locket. A flash of light struck again, destroying Aurora's bindings. She roared, but it wasn't necessary; Eve came in at that second, fully dressed.

"Josephine, where…?"

"He ran down that way!" Josephine gasped.

Eve ran after him, cursing as she did.

"Josey!"

Indiana, Ticka, and Wave were standing in the doorway.

"What's going on?" Ticka demanded. "I felt it! Shadow magic!"

"Ticka, it was Riagán. He tried to kill me!"

Josephine took a few breaths then barked, "Wave, Indie, go after Eve; she's chasing him! I don't want her taking him on by herself!"

She grabbed her clothes and shoes.

Indie ran, but Wave hesitated.

"Josephine, are you okay?"

Josephine pulled on her shoes. "Yes! Go back up the other two! We don't know enough to fight a Shadow magician!"

Wave nodded and ran.

Ticka was wide eyed, as though in shock. She turned to the sounds of foots steps and yelled,

"Armand, go find my brother now! Beware; he may be under a Shadow Curse! Get the magicians! NOW!"

Armand was in the doorway for a brief second. He was as tall as Ticka with short red hair, wearing guard clothes. He ran back the way he came. Ticka ran back to her room to get dressed. As Josephine and Aurora stepped out, Jonathan and Marie appeared.

"What's going on? I felt Shadow Magic! I think... I can't see how it could have been anything else!" said Marie as Perun with Aeolus appeared behind her.

"Riagán," growled Jonathan.

Josephine nodded, a sick, icy feeling in her stomach. Jonathan had been right about the prince of the Dananns.

"I've sent my guards out. Indiana, Eve, and Wave are chasing him," called out Ticka, returning in her day clothes.

"Are you all right?" asked Jonathan.

Josephine glanced over Aurora, seeing no obvious injuries, nodded.

"Yes, I'm fine. The necklace activated itself and protected me. It scratched his face."

"Good," snarled Marie.

They heard a dragon's roar coming from the garden grounds.

"Looks like Eve caught up with him!" growled Perun.

The six of them ran out, swords drawn.

Eve ran, following Riagán's scent with FireWind right above her in the sky. She let out a whistle and Flash came running, chirping, and then went back the way he came. She heard Indiana coming, but she would not wait for him. Eve turned into the east entrance of the gardens.

Riagán was standing and searching about for something. Eve drew her sword and swung at him. The prince dodged her swing. He hissed a few words. Five creatures appeared out of the shadows that were around Riagán, twisting and curling until they created a solid shape. They were like gigantic wolves; they snarled and hissed at Eve, their mad, white eyes glaring. Eve skidded to a halt.

The wolves lunged at her, snarling. She swung her sword and cut each one of their heads off, but they grew back. Eve was trying to figure out what to do when suddenly the dagger on her hip started to glow. Eve jumped in surprise, then grabbed the dagger. Her senses detected that the dagger had gotten longer and more elegant when the Shadow wolves made another mad dash at her. She swung the dagger, and this time the creatures slithered away and dissipated. Once all five creatures were gone, the dagger stopped glowing and returned to its normal appearance. Eve placed it back in her belt and glared. Indie was behind her and had witnessed the whole thing.

"Eve, what was...?"

Without turning, Eve answered, "The Shadow magic activated the Dragon magic in the Vanora crystal. Come on, let's see if we can find him."

A thunderous roar echoed through the palace. They looked skyward to see a black scaled Dragon flying up and over the protective wall of Tailltiu City. Eve could tell that the dragon's partner and Riagán were on its back.

"Curse it all! No way of chasing them!" snarled Eve.

Indie shook his head. "Even if you could, what good would it do? You and FireWind don't have any training, you know."

"I know that!" Eve snapped, whipping around to head back into the castle. Wave was standing with her arms wrapped around herself. Eve's face softened as she walked up to her best friend, hugging her and pulling her back to the castle. They ran into the others as they went.

The queen was calm, but tears were threatening to leak out from the corners of her eyes. The king and Gazelda had yet to come into the dining hall. Ticka had her back to everyone. She was staring into the patterns of the tapestry. Eve had a small gash on her arm and Wave was trying to patch it up, but her shaking was making it hard. Indie saw this and took over. Eve didn't protest; she was too busy watching Wave.

"I'm useless," Wave muttered, sitting on Hurricane's back. Marie shook her head.

"Wave, besides the cave, we've had no combat experience, let alone seeing Shadow magic. Don't get mad because you're shaking. I'd probably be, too."

Both Aeolus and Jonathan were standing close to Josephine, and he wouldn't let her out of his sight. Jonathan had said nothing, but Josephine felt ashamed. Jonathan was right about Riagán. She was too trusting; there was nothing else to say.

Eve looked over at her and shook her head and spoke for the first time.

"Josephine, do not feel ashamed. He was nice and cunning."

Josephine nodded.

"Too right, Eve," sighed Gazelda, walking in with the king. His face was neutral, but Josephine could feel his frustration and worry underneath.

"Are you sure he wasn't under some kind of curse?" demanded Ticka of Eve.

She shook her head.

"I may not have much experience with Shadow magic, but I can honestly say he was doing it under his own power... his own choice. Eyes weren't glazed over, for a start."

"Was his voice strange?" asked Gazelda, placing a steadying hand on Andromeda's shoulder.

"Nope," answered Indie.

"I don't understand, why he would do this?" demanded Ticka, turning to face her father. "And how did we not know of him using Shadow magic? How did he mask it?"

The king took in a deep breath and said, "I don't know, my little one. It makes no sense that we couldn't sense it."

Josephine walked forward and took Ticka's hand. She smiled at Josephine and squeezed it.

"Could he have... studied it for a while then... just now use it...?" Jonathan questioned in a voice that sounded like he doubted it.

"No. I have seen a few Shadow magicians in my time, only a few, but enough to know that Shadow magicians like Dragon hearts must start small and work their way up in magic. It is not something that can be studied, then just done," answered Gazelda, who was pacing.

"Besides, the way he was fighting, there is no way that was his first-time doing Shadow magic," commented Eve.

"Well... then, I really have no idea. But I'm sad to say this may prove that he's working for Cetus," sighed Gazelda, glancing at Kingdor.

"Yes, I know. I was thinking the same thing, too."

The queen glanced at the two with a frown.

"I don't understand. How does it...?"

Marie let out an "oh!" Gazelda nodded to her to speak.

"Because Cetus was using Shadow magic, and no one was aware or could sense it either, right?"

Kingdor smiled at Marie.

"Very good, Marie. Yes, not James, Mango, Gazelda... no one knew Cetus was using Shadow magic until the Battle of the Betrayed. Either my son discovered the same technique or..."

"Cetus taught him, but how and when?" frowned Ticka.

"I do not know, but I intend to find out. He had been acting like his normal self. I did not notice any change in him lately besides him going out more. He had been doing his studies as normal...," said King Kingdor.

Queen Andromeda and Ticka said neither had seen any unusual behavior from him of late.

"But for now, everyone, let's get back to bed. Josephine," the queen addressed her, "would you prefer to sleep with Ticka or one of your girls?"

Josephine took in a deep breath, then said, "No. I will be fine going back to my room. There's no need."

Jonathan's eyebrows narrowed, but Josephine waved her hand.

"Riagán isn't here, and if he has followers or whatever, I doubt after what happened to him they are going to try anything now."

"Nevertheless, I am going to increase the number of guards around the grounds and the gates," said the king, turning and nodding to his head of the royal guard. He bowed and left the room.

"And also alert the city guards as well. We need to keep an eye out for trouble, though, as Josephine said, there will probably not be anything for now."

"'For now,' being the keywords," sighed Wave.

They crawled into their beds and then got up a few hours later for a late meal.

"You know..." muttered Eve as she stabbed her flatbread and egg with her fork, "for all the trouble we have gone through, we have had little in the way of fights."

Marie glared at Eve as she poured her juice. "Yes. Enjoy it while you can; it's, as they say, all downhill from here."

Josephine couldn't have worded it better herself.

Chapter Twenty-Three
Training in Empathy

It was a long week for Josephine. Not only did she almost get assassinated by the prince of the Dananns (whom, from King Kingdor's investigation so far, the prince had been working alone as far as they could tell; They had found nothing more on how he had contacted Cetus or where he learned Shadow magic or how he masked it), Eve was waking everyone up bright and early, against the wishes of the others, to train in sword fighting (Josephine gained a magnificent bruise on her thigh). She was also learning about magic from Ticka and the king. Though their brand of magic differed from Dragon heart magic, Ticka explained that the primary rules and principles were the same: one's raw power and energy determined one's attack and control over it.

Ticka and Josephine did their lessons at the Shrine of the Phoenix, on the springs. Ticka was also teaching her and the other's meditative techniques. Eve said she didn't need them and would disappear when they started. To Josephine's surprise, Marie and Wave didn't drag her back.

"It's Eve. Her idea of relaxation is practicing with her sword. And she knows most of this, for Great-Aunt Nina made sure. Eve is fire, and fire is the most dangerous next to lightning. If she lost her temper, she and everything around her would be in big trouble," explained Marie.

Jonathan frowned and voiced what Josephine was thinking, "She is losing her temper all the time at Indie. How...?"

Wave shrugged. "I think it has something to do with her state of mind. She may be angry on the surface, but her center is calm or something like that. Whatever she does, she does it well."

Josephine sat down beside Ticka and admired the shrine. It was an enormous statue of white marble of a Phoenix spreading its wings as though it was about ready to jump into flight. The water's smooth surface reflecting like diamonds in the mid-morning sun, making it hard to look at, for it almost blinded the eyes. The statue sat on a platform that stretched across the widest stream of the spring. Josephine walked over and traced her fingers over the vines of the miniature rose growing over the statue, which gave it an ancient appearance. Ticka glanced over to see Josephine and laughed.

"Wondering how old the statue is?"

Josephine smiled and guessed, "Made when the Phoenix died, right?"

Ticka smiled widely back.

"Right. We use magic to help preserve the statue... it's almost in its own time and space." "How is that possible? What do you do?" frowned Josephine.

"Well, our magic is made from the energy from us and around us." Ticka pointed at the statue, "When the statue was finished, a spell was placed on the statue so that it was stuck in the same space of time that the spell was done. The roses on the statue are the same way, for they are wrapped around the phoenix. They grew around it and now are in a permanent state of blooming. They will never wilt, even in winter."

Josephine stared at the red roses in wonder. "I think I understand."

Ticka stood up and stretched, her ruby hair sparkling in the sunlight. "Magic is a fickle and amazing thing, and it takes time to understand it. Even the greatest of witches and wizards never truly understand magic. It, like the world itself, contains many mysteries that we humble creatures may never completely discover and explain."

Josephine nodded. She paused and stared at her friend. She was calm, shoulders relaxed. Josephine hated to bring up the subject, but...

"Ticka, do you have any idea why your brother... I know it must be hard but..."

She sighed, then sat down. "You have no idea, Josephine. It is like piercing a sword right into my heart. If I could, I would weep and weep till I was drenched in my own tears."

Josephine placed a hand on Ticka, who sighed again. "But as you will find out, Josephine, being a leader means you must give up some things such as mourning. I have no time to be weak. This was a great shock to my people, and they need to know that their faith in us is justified. I will mourn for my lost brother, but later. I must be strong for my people."

"I don't know what I would do in your boots, Ticka... To feel betrayal like that..."

She shook her head. She could never imagine her brothers or Jake ever doing something so extreme.

"Let's hope you never do, Josephine, though sadly, I doubt you will escape it."

"Princess Ticka, Lady Josephine!" The two girls looked up to see the guard, Aillil, running toward them.

"The king needs you at once in the main hall."

Ticka grabbed her sword. "Is it about my brother?"

Aillil half-shrugged. "I think so, your highness. It has to do with the investigation, I believe."

"Thank you, Aillil."

The blonde Tuatha Dé Danann nodded, and the two began their jog back to the city. Josephine noted as they went that before her powers awoke, this jog would have winded her, but now she could easily run five miles without becoming exhausted. It was a satisfying feeling.

Ticka and Josephine met Wave and Eve in the hallway and walked into the throne room to see Jonathan, Indie, and Marie already there with the queen and a young pair of Dananns and, to Josephine's surprise, a faerie. She had long brown-blonde hair and bright ginger eyes. Her wings were twice the size of her body, with colors of pale orange with darker orange in the middle, like a tiger lily. She stood tall as they walked in.

"Josephine, Wave, Eve, this is our liaison faerie, Edythe."

She inclined her head, and Josephine, Wave, and Eve did the same. The king and Gazelda walked in with another Tuatha Dé Danann man. He was as tall as the king, with dark blonde hair. His hair pulled back in a short ponytail with striking bright blue eyes, almost as bright as hers. The Danann's shirt was a faded black shirt with cut-off sleeves. There was a smudge of dust on his cotton pants and short boots. On his large wrist he wore a large chain bracelet. On his belt a curved long sword, and around his neck was a strange knot circle necklace that had a red stone in the middle. The Danann grinned at them and stood in front of King Kingdor.

"Eurus, Bevan, Cori — report, please."

The three Dananns stood straight in front of the king.

"As far as we can find, your majesty, the prince was acting alone," spoke the red-haired girl.

"Yes, we have searched all over, but we can only find vague hints of him doing strange meetings with humans all over the city," spoke the brown-haired Danann Bevan.

"Did anyone get a good look at them?" questioned Ticka.

"Nope. No one did. Vague descriptions of men in long black cloaks with their hoods up. Riagán hid his tracks well. I searched his room again and found a few scorch marks, but besides that, nothing to tell how he was doing Shadow magic. No documents, but I found this."

The blonde Tuatha Dé Danann pulled out a small, circular mirror from his pocket and tossed it to the King, who caught it.

Gazelda glared at it. "He was using that to scry, wasn't he?"

"Looks like it. The thing had a spell on it, but it was broken," shrugged the blonde Danann.

"Eurus, did you find anything else?" asked Queen Andromeda.

He shook his head. "Nope, just that he really like crows, bunch of crow feathers in his room, creepy really. Along with several bottles of Phoenix Spring water..."

Eurus chuckled.

"Hm, yes, thank you, Eurus," the king frowned.

Ticka glared at him. Eurus shrugged. Eurus then noticed Josephine looking at him with a raised eyebrow. He smiled and winked, making her eyebrow go up more. She tightened her lips in distaste at him.

"Well, at least we know how he was getting messages, but when did he start?" commented the King.

Ticka shook her head. Her father stared at her.

"Ticka, is there something you would like to share?"

She went wide-eyed, "No, nothing."

She knew that tone of voice. It was the same one she used when she and Jake had done something they shouldn't have and didn't tell anyone until the problem was out of hand. One time being when they had let out all the horses accidentally and couldn't find some of them. The queen saw that, too, and gave Ticka a severe glare.

"Ticka, is there something that happened that you haven't told us?"

Ticka tilted her head back and then stared at the floor. "Riagán made me promise not to tell anyone."

"Well, Princess, seeing how he almost murdered your new best friend, I'd share," commented Eurus.

Bevan and Cori gave Eurus a furious glare. The king let out a small sigh.

"Eurus, please restrain yourself."

Gazelda walked forward and placed a hand on Ticka's shoulder.

"Ticka, this is not the time to be silent. If you know something that can help us explain why Riagán has done this and maybe help him, if this is not of his own will, then please, dear, tell."

Ticka nodded her head. She squared her shoulders, took a breath to steady herself.

"He hasn't been the same since we had returned from the Phoenix Mountains a few years ago, when he was thirteen. That expedition to see if we could find a phoenix." she held her breath for a second.

King Kingdor frowned.

"Ah, yes. For his birthday, he begged to go. Continue, Ticka."

"At one point, Riagán left the rest of the group; I was the only one who noticed because everyone else was asleep. I tried to follow him but I lost him and had to go back. When morning came, he was there. I asked him about his disappearance into the woods, but he told me he couldn't tell me that it was a secret. I tried, but he threatened to tell Tina that I was the one who wandered off and you would punish me, Father, and send me home. I was only eleven, so I stopped. For the next three nights, he disappeared and came back. I couldn't understand what was going on. I went through his bag and found that mirror," she pointed to the one in Gazelda's hand.

Gazelda frowned and turned the mirror over again, but found nothing.

"I tried to touch it, and it burned my hand. Riagán found me and was so angry that he hit me across the face. He said that I should never ever go through his things and to forget the mirror that I couldn't, shouldn't, touch it. He threw it into his pack and helped me wrap my hand. We told Tina that I was playing too close to the cooking fire. Riagán never has been the same. He stopped doing so much with me. So distant..."

King Kingdor nodded.

"Yes, I do remember that he was never the same after that. I always put it down to growing up."

The queen agreed.

Ticka was shamed face. "I don't understand why we never saw that..."

Gazelda shrugged. "How were you to know?"

"I should have told someone, but Riagán made me promise. We were so close, so when he asked me to keep a secret, I didn't hesitate. We talked and everything, but it has never been the same since the Phoenix Mountains."

Ticka was twisting her hands.

Josephine walked over and wrapped her arm around her. "I understand, Ticka. I would have done the same if one of my brothers had done something like that."

Ticka gave Josephine a weak smile.

Gazelda let out a humph. "Ticka, what happened, happened. There is nothing to be done about it now except to keep looking," Gazelda looked to the king, and he agreed.

"Eurus, can I enlist your services?"

He nodded. "Of course, but one question: if I find him, do you want me to...?"

Queen Andromeda glared and said in a harsh voice, "You are to *bring him back alive*. Thank you, Eurus. He needs to stand trial. You have been in amongst the islands and Hispania too long; we have laws here. There will be no need for your assassination skills."

Josephine went wide-eyed, as did Ticka.

"I am sorry, my lady. I did not wish to insult you. I only was asking for he is a traitor. Only for clarification."

"That has yet to be seen, Eurus, thank you. You are dismissed."

Eurus shrugged and bowed to the royal family before exiting.

Bevan spoke as soon as the door slammed. "Sir, with your permission, I would like to go after the prince myself, or at least with StarHawk to make sure he..."

King Kingdor shook his head. "No, Bevan, I need you and the rest of the magician guard here. At least for the time being, until we are sure of what is going on. Edythe, I need you to send envoys to your queen and to Diana of the Soli Islands. They need to be made aware."

"Who was that StarHawk?" asked Marie.

Kingdor frowned. "Eurus StarHawk. He is... an assassin. Well, not for us, at least. He grew up in the Sand Strip and was brought up to work with the police force, known as 'The Silver Daggers'. You could say he's a for-hire person. He is the best tracker there is and was here in the city collecting a bounty. I called him to assist."

"He obviously was taught the fine art of tact," snarled Wave.

Ticka let out a sharp laugh. "That is his natural personality. But unfortunately..."

"Sometimes you have to work with unpleasant people," finished Gazelda.

"Rule sixteen," muttered Eve, still eyeing the way Eurus had left. Edythe left the same way Eurus did, to send a report to her queen.

Eve, Marie, Wave, Josephine, Jonathan, Indiana, Ticka, and the Dragons all left Gazelda and the king to sort out what their next move would be. Gazelda wished to meet some old friends in a few cities to the west. She also wished to send a message to the Viken.

"WHAT?" gaped Marie.

Gazelda sighed. "We need to get as many allies as we can, Marie, and that includes the Viken."

"They're pirates, Gazelda," frowned Jonathan. "They gave the Alliance great grief for the longest time, raiding ships. I know they haven't been a menace lately, but what makes you think they'll help?"

Gazelda bit her lip in thought. "I don't know. They are warriors by nature. If there is a good battle, then I am sure they would be more than willing to do so, but..."

"The Viken are going to want some sort of payment," spoke Indie, "usually in the form of leftovers of burned down towns... something along those lines. Don't suppose there is a bribe fund or anything?"

Marie answered, "There was and is some gold left from the old Alliance; in fact, it's here in Tailltiu City, but it wouldn't be enough to buy that kind of help."

"Well, never mind that now. Josephine and I will write up a letter to send to the Viken leader. The problem also is that the Viken, unlike the Dananns, are not united. They have many leaders that feud all the time. We'll have to sort out which one we will contact first. But for now, you lot should go get some more training in," encouraged Gazelda, waving them off as she went to do some more research.

The group was already paired off, Indie and Jonathan, Eve and Ticka, Wave and Josephine taking turns with Marie.

The dragons took turns as well, fighting each other and using their instincts to guide them. Josephine smirked as she watched them. The dragons almost reminded her of kittens playing; only, of course, the dragons were much bigger, with sharper claws and fangs that could tear you in half. FireWind was the best fighter, but in the air, she would lose to Aeolus, and if she wasn't watching, she'd lose to Perun, who was the fastest. Hurricane was having a hard time; she didn't enjoy fighting much nor fighting on dry ground.

Aurora did not like it, but was more confident. After Riagán trapped her, she became more focused and was doing better. Josephine felt the same way as she and Marie dueled. They went on for a few minutes, tied, when Jonathan unarmed Indie.

"HA! Finally gotcha!" he laughed.

Indie chuckled and went to pick up his sword. "Yeah, after what, thirty losses?"

Jonathan snorted, "Nice try, three losses. Loser."

Indie smirked, then glanced over to Eve and Ticka's duel, a mischievous grin on his face. Marie and Josephine watched as Indie came up and grabbed Eve's sword from her hand and held it up high out of her reach.

"You know, all it would take to beat you is grabbing your sword and holding it," he smirked, waving her sword out of her reach.

Eve's eyes became slits, and without hesitation, she crushed Indiana's toes with her heel and took a fist full of his shirt to yank him back down so she could get her sword.

As Indie cussed, Eve snarled, "My sword isn't the only weapon I've got."

Jonathan was silently laughing with Marie. Josephine shook her head.

"Really you two, must you carry on like that?" frowned Wave.

"Yes," the two answered. Wave sighed, glancing at Josephine.

"She's right, cut it out. Work on opposite sides of the field if you must. Now is not the time for this."

"I'll cut it out once he stops being an idiot," muttered Eve, walking over to FireWind and Aeolus.

"And I'll cut it out once she stops being such a nut job," muttered Indie, walking over to Ticka to take Eve's spot.

Josephine looked at Jonathan, who shrugged.

Eve once again caught herself thinking about Indiana Phoenix. She was lying in her bed and listening to the birds rising with the sun. She growled out loud, turning to lie on her left side, away from the sunny window.

"*Why can't I stop thinking about that idiot!*" she thought.

There was nothing really amazing about him except that he seemed to be the most annoying man in the world. The incident with her sword was outrageous. If he was trying to be funny, he failed miserably. Eve had seen him but had given him a benefit of doubt by letting him do whatever but of course he proved he didn't deserve it. She already had a tough time being petite and appearing so young to get any respect and have this cute but irritating... Eve blinked, then shook her head. Had she just thought that Indie was cute?

"*Okay, no denying that Indie is good looking, but looks aren't enough to make up for his horrible personality.*"

Eve tried for several more minutes to sleep but gave up and got dressed, making sure not to disturb FireWind. She pulled out her sword from under her bed, grabbed her boots then snuck out.

The grass felt good under her feet as she walked to the clearing where they had all trained for the last few days. She stepped over a bush, entering the clearing. The group's practice dummy (a thick branch shoved into the ground with an old pumpkin as its head and a holey oat bag for a tunic) was standing in the middle of the clearing.

The Dragon heart closed her eyes to take in the ringing sound that her sword made as it was released from its sheath. She then placed the tip of her broad sword under the dummy Cetus's chin. Jonathan had voted to call the dummy Lord Wilson, but Marie thought it best to dub it Cetus. Eve felt like seeing it as Riagán, wishing she could take the traitor on again. Eve drew her sword back and took a breath. But she then heard a snap. With lightning reflexes, she whirled her sword around to meet Indie's.

"You idiot! You should know better than to sneak up behind a swordsman! Get your bloody head ripped off!" she growled.

"Funny, I thought that's what you were trying to do to me yesterday."

Eve glared at him and put her sword away. She did not want to practice with him around. She turned to leave when she felt a brush of fingers on her wrist.

"Practice with me," he said, staring into her eyes. It wasn't a question but yet not a command.

Eve studied him for a moment, letting the words float in the air.

"All right, but I don't have my boots on. Let me put them back on."

Indie shrugged.

"You know, you have extremely tiny feet for a girl."

Eve's eyebrows disappeared behind her bangs. "Is that a compliment or what?"

Indie's mouth twitched a little, then he said, "Take it as you will, as you do anyway."

Indie pulled on fingerless gloves as Eve studied him a little closer. His muscles were cut, and he had the body of a swordsman. She noticed for a brief second that Indie had shiny scars on his hands. She had never noticed that before. Indie picked up his sword, and Eve nodded.

The two walked in a circle, eyes never wavering, as though they were two large cats eyeing each other in the wild. They did this for at least a good few minutes, the cold dew covering their shoes as they walked. Neither made a sound, their breathing quick as well as their heartbeats.

CLANG!

In a half a second, the two swords met in midair, and then they came apart, only to meet again with a resonating ring. With that, the dance began.

And what a dance it was! Eve found when they were concentrating on sword fighting and not poking fun at each other that the two were well matched. Though Eve saw some gaps in his general defense, she thought that Indiana was perhaps the best swordsman she had ever dueled. So far in her brief life, at least. She had thought before that Jonathan was a bit better than Indiana, but that was not the case as they dueled. She realized Jonathan had been serious when he said he had lost so many times to the man before her. The dance went on for a while, but neither was aware of the time, just each other's movements.

Then, with one great swing, Eve beat Indiana and sent his sword into a tree. Indiana laughed, surprising Eve. He was still chuckling as he pulled his sword out of the tree. This whole time, Eve had yet to hear him give out a sincere, cheerful laugh. It was a wonderful sound. She couldn't help herself and smiled back at him as she took a drink of water from her waterskin.

Then the question in her head came out of her mouth without warning, "Why do you have such an attitude?"

Indie smirked. "You tell me why you're a hoyden, and I'll tell you why I have such an attitude."

Eve snorted at his reply. "I'm only saying you have such a pleasant laugh, and when you aren't being so sarcastic, you are an excellent swordsman."

Indie shrugged, not answering her question. With that, they practiced some more. The two found their duel was more like a dance the longer it went. The sounds of their feet moving through the grass, each movement precise and smooth. Eve decided to end the dance.

She made to do a simple sweep to take out his sword, but Indie blocked it.

"It'll take more than that, firefly."

He switched hands and went with a back slash against Eve's broken guard, but Eve was able to block it.

"Firefly?" she questioned as she countered with a quick step strike against his guard that shook, but it held.

"You are a fire dragon, and when you use your sword," he made a switch back to his right hand to attack but ended up blocking instead, "you fly."

"Huh. I have to give you credit, Indiana," she said as she sliced through his parry then tucked her sword under his chin. "That is a good one. See, once you try at it, I can actually begin to slightly put up with your company."

Indie smirked for a brief second, and then it was gone. They put their swords away in silence. The two headed back to the castle for breakfast. Eve noticed the burn marks on his hands again and found her mouth acting before her better judgment.

"What happened to your hands?"

Indiana stared straight ahead. "They got burned when I tried to save my parents from the fire."

Eve took a sharp intake of breath. "I'm sorry."

Indie glanced at Eve's sad eyes and smirked. "It's okay. Let's go get some breakfast, eh?"

Eve smirked back and nodded, noting for some reason that his hazel eyes were bright in the morning light, not realizing that Indie was thinking the same thing about her green eyes.

The two wandered in as the rest were sitting down to eat. Josephine pulled her bowl closer, then glanced over at Gazelda, who nodded. Josephine sighed and cleared her throat as Ticka sat down beside Jonathan.

"I hate to do this, but our breakfast is going to double for a meeting."

Indie smirked. "Sounds good to me."

Gazelda continued, "First order of business is going to the Centaurs. We will have an official council meeting with them, and from what their letter said, they will officially declare themselves as allies."

Everyone smiled, but Josephine knew what she would say next would take those smiles right off.

She took a breath and said, "Once we are done training at the Centaurs, we will need to head as quickly as possible to the next ally..."

Josephine felt wary as the others looked at her.

"The Faeries, right?" asked Perun.

"No... the Viken," muttered Gazelda.

The reaction was exactly as Josephine had pictured it. All the spoons and forks dropped, sending food across the table. Several yells of protests rang out.

"No way, they are murderers, pirates, we can't!" complained Eve, glaring at Gazelda and then Josephine.

Gazelda swallowed some of her juice, then said, "We have no choice. Look at it from the military perspective. With the Centaurs, the Faeries, and Dananns, we have, oh, about three hundred thousand troops, maybe a little less. We have no idea what kind of army Cetus has built since his defeat. He has had sixty years to make contacts and store supplies. He is an expert at keeping an army secret. That is what got us! We did not know what army was against us till they were marching up to the gates!"

Gazelda realized her temper and sadness had gotten her carried away a little. She took a breath and said in a calmer tone, "We don't have Red Rose's troops this time, at least not in the numbers we had in the old alliance. Cetus will probably have the king do a draft and force all who are able in the kingdom to join. The other part of the large problem is we don't know how many Dragon Knights he has enrolled to his side, either. He has been searching just as hard as I have to find the new generation."

Eve twitched, as though she was going to say something. She bit her lip instead and stared down at her bowl. Indiana caught the movement, as did Josephine, making both wonder what was wrong.

"Did you want to say something, Eve?" Josephine asked in a soft voice.

Eve glanced up and shook her head. "I understand all of that, but the Viken are mercenaries; they aren't reliable."

"Did you get a message? Is that why we're going?" sighed Jonathan.

"We don't know that for sure. I know their track record is against them, but then again, not. And as for the message, I sent it this morning," said Gazelda. She spoke again, seeing what Jonathan was about to say, "They love battling; at least they did when the Dragon Heart Alliance was still strong. We can use that to our advantage. It's been a long time since they have had a good battle with somebody other than blood feuds with other Viken villages."

"We'll just have to make do with what we've got. Perhaps the Centaurs can give us some information on their traditions?" asked Josephine, trying to keep up everyone's spirit.

Wave noticed the effort and smiled.

Gazelda smiled, too, but with dark humor, "The Centaurs most likely will. They are more informed and bigger scholars than even the Dananns. Jabari will help."

Gazelda's smile became wistful. Her eyes glazed over as she was remembering something.

Wave and Marie glanced over at Josephine, noting this change on Gazelda's face, her emotions wistful.

"Who is exactly this Jabari?"

Gazelda returned to the present and said with a smile on her lips, "Jabari is the son of the last leader of the Centaurs, Cyllarus. The Senate elected him after his father died about ten years ago at the good old age of ninety-nine. Would have lived longer if he hadn't been so in love with his wine."

Marie asked Gazelda, thoughtful, "Do you know Jabari well?"

Gazelda let out a sharp laugh. "Oh, very well. He's my best friend, you could even say. We fought many times together. He is a good-natured soul and even more level-headed than his father was."

"How well is well?" giggled Wave.

Gazelda's lips became a hard line. "Well enough. Come on, let's get going. I want everyone packed within two hours."

Gazelda chugged the last of her juice, then went on her way.

Wave and Marie busted into a fit of giggles.

"Sounds like Gazelda has a thing for Jabari," giggled Marie as they stood up and went towards their rooms.

"Really, can a Centaur and a Unicorn have a 'thing'"? teased Indie, who earned a smack on the arm from Eve.

"Cut that out, you idiot. What kind of stupid question is that?"

"A curious, stupid question."

Everyone groaned as Eve smacked Indie again.

"Gazelda can love whoever she wants. Doesn't matter, nor is it any of our business."

"You didn't think that when she held back everything about her being Fair Lady," Indie pointed out.

"That was different; that involves Alliance business. This is her private life, and we need to keep our noses out of it," Eve snarled.

"Let me guess, you've already tried to fish out her previous love life and got nothing, right?"

Eve grunted, "Yeah, pretty much."

Indie said nothing, but had a small smirk on his face.

Chapter Twenty-Four
Jabari, Leader of the Centaurs

The Dragon Hearts, along with Indiana and Gazelda, walked to the guardian forest of the Danann city. Josephine could barely keep back her tears. Ulysses and Starlette had decided it was best to stay in Tailltiu.

"If something happens, we can come to you faster than Mirage could," Starlette smiled, though she was crying big tears from her sunshine eyes. Josephine felt so empty. She and Starlette did everything together, no matter how much Starlette thought it was crazy. Starette was her anchor.

Josephine said as such to her in which Starlette said, "I know, but you have Aurora now, who is a much better fighter than I am, and you are a Dragon Heart. The two of you need to bond."

"I know, but you are my closest friend," Josephine said in a weak protest. Her heart breaking.

"Yes, but you being a Dragon Knight is more important, and it's better that you go on without me for now."

It was no easier for Ulysses and Jonathan, though they didn't cry. They were silly like that.

"Just make sure not to run on the bad side of any pixies," Ulysses chuckled, as did Jonathan.

"No, I won't, not like you did that one time."

With heavy hearts, Josephine and Jonathan hugged their friends and then walked down to join the others. Ulysses and Starlette walked to the highest hill and watched as the group left the city, becoming little dots in the distance. Starlette did not move until Ulysses came back much later to tell her it was time to eat.

XXX

Ticka took them to the edge of the forest, right where the main trade roads were, and before leaving them, she gave the group some parting gifts. She gave Josephine her hunting knife and Indiana his sword back, but with a modification. Both the knife and the sword now had an iridescent sheen to the blades.

"I had them enchanted with the Phoenix Spring's water. They are strong enough to stab any Shadow creature. Not as powerful as the swords that you all have, they were forged with Phoenix water or Unicorn magic, but effective."

Josephine and Indiana took the gifts, humbled.

"Thank you so much, Ticka," Josephine smiled, hugging the Tuatha Dé Danann princess. Indiana smiled and said, "Thanks."

Gazelda smiled at the gesture that Ticka had done, trying to make up for her brother, no doubt.

Her smiled slipped away. "Have any more shadow creatures been spotted?" she asked.

"Vague reports here and there. A few travelers and Mirage just arrived.

Indie muttered, "Dang, that bird can get around."

"She thinks she saw something on the way here, but for all she knew, it could have been a bear. She was flying so high. Same sort of stories from the travelers," shrugged Ticka.

"Right. In other words, stay close together and stay in the sun," grumbled Eve, pulling her pack tighter.

Ticka and Josephine hugged and told each other to be safe. With that, the group left, with Ticka waving behind them.

It was only a three-and-a-half-day ride from Tailltiu City to the Centaur's home, which was known simply as Chariclo's Sanctuary. Gazelda again talked fondly of the half-horse humans.

"Jabari was still a teenager when the last battle happened. He became the leader like I said, ten years ago when his father died," she sighed, "He is a fun-loving person but can become very dangerous if provoked."

"Now, you say leader, not king?" Aurora remarked from beside Josephine.

Gazelda nodded. "Yes. Centaurs elect leaders to enforce their laws and such. Anglii is only a continent, and everyone who lives here is not united. The Centaurs, Dananns, Humans, Viken... all see themselves as separate countries."

"That is why the Dragon Heart Alliance was made to bring them together as a united country," Josephine said.

"It's the same with all the other continents. In Francia, for example, the humans and the unicorns do not see themselves as one people outside of the Alliance," Gazelda explained.

"I've never seen a centaur before," remarked Marie thoughtfully.

"I have," grumbled Indiana as the group reached the end of the dirt path they had taken.

"What was he like?" asked Wave.

Indie's face went into a scowl. "A drunken idiot who wasn't watching what he was doing and nearly took off my head. Ironically, he was the one who taught me how to use a bow."

Gazelda had a small smirk on her face and asked, "What was his name?"

Indie smiled with more fondness than annoyance and said, "Eton. Couldn't hold his liquor but..."

"Sure knew how to fight," finished Gazelda. "He taught me how to fight as well. Darn outstanding teacher, but like you said, couldn't hold his liquor. Got him into trouble once with Pan the Faun. Long story short, they both wanted the same faerie, and it came down to them fighting; both lost the girl and gained large scars for it on their backsides. And I might add it was the faerie who gave them the scars," Gazelda's smile lingered as they took in the scenery.

It was all wide-open forest with TitTo Lake to their left. It was midday and the sun shining; the lake reflecting its rays.

"So where do the Centaurs exactly live?" asked Eve, jumping down from FireWind's back. Gazelda nodded with her horn, pointing towards the lake.

"They live throughout these woods. Beyond the lake and a little further is their small town of Celous. All I can say is that it is made with some beautiful craftsmanship. You'll like it more if I don't say anything."

"LADY GAZELDA!?"

Gazelda turned her head back towards the lake and so did the rest of them to see a young girl, her upper half human, the lower half a chocolate brown mare. Her human face was soft and sweet. She had brown eyes and bright yellow hair.

"Daylen!" Gazelda yelled back grinning, "How fare you and your uncle?"

"Very well, Lady Gazelda! Come, Uncle Jabari, and the rest of the Senate are waiting for you!"

"Lead the way then, if you could, please, Daylen," smiled Gazelda, and with that Daylen nodded her head much like a horse, and she turned on her hooves, going at a slow trot with the rest of them following, Gazelda in the front and the dragons in the rear.

A marble path guided them to the northern front of TitTo Lake, which seemed more like a large pond than a lake to Josephine. When they stopped, Josephine had to do a double take. Beneath the edge of the lake were two large marble columns that stood on either side of a pair of doors. The face of the doors was adorned with a crescent moon, a centaur shooting an arrow with it.

Daylen knocked on the door three times. They opened with a large, squealing noise. Daylen walked in first, her hooves echoing off sand colored marble floors. Gazelda continued on, still in her normal form, so they walked in right after her. Josephine felt her jaw drop.

The room was similar to one in a castle, only it was circular in design. It was a well-crafted combination of wood and stone, with art crafts of oil painting and marble statues decorating the room. The scent of leather and parchment saturated the whole air. The decor reminded Josephine of the art of the people from the Hellos Islands. There were a few Centaurs in the room, two men and one woman. The woman's skin was tanned; her hair, both horse and human, was dark as midnight as was the tunic she was wearing, while her eyes were a deep shade of blue. The one man standing beside her had silver streaks through his yellow hair.

His head turned, his bright green eyes going wide. The other man was standing at the entrance into the next room. He was even taller than the others and had tanned skin and green olive eyes, brown hair and was shirtless, with leather belts crisscrossing across his solid-muscle chest, a battle axe on his back. On seeing Gazelda, his smile stretched over his face.

"Gazelda, you old colt!"

"Jabari, you overrated warhorse!"

Gazelda went forward and Jabari hugged Gazelda around her neck. He pulled back to appraise Gazelda.

"You look as wonderful, beautiful, and as intimidating as always," Gazelda chuckled.

"And you are as charming as always."

Jabari walked forward, now appraising them. Josephine did what she could to keep herself from squirming under his gaze. He turned to Gazelda, a frown on his face. Josephine held her breath.

"This is what I have to work with?"

Gazelda rolled her eyes.

"What did ya think, that I would bring fully trained knights to you? Really?" she snorted.

Jabari snorted as well.

Josephine could feel that the others who had been confident now were a little on the worried side. Well, except for Indiana, he seemed bored.

Another sigh escaped through the centaur's nose. Josephine, at that second, saw Gazelda shaking her head to herself from laughing. Josephine then realized it was all a ploy. She had to cover her mouth to stop herself from laughing.

"All right, I guess I've seen worse. The normal one is a smart-mouth type, but I've seen plenty of those in my time."

Indie smirked.

"The Grace; I am assuming, is hotheaded; one joke about her height ticks her off."

Eve's eyes went wide and then narrowed, an 'humph' emanating from her lips.

"The light brunette looks a little too nice to be a Dragon knight."

Wave seemed like she did not know if she should be insulted or not.

"The royal looks good enough, but still is a little on the soft side."

Jonathan chuckled, catching on to what Jabari was doing.

"Same with the dark-skinned girl, who is the intellectual, I assume."

Marie's eyebrow went up, a tiny "huh" escaped her lips.

"And last but not least..." Jabari walked closer to Josephine.

She straightened her posture a little, meeting Jabari's stare.

"You seem like a capable girl, more of a diplomat than a fighter, but with a little training we should stomp that right out," He winked.

Josephine silently chuckled.

Jabari nodded to the other Centaurs, and they came over. "Let me introduce two members of the Senate and my dearest friends, Soterios and Rhode."

Rhode spoke with a wonderful accent, like Jabari. "Welcome, Dragon hearts, to Chariclo's Sanctuary. This is Chiron's Keep or library, as we now call it, for we converted it into one. I am one of the members of the Centaur Senate, as is Soterios."

Soterios smiled, "I am the head of the army, the commander general."

He smiled, and Josephine smiled back. She liked Soterios. He was big and intimidating, but his warm voice balanced that unease cause by his great height.

"When will we talk to the Senate?" Josephine asked, glancing back at Jabari.

"Tomorrow. Most of the Senate wished to converse tonight, but some of them," Jabari muttered, venom coming into his voice, "are still unsure about rejoining the Alliance so they requested for another day, but I doubt they will say no. Tomorrow you will have to talk to the whole of the Senate and then, you'll have to wait till around two to three days to vote. Sadly," he sighed.

"Why does it take so long?" inquired Wave.

"Because the Senate works as a unit. Jabari is the leader, but he needs the support of the Senate to do so," explained Rhode.

"Could you perhaps brief me on your laws and procedures?" asked Josephine.

Jabari smirked, "I could," he chuckled.

Josephine blinked, then understood the answer.

"Sorry, will you help me understand your laws?"

Rhode smiled, as did Jabari, but then his face went a little bleak, "You will find that details are everything; one little misstep and everything you are working for could fall apart. Thin ice, devil in the details, and all that; politics are pointless, but it is a game many love to play."

Josephine nodded, trying not to let the unease in her stomach creep into her throat.

"But for now, let's get you all settled into rooms and fed," Jabari left the Dragon Hearts in Rhode's and Soterios' care, for he had to attend meetings with the a few Senate members.

Rhode led them to some small rooms for one of the eight main hallways of the keep. It was covered with the same motifs that decorated the main entrance hall. It was also large, which surprised Josephine, but when she looked at Rhode, she realized it only made sense that everything would be wide, for the Centaurs themselves were.

"Uh, what are the dragons going to do?" questioned Eve as they stopped to pick out their rooms.

The hallways were wide but not wide enough for large, fire-breathing lizards.

"We have special accommodations for your partners," smiled Rhode.

Special were the accommodations. The dragons were sleeping in bungalows made of the finest iron work. Creeping vines grew all over the openings, and they trimmed the vines in such a way that the Dragons could pull them down to cover the opening to get peace. The forest beside the lake was large, so the dragons could freely hunt in the forest without worries.

Perun wanted to fish in the lake, but Rhode kindly explained that it was an empty lake. It was a special lake that contains the tomb of Chariclo, the beautiful maiden that had fallen in love and married the leader of the Centaurs many centuries ago when the Centaurs were searching for a new home.

Hurricane asked if there was somewhere else, she could swim. Rhode said that TitTo Lake, east of the town, would do well for them.

Josephine smiled as she laid her head down that night; she knew she was going to like it with the Centaurs.

"All right everyone, time to teach you how to fight properly."

Indiana yawned, then mumbled in a low voice, "Couldn't you've done that a little later in the morning? Why is training always in the early morning?"

It was dawn when Jabari gathered the five Dragon hearts and one human standing before him. They spent the day before listening and talking with the Senate. It had gone much more smoothly than any of them had dared hoped. Josephine remembered how the large lay out of the government building had been slightly intimating. The officials sat behind large raised wooden benches in what was the keep of the underground castle. The floor and stairs were crafted of white and gray marble.

Josephine made a simple request of the Centaurs to please assist them, the Dragon hearts, in rebuilding the Alliance with them and the Dananns and what was left of the Red Rose Kingdom. Jonathan, too, spoke, as did Gazelda, to give testimony to what had been going on and that they needed to join forces. They explained that this was in the best interests of the Centaurs if they wished to remain free. It took an hour after that for speeches from various officials. It would be another day or two before the vote.

"We learned to fight in Tailltiu City," spoke up Wave.

Jabari snorted. "I know the Tuatha Dé Danann's fighting style, and those sticks they call swords," he chuckled. "I will show you how to shoot heavy crossbows, use large broad swords and axes."

Wave's eyebrow went up when she heard the word "axe," while Jonathan shot Indie a grin, which he returned with a scowl. Jabari did not miss this.

"Come now! You haven't even tried yet! Part of being a warrior is not just about how many fighting styles you know, it's whether you have the right state of mind to use it to keep you and your comrades alive."

When Jabari turned to walk to the training grounds, Eve muttered, "That may be true, but I still think I'll prefer the Dananns' style."

In the end, Josephine had to agree. Jabari had them do large amounts of muscle strength training. It was nice to find out the limits of their strength. Jabari took them to a large, empty field, and all in a row were five rocks. Jabari, first, had them test their upper body strength. Josephine found it funny that she could lift a boulder that weighed at least twice as much as the largest male stallion. Of course, Jonathan had to show off that he could lift four times that. Marie could lift just as much as Josephine, while Eve and Wave just a little less than the other two. So, Jabari ordered that every morning, they had to lift boulders for an hour. Indiana laughed, but then Eve laughed because Jabari told Indiana, he too, would lift weights, only they would be smaller to start with and would build up that way. So Indiana would stand to the side and do his excises while the Dragon hearts did theirs. The dragons too, lifted rocks with their front claws and tails.

The first day they all did this, everyone thought that their arms, or in the Dragon's cases, claws, would fall off.

This went on for two weeks and in that short time, Josephine could see her muscles become more defined and cut, and Aurora, too, became more muscular under her ice-colored scales. Even Eve was gaining a good amount of muscle, which she complained about that because her feminine looks were fading. It wasn't so bad for the other girls, even Wave, because they were much bigger and broader than her. Indie stuck his foot in his mouth by saying that now she looked more like a satyr, to which Eve repaid by throwing a ball shaped rock and hitting him square in the arm. Three days later, the bruise was still there.

Over the month that they were training, Josephine felt an issue creep up into her mind, and it gnawed at her every time they practice their shooting or swordplay, the issue that she would have to kill other people. Josephine had killed deer and other types of animals for food when she and her brothers went hunting in the fall, and she had helped put a few horses down that were in too much pain to be able to recover from their injuries that would never heal. But she had never killed to be mean, not even when a garter snake crawled into her boot and bit her when she placed her foot inside. She just took the little snake outside and let it go. She had never killed or ever wanted to kill another person before. Though Josephine had said she would kill Cetus during many of their debate sessions, it was hard for Josephine to imagine killing someone and really didn't want to. Taking the head off a burlap bag dummy was one thing, but to take a human's head off was another thing. Even the thought of killing a troll made Josephine's stomach turn. She had been taught to love and appreciate all life and to never kill in malice or, for pointless reasons, even the most annoying little spider.

In the middle of that, the Senate finally called to vote on joining the Alliance.

Josephine bit down on her lips as she counted, along with the official, the hands for "Yay."

"Seventy to thirty, the motion has passed for the Centaurs to rejoin the Dragon Heart Alliance to call the Dragon Hearts and Dannans allies officially once again!" called the official.

Josephine was surprise that so many were opposed to joining up, but Jabari wasn't nor, was Gazelda. Jabari said that many were not in favor of war, no matter what, and various other self–interests.

"In other words, if we go to war, they would have to fight and train, and they don't want that," explained Jabari to Josephine. "There is a law that if a war comes, half of the Senate—usually the younger members — must go fight. All those who work in the Senate must serve in the army for a time. It gives them a better understanding that the army is something they must be careful of, for they hold the warriors' lives in their hands. It helps keep them humble to some point."

Josephine found a chance to talk to Jonathan when the two were sitting out on the stone wall that surrounded the small village, observing the lake as the sun set. They had just eaten dinner, and the others had dispersed to individual activities; Wave was swimming in the other lake with

Marie, Perun, and Hurricane, while Eve was reading in the library, and Indiana had disappeared to parts unknown. Jonathan was lying on his back, his feet on the wall's edge, with Josephine sitting beside him, her hands in her lap. The wind was blowing hard, but not too hard; it was making the grass and water ripple in waves, the smell of the flowers riding on the wind to their faces. Josephine started the conversation slowly.

"It's amazing here," she murmured, feeling slightly stupid saying something so obvious.

Jonathan felt her slight embarrassment and smiled, saying, "It really is. So calm and peaceful."

He looked at Josephine to admire how the wind was blowing her free hair, almost as though it were a wild kite. It was inky black, but Jonathan saw the hint of blue that glimmered in it. Aeolus smirked at the feelings of affection that were coming from Jonathan. He and Aurora were lying on their stomachs beside the lake, also enjoying the calm spring evening. Even so, he could feel some tension from Josephine. She could also feel Jonathan's confusion at that. Jonathan smiled.

"A bronze coin for your thoughts?" he whispered; his voice almost lost in a gust of wind.

"Jonathan, have you thought at all about what we must do?"

Jonathan said, "Many times. I have a feeling there is one specific action that is troubling you, Ice Queen?"

"How will I fight?"

Jonathan knew what she meant but still tried to keep it light-hearted.

"With your sword, however, from what I've experienced, your fists are just as good."

She shook her head. "Jonathan, I'm not a soldier, regardless how much Jabari and Gazelda have taught me. The most I've ever killed was a rattlesnake that almost bit my friend Jake once. And defended myself against that gargoyle. I've never killed anyone in the way we are going to in battle. How can I kill a human being or similar? Could I slaughter even a troll?"

Jonathan let a breath out. "Ah. I see."

Jonathan glanced over to their dragon partners, then back to Josephine's somber expression.

"I understand what you are worried about. Trust me, the thought of killing anyone, troll, soldier...it makes my stomach and my mind sick."

Josephine nodded in agreement. "I don't understand how any of us can do this. Eve is so eager for battle."

Jonathan chuckled and glanced in the general direction of the library.

"I wouldn't say that. She likes to battle, but not the type of battle I think you're thinking of."

Josephine gave him a raised eyebrow. "Come again?"

Jonathan laughed. "True, Eve was brought up as a warrior, but I don't think she takes too much pleasure in it. I think there are other things she'd rather battle."

Josephine shook her head. "I don't get it..."

Jonathan smirked and nodded his head towards Indiana, who was walking to the library. Josephine followed his nod and let out an "ah". She grew up with three brothers; she got the picture.

"You really think that?" she chuckled.

Jonathan shrugged, "Personally, I think it is mutual," he smiled.

Josephine rolled her eyes. The moment of amusement left her. Her smile faded away.

Jonathan sat up and placed a hand on her shoulder. "I forget that you're not accustomed to this. I was trained to fight and, more so, to kill. When you are a royal, death is something you have to deal with, whether your enemies are from another kingdom or even your own kin."

"Who killed who in your own family?!"

Jonathan sighed and closed his eyes. "One of my close uncles, a few distant aunts and many cousins. My father had two brothers, and my Uncle Dion was tired of my father favoring the youngest, Amédéé. He was my favorite uncle, Holly's father. He was a gentleman and looked after his people until Uncle Dion wanted the inheritance all to himself, as well as influence in Red Rose court."

Josephine felt ill in her stomach. "He killed his baby brother? For money? I guess what my Aunt Shelia said about royalty being blood thirsty was true; she was not exaggerating the truth."

Jonathan nodded. "In the end, justice came to him. Uncle Dion died of the bloody cough a year later and the money went back to my cousins, for he had no heirs. I am curious. How does your aunt know?"

Josephine smiled, "She used to work in the Red Rose kitchens once upon a time, when my uncle was alive and was part of the Calvary. He died when I was still young from an illness. Aunt Sheila came to live with us not long after that."

The two let a moment of silence take the air. Jonathan then broke it, "I cannot tell you but where I stand, Josephine. I do not wish to kill, but if it is what I must do to protect my kingdom and my friends and family, so be it. I will not kill with malice, and I will mourn all who die at my hands. That is how I see it. It is up to you how you will cope with the certain deaths that approach."

Josephine said nothing; she pondered over what Jonathan said. Josephine turned back to him after a moment and said, "I see what you say, but it will take time."

Jonathan sighed and sat up, giving her a sad expression. "I don't think you'll have much time to think about it."

They said little until the last of the orange sky faded into the inky black night on the lake's mirror. Though the warm color meant a sailor's delight, Josephine felt nothing but foreboding anguish waiting for them.

Josephine and Jonathan were in the library talking to Rhode when they heard a gigantic crash of hooves on marble.

Josephine felt cold, sickly cold. Her eyes went wide. Jonathan and Rhode both give out a shocked gasp. There were several other centaurs standing in the grand hall with their weapons drawn. There was a shadow creature in the shape similar to a wolf standing in the middle of the hall. It glanced around in quick, jerky movements.

Jabari came from the front doors and yelled, "Deliver your message, Coyote, then leave these hallowed halls of my ancestors!"

The coyote faced Jabari. Eve and Wave had entered the hall behind the leader as well as Indie and Marie, who had been training outside. Josephine shuddered when the creature talked; it reminded her of someone's voice, but it was warped, harsh and loud.

"You are Jabari?"

The leader of the Centaurs' eyes narrowed. "I am."

"Josephine Drageon, is she here?"

Josephine felt the blood leave her face. Jonathan's arm came up, but Josephine had already stepped forward to stand beside Jabari.

"I am here." She tried to sound brave, but there was a touch of fear in her voice.

Gazelda, by this time, had joined the rest of them and placed a hand on Josephine's shoulder. Josephine appreciated the support.

"I am a messenger from Riagán on behalf of Cetus, the Lord of the Shadow Dragon Knights."

"That's what he's calling himself?" muttered Gazelda, so low that Josephine almost didn't hear it.

"He says this: There is no need for bloodshed. Come to me freely, young Dragon Knights. I will teach you the true meaning of power. The Dananns, Centaurs, all of them who call you an ally, will use you for their own ends. They do not see me as a threat and see you as merely pawns to advance their influence in Anglii. Unless, of course, the Centaurs wish to join Cetus's new kingdom. I stress again there is no need for bloodshed, fellow creatures of the earth. To warn you, the Dananns are receiving a similar hand of friendship from us, and if they do wisely join, then you will gain another enemy. All you must do to signal your alliance is to send a messenger to the northern ridge of the Phoenix Mountains, the mountain of Ember Falls. I and my master are looking forward to your answer."

With a shiver, the dog made its way to go past Jabari. He swung his axe and beheaded the Shadow creature. It dissipated like fog into nothing. For a moment, no one spoke. Then Eve said,

"Somebody is full of himself."

Chapter Twenty-Five
Justification

It took two hours for the Senate to assemble. It was loud in the assembly room; everyone's voices were echoing off the marble walls. They all had the same tone. Worry.

The dragons were sitting right behind Josephine and the other five, while Gazelda was near the top of the room, sitting beside Soterios with his second in command, Aello. She was wearing a blue tunic and a short sword, talking in a rushed voice with Gazelda. Gazelda was calm, but Josephine could feel the concern under the surface. Josephine tapped her foot on the floor, impatient for the meeting to start. Jonathan leaned to Indie when he tapped him on the shoulder.

"What's the point of all this?" Indie waved his hand in the air. "They have already voted and joined the Alliance, so what's the big deal?"

Jonathan said, "Yes, but they now have to figure out what they will do now that Cetus has sent an offer."

He looked at Jonathan in disbelief. "You're telling me they got everyone together just to vote that they are going to say no to somebody?"

Jonathan smiled. "More like how to nicely tell him they got a better offer."

Marie added, "Also, to decide what to do about him. He gave away his hiding spot."

"From what I gather from some of them is that they don't see Cetus as a threat," muttered Aeolus.

"How can they not see him as a threat?" muttered Hurricane.

"They look at it this way: Cetus got his power back, yes, but still recovering. What guarantee is there that he hasn't gone mental? He is old and does not have the army he once had. They did not see him at the cave like we did," Josephine commented.

Jonathan muttered in an icy voice as the reader stood to announce the beginning of the meeting, "Cetus has proven to be a threat and did many crimes against many kingdoms. He needs to be taken in before he becomes what he once was, but when have politicians ever been smart enough to see the bigger issue?"

Jonathan and Josephine turned out to be right. The few who had voted against joining the Alliance were downright passionate about not answering Cetus. To ignore him. One senator in particular was loud about it:

"Cetus is dying from his Shadow magic, just like those of old. We have no fear of this... man."

He didn't dare say Dragon Knight because when another Senator had called him that, Gazelda in a low but dangerous tone informed the Senator that "Cetus is no longer a Dragon Knight due to the fact that he was stripped of his titles after the Battle of the Betrayed and because he also has no Dragon partner."

Many nodded and murmured agreement to that statement. It killed the Senator's argument.

"If nothing else, why don't we, instead of offering a hand with a sword, why don't we give a hand of peace?"

Josephine felt a shock from every one of her friends.

"He didn't!" gaped Eve.

"He did," growled Jonathan.

Senator Nikator went for almost an hour, giving reasons to not attack/capture or kill Cetus. To give Cetus empathy. When Jabari got up to give his speech, he gave a long look at Gazelda, then spoke.

"Many of you have heard the argument to show Cetus empathy. He has not earned it. He killed the king of Red Rose Kingdom and almost killed James Dracolas, his own master."

Jabari glimpsed at Josephine then said, "He also is indirectly at fault for many murders, including those at Drake City when it was but a large village, the young Dragons Hearts who died trying to defend the village and not including the death of Dragon Heart Master Michael Grace." Eve stiffened at the mention of her great-grandfather's name. "We can't show him mercy just because it happened sixty years ago, and murder is murder no matter how long ago. Many of our own were also killed in the Battle of the Betrayed. We cannot let one murderer go; for many will think that they can change the kingdoms and get away with it. Think of the families that were wiped out. That is what will happen to us if we sit idle. We must tell Cetus that we will not join his twisted order, that he will pay for the lives he stole."

It was another hour before the Senate made their final decision.

Josephine finished packing and was sitting with Aurora beside the lake wall. Wave and Hurricane joined them.

"What do you think of us leaving like this?" asked Josephine in the quiet twilight.

Wave shrugged. "I think it's logical. If we leave sooner than later, Cetus is less likely to ambush us. Plus, the Centaurs need to get their army ready. We need to contact the rest of the Red Rose army and the Viken."

Josephine took in a breath.

"It's okay, Josephine, we have Gazelda," Hurricane whispered.

Josephine didn't say anything, but nodded. Wave reached over and wrapped her arm around Josephine's shoulders.

"Is the killing thing getting to you?" asked Wave, her blue eyes kind.

"I guess so."

Wave nodded. "I know how you feel. I'm already having nightmares." Wave placed her other hand on Hurricane, who nudged her.

"I can't stand the thought of taking a life. I won't take unless I have to. I loathe doing it, but I am going to be a knight, so I have to accept what comes with it."

"Sounds about right."

Josephine smiled, wrapping her arm around Wave's shoulder.

They left after dawn. Jabari saw them off with a hug and a reassurance that the Centaurs were going to help.

With those words, the Dragon hearts, dragons, Gazelda, and Indiana disappeared into the bright rising sunlight.

Chapter Twenty-Six
Longing

The next few days were hard on Josephine. The group cut through a few of the smaller towns on their way to the Viken. They passed a few miles north of Wind Sage. Everyone, even Indie, tried to keep up Josephine's spirits. The knowledge that her family was home and safe made her feel a little better, but she still longed to hug her mother. Aurora helped her to not brood on that too much and to concentrate on her training. Every night after they ate, each of them, even Gazelda, would take turns practicing their sword play and target practice. Unfortunately, it didn't stay in practice for long.

It was the eighth night after they had left the centaur's home. Everyone was gathered around the fire. Indiana was whittling something with his hunting knife. Flash sitting on his shoulder asleep. Eve was lounging on FireWind's back.

Gazelda was crouched over a piece of parchment, a charcoal pencil in her human hand, muttering to herself as she wrote. She was so engrossed with what she was writing that she had inadvertently given herself a charcoal mustache. Marie was reading a small, red leather book by the fire, leaning on Perun's side. Josephine was stroking Aurora's head, not really thinking about anything. Jonathan and

Aeolus were scouting ahead, keeping an eye out for Red Rose troops, Shadow magicians, and anything else that could be a problem for them.

They had a few blink-of-an-eye-glances of shadow creatures snaking around the forests. Shadows themselves were just as dangerous by themselves as those controlled by a magician. Mango gave them plenty of stories to fuel everyone's imaginations and make them jumpy. Also, the soldier from the mines still haunted the edges of Josephine's dreams. Gazelda was the calmest about it all, she of course having experience with them.

Indiana put down his project, then gently put Flash on the log before standing up and stretching. He chuckled at Gazelda's mustache and pointed it out to her.

Gazelda jumped when Indie called her name. Aurora tilted her head to the left and then asked, "What are you doing there, Gazelda?"

She took a handkerchief to wipe her face off, then rolled up the message she was writing.

"Trying to get some reinforcements," she mumbled.

Josephine watched as Gazelda folded the message to impossibly small portions.

"Okay, so why are you folding it into oblivion?" queried Indie.

Gazelda let out a small, extremely high-pitched whistle. A green and blue blur flew out of nowhere and stopped short of Gazelda's face. Everyone blinked, then looked to see it was a hummingbird. It was floating in one spot, flapping its diminutive wings to stay airborne. Its feathers looked as though they were polished velvet, shining in the firelight.

"So that my messenger can take it. I don't know the next time we will see either Jessie Bell or Mirage, so best to use the messengers of the sun."

Indie's eyebrows went up. "That little thing is going to take a message for you somewhere across Anglii?"

Gazelda snorted with a sly grin. "Yes, this little thing is going to take my message to someone in a city in Anglii. Hummingbirds are small and fast and, unlike pigeons, are less likely to be spotted by someone and less likely to be eaten."

Indie shook his head. "That bird is too small! It'll get eaten! It's too weak!"

Gazelda chuckled. The bird let out a humph noise, to everyone's surprise, and then whipped around Indiana, and with its long, thin, needle beak, it bit him right on his rear.

"OW HEY!"

Eve fell over laughing, tumbling off FireWind's back. Gazelda chuckled as the hummingbird, whose feathers were all puffed out, flew back to her. She stroked its head.

"Just because one is small does not mean it does not have the power to defend itself."

"Rule... seventeen! And rule eighteen... never mock the power of... a... *hummingbird*!" choked out Eve, wiping the tears off her face.

Indie was frowning and had a slight red tint to his ears.

Gazelda blew a kiss to the little winged creature before it flapped away into the darkness of the forest, heading northwest, the same direction that they themselves were going. Josephine had asked Gazelda earlier in the day where they were going. She replied she didn't know herself until she heard back from a few people. Josephine wondered who exactly Gazelda was trying to contact.

"Gazelda, how do you get them to do that, the humming-birds?" asked Marie, putting her book down.

Gazelda gathered her writing utensils, placing them away in her pack.

"Whistle like I did. The hummingbirds will hear it, and if it does not have a message, it will come to you. Humming-birds come in handy to send quick messages, though if you have a really long one, it's best to send a pigeon or deliver it yourself. They can only carry so much weight, which isn't much. Talk to it in Dragon tongue and you'll be good to go. Just make sure you tell the poor thing where to deliver it. Sometimes they can be so enthusiastic that they'll fly off before thinking, and also, only send one message per bird; they are smart, but they still can't handle more than one place or trip at a time."

As Gazelda sat back down, they heard Jonathan running beside Aeolus. Josephine picked up their emotions, and they were anxious.

When they burst into the camp, Eve was still giggling and didn't notice their anxiety. She said, "Hey, Jonathan, you missed something great! Indie just got bit on the–" Eve stopped, finally tasting the climate. She jumped and pulled out her sword, and everyone else jumped up, hands on their hilts.

"What's wrong?" asked Hurricane.

Jonathan doused the fire and whispered into the dark, "There is a large group of trolls being led through the forest by two people, one a woman about our age and an older man, both on horseback."

Marie passed him his pack as Eve whispered, "How far away are they?"

"About a half a mile from here, and coming fast; they're heading northeast from northwest, towards Red Rose City as though coming from Drake City."

As Josephine jumped on Aurora's back, Josephine heard a clicking of hooves, then Gazelda's voice.

"Just disappear into the woods. Do not ambush them!" Gazelda whispered as she ghosted into the woods.

Marie and Perun pushed the horses out to encourage them to bolt. She heard them run in a westerly direction. That was going to be a pain to get them back.

Josephine felt Aeolus's breath as he moved himself closer to her and Aurora. They, too, ghosted into the woods. Josephine and Jonathan jumped up into a tall oak while Aurora and Aeolus buried themselves in the thick bushes. She could not hear Gazelda, but she heard Eve and Indie go into a neighboring tree with FireWind crouched behind it. Marie and Wave went with their partners across from them, staying low to the ground. Josephine tried to slow down her breathing to stay as quiet as possible. She heard the others doing the same.

The group waited only for five minutes when they heard the stopping of a small army. The smell hit them before the Trolls came into view. They smelled like meat that had been left in the sun to rot. Josephine had to swallow a gasp and some bile from her stomach. The drawings of trolls she'd seen captured their appearances perfectly. The trolls stood from between five to eight feet tall. Their skin was like yellow glue that had been boiled, then left to harden. Their faces were like many layers of fat, showing many chins, and their eyes were only red, angry slits in their faces, with hair that was mostly black or brown and unwashed and short. Their hands were long and so were their green-yellow nails. The trolls were carrying a large array of weapons and armor, but mostly shields, fat broad swords, crossbows, and lots of axes.

Josephine was able to pull her handkerchief to her mouth to filter the smell. The trolls kept going until two horses came galloping around them faster than the trolls' march and came to a halt in front of the line. Leading them was a raven-haired woman on a white stallion, whilst the man was blonde-haired and on a black stallion.

The man yelled to the trolls, "HALT!" and they did with a large chorus of banging from their armor.

Jonathan and Josephine both winced at the noise. As did the woman.

She whipped her head around and yelled at the man, "Archimago! Watch what you are doing! These stupid brutes need a warning!"

The "stupid brutes" glared at the woman that had to have been a noble woman. She wore the finest red and black silk traveling dress and a black velvet cloak. The woman had a young but hard face and deep violet eyes. Josephine noticed that the woman had an accent. When she spoke again, her special Dragon sense realized that the woman was speaking in a language other than Anglii; it was Francian.

"Sorry, *Lady* Claudette," the man Archimago sneered at the word "lady".

The lead troll sniffed the air and spoke in his own tongue, "There is a fresh camp here, and the scent of dragon is heavy."

Lady Claudette did not understand a word and made an impatient noise. Archimago looked thoughtfully at the troll and nodded. He turned with a crooked grin.

"Luck has fallen upon the careful. Our general says that dragons have been here, and the camp is fresh."

Claudette turned around and muttered something under her breath that Josephine did not catch. The fire that they had put out glowed again, a ghost of its former glory a few yards away from the new-comers and their small platoon. Wave sucked in a gasp.

"Well, what do you know, thank the *monsieur pour moi,*" she smirked.

Archimago grumbled a few expletives to himself.

The head troll turned to Archimago and asked, "Do you wish for us to flush them out?"

Josephine felt the blood drain from her face. Claudette smiled as Archimago repeated the question.

"Yes, I dare say Lord Cetus will find this a delightful gift indeed."

"Run," muttered Eve, who had already begun to walk backwards, dragging Indie with her. Aeolus and Aurora, as carefully as they could, put their heads up so Jonathan and Josephine could climb down.

"We have to get out of here before they can get behind us!" whispered Eve, but it was no good. Half of the trolls pulled out arrows and set them on fire. The furious volley landed beyond the trees that they were hiding in. The fire sparked a little and picked up speed. The grass was still on the brown side, so the fire devoured the ground. Eve and FireWind both chuckled in unison.

"This little flame is..."

Claudette yelled something, then the blaze crackled, and shadows oozed and infuse themselves into the fire. As soon as the fire was completely black, it hissed and grew tall until it was higher than the trees. The group of teenagers whipped around to see trolls hacking at the bushes to get to them, yelling as they went.

"Only one option now!" growled Jonathan, pulling his sword.

Eve and the others followed Jonathan's lead, pulling their swords and charging forward. Perun and Aeolus jumped into the air and tore through the trolls while FireWind, Hurricane, and Aurora attacked them with their tails and claws on the ground.

Josephine sucked in a breath when her first opponent came charging at her with a large battle axe. She stopped running and held her ground. The troll brought his axe down over his head. Josephine ducked under his arm and shoved her sword into his abdomen through his leather jerkin. He let out a roar of anger when Josephine pulled her sword out. She had to tuck and roll to get out of the way of his massive arms. Josephine glanced back at him, trying to figure out how to take him down, when she heard something coming up from behind her.

Another troll, this one welding a broadsword, was racing towards her. Josephine jumped out of the way, but the sword troll still grazed her arm. Josephine tried to ignore the blood that was trickling down her left arm while trying to figure out how to take the two down.

She sheathed her sword and pulled out her bow and arrows. The two Trolls rushed forward again, but this time Josephine held her own and placed an arrow in the broad sword troll's forehead, killing him. But that was when it went downhill, because she broke the string on her bow. The axe troll roared with triumph, thinking he had her, but Josephine was able to pull out her sword to cut the troll's wrist. This time Josephine shoved her sword up into his rib cage, finally killing him. Josephine took some deep breaths. She saw that the others were doing a better job of keeping up with the trolls.

Jonathan and Indie both had killed the three that had slipped past Aeolus, and between Wave and Marie, the girls had gotten four. Eve killed the remaining few that FireWind had not gotten with her flaming breath. Gazelda let out a scream in her unicorn form as she shook the blood off her horn. Aurora ran behind Josephine and placed her nose on her shoulder.

"Josephine, are you okay?!"

Josephine still was trying to recover her breath, so she nodded.

Jonathan ran over and took a stand beside Josephine, Aeolus right behind him. Claudette glared at the children in front of her. Between them and the dragons, they had killed their entire platoon, save for the six that were now retreating behind her. Archimago was walking backwards slowly to the trolls. Claudette hissed through her teeth.

"You little fools will pay. You are good at the sword, I see, but you have no... experience in battle; already out of breath." She grinned, looking at Wave and Josephine, who were cut up and panting from exhaustion. Claudette flipped back her black hair and dismounted her horse. She sauntered towards the teenagers, who shrunk back and tightened their grips on their hilts.

The dragons growled warnings to her from behind their partners. She paused and said, "Come now, young Dragon Knights, if you come with me, Cetus will take you under his wing and you will become strong and may rule this entire land someday!"

She waved her hands in the air as if to welcome them with open arms. "But if you resist, I will promise you that Cetus will enslave you, and death will seem so pleasant comparatively."

"And what? Become an ugly old hag like yourself? No thanks, *Madame,* we'll pass," snarled Eve.

Claudette let her arms drop. She snorted and said, "Fine. I don't care either way. But just so that you are aware, *l'âme du petit dragon roux,* I hold the same beauty that I had when I was sixteen, one advantage of being a Shadow magician. I, at least, need not a Dragon Soul with lizard eyes to keep me young!"

At that second, a sword came from behind Claudette. The sword's edge was tight against her throat. Josephine blinked, then straightened up in surprise. It was Gazelda in human form! Gazelda had somehow snuck up from behind Claudette without anyone seeing her.

"Claudette, we meet again. You look the same as you did when I fought with you in WarWink."

Claudette's lip curled over her teeth. "Ah... yes, it was only a few years ago when you tried to steal from my father's estate."

Gazelda's eyes narrowed, then relaxed. "Ah yes. Your father had something of mine that I wanted back. Two things actually, I got my sword, but I still did not get my hands on the other item..."

"That Vanora object is ours! You have no claim to it! The crown belongs now to Cetus, the rightful welder!"

Gazelda snorted. "Rightful? Hardly. He cannot use it, can he?"

Claudette froze. Josephine smiled, as did Gazelda.

"Cetus, when he killed King Nicholas, gave up all the rights he had. Now, Claudette, are you going to tell me what I need to know, or will I have to kill you this time?"

Claudette didn't bother to respond. She whipped around, slashing down at Gazelda with a jeweled dagger. Gazelda stepped to the left, knocking the dagger out of her hand. Claudette pulled out her rapier and whispered to it. A long shadow snaked around the blade of the sword and encased it. With that, she and Gazelda began their sword dance.

Josephine was so engrossed with Gazelda's fight that neither she nor any of the others noticed what Archimago was doing until the dragons roared out in surprise. Eve and Marie tried to cut away the Shadow flames, but the binds did not fray. The six of them turned to see the last of the

Trolls rushing at them, weapons drawn, Archimago behind them.

Archimago jumped, and his sword flashed in the dark firelight as it came down on Eve. Eve jumped back, killed the troll with an upward thrust, then jumped on the troll's back to engage the Shadow magician. Unfortunately, Indiana whipped his sword sideways to block him and caught Eve in her left arm, sending them both tumbling down. Archimago cut Indiana on the face, and as he went to give him a death blow, Wave appeared out of nowhere, cutting Archimago across his chest.

He hollered in pain and grasped at his chest, muttering words under his breath, trying to heal the wound. Wave brought her pommel down on his arm with a resounding crack, breaking his elbow.

Josephine finished off her own troll with her sword, then took a slash at Archimago's other side. But a Shadow hawk came in front of her sword, taking the blow, dissipating. Another hawk then hugged itself around him, healing his wound, absorbing into his skin. He shuddered a few times, then stared at Josephine, who stared in fear. His eyes were no longer blue but a red black. He blinked, and they returned to his inky blue color.

Marie and Perun charged. Archimago pulled the Shadow fire over himself like a cloak and sent the two back into Josephine and Aurora. Jonathan waited till the last second and began a nerve-numbing duel.

Josephine broke her concentration for a second to see how Gazelda was doing. Claudette was snarling as she and Gazelda went sword to sword. Claudette was losing, and she knew it. She waved her hand to have a shadow flicker embers at Gazelda's to attack her from behind.

Josephine did not think as she ran forward to knock Gazelda out of the way when it happened. The necklace flashed and Josephine felt cold, but it was the comfortable cold that she had felt when she first touched the necklace. It glowed and the shadow flames turned into a wall of white-blue aura.

With one last pout of anger, Claudette slashed at Gazelda with her cursed blade. Archimago saw the entire scene from the corner of his eye and took that as a sign to retreat. He was losing his duel between Jonathan and Marie, so the pair of Shadow magicians both called out. Shadow creatures appeared, a hawk and a fox, taking them and melting into the darkness, with one last call from Claudette:

"Next time we meet you, you will lose your lives!"

Indie spat on the ground and answered into the darkness, "Wanna bet, ya crazy wrench?"

In the end, the damage wasn't as bad as Josephine had feared. Eve had a nice long gash on her arm, but it was shallow. Wave only had to put a little bit of ointment on it and a bandage. Gazelda's was also shallow, but Josephine was in shock when she saw black tinting on the skin.

Gazelda cleaned her wound and said, "This is what happens when one is cut with a shadow; it is infected with it and if not for the fact I am a unicorn and she only grazed me, I would be in deep trouble right now. It will dissipate in a moment or two." Gazelda wrapped it with a scrap piece of gauze then sighed.

Perun and Aurora with Jonathan found the horses. They thankfully had not run too far off, finding a little pond to drink from.

Eve was muttering some choice swear words as Wave cleaned her wound. Josephine grasped at the necklace around her neck. It was cold to her touch, but it did not glow like it had when Josephine had run to Gazelda's aid. She looked up to see Gazelda staring at the necklace.

"I am at a loss as to why the Vanora necklace activated. It should only react when you pour energy into it. Of course, you have so much raw energy yet to be tapped into. Maybe that is why it's glowed like that twice now... yet again, both times you were in contact with Shadows, so that is also maybe why." Gazelda sighed. "Well, we have no choice now. I wanted to go straight to the Viken, but we are going to need to take another route. I have old contacts in the cities I wanted to see anyway... get a few more eyes on the roads."

Marie rubbed Perun's neck, then said, "But we'll be more likely spotted if we go into the cities, especially Jonathan."

Jonathan nodded in agreement.

Gazelda shrugged, "True, but it will be harder for them to fight us in the streets than in the forest. They have to be careful; people are easily scared and are known to cause trouble in large groups if threatened. Not to mention that when the people see the king's soldiers, they wouldn't want to be involved with anyone they were looking for, so no one will speak up..."

"And if their families are threatened, they'll speak quicker than a jackrabbit that's spotted a lettuce patch," said Wave.

Gazelda sighed again. "We'll have to risk it. I have to talk to my contacts face-to-face. It's the only way I might get them to help. Plus, thanks to the wonder duo, Cetus will figure out really quick our route. So that means that we need to go to—"

Eve's head snapped up. "You aren't going to say Drake City, are you?"

Gazelda let out a breath. "Sorry, I have a friend there, and I have to talk to her."

Eve let out a growl, then a moan when Wave tied off the wrapping.

"Curse it! Indie, I could just keelhaul you."

Indie glared. "Me? What the heck did I do?"

Eve let out a small "huh," before saying, "What do you think? This cut on my arm, you idiot!"

Indie rolled his eyes as he picked up Flash and petted him. "It's just a scratch. Don't be such a little girl."

Eve curled her lip.

"Look, it wasn't my fault. I didn't think you'd jump forward so fast, so I mistimed it. But at least Wave got a good attack in," Indiana grinned at Wave, who blushed.

Eve dropped the snarl for a second and smiled at her friend, "I have to agree, you were fantastic, Wave."

Josephine nodded. "Yes, much better than me, at least." She sighed at her own poor skill. She wasn't fast enough on her feet.

Jonathan wrapped an arm around her shoulders, "It's okay, Josephine, practicing and fighting are two different things."

Gazelda nodded, "Yes, quite right. It'll take time. Skilled warriors aren't made overnight."

Eve smiled. "Rule nineteen. And back to Indie's inept timing..."

Indiana sighed, "Look, I get it, I made a mistake, and we got beat up and had to have Wave save us," Indie turned to look at Wave with a big smile, "Again, nice save, by the way."

Wave blushed.

Eve grimaced at Indiana, but nodded. "Yes. Thank you, Wave, you were great. A good friend, as always."

Wave shook her head. "You would do the same for me."

Eve smirked, "Always."

"There, all made up. So, now you don't have to hold that little mistake over my head."

Eve's eyes flashed red. Marie groaned. Josephine shook her head. Why wouldn't the two drop it?

"Wave wouldn't have had to make the save if you hadn't made that mistake! I told you repeatedly when we were training that you needed to work on your general defense and timing, but no, you ignored me!" Eve stood up to glare at Indiana.

He snorted, "Look, sweetie," Eve's eyes became slits, "I get it you're good and that you are from one of the oldest Dragon heart families. Sorry I don't apply to those high standards."

Eve shook her head. "What makes you think I hold you to the same standards as my own?"

Indiana laughed, "You set the highest bar for yourself, don't you?"

Eve opened her mouth, shocked, then said, "Of course. But that is myself. I hope that my fellows set high standards for themselves but they have their limits as I do and I won't hold that against them when it is training but in BATTLE we must depend on each other for our lives and it would help if someone would remember that!"

Indiana smirked. "You don't think I care for everyone else?"

Eve snorted, "I don't know, do you? You wander off all the time and sneak back as we travel; you make sarcastic comments all the time and show no respect for anyone else's thoughts! I don't even know why you are still around?"

Indiana slowly turned his head. Josephine blinked when she felt the emotion coming from Indiana; it was serenity and somewhat sadness.

"Because I believe in Josephine; I've seen and heard things. I want to do what I can to help keep Irene safe, and I trust Gazelda. Sorry if you can't see that."

With that, Indiana walked off into the ruins of the camp with Flash walking behind him. Eve was abashed for a second, then anger grew in her face again. Josephine was touched by Indiana's statement.

"I'm going to sleep," snapped Eve. She walked off to a corner of the clearing, pulled a blanket over herself, and curled up into a ball. FireWind sighed and walked over and curled up beside Eve, not daring to say a word.

Gazelda, too, sighed and waved to everyone to go to sleep. She leaned up against a tree as the others found various spots to lie down. Josephine gazed into the darkness one last time before sleep took her, worrying about how they were ever going to fight Cetus if they kept fighting each other.

Chapter Twenty-Seven
Thief of Drake City

J osephine was glad that they had gotten to Drake City. She, with everyone else, was tired of Eve and Indie snapping at each other like fighting cats. When they weren't spitting, a stony silence surrounded the group.

Josephine's enthusiasm didn't last long once she had gotten a good look at the city. It was dingy, to put it mildly. The smoke from the factories covered the windows of the building and homes in gray soot. She couldn't sort out the distinct smells, but they all made her eyes water. The Dragon hearts, dragons, Indiana, and Gazelda stood in the woods, away from the entry road to Drake City.

"All right, here's what we are doing. This is a really tough city." (Indie rolled his eyes to the heavens) "Wave, Josephine, and Marie, you three get food and whatever else we need, and Jonathan," she glared at Eve and Indiana, "with Eve and Indie will scout out for information and a map of the surrounding area, especially the Sugar Lily Forest."

"Oh, goodie," muttered Jonathan to Josephine, who elbowed him.

"What about you?" asked Marie, placing Flash on Perun's head so he wouldn't follow them.

"I must talk to someone," said Gazelda, turning around and becoming a human.

"Who?" asked Indie, but all Gazelda did was pull her hair over her ears.

Without turning around, she said,

"Aurora, you are in charge. Please, you lot, make sure you stay out of sight." She walked forward then called back, "Come on now, it's getting to be almost afternoon."

Indie shrugged at Josephine, who shrugged back.

The Dragon Warriors grabbed their packs and entered Drake City.

As the three girls went deeper into the heart of Drake City, the more amazed Josephine became at the unkind condition of the city. Trash was scattered all over the streets, which were nothing more than muddy roads. Houses and businesses were in bad repair, with cracked windows, faded chipped paint, covered in a thick layer of soot. The people reflected the town; half of them were in tattered clothes, the other half in fine silk.

"What has happened to this city? From what I understood, this was a beautiful town," remarked Josephine as they walked up the main street where the vendors were set up.

"Lord Vanell. This town was already having a hard time, for it was destroyed by the Shadow dragons sixty years previous. Then when our lovely king made Vanell the Lord of this city, it plummeted into the dirt," said Marie as she paid for some herbs for medicine.

"Total blight for almost nine years," added Wave as they moved along.

What Wave, Marie, and Josephine didn't notice as they were talking and shopping, was that they were being watched by a pair of hazel eyes. Her look and stature showed she was a Jinzhou girl, for her eyes were almond-shaped. Her silky, ink black hair that was dull with grime was tied back with a piece of cloth, and her clothes sagged from her skinny body.

She was crouched behind a cart, her eyes following the black-haired girl's silver heart locket. The young girl hated to steal, but she hadn't eaten for two days. Her stomach was begging at her. She never stole from anyone but the rich people who stupidly wore their finery around the poorest parts of town.

The girl and her two companions walked towards the Jinzhou girl's hiding spot.

"It's so horrible. So many of these children are orphans, you can just tell," muttered Josephine as they saw not far ahead of them two young boys sitting on the side of a building, heads bowed in defeat.

"Indeed, most of their parents have probably died, either from overworking in the factories, sickness, or heaven only knows what else," sighed Marie.

"*Just a little closer...*" thought the young girl, kneeling to run for it.

"I wonder if Eve has killed Indie yet?" said Wave, trying to change the subject.

"I wonder how long it'll be before the two get together," laughed Marie.

"And I wonder how long it'll be before they find out about your bet and then mar you," added Josephine with a smirk.

"Never, if a certain Drageon doesn't want her butt kicked and handed to her," mocked Marie.

Josephine laughed. The young girl took her chance. She ran forward, running into Josephine, then kept moving without looking back.

Josephine felt a surge of pain, and it wasn't from the girl running into her. Josephine placed her hand to her neck to find the Vanora necklace gone.

"My necklace!" gasped Josephine.

The three of them ran after the girl. She weaved in and out of the crowd and cursed when she saw that the three were still on her trail. The young girl ran down an alleyway, then cut across another street that was near the higher end of town. As she turned, someone grabbed her arm and yanked her into a doorway.

"Well, well, what do we have here? A street rat on the finer side of town?"

The girl gasped. It was the lord of the city, Vanell! He snickered, yanking the necklace from her hand. She tried to kick him, but he kept her at bay.

"How do you get your little grimy hands on this little trinket?" he gaped, his big mouth open. The girl spat at him, and with that, Vanell smacked her on the head. It was the last thing she remembered.

Josephine, Marie, and Wave came to a halt. They were obviously on the richer side of town.

"Where...?" said Wave. Marie blinked.

"There!" Marie pointed to the side of a house. They rushed over to find the girl out cold, an angry red mark on the back of her head.

"She's okay, just knocked out," said Wave, rubbing the girl's head.

Josephine glanced around, then growled, "It's gone. Who-ever knocked her out took the necklace."

"You don't think she worked for someone?" asked Wave.

"I dunno, but we won't know for sure till she wakes up. It's not safe to stay around here, so let's take her back to the dragons," said Josephine, staring down the street.

"Right," said Marie, picking her up.

As they left, a blonde-haired girl watched them disappear into a dark side street.

"Wow, did you see that black-haired chick? O, I think I'm in love," smirked the young man standing beside her.

"Shut up, Cameron, you bloody pig," she said in a bored voice.

"Aw, come on, sis..."

"Didn't father tell you to contact Cetus to let him know what we have?" she sneered. It was a wonder her brother could read; he lacked such basic intelligence.

"Yeah, he did. I wonder what my cha- "

"Zero, Brother."

The man shrugged and walked off. The blonde snorted. As she watched the back of the girls, she rubbed her wrists, lost in thought. Once they were out of sight, the blonde girl then walked after her brother towards the largest and grandest home in Drake City.

By the time they had gotten back to Aurora and the others, the rain came down in a lazy drizzle.

"Who is that?" asked Perun as Marie placed the young girl on the blanket that Josephine had pulled out.

"A young girl, probably an orphan, who stole my necklace, then it was taken from her," answered Josephine, putting her quilt over the Jiuzhou girl.

Eve, Indie, and Jonathan arrived not long after. The three girls told them what happened, then repeated it once again when Gazelda arrived. Gazelda appeared dismayed over something, but turned to the matter at hand.

"Great, what are we going to do? We have to get that necklace back," muttered Eve.

"Well, until she wakes up, we can't do much," said Marie, nodding her head back to the girl.

"She's stirring," muttered Aurora.

The young girl sat up, then rubbed her eyes and her head. Once she saw them, she backed up against a tree, shaking and crying, her skinny knees hitting against each other. Josephine sensed her crushing fear.

"It's alright, you're safe," whispered Josephine, walking towards her, then kneeling in front of her. "You're safe."

Aurora snaked her head around Josephine to lay it on the blanket. The young girl's eyes got wide.

"It's alright, young one. I will not hurt you, nor will anyone else," Aurora whispered.

The girl looked over everyone's faces, seeing only concern, not anger. She reached out her hand to pat Aurora on the head. She smiled and made a purring noise. The girl smiled, too.

"My name is Josephine Drageon. What is your name?"

She did not answer right away, but kept patting Aurora. Then she said, "Jun. My name is Jun."

Aurora opened her eyes. "Mine is Aurora."

"Jun, I have to ask..."

"My parents are dead," Jun whispered, her words gushing out in despair. "I was four. I–I've been on the street since. I was hungry; I haven't had anything decent for a while. I usually do odd jobs but it's been hard lately. I only steal if I have to. I'm sorry..." Jun said, her eyes full of tears.

"I understand."

"Jun dear, I am Wave. Did you know who hit you and took that necklace?" she asked, taking a seat beside Josephine.

Jun nodded. "Lord Bram Vanell."

Josephine's and Wave's eyes went wide. They whipped around to see the other's faces of shock and anger.

"Oh great. Vanell has got connections," snarled Eve. "Of the dark and evil kind, as in Cetus."

"We'll have to get the necklace back tonight," said Gazelda. "We'll have to sneak into his mansion; shouldn't be too hard because he's paranoid, but cheap. His guards are not known to be the greatest of warriors."

"Do we have to, really? If he can't use it..." started Indie, but Gazelda cut him off.

"Then WE can't. We have to get the necklace back."

Tears fell down on Jun's face. "I did something really wrong, didn't I? I messed up really bad this time. Stupid..."

Josephine pulled Jun into her arms. "Shhh, it's all right, you can help us get it back," Josephine said.

Jun sniffed, "Really?"

"Yes, do you know where Lord Vanell lives?"

Jun nodded. "Yes, on the highest hill in the richer district of town. He has guards who look after the front entrance of the mansion, but that is it. He has blind spots around the place. It's easy enough to sneak into the mansion from the side of the servant's entrance. The guards change every three hours, and most of the time there is a five-minute gap before the next set of guards comes. I've worked at the mansion a few times as a dishwasher and odd-job girl. I know the layout of it pretty good. Many of the other servants and such have always muttered that one day they would storm and raid it, but no one ever has because of Vanell's children."

Gazelda blinked. "Well, I dare say that is more than enough information to help us. Jun, you are a remarkable child."

Jun smiled widely, something she hadn't done in a long time.

"There are also many secret escape routes. In the early days, Vanell was a little more paranoid than he is now, and so we could go through those, too, if we need to."

"Why isn't he still scared stiff?" frowned Indie, "The people of this town are getting more desperate by the day."

"True, but that was many years ago. His children were still young but now..." Jun sighed.

"What do you mean?" asked Jonathan. Josephine had a feeling she knew why Vanell wasn't worried about being overthrown.

"His three children are Dragon hearts, like you. They each now have gigantic dragons that fly around here all the time. The two sons terrorize people. There is also a girl, but nobody ever really sees her around. Cameron, Cutler, and Shayla."

"Did you know this, Gazelda?" asked Eve.

"Hm, I knew Vanell had children. Heck, I knew Vanell's great-grandfather; I fought verbally with him a few times, a pain—he gave money to Cetus's cause. His descendant is a stupid moron. I've only heard rumors. I knew there were three of them and their names, but not much else. I have been abroad until only a few years ago after Maruko was murdered. Cetus probably has been training them. Bram is walking in the family's footsteps for sure. Even if I knew sooner they were Dragon hearts, it wouldn't have made much difference. There would have been no way to get them to come train with Eve and the others. Bram wouldn't have allowed it. Heck, he'd probably would have killed me on the spot."

"Great, so they probably have control over their elements," muttered Jonathan.

Eve shook her head and so did Gazelda.

"Not necessary. Elemental magic is hard. Even though Cetus was great at it, doesn't mean the students will grasp it. Seeing who their father is, I doubt that highly. Even though you lot can't do elemental magic, you'll still be able to fight their Shadow magic easily. I think."

"Think?" asked Marie, raising an eyebrow.

"Well, better to avoid a fight at all costs. With Jun's help, I hope we will." Gazelda smiled at Jun, who smiled back, but with her eyes down.

"Now then, let's get busy. It's been a while since I've snuck into a castle and my skills are rusty, nevertheless, I dare say we are up to the challenge."

Chapter Twenty-Eight
Sneaking Around and Apologizing

T he first part of their plan went extremely well. As Jun had said, there was a gap between the shifts of guards. The dragons flew high over the city to hide on the northern edge in the forest, ready and waiting for a signal if something went wrong.

The group climbed over the wall with ease. Jun led the way into the castle's large kitchen. She tried to say sorry again and again as they went. Josephine, though, told her it was somewhat an accident, and that there was nothing more to do but to fix the problem. Jun nodded and became quiet as they reached the wall. As they climbed over the wall, Jun showed she had some talent. She jumped off the wall, doing a no-hand flip, and landed like a cat on her feet. Everyone stared at her in amazement.

"What?"

Wave shook her head, "That was fantastic, Jun. I do not think even I could have done that flip."

Gazelda looked at Jun with curious eyes. "Jun, do you know exactly where in Jiuzhou your family came from?"

Jun shook her head. "I am not sure. If my parents told me, I don't remember it. I was too small."

Gazelda nodded her head and turned away. Josephine and Eve exchanged looks at each other, wondering what was with Gazelda, but they didn't ask her anything as they followed Jun into the castle.

No one was around. The kitchen's fire was red coals. Herbs were hanging from the ceiling. The remnants of the evening meal were being eaten by the hunting dogs and a few mice. The dogs didn't even look up to see the newcomers; they kept their noses to their meal. The candles were snuffed out, leaving the room in a peaceful darkness and letting off smoke that wasn't strong enough to cover the smell of sweat and rotten meat.

"Marie, Wave, you two say behind and be look out," Gazelda whispered.

The two nodded, sneaking off as the rest followed Jun into the vestibule. It was the primary connection to the other parts of the castle. Through one doorway, Josephine could see the grand staircase; the one they had just come through was the pantry, and then there were the front doors and a closed door to the left, which was a tower.

Gazelda nodded, "All right, if I remember rightly, mind you, it's been a while since I was here last; the armory is that way past the stairs."

Jun nodded her head to confirm Gazelda's thought. "That is probably where Vanell is keeping it, but then again, he might have it on his person. I'll head upstairs and poke around while the rest of you look around down here. Split up, then meet up in an hour. That's probably how long we have."

Gazelda pulled her hood of her cloak over her face and slinked up the stairs, out of sight. Jun watched Gazelda disappear with her jaw slightly hanging. Josephine smiled and with a light touch closed it. Jun blushed and looked down. Josephine was happy to see that Jun looked much better than when they had first seen her. Her skin had more color now that she had eaten a proper meal, and she was wearing some of Eve's clothes and her hair was now clean and done up in a braid. Eve had even given her a small knife that was now in the pocket of her vest.

"So Jun, were do we go now?" asked Josephine.

Jun pointed behind her back. "We should go that way. It goes straight into the armory and the Keep. That door–the closed door –is the library tower. There are a few trap doors that lead to other parts of the castle through an under-ground tunnel that also is the link to the cellar."

Eve pressed her lips together, then nodded. "I suggest that Indiana and I, with Jun, go to the dining area and explore the west side, while you and Jonathan go to the armory. It's a straight path from the stairwell, right, Jun?"

Jun nodded.

Josephine took a deep breath. "Okay then. As Gazelda said back together here in an hour."

With that, the five parted into the inky dimness of the castle.

Indiana sneaked a few glances at Eve as they followed Jun into the dining hall. He was racking his brain, trying to figure out why Eve decided to come with him. She was as good as or better at fighting than Jonathan. He would have thought Eve would have wanted to go with Josephine to make sure she was safe. Not to mention the fact that she was angry with him. The two had kept a stony wall of silence between them as they'd gone through the city earlier with Jonathan, driving their friend a little crazy.

Eve caught his eye. She stopped walking, and he did the same.

Jun was frowning in the dark. "I can't see anything."

Eve smiled. "I forgot you two aren't Dragon hearts. Here, let me."

Eve knew enough about her powers to know how to make a spark and not set everything aflame. She snapped her fingers, warmth coming to the tips of them. A glint of light came, and then the candle took hold of the spark and gave the room a small glow. Eve continued to snap her fingers until all twelve of the candles in the candelabra were lit. Eve took a second to listen to them flicker, enjoying the fizzing sound they made.

"Much better," grinned Jun, and she looked around the enormous hall. She found a bowl of fruit that had been left out, so she took a plum. Jun wandered over to the two tapestries that were hanging at the front of the hall and studied them.

Eve studied them as well. The one on the left was mostly red, while the other was mostly blue. The red tapestry looked to be depicting when Taranis had battled Zankeno. The other seemed to depict when the first six elder dragons rose from their elements. The detailing impressed Eve. As she stared at the Taranis tapestry, something seemed off about it. The item around his neck looked to be a crystal, maybe the Vanora crystal, but she couldn't be sure. Zankeno had a dragon behind him screaming and blowing water–fire. But Zankeno wasn't a Dragon heart, so that made no sense to her. Also, the stitching seemed to be raised higher in certain spots. Perhaps it was the fight between Taranis and Kegan? If so, that was a rare thing to see.

"Eve, I want to ask you something."

Eve tore her eyes from the wall to look at Indie. He was frowning.

She rolled her eyes. "Well, go on and ask; heaven only knows why you decide now to bother requesting things. Normally, you do as you want."

Indie chuckled without smiling. "I was wondering something. I thought you did not trust my sword skills."

Jun kept munching, keeping her focus on the tapestry, trying not to listen.

Eve tilted her head in confusion. "What makes you think I don't trust your sword skills?"

Indie raised an eyebrow. "Is that not why you yelled at me the other night in front of everyone, because of the mistake I made with Archimago?"

"Ah, that. I was mad at your mistake, nothing more. You have skills, Indiana. Though maybe it was best we did trip, because Wave came out of her shell a little and fought back hard. Believe me, it was not just your misstep I was ranting on, it was also my own mistakes. I am bad about... pointing out everyone's weaknesses. That is what makes me a good teacher, but sometimes a terrible friend. I also should have let the subject rest, but I instead dragged it out. Forgive me, Indiana."

He smiled. "Forgiven. And I'm sorry, too. I will work on my footing. As you said, in battle, we must count on one another."

Eve smiled back at him. It was nice to know that they could work things out without yelling. Eve was even ready to say that when she heard footsteps. The three ran to the far side of the hall and jumped behind a covered table with bated breaths as someone walked into the dim candlelight.

Josephine and Jonathan followed Jun's instructions and found the armory with great ease. There were two large wood and iron doors, but Jonathan, with quick, steady fingers, picked the locks. Josephine laughed as Jonathan put away his two steel picks.

"What?" he whispered.

"A prince that is adept at picking locks?"

Jonathan smirked.

"You never know when you'll need to pick something. Besides, I learned how to do it so that my brothers and I could sneak out at night and ride the horses. I had to figure out how to get the padlock off." He smiled widely, which made Josephine smile as well as her heart skip a beat. The two, with as much care as they could, opened the door and slipped in.

There was no light, so Jonathan used a match to light two torches. The armory was large. Much of the weapons like the axes were on mounts on the wall, while things like the chain mail and the pikes were on stands.

"For such a small castle, this is a large armory," murmured Josephine as they made their way through the room to find the necklace.

"After Drake Town was destroyed and then rebuilt as a city, they made it more of a military fort, and for a long while they had a standing army. Vanell, a few years back, disbanded it. This, I am assuming, is the leftovers that Vanell took for himself and his personal guard."

"Well, if nothing else, he has looked after it all, or at least his servants have."

Jonathan agreed. The two picked through everything. But in the end, they found nothing.

"Well, I guess Vanell has the necklace on his person or in another room somewhere, because it sure to heck is not here."

"Right, let's go join back up with Marie and Wave to wait for everyone else; maybe they had more luck."

The two locked the armory back up and headed back to the kitchens. When they reached the hallway, heavy footsteps echoed on the stone floor from the other direction. Jonathan fell back against the wall while Josephine whipped around the corner of the entrance to the grand staircase. Jonathan tossed himself so hard against the wall that he fell through a hidden trapdoor into an inner parlor. Josephine saw it, but she didn't dare move because she could see a shadow of a person coming towards her. Jonathan moved a smidge out of his spot to hold a finger up to his lips. She nodded, and the two waited with tense muscles as the figure slinked closer.

Wave and Marie were waiting with clenched nerves for the others to return. It had been about twenty minutes since they had disappeared into the inner rooms of the castle.

Wave and Marie would share anxious glances every so often and see the worry on each other's faces. Marie nibbled on her thumbnail. She then heard something. Wave met her eyes. The two walked slowly back away from the torchlight and into the camouflage of the shadows. They watched as four armored guards and a set of twins their age, also wearing armor. One was a boy; the other was a girl, both with black hair and dragon-shaped eyes. They momentarily stopped breathing until the group left and entered the main hall. Marie and Wave exchanged worried glances.

Marie gulped. "We're in trouble."

Chapter Twenty-Nine
Lord Vanell and Family

G azelda was digging through the bedrooms when she heard a noise, a noise she knew well, a group of soldiers marching. She dropped the drawer she was going through and ran down the stairs of the north tower that came out to the servants' chambers. Gazelda dashed through without pausing and found herself in a long hallway full of paintings. She cursed when she could not find a door at the end of the way, and when she turned to go back, she heard the door close and a click of a lock.

Lord Bram Vanell smiled at her. He drew his rapier and strolled towards her. He was wearing a puff sleeved shirt and leather breeches. With a flick of his wrist, he bowed to her. Gazelda scowled, then pulled out her blade.

"Fair Lady Gazelda. How good to see you again! Last time you were here, you were posing as a gardener, I believe."

"And I defeated you then at the sword, if I remember correctly. I will beat you again, Vanell; you are too flashy to be a real swordsman."

Vanell's lip curled for a second, then he smiled. "And here we are again. You are trespassing in my home, trying to take something from me."

Gazelda snorted, "You forget last time, and this time, too. I am here to claim back something that belongs to the Alliance."

It was Vanell's turn to snort. "The Alliance? It is no more. It is just a bunch of mere children who think they can be knights."

"Enough chatting, Vanell; let's duel so I can crush you and get back to fighting Cetus. Shall we?" Gazelda moved her head back and forth mockingly, imitating Marie.

Vanell shrugged, "Fine. But you should know your knights are outmatched. My sons and daughter are not the only Dragon Knights here."

Gazelda glared. "What are you talking about?"

"Remember Jewelvana Garcia?"

Gazelda blinked. "Can't be…"

Vanell smiled, "Her great-niece and nephew, they are twins. Fire and earth, Lupita and Raul."

Eve, Indie, and Jun dived out of the way as arrows flew at them. Indie and Eve then both found swords in their faces as Jun was staring up at the end of a staff with a blade.

"Get up," barked the girl that was pointing her sword at Eve.

The trio slowly rose to see who was brandishing steel in their faces. The girl who had spoken had dark tanned skin, as well as the boy whose eyes were on Indiana. Both had black hair, heart-shaped faces, and brown Dragon eyes that were full of annoyance.

"Who are you two?" asked Eve in Dragon tongue. The girl answered.

"I am Lupita Garcia, and this is my twin brother, Raúl Garcia. We are students of Dragon Master Cetus Cyprus."

"And I am Daiyu of the Wing Clan," smiled the girl, who was pressing her staff against Jun's neck. She was dressed in an all-black outfit. The top had long sleeves like on a kimono, but she was wearing tight-fitting pants. Her eyes were the same shape as hers save they were hazel. Daiyu's hair was black as Jun's, but it was done up in a bun at the back of her head.

"And I," came a third voice that became louder as its owner entered the hall, "Am Cutler Vanell. Welcome to my home, fellow Dragon hearts."

Cutler Vanell smiled he entered. He had auburn hair and muddy brown-colored Dragon eyes that were narrowed in self-confidence. He was donning a long, red cape and a broad sword.

"Lupita, Raúl, could you please bring them into the main hall? I dare say father will have Gazelda and the rest well in hand."

Eve laughed. "Your father? Getting the upper hand on Gazelda? I highly doubt that now."

Cutler tilted his head. "Hm, you have a pretty voice to go along with that lovely face of yours." Cutler sauntered over and took Eve's hand and kissed it. Indiana felt like he was going to hurl. As did Eve and Jun.

"Pray tell, what is your fair name?"

Eve snarled, "Eve Nina Grace, Dragon Knight of Fire, second in command to Josephine Drageon, Leader of the Dragon Heart Alliance."

"Ah, such a sweet name."

Eve watched out of the corner of her eye as Wave and Marie approached Cutler and his small army.

She twitched her eye. "Thank you, but no thank you. I am not looking for anyone at present and I don't take kindly to compliments from my enemy."

Cutler blinked, then pulled a sugary frown, "Come now, Eve, if you join us now, I promise you will want for naught, especially if you decide to court me. You don't have to put up with..." He glared at Indiana, "Riff-raff."

Eve sighed. "You know, all these offers are getting a little old. You can tell Cetus and the rest of his minions that we are disinclined to acquiesce to his offers."

Cutler raised an eyebrow, clearly confused by Eve's flowery statement.

Eve sighed. "No thanks, go take a flying leap off a cliff without a dragon. We will never join you."

He leaned in and whispered into Eve's ear, "It is not an offer, but an order. If you don't do it willingly, then you will be forced, and if not, then you will be killed. Killed or be with me. What do you say, babe?"

Eve grinned, then kicked Cutler in between the legs while Marie and Wave knocked out some of the guards.

Seizing his hair, Eve hissed into Vanell's groaning ear, "No. And never call me 'babe' again."

She then decked him on the chin. Indie grabbed the heavy metal goblet on the table to knock him out over the head.

"Nighty night, pretty boy."

Wave and Marie were fighting with the Garcia twins. Jun was struggling to get out of Daiyu's headlock. Indiana jumped forward to help Marie with Raúl while Eve slammed Daiyu into the wall to free Jun. Daiyu didn't even try to fight Eve; she threw a ball of powder down and disappeared out of sight. Jun was fine, so Eve jumped into the fight between Wave and Lupita. Jun watched in awe as the six of them dueled. The young girl had seen more than a few street fights, but the ones fighting either did it with their fists or short blades. This was something fiercer than any of that.

Jun was eyeing them when she heard a moan. She jumped to see that Cutler was stirring. She grabbed the same goblet that Indie had used and hit him on the head.

"And stay down," Jun ordered him.

Josephine watched as the second Vanell brother came into view. He was broad shouldered and brown eyed. His light brown hair was pulled back into a short ponytail. He leered, then whispered, the air becoming an ominous cold. Josephine reached for her sword but it was too late; Josephine's ears rang as she was flung clear into the stairwell, rolling to a stop. She pushed herself up and looked, but there was nothing but dust.

Jonathan, too, had gone, but he hit the wall of the parlor and crashed down on a small oak stand. He winced on as he pulled out some splinters. The Vanell brother walked in, pushing and destroying the fake wall.

"From what Claudette told me, you must be the prince heir, or more like the prince outlaw."

Jonathan wiped the blood off his lip and smirked. "I take it you are one of Vanell's sons?"

The Vanell nodded, "I am Cameron Vanell, Prince Jonathan." He did a mocking bow.

Jonathan stood up and stared at him, eyebrow raised.

"Tell me, the young woman that I blasted into the other room, was that the new leader, Josephine Drageon?"

Jonathan grimaced, "Aye, that was her."

"Extraordinary. She is a rare beauty. Maybe Cetus will let me keep her. Sadly, for you, your life isn't worth anything."

Jonathan tensed when he watched Cameron pull out a knife.

"Shame really."

Cameron tried to channel some Shadow Magic onto his knife, but all he did was burn himself. Jonathan raised his eyebrow at him. Cameron snarled, throwing the knife at him. Jonathan pulled his sword and deflected it with a clang.

"Really? You think throwing a little knife at me is really going to cut it?"

Cameron frowned, "Guess not. Oh, well."

With that, Cameron swung his long sword down on Jonathan, who blocked, and the two began to duel.

Josephine stood but stumbled a little before she could get herself together. As she did, someone descended the grand staircase. Josephine looked up, only to gasp. The woman was bronze-blonde with pale blue eyes. It was the girl from her dream! Josephine was speechless as the girl stopped on the last step. They stared at each other for a minute. She became curious by Josephine's shocked expression.

"Hello. From Claudette's and Archimago's report, you must be Lady Josephine Drageon."

Josephine took a breath and found her voice again. "You flatter me, but I am just Josephine. I am not really a lady."

The girl smirked, "Modest. I like that. I am not really a lady, either. I am Shayla Angelina Vanell of this city. Normally, I would welcome you into my father's home, but seeing how you have come in uninvited; I dare say I need not extend the courtesy."

Josephine inclined her head. "I would not say that. Your father took something of mine, so I dare say he gave me an invitation in an around about way."

Shayla laughed. It was loud and hard. It gave Josephine goosebumps.

"From what those two sad excuses for warriors told us, you were not much of a warrior. But it is obvious what you may lack in sword skills you make up for in intellect."

Shayla stepped off the last step. The two stared at each other for a moment.

"Is this the part when you offer me a place with Cetus's personal guard?" Josephine remarked.

Shayla's eyes flashed and became slits. "I should, but I won't. From the sounds of it, you would decline anyway. I will not waste my breath or yours."

Both girls jumped when an explosion came from the dining room.

"FIGHT ME YOU FLEA-BITTEN WENCH!"

"Cutler," Shayla snarled. She turned back to Josephine when an enormous crash came from where Jonathan was with the other Vanell brother.

"Cameron," she sighed, "My little brothers are not known for their intelligence, I'm afraid."

"I'm assuming you got all the brains then?"

Shayla chuckled, then pulled her sword. "I'm afraid that this is where I kill you, Josephine. Trust me; I'm doing you a mercy. If I took you to Cetus, death would seem like a relief."

With that, Shayla swung her sword down and made a small crater where Josephine had been standing a second before. Josephine swung herself around. Their swords made an ugly ringing sound as they made contact. Josephine focused hard on the battle, trying not to let the sounds of battles in the other parts of the castle distract her. Shayla was skilled and ruthless. She was going to kill her, of that Josephine was sure.

Eve and Indie were finding the same problem with Raúl and Lupita. Both were skilled and were not holding back. Wave and Marie had retreated so that Eve and Indie could take them on one-on-one. As Eve was getting Lupita to retreat, Cutler yelled at Eve, letting off some sort of Shadow spell, engulfing the room with smoke.

Wave and Marie grabbed Jun and ran outside, coughing. Eve and Indie jumped into the hallway, smacking the siblings in the jaws. Lupita tried to slow them down with a small ball of fire, but all Eve had to do was wave her hand to dissipate the ball. Indie smirked, and the two took a stand, waiting to see what the twins would do next. Before they could do anything, Cutler came barging in, knocking the twins into the walls.

"She's mine."

Indie blocked Cutler's sword. "I'm pretty sure that Eve made it clear that she is no one's."

Cutler glared, "First, I'll kill you, then take the Grace."

Cutler swung his sword wide, missing Indie, getting the blade stuck in the wall. Indie blinked, then sighed. He pulled Cutler's sword out, then smacked him in the jaw, then on the back of the head.

"Guy just won't stay down."

"Dragon hearts have thicker skulls than normal, but I think this guy is all skull," commented Eve.

The pair glanced around to see that Lupita and Raúl were nowhere to be seen.

"Where did they go?" frowned Eve, walking forward back into the kitchen. But they heard an earth-shattering crash from the direction that Josephine and Jonathan had gone.

"Come on, we need to find the other three and get out of here. They probably already gone back out to signal the dragons. It's getting too dangerous!" Eve barked.

The two ran towards the stairs where Josephine and Shayla were dueling. Eve let out a gasp. Beside her, Indie fell down. Eve swung around to see Cutler with a bruised mouth snap his fingers to make a spark. He twirled his arm wide, letting loose a whip of fire. Eve grabbed Indiana to drag him out of the way.

Josephine and Shayla had to duck to get out of Cutler's fire whip, which was gouging the walls and sending sparks, burning the walls and rugs. Josephine shook her head to clear her blindness. Shayla took the chance to lunge at Josephine. She deflected the blow, but got a cut across her forearm. It was not deep, but it was dripping down her arm, soaking her shirt. Josephine noticed with terror that Shayla was feeling nothing as she walked towards her, sword raised.

Gazelda found it hard to keep back a sigh as she and Lord Vanell dueled. Like their initial duel when Vanell was fifteen, his moments were still flashy and ill-timed.

They dueled for a few minutes, but once she heard the second and third crashes, she became fed up. Gazelda flashed her sword in front of Vanell's face, cutting off some of his curled hair. Vanell looked up in astonishment. Gazelda punched him in the gut, then whacked him over the head. Gazelda didn't feel like killing the lord. He would be a problem later, she knew, but now was not the time to execute him. She made a note to next time make fun of the lord's overly glamorous hair style. Maybe even get Eve to make it a rule. While battling the lord, Gazelda figured out where the fake wall was. She placed her sword back into its scabbard before running over to the wall to push it.

Josephine held her sword up, ready to block Shayla's blow. Shayla whispered something and then grabbed at Josephine, pinning her to the wall. Gazelda ran in at that moment. Their teacher yelled at Eve, who was trying to help Indie try to fix the cut on his arm. Josephine couldn't hear what Gazelda said, because a dull roar from overhead echoed through the castle. Shayla's emotionless state made Josephine think of something.

"Why do you do this? You obviously aren't like the others. I don't feel the same drive from you, unlike your brothers." Shayla sighed.

Josephine felt tiredness coming over her, the feeling of unwillingness to continue. She realized it was Shayla who was feeling as such. "I am not, but I am not you, either. I am a prisoner to my fate. As are you, Josephine."

Shayla pulled back her sword, but then she dropped it. A high-pitched ringing was filling the room. She ripped the Vanora Crystal necklace off from her neck, dropping on the floor. The stone in the middle was glowing white hot. Josephine dived for the necklace as it fell.

Shayla, instead of reaching for the necklace, picked up her sword. Josephine stood up to meet her gaze.

The necklace glowed, as did Eve's dagger and Jonathan's ring. Jonathan took the distraction to disarm Cameron. He knocked him into the wall. Jonathan did not pause to see if Cameron was alive or not; he had felt a connection with both Eve and Josephine, and from what he could tell of their emotions, both were fighting and losing.

He skidded into the hall where everyone else was. Josephine was standing and facing who Jonathan assumed was the other Vanell sibling. Shayla was glaring at Josephine.

"You truly are the princess of legend."

Shayla's head snapped up, as did everyone else's, because another roar came. It echoed through the roof. A white-blue dragon came bursting into the hall from above, sending everyone scrambling to get out of the way of the falling ceiling. At first Josephine panicked, thinking it was Aurora, but she realized when the dragon stood it was smaller and had a longer face, with a brown leather saddle strapped to its middle.

Shayla jumped on the back of the dragon. Josephine realized was the same one from her dream. It had to be Shayla's partner. The ice dragon jumped up and out, smashing more of the ceiling with its massive wings.

The Garcia twins ran away without a second look at Eve and Indiana. Indiana stayed standing for a second, then he collapsed. Eve rushed to help him up. Aurora flew straight past Shayla's dragon. She touched the ground long enough for Josephine to climb up. Aurora let out a snarl as she jumped up to go after the pair.

Josephine felt her stomach drop as Aurora rose. She crouched on Aurora's dip between her front legs, holding on tight to one of her neck spines, trying to avoid being scrapped raw by her scales or knocked off by her wing joints flapping.

Her scaled dug into Josephine's legs, preventing her from moving them.

When they were clear of the castle, they saw Shayla and her dragon flying west. Shayla turned her head, then tapped her dragon. She did a circle in the air to face Aurora and Josephine.

"Come now, Josephine, Alcyone and I have to leave. I am being merciful today, giving you back the necklace, seeing how it is no use to us or Cetus. But do not press your luck. I can tell that you and your dragon have no experience battling together, let alone in the air. Do not, please, do not press your luck. I truly do not wish to kill you, but if you keep fighting Cetus, I will be forced to do so."

Josephine shivered, not because the air was cold, but because Shayla meant it. She had said it with absolute conviction. The other two Vanell siblings, along with the Garcias, appeared behind Shayla on their dragons. The sister's dragon partner was ruby red like FireWind, while the brother's partner was a dark brown that blended into the night sky.

"Oh, please sister, let me take care of her!" called out Cameron.

Jonathan blinked, trying to figure out how the heck Cameron had gotten out so fast. Jonathan jumped when FireWind ripped out of the front doors. Wave appeared with Jun hanging onto her waist, riding Hurricane, and Marie with Perun.

Jonathan and Eve jumped forward to jump on Aeolus and FireWind. They took a leap into the air, making more of the castle wall crumble. They flew up behind Josephine and Aurora. Shayla yelled out to leave, and with once last warning, Alcyone let out an icy lick of flame, which Aurora matched. The ice fires exploded over the castle, taking tiles off the flanking tower.

Josephine gripped tight onto Aurora's spike, filching at the scratches on her legs.

When the Dragon hearts recovered, the Shadow dragons were already gone, tiny specks in the waning night.

Chapter Thirty
Dragon Knights from the Past

S omeone was cooking; Josephine could smell sausages. She moaned as she rolled over to get up. Every single part of her body ached from the top of her pounding head to the tips of her bruised toes. Her legs and hands scrapped up from climbing on Aurora. She had one deep cut on the front of her right leg that ached something awful.

Jun noticed and rushed to help Josephine up. She smiled, leaning a little on Jun as they walked over to the camp-fire. Gazelda handed Josephine a bowl full of sausages, scrambled eggs and what looked like cooked tomatoes, but Josephine was too tired to think about what she was putting in her mouth. Eve was sitting on her other side. Indiana was lying on a log with his arm over his eyes. Jonathan was sitting on the ground in front of Indiana. Wave and Marie walked back over to take seats in front of Josephine. Aurora snaked her head around, lying her snout on the log. Josephine paused to stroke her head.

"How are you feeling?" she whispered.

"Fine, now that I've slept for a bit. How about everyone else?"

"Not s'bad," answered Aeolus, yawning as he spoke.

Josephine smiled. "I'll say, seeing how I think I saw your tonsils?"

"We've got some nasty scratches from the fights plus flying bareback on the dragons, but nothing too serious," said Jonathan, nodding at the others.

Josephine nodded, rubbing her leg, then asked, "Where are we?"

Marie answered, "Just outside of Alshinella City. Northwest of it, technically."

Perun yawned, then stretched his long body before saying, "Just lucky that there were rain clouds to hide us. It only took us two days to get here."

"Lucky you lot are so big now to support our weight. We lost all our horses back in Drake."

Gazelda took a sip of warmed cider, then sat down across from Indie. "We'll just have to fly everywhere. It's less likely we'll be ambushed, but also less likely that we'll get any messages from anyone."

Marie shrugged. "It can't be helped. Half of Drake City saw the dragons. No way will we escape being noticed now."

Gazelda snorted, "Too true. But we have to go into Alshinella City. Especially you and I, Josephine."

Josephine looked up to meet Gazelda's golden gaze.

Indiana spoke for the first time, not bothering to move his arm, "You want to go into the biggest city next to Red Rose City with troops crawling all over the place?"

Gazelda shrugged. "Nothing we can do about it."

A thought came into Josephine's mind.

"Do you need me to talk directly to your friends?"

Gazelda rubbed her forehead. "To put it in simple terms, yes. Do we need any supplies?"

Wave shook her head. "We have everything that we got in Drake City. We strapped the packs to Hurricane and Perun before we went into the castle, just in case."

Gazelda nodded, then tossed the last of her drink into the bushes, missing Flash, who had a mouse in his mouth.

"Good. Then you lot stay here and be ready to leave at a second's notice. Pull all the ropes and the biggest blankets we got so that we don't have to fly bare back again. If you need to, go into the city and get more rope, but take great care not to be noticed!"

Josephine let out a breath, trying to resist the urge to touch her leg wound.

"If all goes well, Josephine and I will be back before the sun leaves the sky."

With that, Gazelda pulled out a green cloak, and Josephine pulled on her black cloak. Josephine left her bow for Jonathan was going to repair it for her. She took her dagger and her sword, hiding them as best she could under her cloak. Josephine and Gazelda then slipped into town.

It was not until around midday the pair got into the city unnoticed.

"Why aren't there any sentries for the city?" asked Josephine as she and Gazelda slowly walked up the main street.

"Look around you. It's twice the size of Drake City and much less organized. The streets twist and turn and there are plenty of dead ends. There is no way of checking everyone that comes into the city. I think if I remember right, the man who built this city built it in a way to choke off bigger armies. He was a bit...eccentric though and there were never any walls built. There are too many ways to get into the city to be able to have any proper way to check everyone."

Josephine nodded. Even the main street was claustrophobic. Josephine looked up to exhale. There were hundreds of people surrounding them. Smells of all types were attacking her, making her already queasy stomach quiver. When she glanced up again, something caught her eye. A bright yellow something that flew out of her sight over the city. Josephine let out a gasp of relief when they slipped onto an empty side street.

Gazelda smirked at Josephine. She waited for Josephine to catch her breath, and then the two continued on. As they went, Josephine noted the houses were in much better shape than some of the other homes they had passed on the way. It wasn't the richest part of town, but it wasn't poorest, either.

"Who is your friend, Gazelda?"

"He's Turku Blackthorn. He is our first stop."

A few children were playing in the street with a ball. When a young, brown-haired girl with blue eyes spotted them, she called out, "Gazelda!" and ran over.

The other three children also yelled Gazelda's name and ran over to them. There were three girls and one four-year-old boy.

Gazelda smiled at them. "Hello Elizabeth, Mary, Kitty, William. Is your grandfather home?"

They nodded and then the young boy William walked up to Josephine and tugged on her cloak. Josephine smiled and kneeled down.

"Hello, pretty girl. Who are you?"

Josephine laughed. "My name is Josephine. It's nice to meet you, William."

"Come on, Gazelda!" squealed the youngest girl Kitty, pulling at Gazelda's arm.

The children led them inside into an old-looking house. Though it was old, it was well maintained. It was a two-story house with white paint and green trim. The children entered the house, guiding Gazelda and Josephine up a flight of stairs to a large study room. The room was lined with shelves filled with books and payroll scrolls. In the middle of the room was a large oak desk, and behind it was a large chair that was facing the far wall, the back facing them.

The girl named Elizabeth giggled and said, "Grandfather! Lookie, it's Gazelda, and she brought a friend!"

The chair swung around quickly to reveal a tall man with tan skin and bright blue Dragon eyes. Josephine did a double take.

"Gazelda! Long time no see! How are you?"

"Not the greatest, I'm afraid," replied Gazelda dryly. "Turku, this is Josephine Drageon."

Turku did a double take. He looked back at Gazelda, who was giving him a "send the children out" expression. Turku took the hint, sending his grandchildren outside.

Turku sat, leaning against his desk, arms folded. "I take it you're not here for a social visit, Fair Lady," he said.

She said, "Let me guess, you heard about what happened in Drake City?"

Turku rolled his eyes to the ceiling and threw his arms up, "Of course I've heard, everyone has! Though, I have a feeling there is more to the story than what rumors have given. Always is. You never do things quietly or in small amounts, do you?" He shook his head, then took a softer tone. "Even James said so, and he got himself into plenty of tight spots himself," he chuckled.

Gazelda chuckled as well at the mention of the last Dragon Leader, then said, "I am simply doing what I always have done, my job," she said.

Turku nodded. He then turned to Josephine, "So are you the princess that James foresaw what seems like a lifetime ago?"

Gazelda laughed. "It was a lifetime ago."

Josephine smiled shyly, pulling out the locket from under her shirt. Turku took it in his hands for a second. The stone glowed a sea blue, the same color as his eyes, like Wave's. He returned it to her, a glint in his eye. Turku smiled.

"You are a water dragon, right?" Josephine asked.

"I am. Seawind and I were a part of the last generation of Dragon hearts."

Gazelda leaned forward.

"So Fair Lady, how may I help you? Not that I don't already know," Turku sighed through his nose.

Gazelda did not hesitate. "By calling everyone from the old crowd."

Turku raised his eyebrows extremely high and said, "Gazelda, the only people I hear from the old crowd are Sandra and Mina. I heard also once in a while from Rachael, but she died a few years ago."

Josephine blinked. "Sandra... You mean Sandra Heartwell?" gasped Josephine, a realization coming to her. "That must have been her dragon I saw out of the corner of my eye! The flash of yellow! Storm was her dragon, right, and their element lightning?"

"Yes, and most likely. I see Sandra and Storm all the time. Storm is always flying around the city."

Turku chuckled, then frowned, "You know Mina is in Drake City; did you try...?"

Gazelda looked down, then to the side. "Yes, I tried. I just thought maybe an old friend would be better than an old teacher. She turned me down, didn't even let me in her house. She is still upset, even after all this time, over her cousin's death and Cetus's betrayal. Not that she didn't realize that death was a part of the Dragon Knight way of life, that it was something that we all knew could happen, that sacrificing one's life is the risk we take!"

Gazelda blinked, realizing that she was yelling. She took a breath.

"Sorry. Mina never took to being a knight. Well, she was just..."

"Naïve," Turku said, finishing her sentence.

Gazelda frowned. "That wasn't the word I was going to use..."

"But it's the truth of it. Mina was naïve, we all were really, at least about Cetus. But Rook, he died the way he would have wanted to die, saving someone else's life."

Turku rubbed the back of his neck then spoke again, "I don't know why you'd come to me, Gazelda. I was but only sixteen years of age when we fought the final battle. I am but a trader now. SeaWind and I would be useless in an all-out battle. It's been sixty years since we've done any-thing of the sort. We'd be about as useful as throwing a bucket of chilies at a fire dragon."

There was a moment's silence, then Gazelda said, "Dear Turku, please, even with the Dananns, the Centaurs, and maybe, if we are lucky, the Viken. We need more Dragon hearts. Ones who have experience. I'm sure with some refresher training; you and SeaWind will be able to fight again."

Turku was already shaking his head, "Gazelda, I've got four kids, twenty-five, twenty-two, nineteen, and seventeen, and four grandchildren. With the third child to be married next spring. None of them are Dragon hearts, as you know. I just don't have the skills. I can't help you fight."

Josephine bowed her head in defeat.

"But," Turku smiled, raising a finger, "I could help you lot by other means. As a trader, I hear things. I also can send supplies to where you need them. I already trade with the Centaurs and the Dananns and, if I must trade with the Viken to bring down Cetus, then I will do that, too."

Gazelda and Josephine answered with huge smiles.

"That would help us greatly. Thank you, Turku, for your service back then and your service now," Josephine said, bowing.

Turku smiled and laughed, "What kind of Dragon Knight would I be if I didn't help the new generation? As for fighters... have you tried Sandra yet? She has changed little in the past years. She would be itching to go back to the battlefield."

"I hope you are right, Turku. I hope so."

The three talked for a bit longer, giving information on who to contact, then Gazelda and Josephine left Turku's. They started up a dusty trail on a side of a hill a few blocks away from Turku's home and closer to the edge of town. After a steep climb, the two women found themselves on even ground in front of a small cottage. The air was full of spring smells, crocuses, daffodils, and buttercups. The cottage was the colors of sand, and there seemed to be some kind of extension on the back of it. Gazelda tapped three times on the front door, but there was no answer.

Then suddenly someone yelled from the back of the house, "If that's you, Isabella, come back for your flowers tomorrow. Afraid I didn't get time today; Storm was late comin' back from Drake City!"

Gazelda yelled, "Sandra Heartwell, don't jump to conclusions! Don't you remember anything that James and I taught you?"

Josephine heard a gasp, a clunk, and then footsteps as Sandra rushed around her home, and for a brief second, she saw her. A woman slightly smaller than her with blonde hair and bright yellow dragon eyes. She pounced on Gazelda.

"Oh! My dear, Fair Lady! Oh, how I've missed you! Come, you and your friend must come in!"

Before she opened the door, Sandra gave out a roar that made Josephine jump. A flash of yellow came out of the woods. It was the dragon she had seen earlier! This dragon was larger than Perun and wider in the face.

"Storm," smiled Gazelda.

Storm smiled back. "It has been too long and I'm afraid it's not for a trip down memory lane, is it? Not the good ones, at least." He had a deep booming voice that warmed Josephine, even though the tone was sad.

Gazelda nodded somberly. Once they were inside Sandra's small kitchen, with Storm outside resting his head on the back doorstep, Sandra gave everyone tea.

"I know why you're here, Master," Sandra said, sitting down at the tiny table.

Gazelda waved her hand. "Don't need to call me that anymore, Sandra. You were a full-fledged Dragon Master when it all happened."

Sandra smiled briefly, "Old habits and all."

Gazelda sighed. Sandra's face became serious.

"I knew why things were going wrong long before your message. I felt it, that energy that was tainted. I haven't been around that power for a long time, but I felt the Vanora Crystal. Even the earth itself quivered the moment he gained his power. That rotten traitor."

"Sandra, we need your help. We've got the Dananns and the Centaurs, some loyal Red Rose Troops of the prince, and maybe soon the Viken."

Sandra coughed into her tea.

"But that is not enough; we need more Dragon Knights with full training. I've tried, but you are the only one left who I can turn to."

Sandra did a double take. "What about the Dragons? They aren't helping?" she glared.

"No," answered Gazelda, in a hard tone.

Sandra and Storm both hissed, "Why not? They have to train the new Dragon heart's partners! That is how it has always been!"

Gazelda smiled humorlessly. "Part of it is that Cetus brings back bitter memories. His Dragon, Sasha, is the leader now."

Sandra's jaw dropped and just hung. Josephine nodded. Sandra blinked, then looked at Josephine for the first-time noticing her.

"I'm sorry. Josephine, was it? I have taken little notice of you. Are you one of Gazelda's new warriors?"

Storm snorted at his partner's lack of observation. "She *is* a Dragon heart, Sandra."

Sandra blinked, then looked back at Josephine, who was holding out the Vanora Crystal necklace. Sandra's eyes softened and she, like Turku, took the necklace into her hands. And like with Turku, it flashed, this time the color of yellow lightning. She let it slip into Josephine's hand.

Sandra smiled, "Of course, I should have known. Once you get used to your emotion powers, you'll find you'll be in tune with other things such as a person's magical aura. I dare say your power is extremely strong. Much untapped magic. You must be the princess that was in the prophecy. I only heard it, but it was enough. So, what is it you need from Storm and I?"

Gazelda looked at Josephine and waved her hand to go for it.

"Sandra, you did a great service to the Dragon Hearts sixty years ago, so I ask you as a Dragon Heart, both you and Storm, and as the Leader of the Dragon Heart Alliance, will you take up the duties that you had so long ago and perhaps also take on a few teaching duties?" requested Josephine, doing her best to be humble and somber.

Sandra smiled at Storm, who grinned, showing his white fangs. "It'll be different for sure to do teaching duties. Yes, Josephine Drageon, I and Storm will take up the mantle of the Dragon Knight title we left so long ago. You have my sword, my heart, and my loyalty," Sandra said the last part in Dragon tongue and then stood up and took her sword from off the stand over her fireplace and presented her sword to Josephine with a bowed head.

Storm slinked his large head around Sandra to look Josephine in the eyes. "I, too, as my partner, resume my duties as a Dragon heart dragon. I give you my loyalty, my claws, my wings, and my knowledge."

Josephine bowed to both of them. Her heart swelling with new hope.

"I thank you on behalf of the new generation of Dragon Hearts. Your service is greatly appreciated."

Sandra smiled and then sat back down. She took a sip of her tea and then said, "I should warn you; I am not good at elemental magic. I can give you basics, but that is it. I don't do elemental magic because I never had the skill to control lightning. Even with Maynu's help, I just never could get the handle on it."

"That's fine. If you and Storm can give us basics, such as flying on our dragons to fight, that is more than really what we have now."

"Yes, their education has been rather spotty," muttered Gazelda.

Sandra smirked and shrugged. "So? So was Taranis's. He was the first, so he had to learn from everyone. It's the repeating cycle of history. You and your fellow knights may have a better teaching than most of us. Wait and see. If the other young knights are as powerful as you, then we may win after all," said Sandra.

Gazelda nodded, "I hope so."

"All right now, could you catch me up to speed, Gazelda? Do you know who Cetus has from the old crowd? Marcus, Jewelvana, Reed...?"

Gazelda closed her eyes. "Jewelvana is not in direct service to him. She sent her grandniece and grandnephew in her stead."

Sandra curled her lip. "I guess I shouldn't be shocked at that news."

Gazelda agreed. "Marcus and his Dragon partner are both dead. From the looks of it, Reed did it."

Sandra's face darkened. "I'm not surprised at that piece of information. I knew he had become a sword for hire."

For the next hour and two cups of tea, Josephine and Gazelda briefed Sandra on everything that had happened since Ark gave Josephine the necklace. When they told her about the other four Dragon hearts, Sandra laughed.

"Of course, a Grace and a Williams. Wouldn't be the Dragon Heart Alliance without them. It's interesting that a royal is a Dragon heart. The spirits work in mysterious ways..."

Gazelda chuckled and then glanced out the window at the receding sunlight.

"We need to get back to the others, speaking of. Sandra, if you could, would you and Storm go to the Dananns and find out what you can? Then from there connect with the old Indo tribes and Diana? And also, if you can if you run into Mango, please tell her to send me an updated situation message with Mirage. We are heading to the Viken territory. We will need to hold a large summit once we've got all the allies under one roof."

Sandra nodded, "Sure. No problem. I'm still in contact with a few of the tribal elders or their offspring. But I'm surprised Diana hasn't sent word to you. She's like Mango, knows things before we even blink."

Gazelda snorted, "And like Mango, if she thinks she needs to talk to you, she will when SHE wills it. Not when you want to."

Sandra nodded and smiled, "It was nice to meet you, Lady Josephine."

Josephine shook her head. "It was my honor, Master Heartwell."

Sandra smiled, "Need not call me that, Josephine."

Josephine smiled back. "How about I call you Master San-dra if you just call me Josephine? I am not a full Dragon Knight yet and do not deserve the title."

Sandra smiled widely. "You are wise, Josephine. I am happy to follow one such as you. I will let you know as soon as I get word from our allies."

With that, Gazelda and Josephine pulled their hoods over their faces, disappearing into the near dark. As they reached the edge of town, Josephine noticed a flash of yellow disap-pearing into the night towards the east.

Josephine and Gazelda arrived at the camp with a surprise. Ticka was sitting at the fire having a lively conversation with Jun.

"Ticka!" gasped Josephine, ripping her cloak off so she could hug the Tuatha Dé Danann princess.

"Josephine, Gazelda," she greeted.

"Good grief, child! What are you doing here?" Gazelda demanded, sitting down.

"Mother sent me to give you something and also to let you know what has happened."

Josephine glanced at Eve, who shrugged. Ticka didn't miss the exchange.

"I thought it would be best to wait until you and Gazelda came back."

"So, what is going on now?"

Ticka squared her shoulders then began talking in a reporting voice, "The Centaurs sent their ambassador to formally acknowledge both of us are joining the Alliance again. The Dragons sent a messenger to us saying that the Centaurs are now under the same scrutiny that we, the Dananns, are. If any misstep occurs, then they will attack both of us."

Jonathan laughed, "Perfect. Just brilliant."

Ticka tilted her head in agreement. "Yes. The Dragons also warn that if we fight Cetus, then it is best not anywhere around their territory, for they will attack both fighters."

Marie gaped at her. "If Cetus tries to attack the dragons and we try to help, then the Dragons will simply wipe all of us out?"

"Yes," Ticka replied.

Gazelda let out a snort. "Sasha is not wasting anytime making sure that we and Cetus stay away. Then fine, when Cetus attacks them, we will abide by their wishes."

Wave's eyes went wide, "But we can't do that! We can't let the Dragons get slaughtered!"

Gazelda turned to Wave, "But they don't want our help, Wave. I understand where you are coming from, but the Dragons have their own rules and we must follow them. If they plead for help, then we will answer, but we cannot help those who do not wish to be helped."

"Rule twenty," muttered Eve, who was poking at her soup with venom.

"Indeed. Is there any other news, Ticka?"

"Just that Red Rose castle has been abandoned by the king."

Everyone gaped at Ticka.

"What? Cetus isn't going to take it?" asked Marie.

Ticka shrugged, "We do not know. Queen Adriana has taken it back. The queen, along with Sir Lance, stormed the castle in order to take it back when they discovered it was empty save for a few loyal to Cetus who have been locked up. Right now, she, along with some of my father's magicians, is trying to uncover what Cetus is up to, taking the king away. Mango sent us the message that they had taken Red Rose back as went to leave to find you lot. Also, your mother wanted to reassure you she and your siblings are fine."

Jonathan smiled, appreciating the message.

Josephine folded her arms, thinking. This was maybe a good sign. Cetus did not seem to have enough troops or power to keep Red Rose, so he had his troops retreat for the time being to regroup and would simply try to take it back again later. Jonathan voiced what Josephine was thinking, and Gazelda agreed.

"Which is good news for us. I am warning you now that I will leave to sneak about."

Josephine blinked, "What?!"

Gazelda grinned widely at Josephine's face of terror. "I need to do some spying of my own and check back at Red Rose City with the queen and Mango. Josephine, of course, will be in charge."

Josephine had her eyebrows raised in doubt but nodded. Gazelda chuckled.

Ticka spoke, a tender smile on her face, "In that case, you might want to take your sword back, Godmother."

Gazelda did a double take when Ticka reached into her pack to pull out a long sword wrapped in a black cloth. Ticka took care as she unwrapped, then removed the sword from its tan-brown scabbard. Josephine and the others sucked in their breath all at once. The sword was not made completely of metal. Its core was metal, but the blade itself was made of some sort of white crystal; the hilt made of bronze with gold leaf. The blade had Dragon language engraved just below the hilt:

"*For the fairest lady of all.*"

"Pray tell, Gazelda, who nicknamed you Fair Lady?" asked Wave as Gazelda, with bright eyes, took her sword.

"And more importantly, who made the sword?" asked Indiana.

Gazelda laughed, "James Dracolas was the one, funny enough. If I get the time, I will tell you about it. It's quite funny, really. And the person who crafted my sword was a Tuatha Dé Danann. Silvanus..." Gazelda looked almost sad, staring at the sword.

"Wait, the person who created the sword was named Silvanus?" question Eve.

"No. It's the name of my sword. Naoise was the one who crafted it."

Gazelda sheathed it, a far-off look on her face of someone who was remembering her sad past.

"Who was Silvanus?" asked Jonathan.

Gazelda became solemn. She said, "Again, a story for another time."

Ticka eyebrows went down, but she said nothing to Gazelda. Instead, she turned to Jun.

"Jun, I see that you have no weapons of your own. This will not do for our youngest warrior."

Jun's eyes became wide saucers.

"Therefore, I will give you one; a Tuatha Dé Danann weapon," Ticka smiled at Jun's awe-struck face as she pulled out what looked like a short black hide whip.

Ticka stood. "This is something we created a long ago with a little bit of our magic. If you flick your wrist just right..." Ticka rolled her wrist in a downward movement and the whip straightened out to become a staff. "It is a bit better than a normal staff made of wood because it will simply go slack instead of breaking in two. It is yours, Jun. I dare say you have a special soul about you and will make good use of this."

Jun took the whip and gave Ticka a deep bow, then paused before giving her a hug. Ticka took the hug gladly. Jun then ran off a little so she could practice using it. As she was, Josephine gained a worry expression.

"What are we going to do about Jun? They saw her at Drake City, so she's marked."

Gazelda watched Jun with a thoughtful look. "I would take her with me and drop her off at Red Rose City to Mango, but I need to go to other places. I guess you'll just have to take her with you."

Wave protested what Josephine was thinking. "But she's only a young girl!"

At that moment Jun flicked the whip too hard and smacked Indie on the back of the neck.

"OW! Watch it, squirt!"

Jun sucked in a breath. "Sorry, Indie! Sorry!"

Indiana sighed. "She may be a young girl, but she's not that much younger than us, and she has street smarts. Not to mention, the kid can look after herself," Indie glared at her from the corner of his eye, but his smirk overthrew the glare.

Josephine sucked in a breath, but Jonathan spoke. "We'll take her as far as the Viken. If my cousin is still in Cattail Port City there, we'll leave her with my cousin Mary and her husband. If not, then we'll just have to take her to my mother after we see them."

Jun stopped practicing and pranced over to Josephine, getting down on her knees to beg, "Pleeeeease, Josephineeee! I have no family and I promise I won't get in the way! I'll do everything you tell me to!"

Josephine sighed, pulling Jun into a hug. "Of course we'll take you with us. It's the least we can do for your help," Josephine added, "You know, I always wanted a little sister. How about I take you in as... my ward? What do you think, Jun?"

Jun smiled a breathtaking smile, hugged Josephine tightly. Josephine knew she would never let go, nor would she ever want to.

Gazelda laughed along with everyone else. Aurora nudged her. Jun turned and hugged her face.

"Well, that settles it. Now, off to sleep, everyone, we part in the morning."

With that, they went to bed. As Josephine and Aurora were setting up their beds, Jun walked tentatively over and stood looking at Josephine. When she saw the thirteen-year-old, Josephine grinned. Jun smiled widely and tucked herself in with Josephine. She pulled her blankets over her.

"Good night, Little Sister."

"Good night, Big Sister. Good night, Aurora."

"Good night, my girls."

Chapter Thirty-One
Spuck the Sprite

As the sun peaked its rays over the horizon, Gazelda left. Josephine and Eve saw her off, letting everyone else get more sleep. Gazelda told the two to look after everyone and to have faith in themselves and the others before she disappeared into the wood in her Tuatha Dé Danann form. Eve smiled, then swung her arm around Josephine as they walked back to camp.

"You're the big bad leader now, Ice Princess. Feel ready for it?"

Josephine let out a bitter laugh. "No."

Eve smiled without humor. "No choice, though."

"I know."

Eve sighed, pulling back her hair. "We have each other, like Gazelda said. No matter what, remember you have me, Josephine."

Josephine smiled at her second in command. "Thanks, and vice versa."

The teenagers and dragons packed up their gear to continue southwest towards the Phoenix Mountains, home of the Viken. Ticka sold her horse and opted to ride with Wave.

Gazelda had given them tips about how to fly with the dragons, and it was not that much different from riding horses.

Josephine flinched as she mounted on Aurora's back. She'd done just a blanket and a rope before and it hadn't been fun for her or the horse.

"We'll have to keep care of the ropes; our scales will rub them thin..." said Aeolus as Jonathan mounted him. She saw him flinch from his leg cuts he'd gotten.

"Yes. Every few miles or so we'll need to make sure the knots are safe and the rope isn't fraying from rubbing against scales."

"Marie makes the best knots at least, so I'll leave that to you," smirked Eve.

"Yes, I will do that. I can't figure out how you can cut a blade of grass with such precision, but not a halfway good knot," laughed Marie.

"Wow, there's something that the great Eve Grace can't do..." chuckled Indie.

"Keep that up and I'll tie you to FireWind's underbelly," she sneered.

Firewind rolled her eyes. "No. He can walk. I'm not dealing with extra baggage like that."

Josephine took a breath, then took Jun's hand as Marie helped her take the spot behind her. They had just enough rope for all five dragons. The blankets also were just big enough for two people to sit full seat on each dragon. Each of them walked around to make sure the ropes were tight enough.

"Is the rope uncomfortable?" asked Josephine as Aurora walked back to her.

"Sort of. But it's not itchy enough to bother me for now."

Josephine sighed, patting her snout.

Ticka jumped onto Perun with Marie. Then Indie, to everyone's surprise, took Eve's hand without hesitation to jump on Firewind.

As Indie sat behind her, Eve said, "Just watch where you put your hands."

"Yes, Eve," he smirked, putting his arms around her waist the proper way that Josephine's brothers would do when they rode with her.

When the two noticed everyone's stares, Eve and Indie both glared and said, "What?!"

No one said a thing, but Josephine distinctly heard the sounds of coins being exchanged.

"I've never really ridden before..." said Jun. Josephine patted her hands.

"Sit straight like this," Josephine straightened her own posture. "Don't squeeze your legs too much. Bend and squeeze with your knees, with toes up. And you need to relax enough to go with the swaying."

Jun nodded, fixing her own posture. Marie checked Jun before going to Perun.

"Let's walk first to make sure we don't slide off before going in the air," suggested Marie. Everyone nodded.

With Aurora in the lead, they walked down an old forest path. Besides the lack of saddle, the motions were the same mostly as if she was riding Wind drum. Marie supervised Jun and would correct her posture as they went along. They went for a mile and didn't have any major issues.

"We'll go first," said Aeolus. The others nodded.

Aeolus took a small running leap, blowing a bit of dust and leaves on them as he jumped into the air, his large wings flapping. It took a second for Aeolus to adjust with Jonathan on his back, but he was able to gain altitude and fly on the air current.

Josephine smiled as she could feel the joy coming from the wind dragons.

One by one, the other dragon flowed suit. Aurora ran to jump, and Josephine felt her stomach clench, as well as Jun's hands on Josephine.

Aurora leaped into the air. Josephine did her best not to squeeze her legs too hard, but the sensation of coming off the ground overwhelmed her a little. She corrected her posture as Aurora found the current to stabilize her flight. Her wings thankfully did not hit her or Jun, and the ropes were secure enough to keep them from slipping off.

"Just don't try anything fancy until we get proper saddles," warned Marie as FireWind joined them. Indie squeezed Eve's waist hard, which, instead of annoying Eve, made her smirk.

With that, the dragons sped off. They kept lower to the treetops than probably they normally would, just because of the weight of having their partners and friends. The dragons were large but not full grown yet.

They flew for a few hours, and in which Josephine and Aurora enjoyed for the most part. The wind was scary at first, but when she got used to it, she found it exhilarating. It was even more enjoyable than riding on Starlette; the wind blowing her hair back, the steady rhythm of Aurora's and the other's wings. Josephine could feel Aurora's joy at having her riding, which made both equally happy.

As they went along, Josephine found it weird not to have Gazelda's kind yet commanding presence. She was a little unsure how to navigate the mountains, even with Gazelda's instructions, but Jonathan and Indiana were able to keep them on track simply by following the Sugar Lilly River. The river was like a snake, winding slowly and steadily through the land below them. There were a few small cottages and one town along the way, but they were able to avoid them by flying further south, keeping the river within their eyesight.

"How much farther is it to the Phoenix Mountains?" asked Jun when they had stopped to rest and drink.

Indiana pressed his lips. "A good twenty miles, at least. Even at the dragon's current speed, it's still going to take us five full days before we even reach the edge of the Sugar Lilly Forest and then the Phoenix Desert."

"Yeah, then we have to find the Vikens," muttered Marie.

"Shouldn't be too hard to find the blood thirsty raiders," yawned Aeolus. Josephine glared and pointed a finger at the wind dragon.

"I am warning you all right now to cut that talk and/or get it out of your systems now. We will not insult them. We need them."

Aeolus nodded, but Indie curled his lip. The group took off again. They landed for the last time for the night, just before sunset at a curve of the river. Keeping close and staying by the water to reduce the risk of being ambushed by shadows or anything else.

It was late at night when Josephine woke up. The fire had gone out. She could hear her friends' slow breathing, telling her they were all asleep. She didn't know why, but she felt something was wrong. It wasn't the icy feeling of shadows, but her skin was still bumpy. Josephine picked up her sword when she heard a twig snap. She paused, searching in the dark, thinking maybe it was just Eve.

Jun was on her left side, curled up to Aurora with a sugar lily in her fist. Wave was lying with Hurricane, using Hurricane's claw as a pillow on Josephine's right side. Indiana was leaning against Aeolus with his arms folded, frowning in his sleep. Jonathan was stretched out against Aeolus's body, using his arm as a pillow. Marie and Perun were on the other side, curled up in little balls. Ticka was lying beside the two, her hair covering her face. Josephine squinted back into the pitch-black forest.

"Eve, is that you?" she whispered, wondering if it was Eve coming back from watch duty. She heard another loud snap, and this time it sounded almost like a tree branch being broken in two. Then a smell came to her, and it was sour, almost like rotting wood.

"Wake up! There's someone here!" Josephine yelled, grabbing her sword.

A roar went through the camp and jerked everyone else awake. In the blink of an eye, a troll larger than even

Jonathan came crashing through the bush, throwing an unconscious Eve to the ground.

"You call that a Dragon Knight! HA!"

Ticka flashed a spark of magic at the troll, then grabbed Eve. Five more trolls came out of the woods and into the clearing.

"Don't harm the tall raven-haired girl," muttered the troll that had thrown Eve.

"Aye, Sir."

Aurora and Hurricane roared, and Jun screamed. Josephine whipped around to see five more coming at them from behind. They were surrounded.

"They just want me."

Josephine glanced at Aurora for a split second; Aurora's eyes went wide when she felt her emotions.

"JOSEPHINE!"

But it was too late. Josephine jumped over Aurora, gutting a troll as she went. She ran into the forest, Aurora's roar ringing in her ears, the trolls on her heels.

Josephine felt her necklace blaze and ice fire flow through her veins. She knew Gazelda would kill her later, but if she didn't try something, the trolls would kill her here and now. She closed her eyes as she felt ice crystals formed and moved along her arm. Her breathing increased as the ice blazed on her skin. It felt good. She opened her eyes to see a line of ice-colored fire blaze up her arms, pooling into her right hand.

The four trolls that had gotten away from the others hesitated. Josephine stared down the leader to see her reflection. Josephine saw not herself but an angry dragon-eyed girl with flickering flames in her hand, a glare that was more dragon than human. They lunged forward, trying to kill her before she could do anything, but it was no good. Josephine willed the fire to get larger, and it became a blaze larger than an apple. She hissed, throwing it at the charging trolls.

It hit one and caught the one next to it on fire. Josephine then drew her sword with speed unmeasured, cutting down three of the other two trolls who had not fallen back at the fire. She got two in the heart and one in the throat. Josephine stood panting, her sword dripping in blood.

Human foots steps came out of the woods towards her. Josephine looked up to see a red-haired girl smiling. She had brown dragon shaped eyes. Behind her stood Riagán.

"See, they are so predictable. Of course, they would go to the Viken."

The girl walked forward, almost skipping in smugness. Her red hair was not shiny like Eve's or as long. It was cut just above the girl's broad shoulders and it was dull, as though she'd dyed it. The girl had a slight tan and wide lips.

"Josephine Drageon..."

The girl began to whisper and shadows shaped as crows boiled up and surround her. Josephine felt the necklace hot against her chest and channeled her ice magic into it. The necklace's stone shimmered, then glowed bright. That stopped the girl in her tracks. Josephine gave the girl a wicked smile.

"You cannot touch me, Shadow magician."

Josephine hoped this would deter her, but it did not.

"Bloody... one of you trolls will have to take it. Neither I nor Riagán can touch the necklace," The girl made a backhand gesture with her hand. A whip of shadow energy knocked Josephine back into the tree.

Not too far away from Josephine, a sprite of small stature looked up at the sounds of the blast.

"Uh-oh, what fools be running around in the forest now?"

The sprite shook his head and decided he'd better see what was going on. He jumped into the air and flew towards the sounds of fighting. He snapped his fingers and his magic teleported him between Josephine and her enemies.

"OIE! What is going on? Get the heck outta–"

One troll threw an axe at the sprite. Before he could do anything, he heard a voice behind him. He watched as a blaze of white icy fire flew forward, hitting the troll. A red-haired girl jumped to get out of the way of the fire. The two trolls that were left ran away, as did the Tuatha Dé Danann that he saw behind the red-haired girl.

The sprite turned to see a raven-haired girl, who was shaking, gasping for breath. He glanced at the redhead to see crows made of shadows flock around her. Without a second thought, he grabbed the girl, then snapped his fingers. The two disappeared out of sight.

Josephine wasn't sure for how long she was unconscious. She blinked a few times, then slowly sat up. She rubbed her eyes. For a second, she thought she'd been captured and would be in some sort of dungeon, but it was some sort of cove in the trees.

The trees' highest branches were interlaced, creating a roof. It was a single, large room formed by a collection of trees that were growing almost on top of one another. The forest cottage had a small stone cooking pit that sat on the far side of the space.

She placed her hand on the bed to find it was made of a soft moss that felt almost like finely spun wool and a cotton pillow. A few lamps were lit to give more light to the small space. Bits of orange sky shone through the tiny gaps in the leaves. With the small personal touches, the place felt more like a home than just a camp. There were a few little oval frames with pressed flowers and a line with clothes pegged to it. A small round table that looked to be an old tree stump had a tea set resting on the vast surface.

Josephine smelled mint. Her eyes fell upon the individual who was present just before she passed out. He looked about as old as Jun, but was shorter, with black hair and brown eyes that sparkled in the dim lamplight. He was donning a black tunic and pants, with short black boots. His ears were pointed, more severely than a Dannan's.

"Well, well, awake, are we?" he said.

Josephine blinked again to make sure she wasn't seeing things when she realized she wasn't. The boy really was floating over to her to give her a cup of what Josephine guessed was mint tea.

"Yes, thank you... Um... I'm sorry, but who exactly are you...?"

"Oh, pardon my rudeness!"

The boy sat his teacup down and floated a foot from the ground. He cleared his throat, "I am Spuck, the Sprite Goodfellow, the greatest Trickster of Anglii, third of all time, and cousin of Robin Goodfellow the Puck himself. You have heard of me, yes?"

He put his arms behind his back, smiling wide and proud. Josephine thought for a second, then frowned, shaking her head.

"Sorry. No. I've heard of Puck, but not you."

"Young people these days! Surely you heard of some of my adventures with Pan?"

"Sorry, heard of Pan..." Josephine shrugged as a half apology.

".... eh it's okay; I really have not done nothing lately. It's fine."

Josephine dipped her head in understanding.

Spuck floated for a second, then pouted, "Okay, really, NOTHING with me adventuring with Pan? URGH! The idiot is taking all the credit again. Good for nothing goat," Spuck sighed, then regarded Josephine, "You know, it's been a long time since I last saw a Dragon heart in these woods."

Josephine's eyebrow went up, which Spuck saw.

"Oh, yes, Lady Dragon Heart. I've been around for two hundred years and knew my share and was friends with many a Dragon Knight," he grinned.

"Oh," was all Josephine could say. She took a sip of her tea.

"My name is Josephine Drageon, Lord Spuck Goodfellow."

Spuck nodded, "Just call me Spuck. Yes, yes, it's been a while. Probably the only ones who remember me would be the old Dragon heart families like the Graces."

"Hm, really? My friend/second in command is a Grace."

"Really. I wonder if she knows of the time when I made fun of Rodger Milton Grace's Dragon... urha.... yeah anyway..." Spuck laughed nervously, blushing, and then walked over to the stove to poke the fire.

Josephine took another sip. The tea was warm, and it was helping Josephine regain her wits. She stopped mid-sip when she realized...

"The trolls!"

Spuck smirked. "You got them all. I have to say, you look to be a young wet behind the ears Dragon heart. I've seen much in my life, but that was some impressive ice fire. Few young Dragon hearts can do that."

Josephine snorted, "That may be, but I am going to be in trouble when Gazelda finds out what I did. I and my friends aren't supposed to be using Elemental magic. We have no formal training."

Josephine rubbed her hands. They felt fine. There seemed to be no ill effects from her attack.

Spuck glanced over his cup, tilting his head. "Gazelda? As in Fair Lady the Unicorn?"

Josephine stared at the sprite. "Um, yes, do you know her?"

Spuck nodded. "Yeah, back when the old Alliance was around. More acquaintances than anything. She lost a bet to me, if I remember rightly," he smiled, remembering something.

Josephine asked, "Spuck, if you are a trickster, then why are you here in the Sugar Lilly Forest?"

Spuck paused mid sip, taking a deep intake of breath. "I was sort of a reserve warrior back in the day. I was not a part of the last battle; I would have but..." Spuck shook his head, then continued, "After the Dragon Knight Alliance disbanded, I took a break from the world. Sugar Lilly is my favorite haunt."

He frowned at her, putting his cup down.

"But I can't say I'm happy. Seeing you and those trolls and hearing Gazelda's name means that trouble is brewing in Anglii." Spuck shook his head.

Josephine sighed, "Yes, I'm afraid you are right. Cetus has returned with his powers and is slowly gathering his army. I and my fellow Dragon Knights are trying to pull together members of the old Alliance to stop him and bring him to justice."

Spuck laughed. "Yeah, good luck with that. I did not know the little snot, so I definitely have no love for him, but good luck getting justice. The little guy rarely gets such a thing. One of the main things about us tricksters is that we fight for the underdogs."

Josephine stared thoughtfully at him. "Spuck, how did you get me here?"

Spuck puffed his chest out and then explained, "I teleported you. One of my many sprite magical abilities. I can transport anything as long as I'm touching it or I have touched it. And if a magical barrier does not hinder it."

Josephine nodded. "Did you also heal me?"

"Yes, I did. Sprites, like faeries, have a few healing techniques. Mind you, I am not as good as a trained faerie, but I can heal most minor scratches, scrapes, and most major cuts like the ones you had."

Josephine looked at her upper arm to see not even a scar where her two cuts had been, and she also realized her cut on her leg was gone.

"Thank you so much, Spuck. Do you think you could do me a favor and help me find my friends?"

Spuck nodded, "Of course. I know this forest well, and if you are attuned to your dragon's emotions, then we'll find them easy."

"Oh, I can just imagine Aurora's emotions right now," chuckled Josephine as she glanced around the forest, nervous.

Spuck smirked. "Yes, I dare say I can guess that she is not happy right now."

Josephine smiled. She pondered something, "Spuck... you know, we need healers, and someone with your talents..."

Spuck laughed and moved his head back and forth. "Oh, no, thank you. I was a warrior once, and I don't feel like doing it again, thanks."

Josephine pouted, then got an evil idea. She didn't like the thought of doing it, but if she couldn't persuade Spuck, then how could she persuade the Viken?

"Spuck..."

The Sprite turned back to her from his tea cake. "Hmmm?"

Josephine employed her most charming round-eyed expression with pouting lips.

"You said that the tricksters were for the underdogs, right? The weak?"

He raised an eyebrow, "Yesss..."

Josephine smiled, "Well, if that is so, then why won't you help us? I am the leader, and right now, we only have a handful of allies. We are right now weaker than Cetus, who is a mean big guy..."

Spuck frowned, but Josephine pushed on, "Plus, being a great trickster is depending upon your reputation, correct?"

The sprite slowed his chewing.

Josephine could sense her words were getting through to him. "What better come back could be for a trickster like yourself, then to help the underdogs the Dragon hearts? It would be a grand adventure and bring plenty of glory. Just think of all the stories that were told of you when the Dragon Knight Alliance was in its glory, and all your old friends..."

Spuck swallowed. "Yeah, and lots of camping, rain, and smelly horses, old coffee and bloody trolls...." Spuck stopped, then sighed. Josephine was pulling off the greatest puppy-eyed look she could muster. Even Jenn Falcon, master of the puppy-eye look, would have been humbled. She felt his distaste dissipate.

"FINE! Stop pulling the wounded bunny look!"

Josephine smiled widely and hugged Spuck. "Thank you so much, Spuck!"

Spuck nodded, "All right, Josephine Drageon, I swear to once again serve as a warrior of the Dragon Heart Alliance, but I am warning you, I will only take orders from you. I don't take orders from just anyone. And if you can persuade me to come out of my forest to help fight, then you I find most worthy to follow."

Josephine nodded and agreed, and the two sealed it with a handshake.

"Why do I have a feeling that I am going to be chased once again by all sorts of beasts?" he muttered.

Josephine believed it was more a comment to himself than to her, so she stayed quiet as Spuck ran around collecting things to place them in a leather pack. The rest of his belongings he stored in a crate made of untreated branches. He locked it with a snap of his fingers.

"All right, you, let's get going before you trick me into anything more. From now on, leave the tricking to me!"

Josephine laughed, "Yes, Spuck. Maybe I'll have Eve make that an official rule."

Spuck flashed a smile, and with that, the two left the small home in the woods.

"JOSEPHINE!" yelled Aurora into the dim, thick trees.

Aeolus sighed, "Sister, you are going to going to get us killed! Those trolls will come back after us!"

Aurora glared. "What if it was Jonathan?" she snapped.

Aeolus clamped his mouth shut. At that moment, Perun, Jonathan, and Marie walked up to the two dragons.

"Anything?" Aurora asked, already knowing the answer from their feelings and the looks on their faces.

"Nothing," said Perun.

"Where...?" started Aurora when they all heard rustling coming from the trees. The Dragons tensed at the sound, but then Aurora relaxed. She could feel a happy person coming towards her and one slightly annoyed.

"OW! No wonder I just teleport. OW! Stinking burrs!"

Josephine and a small boy came through the bushes.

"Aurora!" cried Josephine, jumping to hug the ice dragon around the neck.

Aurora pulled back to growl at Josephine, "If you EVER do that to me again..."

Josephine sighed, "Yes, I know. I'm sorry."

Aurora shook her head and then nudged Josephine. She smiled. Aurora then looked behind Josephine. She tilted her head at Spuck.

"Oh, Marie, Perun, Jonathan, Aeolus, Aurora, this is..."

"Spuck the sprite Goodfellow, greatest trickster of Anglii, third of all time, cousin of Robin Goodfellow the Puck himself," Spuck said, then bowed.

Jonathan coughed back a laugh, as did Aeolus and Perun, while Aurora and Marie bowed back, then glanced curiously at Josephine.

"Spuck saved my life, you see. But let's get back to the others before we start telling stories."

The others nodded in agreement. Once they were all settled in a deeper part of the woods suggested by Spuck, they lit a tiny fire. Josephine; with a little help from Spuck, explained what happened when she ran off playing decoy. Josephine paused at the point when she used her elemental magic to look at Eve.

"Eve, are you okay?"

Eve came over to the fire, limping badly. "I'm fine."

Indie gaped at her, "All right my... Josey, she's got at least three broken ribs and a bruised hip!"

Eve tumbled down beside Josephine, cursing under her breath the whole time.

"No kidding," grumble Marie. "A hummingbird could kick her butt and hand it to her right now."

Eve snarled at Marie.

"Spuck, do you think you could help, Eve?"

Spuck was playing behind Indie, who finally noticed and took a swipe at him. He stuck his tongue out at Indie, then nodded.

"Broken bones are my specialty."

As Spuck, with careful hands, healed Eve's wounds, she stared at the sprite with a thoughtful expression.

"Spuck... Hey, aren't you the sprite that insulted my great-great-grandfather's dragon and got your keister burned by his fire breath?" She laughed, then groaned.

Indie was silently laughing, as was Jun.

"Shush. You're lucky that FireClaw and I made peace," smirked Spuck, healing her last rib. Spuck double checked his work, pleased with himself.

"I suppose it's my own stupid fault. I wandered too far from our camp. Trolls outnumbered me, and I was too far to call for any of you," she grumbled.

FireWind nudged her, and she smirked, patting her head.

"From now on, we come with you on patrol."

Jun shifted as Spuck sat beside her. Spuck then began playing with her, trying to outdo each other with funny faces.

Wave smiled, then asked Josephine, "You didn't mention how you fought off the trolls and that girl."

"Wait, what girl?" asked Eve.

Josephine described the girl to Eve, who went white in the face. She bowed her head, placing her hand on her forehead. Her emotions crashed into devastation and worry. Everyone stared at Eve, even Jun and Spuck. Wave frowned, then went wide-eyed. She poked Marie, who was still clueless.

"Oh my... We always... but she died..." whispered Wave.

Eve shuddered like she was going to cry, "No, Wave, we assumed she died. We never knew for sure. But now we know... Darcy is alive."

Marie, who was letting off just as much confusion as the rest of them, gasped at the sound of the name.

"Who is Darcy?" asked Aurora. FireWind nudged Eve again. She placed a hand on the dragon's nose.

"Darcy Morgan. Or Diva, as she preferred," muttered Eve.

"I don't understand. Do you know this girl?" asked Jonathan.

Indiana was as lost as the rest of them. Eve looked up with grief and tears in her eyes. Josephine had never seen her like this.

"Darcy was... kind of my sister."

Indiana did a double take. "Wait, what? I thought you said you only had a little brother who wasn't a Dragon heart?"

"Yes, I only have a blood brother. Darcy was more of a soul sister. Like Marie and Wave."

Wave moved to sit beside Eve, putting a hand on her shoulder.

Eve placed her hand over Wave's. "Her parents abandoned her after she was born when they found out Darcy was a Dragon Heart. From what my mother told me, Darcy's mum was... a bit off. She was dedicated to her religion and thought Darcy was a demon. Left Darcy in the snow, crying... anyway, my parents took Darcy in after someone found her, knowing that she was a Dragon heart. Darcy was a part of our family... but it changed. When we turned fourteen, this boy came into town."

Eve's eyes flashed. Josephine could tell this boy, whoever he was, would have been dead if he had been standing there right now.

"He was, like, eighteen, nineteen years old. She pined after him. I warned her not to chase after him. Even without my powers awakened, I could tell he was dark, tainted. But Darcy wouldn't listen. I think... she wanted something I didn't have... I don't know, maybe she was jealous... whatever the reason, she began running off for hours and then would come back and refuse to talk to anyone. One night, I followed the boy and saw him practicing Shadow magic. I confronted him. He would not leave. I overheard him bragging about Darcy. I almost killed him," she snorted.

Wave took a breath and continued the story, "It was not long after Marie came that this happened. We found Eve with bloody knuckles and a few punches to her face. She'd managed to break his ribs, nose, and a few toes. If we hadn't stopped her, she probably would have killed him."

"I would have killed him. I was going to kill him," Eve muttered.

"Anyway, Diva showed up at that moment. We pulled Eve back. Diva went into a rage herself," Wave shook her head, "She was helping the boy up when he said he was leaving. He was planning to leave soon, anyway; Diva was beginning to bore him. Eve attacking him, that was it. When he left, she disappeared the following night. No note. She took little with her."

"We assumed she was grieving over the boy and left. That she had maybe had gone into towards the mountains or into the desert. We tried to find her. Most of the town looked for her, but there was no trace of where she went or what happened to her," added Marie, taking a seat on Eve's other side.

"So great, another snake to worry about," muttered Perun.

Eve bit down on her bottom lip. "Appears so."

Indiana spoke up. "We'll deal with her when we get to her. From the sounds of it, she is a powerful Shadow magician, but besides that, we don't know. No point dwelling on the unknown when there isn't anything you can do about it."

Eve smirked at him, "Rule twenty-one."

Spuck looked curiously at Eve. "Rule what?"

Eve smiled and explained to Spuck their rules of life. He got a wide grin on his face. "Sweet! Okay, rule twenty-two. Spuck only takes orders from Josephine! O, and rule twenty-three, I am the official comic relief of the group!"

Eve laughed and nodded. "Gotcha, Spuck."

Jonathan smiled then turned to Josephine, "Still, doesn't explain that burst of Dragon heart power we felt, nor why the Vanora Crystal objects went off," he commented, getting back on topic.

Josephine gulped, "I... uh..."

Spuck jumped the crossbow before Josephine could stop him.

"She used her ice magic! It was really wicked, too! I saw James use ice magic but not the way like she did... and oh yeah... eh, eh, sorry Josephine..." Spuck retreated behind Jun before Josephine ripped his head off, though that was the furthest thing from her mind.

"YOU DID WHAT?!" yelled Eve, jumping on her feet. Josephine cringed.

"Calm down, Eve. Do you want them to find us?" grumbled Marie.

Jonathan agreed, "Yeah, Eve, cool it. Besides, it was a life-or-death situation, and not to mention my wind powers flared up when the ring went off, almost getting me beheaded by the troll I was fighting. We are going to have to figure out what to do with the crystals."

Eve sighed and sat down. "The crystals are to alert the Dragon heart wearing it if there are Shadows near."

"Yeah, and they are going to get one of you three killed. What if you are hiding and the crystal flashes?" demanded Aurora.

Josephine looked at Ticka, who had said little since Josephine and Spuck had showed up. She had told her that her brother had been with Diva, and besides a pang of sadness, she'd said nothing.

"What do you think, Ticka?"

Ticka pulled at her hair, "I think the reason that the Vano-ra Crystal goes haywire and sparks your elemental magic is because you have so much untapped power. I was thinking about how the dragons are already almost full grown," her eyes flickered to Aurora, then back to Josephine, "The power of a dragon reflects the power of the Dragon heart partner. Gazelda, I know, asked my father about it, and that's what he told her. She; of course, already knew that, but I am guessing that she never saw such untold power in any of her students."

"It would have been nice if Gazelda told us that," mumbled Marie, and Josephine, though filled with guilt, had to agree with her.

"True. But maybe she wanted to sort out what was going on with us and to give us a full answer instead of just a bunch of guesses," pointed out Hurricane. Wave agreed with her.

"Maybe. Tell me what happened after I ran off," said Josephine.

Jonathan gave her the run-down. "When you ran, the trolls on the furthest side chased after you. We did our best to kill the ones in front of us. Aurora tried to fly after you, but the trolls had us pinned in the thicket with no way for the dragons to take off in flight. Ticka took Eve, and between her and Marie, they killed the first line."

Indiana took over. "But there was a second line of ten in the bushes that replaced them. They ran around, trying to get us to split up, and they had a few of their tracking dogs with them. I was able to take the fylgja out with my bow before they could rip Perun and Hurricane to shreds."

Wave continued the narration. "Jonathan and Marie, with Perun, Aurora, and Aeolus, chased after the ones who escaped, and the rest of us took care of the few who were foolish enough to stay behind. We saw no one else besides the trolls."

Josephine nodded.

"We didn't see anyone else, either. My ring flashed, like I said, and it made me stumble. Fortunately, the troll I was fighting did not have good aim," Jonathan smirked.

"How did you control your magic?" asked Josephine.

"I stood still. I thought that a Shadow creature was around, but I didn't see anything. It may have been reacting to yours. After a few seconds of not doing anything, the light went out. But for a second, I felt as though I was feeling someone else's distress other than my own."

Eve frowned. "Did my dagger flash?"

Wave frowned back at her, "I don't think so..."

Ticka shook her head, "I was beside you. I saw Jonathan's ring flash, but your dagger did not."

"Huh. Weird," muttered Spuck, who was chewing on some jerky. Indie noticed and then went cross.

"HEY, THAT WAS MINE!"

Spuck jumped into the air and floated there. "What? It was just sitting there."

"It was in my pocket!"

Spuck shrugged and continued to chew the stick.

Indie glared at Josephine. "There is no way I am going to put with this sprite the whole time we are questing," he said, pointing his finger at Spuck.

"Sour puss," muttered Spuck.

"We need to get to sleep then get the heck out of this forest," said Ticka, glancing at the sky, which was glowing with early dawn light.

They all agreed and put the fire out.

Chapter Thirty-Two
Phoenix Mountains

E ve poked Josephine and Jun awake two hours later. Everyone was jumpy and on edge as they packed.

"So, how are we going to get to the mountains? We are not only lost, but if we fly, I betcha anything that they are going to spot us and attack us. They want us bad," Marie pointed out.

"I know. I just wonder why they want us alive," Josephine muttered.

"I've been thinking about that."

Josephine looked up from her pack to see Ticka walking towards them.

"I think it's your power. From the sounds of everything, all five of you seem to be exponentially more powerful than most of the older Dragon hearts ever were. It's clear that you are of prophecy."

Jonathan walked over. "Therefore, Cetus can't afford for us to be free or alive if not under his thumb."

Ticka nodded, "It makes sense."

"So why not have his students kill us?" countered Wave.

Ticka paused.

"I think I know," said Indie.

Eve raised an eyebrow. "Really? What's your theory, ge-nius?"

Indie smirked, "It's like bosses and street fighting,"

Eve blinked; her eyebrows went further up her forehead. "You are saying there is a connection between the blood traitor of the Dragon Heart Alliance, who is a knight, and a bunch of uncivilized, tobacco chewing thugs?"

Indie shrugged, "Yeah, if you let me explain..."

"Go on, Indie," smiled Josephine.

"In street fighting, there are the fighters, then the fight bosses. The sponsors, if you will. A smart fighter gets a manager to help make sure that he gets the cuts of bets placed on him. A smart manager, of course, looks out for..."

"The strongest fighters," finished Jonathan.

Indie dipped his head, "Exactly. Diva, Shayla, they are a bunch of small-time fighters. Shayla doesn't seem to follow orders well, but it sounds like Diva and the Vanell brothers are incompetent fighters who follow orders," said Indie.

Josephine caught on to Indiana's point. "We are his prize. There is no point in trying to take over Anglii or any other kingdom, for that matter, if we are running around and not under his control. That's... that's why he retreated from Red Rose; he did not have enough soldiers to protect it! He must have been heading to the Phoenix Mountains when we crashed in at Drake City! That's why..."

"There were so many Dragon Knights there!" finished Wave.

"He was nearby..." muttered Eve.

FireWind interjected, "That would also explain why there are so many trolls around here. He must have had the troops split up to make it easier to get to the mountains without being seen and search for us."

"Which means we have to get to the Vikens, and fast. They wouldn't dare try to attack us if we are with the sea raiders," said Indiana.

"One problem, the moment we go into the air..." started Aurora.

"They'll attack us, and we have no way of fighting in the air," growled Josephine.

"Can't Spuck get us some of the way there?" asked Jun.

The six teenagers and five dragons stared at Jun with wide eyes. Jun took a step back, a little startled by their looks.

"What?" she demanded in a high-pitched voice.

"Squirt, remind me to treat you after this," laughed Indie.

"Spuck!" called Josephine.

Spuck came floating above Aurora.

"Yyyyeeesss?" he smiled.

"Is there a way for you to teleport us to the Phoenix Mountains?" asked Josephine.

Spuck frowned, "I could. I've been near there. Only on the edges of the desert were the start of the rocky trail that leads into the mountains. I've never been to any of the Viken villages."

"That's fine. I think it would be best for us to walk in than drop in. I don't think warriors like them take well to surprises," Josephine smiled at the comical image that had popped into her head of them falling on top a few Viken warriors.

"The best way is to do a few at a time. It's too much to do everyone at once," Spuck emphasized, waving his hand at their group.

"Have you ever teleported with a dragon?" asked Aeolus, wagging his tail and frowning.

"Oh yeah, with his partner, sure. Of course, we were being chased at the time and..." Spuck's voiced faltered, which made Indie to start not liking the plan.

"And what?" demanded Indie.

Spuck winced. "I teleported us into a pigsty. The pigs weren't the only ones who were not impressed."

He saw the looks on everyone's faces and waved his arms in the air.

"No, wait! It's all right! As long as arrows and trolls are not coming after me, I'll be fine!"

Everyone nodded and got ready, but Indie said to Spuck, "If I end up in a pigpen, Spuck, I'll kick your butt."

Fortunately, Indiana did not have to kick Spuck's butt. Spuck first teleported Eve and FireWind with himself to make sure that where they were going was safe. Once they were sure, Spuck came back for Marie, Jun, and Perun, then Josephine and Aurora, taking Jonathan, Indiana, and Aeolus last.

"Not bad Spuck," commented Jonathan.

Spuck held his hand up in an okay sign. He was panting heavily. It took them well past the morning to get moving because it took a large amount of Spuck's energy to transport so many. Spuck had to rest between each of them so he could do the next one safely. Spuck rode on Aurora's back as they walked towards the winding trail that led straight to the mountains.

First thing Josephine noticed when she arrived was that it was hot. It was hotter than she had ever felt back home during the summer, or even more so than when they had traveled through Mango's Desert. Josephine was sweating so badly she ended up going barefoot and changed into one of Marie's short sleeved tunics. Jun, Indie, Aurora, and Spuck weren't too thrilled with the heat, either.

Eve and FireWind, on the other hand, were enjoying themselves, to put it in mild terms. They were sprinting ahead of them on the rocky trail. Jonathan, Marie, and Wave did not find the heat too unbearable.

The other major thing Josephine noticed was the mountains. It was hard to miss the massive rocks that were looming over them already. They had to be twice the size of the Clocha Móra Mountains. They continued until the light faded. The group had made good time and was now deep into the Phoenix Mountains, following the rock laden trail.

"Any idea where the Viken are?" Spuck asked as they made camp.

The group decided to climb up the one side of a mountain to take refuge in a cave that overlook the mountain side. It was cooling down extremely fast, making Josephine feel much better. Flash crawled up first, and then in a line, the dragons slithered up the side and into the caves.

"Not really. According to Gazelda, they live in small villages all over the range. We're just going to have to follow the paths until we find one."

"Anyone besides me half expecting them to draw arms against us the second they see the dragons?" asked Indie, as he and Marie started pulling together dinner.

"I know, but I don't know how else to approach them. It's not smart to go in with no weapons or just one or two of us.

Like you said, we do not know how they will take us," sighed Josephine as she pulled her hair back into a ponytail.

"I think it'll depend on how long their memories are," commented Spuck, "If they remember that the Dragon Knights used to fight them and burn their ships when they were pillaging towns, then we're in trouble. If not, you may have a sporting chance."

"Thanks, Spuck," chuckled Josephine in a sarcastic tone.

"You never fought them when you were in the Alliance?" asked Jun to Spuck.

"Nope. I was just a back-up warrior. Did little things if they were too small for the Dragon Knights to deal with or if everyone else was busy. Never fought in any major battles. Fought a few trolls and a leprechaun..." Spuck laughed at some old memory and shook his head.

"I am guessing we are going to do this blind," said Aurora, who sat down behind Josephine.

"Looks like it," said Josephine dryly. Josephine glanced over to see Jonathan helping Jun with her nightly fighting lessons. Indiana, Jonathan, Ticka, and Eve would take turns each night helping the young girl learn how to protect herself. Eve had a good laugh when they were showing her how to punch. Jun, by accident, got Indiana in the face.

Jonathan was showing her how to hold a sword. She wasn't using a sword, but a stick that Spuck had been using as a walking stick. Jonathan was pulling and pushing at her legs to help her move into the proper stances. It was a good thing they were helping Jun, because it helped the rest of them to remember their mistakes at the same time.

"You know, there is something I still don't quite understand..." murmured Aurora.

"What's that?" asked Josephine.

"Why is Shayla with Cetus?"

Ticka bit her lip. "I have a theory that maybe she had been made to swear an oath of some kind."

Indiana shrugged. "Why doesn't she just break it?"

Ticka shook her head, "Magic oaths are binding. Breaking certain oaths, depending on the person or magic, can be different. In Shadow magic; however, there is but one penalty if you break your oath."

"Death, I am guessing?" asked Perun.

"Yes. Shayla may have no choice if Cetus used a death oath of some sort. Though it is not really his style to use it."

Jonathan turned to look at Ticka while Jun was swinging her sword stick. "What do you mean? How do you know it's not his style?"

Ticka leaned forward to the fire, shadows dancing across her face, making it seem darker than it really was. "I read up on Cetus in the *Dragon Heart Chronicles*. He is a man of fancy speeches and empty promises, and if you don't do something, then he kills you. Death oaths, especially in shadow magic, can backfire on either person. Cetus does not seem like the kind of person to do that."

"No, he is not one who wants to risk his life," growled Eve.

Spuck tried to take some vegetables that Eve was cutting, but she saw him out of the corner of her eye and slapped his hand.

As he rubbed his hand, Spuck commented, "Sounds right. Like I said, I was not around the Alliance much and I wasn't close with him. But I met him a few times. Very cunning, silver tongued almost. He has the hard face of someone who prefers to talk you into something rather than threatening you by sword point. I never liked him as much as the others. Sandra Heartwell and Storm were my favorites. Always laughing about something," Spuck smirked.

"So why does Shayla stay? From what little I could get, there is no love for her brothers," sighed Josephine. "She is a formidable fighter; why not just leave?"

"Cetus may have something else over her head," commented Wave, "Maybe her mother? Or someone she loves deeply?"

"No; I don't think so. Shayla's mother, Bram's wife, died when Cutler was born. As far as I could gleam from the local gossip, Shayla has never had any suitors or anyone calling on her," said Ticka.

"Then why?" asked Jonathan. He walked over, being relieved of duty by Indie, who Jun accidentally hit when she was swinging; Jonathan sat and then gave something for the rest of them to chew on.

"Maybe she can't because she has nowhere to go."

Josephine raised an eyebrow. "It may be tough to leave but..."

Jonathan shook his head. "You're thinking like yourself, Josephine. You have a good home and family. But think about her life. She's probably been under Cetus's and Vanell's thumb from the moment she was born. Shayla had no choice. She can't leave because Cetus and her father have worn her down. Shayla has never had freedom in the realest sense of the word. I bet she wants to leave, but

Cetus and Vanell have had control over her for so long, she wouldn't know what to do if she was free."

Everyone went quiet. Josephine stared at the sparking fire. It was true, maybe. Cetus and her father didn't need to chain her physically because they had her chained mentally. But there was something missing in Jonathan's theory that didn't quite sit flush with Shayla's personality.

"I think you are partly right. Maybe she just doesn't have anywhere to run and thinks that. Why bother running if they'll just bring her back," suggested Aeolus.

"Seems more likely to me," agreed Josephine, "May explain why she had manacles on her wrists in my dream."

Everyone stared dumbfounded at Josephine

"Oh, I didn't mention that, did I?" smirked Josephine.

"Yeah... no," said Aeolus.

"Why...?" started Jonathan.

"I don't know why. It was while we were still at the Dragon's home," said Josephine.

Marie pressed her lips, "Hm, you do seem to have some powerful sense of foresight, but it only seems to be in your dreams and other certain points of time. That can be bothersome."

"I know, until I saw Shayla, I didn't know if it was a dream or a vision," sighed Josephine.

Jun and Indiana had stopped practicing, moving to sit on the other side of Jonathan. Indiana was leaning back, still chiseling away at the same piece of wood, only now it seemed to have more of a shape. It reminded Josephine of Flash.

"Well, there is nothing really more we can do for the time being, so let's eat and get to bed. Tomorrow is going to be long."

Chapter Thirty-Three
Village of Warriors

The group of teenagers, dragons, and one sprite packed up and left as the sky turned orange. It was the only way they knew for sure that it was dawn because the mountains were so tall and tight together that they blocked out the sun; all you could see was its rays. It was now extremely cold, and as they walked, their breaths would become little clouds. The group continued on the rocky trail that they were following until...

"Oh goodie, a fork in the road," groaned FireWind. The group stopped in mid-step. The trail split into two directions, one going in a northwest direction, the other going more southeast.

"Guess it would be too easy if there was a sign that said, 'Viken village is this a-way'," said Spuck.

"Should we risk flying up to see if we can spot any villages?" asked Jonathan to Josephine. The reason that the dragons were walking was to make sure that they wouldn't get shot down.

"Looks like it. I did not want to risk it, but now..."

"Let's do it like this. Jonathan and Aeolus will go on that route," Perun nodded his head northwest, "And I and Marie go that way. We are the fastest flyers."

Josephine agreed it was the best plan. "If you see a sign of a village, fly straight back here. Do not go near it," she ordered in a firm voice.

"Yes, Lady Josephine," teased Jonathan as he and Aeolus jumped into the air and flew down the trail.

Josephine felt her stomach lurch as she watched the two, not just because she was worried about them but also at how graceful they looked when in flight, like a bird of prey. Marie and Perun flew off, but they were more like an arrow from a bow and became nothing more than a yellow blur in the sky. Josephine and the rest sat on the ground, waiting. Jun followed Flash around as he picked at the ground, scrounging for a few little bugs that were hiding in the tough grass. An hour went by, but neither pair had returned.

"I wonder how far out the Viken villages really are," commented Indiana.

"Far, they are raiders of the sea, so makes sense they would be closer to the edge of Anglii," said Wave.

"How far in are we, anyway?" asked Eve from on the top of FireWind's head.

"I have no idea; we've covered several miles in a short amount of time," said Josephine.

Ticka shrugged from beside Josephine.

"I would guess almost fifteen miles if I looked at that map correctly," Aurora suggested, as she stretched out her back.

"I hope they get back soon; it's risky standing in one spot too long," said Hurricane, looking in the general direction that Perun had flown.

"Me, too," agreed Josephine.

"Not to mention that we are getting dangerously low on supplies. We're good on the water because of that small spring, but food, not so much. There's just so little game around here...," said Indie.

"Not to mention vegetation," added Eve.

Indie laughed. "I thought you'd rather eat a deer raw than eat anything green," teased Indie.

Eve let her lip curl up over her teeth. "I hate rabbit food, but if I have to, I'll eat it. I'm not so picky that I'd stupidly let myself starve just because I don't like it."

Indie didn't say anything to her; he chuckled. Spuck was lying flat on the ground, watching a few ants walking in a line in the sand. Flash noticed and he, too, watched the ants from the top of Spuck's head. Flash watched and waited, then suddenly with a tongue like a frog unfurled it to scoop up the ants.

Spuck blinked. "Hey, neat! Do that again, Flash!"

Jun giggled, walking over to watch Flash with Spuck. Josephine laughed and turned back to see something coming from where Jonathan and Aeolus had gone.

"Hey, I think they're coming back!" said Josephine, jumping up in relief.

FireWind smiled, "Hey, talk about good timing, here comes Marie and Perun."

Sure enough, when Josephine turned around, she could see a yellow dot coming in fast to their spot.

"See what? I can't see anything," complained Jun, who was squinting her eyes.

"I don't think you can see them yet, Jun," smiled Josephine, who saw that Indie was also squinting his eyes.

"What's the story?" asked Spuck impatiently as the Dragons landed, kicking up mini tornados of sand.

"We found a town about ten miles that way," said Jonathan, pointing his thumb behind him.

"Better than us. There is a town, but it's much farther than that," sighed Perun. "We just barely saw it as we turned around."

"Guess we win," smirked Aeolus. Perun rolled his eyes.

"Whatever, come on, let's get going," grumbled Eve as she jumped off FireWind's head to pick up her pack.

"Are we going to fly most of the way to it?" asked Ticka.

"I think we will, since Jonathan and Aeolus did and didn't get shot at, so let's go," nodded Josephine.

Indie joked, "Of course, we could get shot at because they see Jonathan's ugly face."

"Har, Har, Indie," Jonathan said back.

"Come on, boys, let's go," barked Eve.

Indie and Jonathan did a mock salute to Eve, then Indie climbed aboard Aeolus. Eve rolled her eyes.

"Great, Jonathan is becoming another Indie. He's going over to the dark side."

Spuck smirked.

"Hey, I'm the funny one around here."

"You'll be the dead one if you don't move it," smirked Eve.

Spuck blinked to see everyone was already a few feet above and away from him.

"YIPE! HEY, WAIT FOR ME!"

They flew at a steady pace, following the serpentine trail through the rocky Phoenix Mountains. It was all quiet expect when Spuck started asking if they were there yet. After the third time, Indiana threatened to throw him into the Viken village so that the inhabitants could eat him for dinner. After that, Spuck began throwing rude faces at Indie until Josephine caught his eye. Taking the hint, Spuck took a seat on Hurricane's tail and became still.

"Where do you think the Phoenixes live?" asked Jun, yelling into Josephine's ear over the wind.

"Not sure. Probably not anywhere near the villages. Somewhere deep in the caves, maybe. No one really knows," Josephine called back. She made a note to ask Ticka about the fire birds, but it got shoved far away in her mind the second they saw a small gap in the rocky terrain.

A village was nestled in a large, hilly clearing with a few bushes. There was a break in the rocky terrain. A few scraggly trees scattered around the area made it easy for Josephine to find the sun's location in the sky. The dragons landed high on a cliff, out of sight of the village's gates.

"All right, any ideas?" asked Josephine as Aurora folded her wings.

"Well, we can't go marching in," sighed Eve.

"How about you, Ticka?" asked Josephine.

Ticka thought for a moment. "I think it would be best if you, Aurora, Jonathan, Aeolus, and myself go. We are the ones with the highest rank (no offence, everyone), so it stands to reason the leader of the village would only talk to us. If we can talk to him without the Vikens pulling their battle axes on us, then everyone would be safe to come."

Eve frowned. "I don't like it, if they do..."

"Then I think we two dragons with our fire breath will hold them off," said Aurora in a gentle tone.

"Good point," said Eve, though Josephine could feel that she still wasn't too ecstatic about it.

"You'll be right here and you'll know if something goes bad," pointed out Jonathan.

Eve let out a sigh and nodded.

"What do the rest of you think?" asked Josephine.

The emotional air was neutral and agreeing. Jun and Spuck nodded.

"I think it sounds logical," said Marie.

"It's the best we've got, so..." said Wave, shrugging.

"Fine then. Let's go meet them. The great sea dogs warriors."

The three of them decided it was best to walk in on the dragons. As they went, Josephine felt her early breakfast churning in her stomach.

"I really wish Gazelda was here," Josephine muttered.

"I know, me, too," sighed Aurora.

Ticka hugged Josephine from behind. "It'll be fine; we are here supporting you," she said.

Jonathan nodded, as did Aeolus. Josephine took in a breath, concentrating on Jonathan's and Ticka's calm mind-sets to relax. When they walked over a small hill, they reached the large log fences that marked the entrance of the village. It sounded very much alive from the feelings Josephine felt emanating. Happiness, disappointment, frustration, loving. Smoke was rising from the cooking fires into the Phoenix Mountain sky that was becoming bluer as the sun went higher. The sounds of iron being struck and goats munching on straw, letting out a bah once in a while.

There were no guards at the entrance. Aeolus and Aurora came to a halt.

"Should we knock?" asked Aeolus.

"Wish we could know if they received the messages that Gazelda sent," said Ticka. As she said that, a giant-sized man came lumbering through the gates.

He didn't notice at first the two dragons standing there. He was inspecting the gates to make sure they were sturdy. When he turned to close the door, he blinked, finally seeing them. Aurora and Josephine shared a nervous glance when the man did a double take.

"Am I in a dream, still drunk, or I am really seeing two dragons with their partners and a Tuatha Dé Danann?" he asked in a slow voice.

Aeolus choked back a laugh. Ticka dismounted and walked at a tempered pace. To Josephine's surprise, she spoke in the same language as the Viken man.

"I am Ticka Walsh, the Princess of the Kingdom of his majesty Kingdor Walsh. This is Josephine Drageon and-" Ticka paused, trying to think how to phrase something, then said, "the heir of Red Rose Kingdom, Prince Jonathan Falcon. With Aurora the dragon of ice, and Aeolus the dragon of the wind."

The man nodded. "Alright, I am not dreaming, though I still feel a little drunk."

Again, Aeolus choked back a laugh.

"I think my king of this village is expecting you. All the kings of the Viken are. If you do not mind, may I first go to him and tell him you are here, then come back to bring you in?"

Ticka smiled. "Not at all, my good man. It is a wise thing to do. We will wait."

The man nodded and went in. Aeolus let out the laugh he had held back.

"Drunk? I guess the Viken have changed little."

Josephine smirked. "No. Viken, just like all of their fellow Angliians, like their hard drinks little too much."

They waited for what seem like hours before the man came back. Josephine was able this time to take in his appearance. He was wearing a long green tunic, chest plate, and brown trousers. He had long brown hair and a long beard, and both were braided. In his beard was intertwine strands of light red, brown, and yellow thread. He was fairly muscular, though it looked as though he had a slight middle-age gain at the waist.

"Our King, Herleif, will meet with you right now. He is curious why there are but three of you when the message from Gazelda Fair Lady said there were five of you Dragon hearts with five dragon partners."

Josephine asked, "What is your name, if I may ask?"

The man tipped his head. "I am Bjarne, son of Einar, my lady."

Josephine smiled. "Could you, Bjarne, please let him know the others are here, if he so wishes to meet them. We thought it would be more... courteous if it was us five to start with."

Bjarne gave her another bow of his head, then disappeared. It did not take as long this time for him to come back.

"My king says that is fine, just fine. Bring your fellows so that you all may speak in the Great Hall with him. He will wait for you."

"Thank your king for his kindness and patience. We will come right away. And thank you for speaking for us, Bjarne."

Bjarne smiled despite himself. "Thanks very much, Lady Drageon."

With that, Bjarne left. Josephine glanced at Jonathan, who turned and let out a loud whistle. Within a few minutes, the others appeared.

"So, what did their king say?" asked Jun, jumping down from Hurricane.

"That he would like to see all of us in his Great Hall," smiled Josephine.

Bjarne returned then pulled open wide the gates so that the dragons could walk through. The village was made of many one-room houses constructed of mud, sticks, and stone. They were arranged in a semi-circle around what must have been the main town fire. They walked at a careful pace, getting many stares from behind the buildings. A few children stared wide-eyed at them. They, like the adults, wore various tunics, homespun dresses, with many layers. A few here and there were donning animal skins, but not many. She also noticed that the Viken were a big people, in both height and weight. Even the women were large. They carried themselves proudly as they attended their tasks.

Bjarne led them to the edge of the village where an extensive building stood. It was made of the same materials as the others, but it was built twice as long and as tall.

"Here is the Great Hall of our village. The king is sitting inside, waiting for you," Bjarne informed them.

Perun looked at it with awe. "We will all fit."

"Nice, isn't it?" smirked FireWind.

The dragons waited for everyone else to go in, and then they followed behind, going in two by two with Hurricane last in line.

The hall was amazing. They decorated the wooden posts with engravings of what Josephine assumed was their writing system. There were also several tapestries with battles depicted in great, stunning details. There were three long oak tables pushed aside so that the Dragons could come forward to where the throne was. The man sitting in the large chair decorated with furs was, Josephine assumed, King Herleif.

He was wearing a chest plate, and under his helmet was brown hair to go with his short brown beard that had gold and red thread woven in with a few black beads. There was a woman sitting beside him using a small hand loom to weave something. She was bigger built than Marie, but no less beautiful. Her hair was the color of a pale yellow, and she was wearing a circlet made of cloth, with an elaborate design embroidered with small beads. She was wearing a similar dress as the other women, only hers was a bright blue, while the others wore shades of reds, browns, and greens. She had blue eyes, while the man beside her had caramel brown eyes. He stood and spread his arms wide.

"Welcome! Welcome, Dragon Hearts, Dragons, and the Princess of the Dananns. This is my great hall! I am King Herleif and this is my fair wife, Matilda."

The woman placed her loom on the stand beside her, then stood and tipped her head in a bow. "This is an honor, indeed! Never have the Dragon Knights come to the people of the Vikens in peace! Pray tell me, which of you are Josephine Drageon and Gazelda Fair Lady? Could you please tell me all of who follow you here?"

Josephine stepped forward in the line the group had made, with Aurora stepping right behind Josephine.

"I am Josephine Drageon, Leader of the Dragon Heart Alliance, fair king. Our mentor, Gazelda Fair Lady, could not come with us due to some troubles we had."

The King nodded. "Ah yes, we may not talk with our cousins of Anglii often, but a few come here to trade and are kin. Word came to us that Cetus, once of the Dragon Knights' ranks, had risen from the dark shadows once more. Not only that, but word came that you lot destroyed half of the lord of Drake City's home!"

The king let out a booming laugh that filled the hall. Josephine could feel joy and envy coming from the king as he shook his head. "What I would have given to see that!"

Josephine blushed a little in her cheeks. "Yes, my good lord. We lost something, and we had to retrieve it. Lord

Vanell wasn't too willing to give it back." Josephine could feel embarrassment and shame coming from Jun.

The king laughed again. "Yes, indeed? Remind me never to steal anything from you, Josephine Drageon!" he laughed.

Josephine smiled in relief. At least this king was easy-going. Maybe they had a chance after all.

"Come now, who is the rest of your Alliance?" he asked.

Josephine smiled and pointed. "This is my dragon partner, Aurora the ice dragon."

And with that, one by one, she introduced the dragons and Dragon hearts first. When it was Ticka's turn, Ticka walked forward and bowed to the king and queen.

"As my father's heir, I am representing his kingdom."

King Herleif nodded.

"Indeed, it has been a long time, longer than the time before the Last Battle, that our two people have spoken. Please, let your father know, Princess Ticka, that at least my clan is honored to be called 'friend' by him."

Ticka bowed. "It would be my pleasure and honor to do so."

Ticka stepped back as Josephine introduced Indiana, then Spuck.

"Spuck the sprite... ahaha! I remember my grandfather telling me a story about you; did you really insult a Grace's Dragon and get your back-end burned?"

Spuck blushed angrily and mumbled something, but Josephine didn't quite catch it. Spuck sighed, then said in a louder voice,

"Yes, it was an accident, but, yes, I did."

King Herleif nodded. "I understand. The little things can set off some of the kings of the other clans and whole blood feuds will flare up! I, unlike most of my kinship, have thicker skin. So do not fret about that round me. I enjoy a good-humored insult! Though it's best not to insult my wife; she does not take to that too well."

Spuck smirked and nodded, then shrunk back. The queen raised her eyebrow but said nothing to her husband. Jun shifted her feet and hid into the shadow of Perun.

The king still noticed. "Come now, youngling, what is your fair name?"

Josephine saw the terrified look on her face but nodded her head to Jun to come forward.

"Your Majesty, this is my ward, Jun. She helped us find our missing item in Drake City."

Jun blushed a bright crimson, staring straight at her feet.

Herleif looked at her with interest. "Indeed? Well, you must be a great warrior in the making, young Jun!"

Josephine nudged her with a light tap.

"Thank you, your majesty. But I'm not that great. I can fist fight well enough–"

"Tell me about it," muttered Indiana.

"–But I am not that great at using a sword," she said to her feet.

He smiled. "It is fine, Jun. Not everyone is meant to use the same weapon. I am sure you will find yours. As Josephine's heir, I am sure she will see to it."

"I will indeed."

"Come now, I find talking about such serious things as alliances and wars are best done over a hot meal and a large tankard of mead! My dear Matilda?" He looked at her and smiled widely.

"My cooks are at it, and now that I have met you all," she said, nodding to the Dragon hearts, "I will go join them to help them finish the feast." With that, she turned and left through a side door into what Josephine assumed was the kitchen. There was smoke drifting lazily through the door with the smell of sharp spices.

"Wait till you sample my wife's cooking! None of the other kings can boast about their wives' cooking like I can! She is the best! Every year when we have the meeting of all the villages, they have a cooking competition and she has won every year since I became king. You are in for a real treat!"

King Herleif did not exaggerate. When the first course came out, Josephine almost let her jaw go slack. There were many fish dishes, such as Salomene; fish cooked in a sauce twice over, cod, and a few other dishes that Josephine could not name. There was also salted venison; some were cooked whole and given to the dragons whole, which they enjoyed with great gusto. Presented were also some pork and meat pies. There were some cooked vegetables, but mostly cabbage dishes. Everyone tried to eat slowly to enjoy the first home cooked meal they had had for a long while that wasn't a stew. They talked little as they ate the first course. Josephine was enjoying herself. With the Vikens, it was rude to eat alone, and everyone, even the servants, ate at the Grand Hall table. It was a sign of a great and wealthy king of the Vikens if he helped to provide for his people at his own table. When the second round of food came was when it became interesting, for food from other lands was put on the table.

Queen Matilda placed a particular dish in front of the dragon hearts. It was made of meat, but Josephine wasn't sure. It had spices, and it looked almost like a stomach or something. Josephine looked again, and she knew it was some sort of animal stomach. She almost gagged. Everyone else looked at each other with various looks of disgust or curiosity. Spuck didn't hesitate and took one of the largest pieces.

"What is this? It tastes familiar..." said Spuck thoughtfully.

"Spuck, you are disgusting, you know that? Though it looks familiar..." muttered Indiana.

Jun glanced at Josephine.

"Try it," was the only thing she could say. They all took a bite. Wave almost threw up. Indie was slowly eating, but he didn't seem disgusted as Marie did. Eve was chewing, but from the look on her face, it wasn't that great to her. Josephine found it had almost a nutty taste. She did not, however, think she liked it. When Queen Matilda came back, she smiled at Spuck.

"My lady queen, what is this?"

"It is from Ériu! Haggis!"

Spuck smiled. Eve smacked herself on the forehead.

"Boy, it's been so long! Though this seems to have a different spice taste than some that I've eaten in the past."

The queen nodded. "Yes, I cook it with a few things that the Ériu don't. Like mushrooms." Spuck nodded and began eating it again. When the queen left, Jun looked at Spuck with a frown and asked what everyone else was thinking.

"Dare I ask what it is made of?"

Eve gagged and answered Jun, "Gah! I know what, sheep's stomach!" She covered her mouth. "My grandfather makes it once in a while because our family is originally from Ériu. It's been a few years since he made it. I forgot..."

Indie flinched. "I knew of it, but never ate it."

Jonathan smirked at Josephine. She replied in kind.

"Yuck. I am not eating anymore," muttered Jun, pushing the Haggis over to a corner of her plate.

Wave nodded in agreement. "It's not my favorite for sure."

Spuck blinked with his mouth bulging. "What? Are you crazy?"

Jonathan raised an eyebrow. "You really like this?"

Spuck nodded. Without hesitation or waiting for another cue, everyone scraped their Haggis onto Spuck's plate. Spuck blinked, then shrugged and continued to eat.

Indie shook his head. "Spuck, you are insane."

Spuck wrinkled his nose at Indie, and without a pause devoured the dish. The second course was taken away, and the third began with the lighter dishes that were mostly pastries. It was then the king began talking business.

"Now, Lady Josephine..."

Josephine turned from her conversation with Queen Matilda to look at the king.

"I should let you know how my people work. There are several kings who live throughout the land here. Whoever is the richest and can boast of many loyal followers is named the King. Once a year, all the kings and people gather in a meeting that last for a week. It is then that we do council and address concerns and so forth. Luck is not with us in that we just had our spring meeting, but a full moon ago. The Phoenix Mountains are harsh, and it is hard to contact all the villages. I am afraid there is no actual way to get word out to all the villages. Not only that, but some clans feud with others, so I doubt highly that you would get the whole of the Viken to come to your cause."

Josephine took a breath, then nodded. "I understand, King Herleif."

The king took a swig of his mead and then said, "However, I can call upon several of my kin to help. Also, a few old war friends. I dare say that most of the villages here on this side of the mountain and the coast will come to your aid. It has been a while since we have seen any good battles!"

Josephine heard Eve's cough and knew what she was getting at.

"My king, I thank you for your help, both yours and your kin's. But there is one thing that we must address."

King Herleif nodded, a small wave of curiosity coming from him.

"It's about the Viken's love to... pillage."

The king smirked at Josephine.

"Ah. That. Sad to say that the Viken's days of pillaging have declined over the years..." A wistful expression came over his face. "It has become harder to do what our ancestors did. The natives of the other lands have grown in strength, and because of the last blood feud between two of the strongest villages, the number of our ships have been cut down. Due to all of this, we have started to trade more with many people, especially those of the Helios Islands and Ériu. We sometimes pillage, but it is rare nowadays. It is more profitable to trade than to take."

"This makes us much more at ease, but, my king, do you think that you could... ask your allies and kin to refrain from doing any raiding?"

King Herleif smiled and waved his hand.

"Of course! But if there is anyone you need us to raid..."

Josephine smiled. "We will let you know at once."

The king smiled, then he frowned.

"I will tell you, Josephine Drageon, why I was so willing to talk and join your alliance. I lost a nephew a week ago to a Shadow creature. He was hunting in the northern area of the mountains. His throat was cut and his eyes were gone."

Josephine shivered.

"He was my younger brother's eldest and only son. Shadows have claimed many of my people's lives in the last few months, and it is only increasing by the day. My people were proud warriors, Josephine, but now they fear their own shadows. We join to not only protect but to gain back our glory. I want revenge for my nephew. I tell you this, Josephine, for this is also a warning to you to keep your word and do things that honor us. We do not take well to oath breakers."

Josephine bowed her head. "I will ensure that we honor you as long as you honor us, good King Herleif."

After that, the king asked for several of his servants to leave in the morning to contact his cousins, brothers, sister, and his old battle companions to ask them to join the Dragon Knights. King Herleif told Josephine that most of them would probably come to swear alliance with her over the next week. Josephine wished to return to the Dananns as soon as possible so that they knew what was going on, but she knew this was more important.

"Of course, my king. We will wait as long as we must."

That night, the Great Hall was done up as a large bedroom for everyone. The Viken placed out the biggest blankets they had for the Dragons to sleep on. They didn't mind sleeping on the floor, but the queen would not have it. The Dragons took the blankets without further comment to the queen.

"She is scary when she wants to give you something," said Perun as he straightened out his blanket on the floor.

"No kidding. I like to see Lord Vanell take her on," said Aeolus.

Jonathan laughed. "She'd chop him up and cook him in a stew before he could draw his sword."

"That's something I would pay to see," laughed Marie.

"Ditto," smirked Eve and FireWind.

The Dragon Hearts pulled out their bedrolls and, with the extra blankets their hostess gave them, each made their beds beside their dragons. Jun snuggled up with Aurora and Josephine while Indie just flopped between Aeolus and FireWind. Ticka decided to sleep on the other side of Josephine. Spuck, apparently, for reasons left unexplained, would not sleep on the ground and asked Aurora if he could sleep on top of her. Aurora said it was fine.

Spuck straighten out on Aurora's back, curling up in the spot where Josephine normally sat. Within five minutes, Spuck was snoring.

"Wonder why he doesn't like sleeping on the ground?" pondered Wave.

"Probably pulled a prank on someone and then they got him back or are planning revenge on him one of these days," muttered Indie, glaring in the general direction of the sprite.

FireWind sighed, "Really, are you going to hold a grudge against him just because he took your jerky?"

Indie looked at FireWind with utter disbelief, "Of course not! He's cheerful and pulls faces when he thinks I'm not looking and tried to slip haggis into my pie. Those are the reasons why I don't like him."

"But I'm cheerful," frowned Jun.

Indie laughed at her face. "Very cheerful, but that's okay on you, squirt."

Jun smiled, then settled down in her bed to sleep.

"When did he try to slip haggis into your pie?" asked Josephine. She couldn't remember see him try.

"When you were talking to the king about the different clans," Indie muttered with disgust.

"That reminds me, we'll need to ask for each of the flags of the clans so our allies know which ships not to shoot at."

"I just thought of something," said Marie.

"What?" asked Perun. Marie sighed and leaned against Perun's leg.

"If Cetus is in the Phoenix Mountains and the Shadow creatures have increased in numbers, it makes me wonder if Cetus has shanghaied the Northern Clans into fighting for him."

Josephine dropped her blankets, and Wave let out a small gasp.

"I didn't even think about that," said Eve, coming around FireWind.

"Neither did I. This could cause problems with our new allies if they have to fight their kin," said Josephine.

"Do you think Cetus would make them swear Shadow oaths?" asked Hurricane.

"I don't think so. Remember what I said about Shadow oaths? He'd more likely try to take them over with a Shadow possession than an oath."

"What happens when a Shadow takes you over?" asked Jun.

Josephine hugged herself tightly. Mango had all too graphically explained what happened. Josephine watered it down for Jun.

"It takes over the person's body, and their eyes become black. Their voices also change, and they become mindless. Whoever controls the Shadow also controls whoever's body that has been taken over."

She could feel Jonathan clench in pain, thinking of his friend Jamard.

Jun gulped. Josephine patted her on the head. "It will be fine. Don't think about it. Think of happy things as you go to sleep."

Josephine hummed a lullaby that her mother had sung to her, and within minutes Jun dozed off.

But before she fell asleep Jun muttered, "Good night, sister."

Josephine stopped humming. "Good night, sister."

"Nice save," commented Jonathan once Jun was out.

"She doesn't need to have my nightmares," said Josephine as she finished making her bed. Jonathan agreed.

"No kidding," said Wave. "Do you think Mango told us all the gory details just to torture us?"

Marie shook her head. "No, I don't think so. She didn't want to sugarcoat it for us. Not that you've done that with Jun," Marie said hastily.

Josephine understood.

"You'll have to tell her the whole of it later on, but I think just telling her the basics was fine," commented Indie from his bed.

Josephine shuddered.

Shadows taking over a body was something she hoped that none of them see again. When a shadow takes over a person's body and the person has a strong to fight back... it was bloody. Mango said much of the time, the bodies would be damaged and the person's mind would break, and they would become insane. Mostly when a shadow left a person's body, they would die, and those who didn't would do so in a few minutes, unable to move or do anything. She glanced at Jonathan, worrying about his friend.

Josephine pulled her blankets over herself to block the images from her mind. She listened to everyone slowly falling asleep, one by one. Once Jonathan fell asleep, she dozed off, listening to his soft breathing. No louder than the breeze floating through the hall.

Chapter Thirty-Four
The Challenge of Wills

T he next few days were frustrating for Josephine. Not because she had to meet with all the other kings of the Viken. No, she found that entertaining. The Vikens' idea of ceremony was talking over a meal. Marie and Wave both complained that they would have to train twice as hard to keep all the weight off. Josephine felt the same way.

Eve did not complain; in fact, she began teasing everyone. No matter how much she ate, she did not gain any weight. She especially teased Indie, who would retaliate by poking fun at her during their nightly sword sessions. This, too, was entertaining, and sometimes she would just sit and watch them to take her mind off things. Jonathan would see this and would poke her into practicing with him, which she found useful and also nice because she was spending time with Jonathan. The thing that was frustrating to the Drag–on heart leader was that they had no word from Gazelda, or anyone. Ticka had sent a pigeon to her father, but there was no reply yet from the Tuatha Dé Danann king.

Everything was going well until the last of King Herlief's friends came. His name was King Verner, son of Gunnar. He was the youngest of the rulers, only two years older than Jonathan. His father died last spring, leaving him to become the new leader of their village. King Verner, like a few of the Viken, had the mindset that anyone who was Anglian was weak, in other words, not Viken. She could feel the utter disgust coming from him when they locked eyes. After Josephine introduced herself and the other Dragon Hearts, King Verner unleashed his opinion of Josephine on his father's friend.

"This is the girl we must rely on to keep us safe! My village is one of the furthest out along the western ridge. My people are being kept inside their homes because of the shadows. The shadows belonging to that of a Dragon heart traitor. You want me to give my warriors to the order of a mere girl? My youngest sister could beat her, and she is of only eight years!"

Josephine felt her face flush, as well as Eve's temper.

Josephine tried her best to keep her voice level. "My Lord, I may be young in years, but I am only slightly younger than yourself. I assure you I can lead. You will still be in charge of your own warriors."

King Verner shook his brown curls. "But I will be led by you."

Josephine narrowed her eyebrows just a smidge. "In a way, yes. But I do not understand, King Verner. Why do you oppose me?"

The young king sneered, "Women of Anglii are soft and fearful, unlike the shield maidens of our people. I refuse to put myself or my warriors under the directions of a woman who is not my kin. You know not our people's traditions or the way of the warrior."

Josephine made her face neutral. "King Herlief is helping me understand your—"

King Verner jumped to his feet, waving his hand angrily around. "You could know everything about my people, but it makes no difference! You are not of Viken blood! Just a soft Anglii girl with a big pet lizard pretending to be a knight! You have no experience of being a warrior! Anglii has proven that its people are nothing more than gutless wyrms!"

Aurora let out a low rumble, as did FireWind, Aeolus, and Perun. Eve snarled and put her hand on the hilt of her sword. Josephine caught her eye and glared. Eve got the hint, as did the dragons, and they all backed off. Jonathan was calm, but Josephine could sense his anger below the calm surface. Only Marie and Wave seemed to keep their cool along with Hurricane, Indiana, and Ticka. King Herlief narrowed his eyebrows.

"Verner, do not make a fool of yourself. I have seen Josephine train; she is more than able to take the mantle of leadership."

Verner said, "As for you, my father's old friend, how could you let this mere child... hoodwink you? Dragon heart or not."

The older king sighed, "Verner, just because your father saved my life does not mean I will respect you if you are not deserving of it. You do not even have enough hair to cover your face. I would not be complaining about her age."

Verner glared. Herlief matched his stare.

"I have listened to Lady Josephine, Prince Jonathan, and Princess Ticka. From their accounts, I believe it is in our people's best interest to join with our old enemies to ensure that we live. You, being one of the kings, know that our people are beginning to fade."

"Indeed. My village has been doing fine up till now."

Josephine knew that this would not be the last time someone like Verner was going to challenge her leadership. She had to think fast. He reminded Josephine strongly of a few of the boys from her hometown. It was then the idea popped into her head. Without smiling; though she wanted to, she stood to meet King Verner in the eye.

"King Verner, I wonder, as a warrior, would you agree to a warrior's challenge to quell your worries over my abilities to lead?"

She could feel the confusion from everyone but one. Indie was smiling from ear to ear.

King Verner frowned. "A warrior's challenge? What are you suggesting?"

Josephine cracked a small smile. "I understand the Viken enjoy a good spot of sparring. I suggest that you and I, in one week's time, have a wrestling match."

Eve now was wearing a smile, as was FireWind. The others were not too sure about Josephine's plan. King Verner was dumbfounded, but quickly recovered.

"Sounds fair, Josephine Drageon. I accept." The king grinned widely, as did Josephine.

The king wouldn't know what hit him until he was kissing the ground.

"Have you lost it?" demanded Wave as the group went to the town's well to talk in private.

"What are you talking about?" asked Josephine in an innocent tone of voice. Wave groaned while Indie laughed.

"You can't wrestle King Verner!"

"Looks like she is from where I'm standing," laughed Indie.

Wave shot him a look that made even Eve seem like a fluffy bunny.

Josephine sighed, "Wave, it's the only way. Besides, I think I am more than capable of taking him on; he is big, but not *that* big."

"Careful, he might crush you with his colossal ego," joked Spuck.

Josephine stared at Jonathan, waiting for his opinion.

The prince rolled his lip then said, "I'm not too sure about this, but if you can take him out, you'll earn respect with not just the Viken, but some of the other allies, which is key to help keep everyone in line."

Josephine grinned, "Oh, come on, have a little faith. I am Wind Sage Village's best wrestler for a reason. You forget; I have three older brothers. I may not be the best when it comes to sword fighting, but when it comes to fist fights and wrestling, I'm the best."

Spuck and Indie both grinned widely. Jonathan smiled, too, but Wave still wasn't happy.

Josephine sighed. "I'll practice with the boys."

Wave glanced at Indie and Jonathan, then back to Josephine with a frown.

"I still don't know about this..."

Eve interjected, "Wave, it's the only way Verner is going to shut it and listen. Actions are favored over pretty speeches here. I am sure maybe King Herleif's nephew Ralf would like to help; he is almost the same weight and size of Verner."

"I'll help as well, Wave," smiled Ticka.

Wave let out a breath, "Okay, fine, as long as you have help, I suppose there's no point in arguing."

Josephine smiled, draping an arm around Wave and squeezed her friend's shoulder.

"It'll be fine."

In the end, though, Ticka could not help. King Herleif received via pigeon a message from King Kingdor asking Ticka to come back as fast as she could. All the message said was that Shadow creatures were increasing in number and that he needed her and her magical abilities. At first Ticka wasn't sure how she was going to get back, when Josephine got an idea.

"Hey Spuck, could you teleport Ticka to Tailltiu?"

Spuck scratched his chin. "I have never been to Tailltiu City. I could take you to the Centaurs' home, and then you could ride over to Tailltiu."

"Sounds good to me," smiled Ticka. With a snap of Spuck's fingers, Ticka disappeared to the Centaurs' home. With her, she took a scroll with a run-down of all the Viken allies and information that they had gathered for both Jabari and Kingdor.

Once Spuck was back in a blink of an eye, Josephine set off to the Viken's training field to practice her wrestling;

whistling as she walked with a smile on her lips, with the others right behind her.

Chapter Thirty-Five

Practicing the Destruction of One's Ego

Josephine braided her hair, then pulled it into a bun. She stretched her arms.

Indie smiled, "If you don't mind, I'll go first."

Josephine smirked and noticed that Jonathan still didn't look too happy, but was smiling despite his emotions. Eve was as eager as Indie while Wave still was not too keen on the whole idea. FireWind came towards them, with Ralf walking beside her.

"Found him," she said with a big grin.

Ralf nodded to Josephine. Ralf looked much like his uncle, only he had broader shoulders, no beard, and bright green eyes.

He turned to FireWind, "Next time, Lady fire dragon, simply ask someone where I am instead of poking around in all the buildings."

FireWind coughed, dipped her head down. Josephine laughed at FireWind's embarrassment. Eve chuckled as she sat on her dragon partner.

"All right then. Ralf, thanks for helping."

The young Viken nodded. "It is my pleasure. I, myself, do not think highly of King Verner, so it will be good indeed to see someone put him in his place. He underestimates everyone but his own abilities. It will be fitting to see you teach him some respect."

"Thank you, Ralf. Now, are there any special rules to wrestling that the Viken have?"

Ralf shrugged.

"Only that there are no rules, really. Most of the time; although we don't bite our opponents or kick them between the legs. It's more out of respect. Though, now that I think about it, the primary rule is no weapons and no magic, but of course, our people don't have any magic like the Dananns. Everything else is fair."

Josephine nodded, "Okay then. Indie, are you ready?"

Indie had taken his leather jerkin off and was wearing an old cotton shirt with no sleeves. To Josephine, his arms looked like coiled whips ready to snap forward at any second.

Josephine walked forward to face him. She held back a laugh when she remembered she was a whole four inches taller than him. Of course, that didn't really mean much, but she still found it funny, for she saw Indie as a brilliant swordsman and therefore he always seemed so tall that she kept forgetting. Maybe it had to do with the air of confidence he always had. Marie walked over to stand a little off and between the two.

"I'll judge if you want. I've had to judge for Eve's fights with all the boys back home so many times..."

Eve let out a triumphal chuckle. "Only sad part was that after the first few fights, they gave up," she pouted.

Indie gave Eve a side glance but stayed quiet. Josephine clapped her hands.

"Okay, come on, ready to be defeated, Phoenix?" Josephine teased.

Indie chuckled as the two crouched. "We'll just see about that."

Marie sighed, "Okay, GO!"

Josephine lunged forward, and fully focusing on her senses. As she grabbed Indie's shoulders, she could feel the blood pulsing through his body and could feel the way his muscles were tense. Josephine also could feel how uselessly Indie was pushing against her. He was like a mouse trying to shove a boulder out of the way.

Josephine took her leg and swept it under Indie's, knocking him off balance. She grabbed his arm and twisted it, placing him face down on the ground and stuck her elbow in the middle of his back.

Indie coughed, "Okay, yeah..."

Josephine laughed, helping Indiana back on his feet. He smiled, shaking his head.

"Remind me to never challenge a Dragon heart to a wrestling match, only sword fights."

Josephine laughed, seeing the disappointed look on Eve's face.

Wave still was not convinced. "Sure, she can fight Indie; no offence, but you are not built like a Viken."

Marie shook her head at Wave. "Are you trying to make Josephine feel so bad that she fails because she doesn't think she can do it? Wave, stop it and let her practice."

Wave's face went pink, "It's not that, I'm worried for her!" she pouted.

Josephine walked over to Wave and placed a hand on her shoulder. "I understand, and thank you for caring. But, Wave, really, this is going to be fine. Wait and see. Have a little more faith."

Wave sighed.

Josephine grinned widely, like a cat. She turned to the others. "All right, which of you boys wants to be destroyed next?"

Ralf looked at Jonathan and gestured that Jonathan go.

Jonathan raised his eyebrow at him and chuckled, "I'm guessing it's me."

Jonathan was nothing but happy and a little nervous as he walked to meet Josephine in the middle.

"Now don't go easy on me, Mr. Wind Prince, just because you have a crush on me."

Everyone busted out laughing. Jonathan tried to look cross at Josephine, but he wasn't doing so well keeping his face straight.

Marie chuckled as the two crouched. "Ready?"

Josephine and Jonathan smirked at each other.

"Ready."

"Go!"

Jonathan was stronger than Indie. Both grabbed at each other's shoulders and found neither was willing to give ground. Josephine and Jonathan shared one grin before Josephine twisted herself in and under Jonathan's arms, making him lose his footing, and before he could save himself, Josephine placed her right leg under his left leg and slammed him down on his back on the ground. Jonathan tried to get back up, but Josephine had her knee in his leg and one arm pinned behind his own back, the other was in her hands, and the elbow in Jonathan's shoulder. Josephine could feel and hear both their hearts beating a thousand miles a second. Josephine took in that everyone was laughing and clapping.

"Ice Queen, one, Mr. Wind Prince, zero," smirked Marie.

Josephine quickly detangled herself from Jonathan, then offered him a hand up, which he took.

"You were not kidding," He laughed a little breathlessly.

Josephine grinned, "Told ya."

Spuck let out a whistle, and everyone turned and stared. Spuck looked left then right, and then in a last ditched effort whistled, looking up.

Indie shook his head. "Rule twenty-four: Whistling only makes you look guiltier."

Spuck stopped whistling to roll his eyes at Indiana.

Josephine chuckled, then glanced at Jonathan, who smiled back.

"So, Ralf, ready to lose?" laughed Eve.

Ralf shook his head. "If I did not know better, I would say you were a Viken, Josephine. Very good indeed."

"Helps when the person you're wrestling is a little on the softy side," teased Indiana.

Jonathan rolled his eyes.

"Lookie who's talking, *Marilyn,*" mocked Eve.

Spuck choked on the piece of taffy he was nibbling on. Jun slapped him on the back.

Spuck whispered a "thanks," then said in a raspy voice, "What do you mean by Marilyn?"

Indie's face had gone white.

Eve smiled widely. "That is Indiana's middle name. Indiana Marilyn Phoenix."

Spuck matched Eve's smile. "Realllly?"

Spuck rattled off a bunch of "girly" jokes. Everyone sighed as Indie lunged at Spuck, then chased him around the clearing.

Eve shared a look with FireWind. When the two passed the Dragon Knight and the Dragon, FireWind grabbed Spuck's shirt with her teeth while Eve grabbed Indie's shirt. Eve promptly smacked the two on the back of their heads. Spuck complained, but Josephine only shrugged.

"You were asking for it."

Spuck pouted as floated in the air, folding his arms and legs with a disgruntled face. Indie wisely took what he got, saying nothing as he rubbed his head.

Aurora sighed, "Anybody besides me thinking this is going to be a long week?"

Josephine's only reply was laughter.

Chapter Thirty-Six
Strength of a Dragon, Grace of a Woman

For Josephine, the week went much faster than she would have liked. In some ways she was happy, because it meant that the match was closer, and the sooner it was over, the quicker she and the others could go back to the Dananns. On the other side of the coin, she wished it would last longer, for she was having fun with everyone, especially Jonathan. When they would practice, they would talk about anything and everything. The last conversation had been about their siblings. In the end, they figured that Jeremiah, Jonathan's book worm brother, would get along nicely with Matthew, Josephine's eldest brother, who also was a bit of a bookworm. Josephine explained how Matthew was the one who enjoyed reading legends with Josephine when she did her lessons.

"Grandfather was always the one who told us legends for bedtime stories. When he died, Matthew sort of took over that role."

Jonathan nodded. "Jeremiah loves studying the ancient legends. His dream is to go exploring around the earth, trying to find out if any of them are true. Though I don't know if he'd be up to it. He's definitely a scholar kinda person. He can be a little snotty at times." Jonathan grinned.

Josephine smiled back. "Matthew would help keep him in line, then. He is gentle and sweet, but knows when to be stern. He had to know when to be stern, seeing how he helped to look after me, Timothy, and Ronald. The trouble-makers."

Jonathan laughed. "In that case, no doubt they would get along with Jenn and Jordan. They are the troublemakers, along with me." Jonathan let out a frustrated sigh and rubbed his sword with a little more force than he had been.

Josephine shared a sad look with Aurora. "I highly doubt that you were troublemakers. You were just doing what you could to fight your father's unjust ways...?" Josephine turned the statement into a question.

Jonathan sighed, glancing at the Viken village. "Yeah, we tried to fight back as best we could."

Josephine laid a hand on Jonathan's shoulder, "You will get back your kingdom."

He smiled and raised an eyebrow. "Is that an order or a statement of fact?"

Josephine removed her hand and gave Jonathan a half-shrugged.

"Both."

Jonathan smiled and went to say something, but Jun and Indie appeared to practice sword fighting, so the two went back to practicing themselves.

Ralf's time was split between helping his uncle and assisting Josephine's training. Josephine had beaten him every time, but she wanted to keep on her toes for any possible underhanded tricks. Ralf had developed a reluctance to practice with her due to Josephine's above -average- Viken strength. By the end of the week, he had a magnificent bruise on his arm from when Josephine punched him a little too hard.

She also had Jonathan's help. However, his attempts to be underhanded were complicated by their awkward falls, causing him to blush due to his gentlemanly nature. It did not help that someone always seemed to be conveniently nearby watching, making Jonathan even more reluctant to practice with Josephine. Which frustrated her, for her losses to him made fighting him more useful.

The night before the match, Josephine had wandered off to the small hill that was just beyond the practice area. She had just left dinner. She found that her stomach didn't feel up to eating much because of her nerves; it also did not help that Spuck had challenged a young Viken warrior to a haggis eating contest. Josephine knew she was not the only one that had jumped ship when Spuck and the warrior had started shoveling down.

Josephine took a seat on a rock overlooking the mountain range that stretched to the edge of Anglii. She could just see the horizon of the ocean. A stiff wind blew over Josephine, making her feel at ease. It was after sunset, and a few stars were shining in the black fabric of the sky. She turned her head to find the Dragon Star. Josephine let out another sigh, and then at that moment, she realized that the wind was still blowing. She tilted her head back to see Jonathan and Aeolus smiling at her.

"Hey, thought we were not supposed to use our elemental powers," she complained.

"The dragon is doing it, not me," laughed Jonathan as he sat beside Josephine, who pulled her legs close to her, resting her chin on her knees.

Aeolus smiled and retreated to the great hall. As he went, he saw Aurora watching the two. The pair smiled, then walked back to the village in a happy silence.

"Ready to kick some kingly butt?" joked Jonathan playfully, nudging Josephine.

"I guess so," she smiled.

Jonathan laughed. "Maybe I should give you some incentive."

Josephine's eyebrow lifted. "Like what?"

He took a breath. Josephine could feel him pushing back a nervous feeling that piqued her interest.

"If you win tomorrow, I'll give you a victory flower and a kiss."

Josephine blinked and laughed. She could feel he was unsure how to take her reaction.

"Should I be insulted that you are laughing?"

Josephine took a breath and shook her head. "No. Unless you weren't serious?" She giggled.

She had no idea why she was laughing. Must have been built up nerves. What she did know was that she could not take her eyes off Jonathan's brown eyes.

"No. I was serious," he told her, keeping her stare.

Josephine leaned forward; their noses almost touching.

"Then, I would like to take that prize."

Jonathan matched her grin. "I will be willing to give it."

"I bet," she laughed.

Josephine got up and put her hand out to him. Jonathan gladly took it, and the two walked back to the village, not saying a word. Their shared emotions creating an over-whelming sense of bliss.

Josephine was up early the next morning, unable to get anymore sleeping done. She and Aurora sat outside the Great Hall, waiting for everyone else to get up and join them. Eve and FireWind were the first, with the others not far behind them. The main courtyard in the middle of the village was where the match was to take place. Of course, all the inhabitants and visitors were gathering around the rock circle that was the arena. Josephine and her cheering squad, as Spuck dubbed them, stood at the top of the circle, waiting for the kings. Josephine stood, tapping her foot.

She wasn't too eager to do this, even though she knew she could beat the young king. What concerned her was Ticka and Gazelda, whom they still had not heard from for over a week. Aurora felt all of Josephine's pent-up emotions. She snaked her head around, placing the tip of her nose on Josephine's shoulder.

"It's okay."

Josephine let out a snarky laugh.

"One Dragon's opinion."

King Verner and King Herlief finally appeared from the main hall, both wearing black and gold clothing with a phoenix and a boar emblazed on the front. King Herlief whispered to King Verner. The younger king shook his head and whispered harshly back. Josephine leaned slightly towards them. She heard the younger king whisper,

"I don't need advice from *you*, King Herlief. You are foolish enough to help the weak people of Anglii. I will show everyone that they are not worthy of our battle axes."

"This is not about worthiness; this is about surviving!" snapped King Herlief.

"Yes, and we can survive without the wyrms and their humans; we have been doing it for centuries, so why bother? I am going to prove this, so don't bother trying to stop me."

King Herlief opened his mouth, then closed it, deciding it was a lost cause.

As King Verner walked into the hand drawn ring, Josephine took a breath. She glanced over at the others with a small smirk before going forward. Spuck gave Josephine a quick thumbs up while the others gave her smiles. She could feel every single one of them believing in her. It helped her walk with confidence, her head high.

King Verner said nothing as Josephine stood in front of him. King Herlief glanced warily at his wife as she stepped into the ring. Traditionally, it was the leader of the Shield Maidens who oversaw events between warriors, and the leader is almost always the king's wife. Queen Matilda gave Josephine a secret smile before turning to the rest of the spectators.

"Welcome, one and all! A warrior's challenge never before seen within our people's times! King Verner and Lady Josephine have agreed to a wrestling match to help quail the fires in the way only our people can understand! With honor in a fair fight!"

Several cheers came from the crowd. The queen waited for them to abate before continuing.

"The match will go on: The winner will be whoever can keep their opponent down for thirty seconds, or if the opponent is out cold or dead, whichever comes first."

Josephine noticed Wave staring nervously at Eve, who was smirking. Eve sighed, shaking her head at Wave to calm down.

Queen Matilda saw this and added, "However, in this match it is greatly frowned upon to kill," she looked at both warriors who nodded their understanding of the rules.

"I'll say 'frowned upon'. I'll rip his head off if he tries," growled Aurora.

Perun twitched his tail. "I doubt he'll go that far, and we can't. As good and easygoing as King Herlief is, if the code of the warrior is broken, he'd have to punish you for interfering."

Aurora humphed as the queen explained those very rules. She would not let some stupid warrior code stop her from protecting Josephine if she got into trouble.

"*But*," Aurora thought smugly to herself, "*King Verner will never be able to get that far.*"

The two fighters stared at each other as the queen went over everything. King Verner was sure of himself. Josephine held back a smile. Just like any other man or woman—that overconfidence would be their downfall. Josephine was confident, but not stupid enough to think there wasn't a chance she could lose. The childhood lesson about over- and under confidence, ingrained into her by her grandfather, was what she was relying on in this fight.

Queen Matilda finished talking, then turned back to the opponents.

"Now, those are the conditions of the match. Do both warriors agree to uphold the conditions?"

Both said yes, though Josephine noticed that the "yes" from King Verner was bitter. He turned his blue eyes to Josephine. She saw they were hard with anger. He tightened his ponytail as the two crouched down in front of each other. Josephine felt the others stiffen as she did.

The queen yelled, "Then let round one begin!"

King Verner was already launching himself at Josephine as the queen shouted "begin".

Josephine rolled under his grasp to stand on the opposite side. She would not confront him straight on from the get-go; there were two more rounds to go, and she needed to conserve her strength. King Verner glared and Josephine answered with a smirk. The other part of the plan was to make King Verner lose focus—he was short-tempered. Eve told her that those who are short-tempered are the easiest to become wild and lose precision.

"As a Grace, that's your main motivator," smirked Indie.

"Please, not in battle. I know better. I never let my enemies make me lose my balance like that."

Eve was watching Josephine, pleased. Every time King Verner would make a grab at her, Josephine would twist out of it, and when she could, she would grab at him. They would push for a few moments before moving back. King Verner was tiring of this, so when Josephine tried to retreat, he brought his fists together to swing down hard. Josephine was able to roll out of the way, his knuckles scraping her hair.

She brought her arm up to block another downward hit. She shuddered at the bone-numbing impact. Josephine knew she had to finish it fast. She came from King Verner's left side and saw him blink in surprise when she wrapped her leg round his, then pulled him down and placed her elbow against his throat. He tried to get up, but Josephine was stronger and had more energy. After the five seconds he gave up, and the queen declared Josephine the winner of the first round.

Josephine offered a hand to the king, but he ignored it and went back to where King Herlief was standing. Josephine shrugged, going back to her friends. Aurora touched Josephine on the head with relief.

"WOO HOOO! You did it, Josephine!" cheered Spuck.

"Don't get too excited," sighed Josephine. "My arm's hurt."

Aurora blinked and then snarled.

Wave took Josephine's arm, "It's not broken, but he bruised bad with that downward hit."

Indie narrowed his eyes. "You think you'll be able to keep going?"

Josephine shrugged. "I have to, though I might lose this round. I don't like the thought of being tied, but I might have to let him beat me, so I get my strength back in my arm. If it gets hit like that again, I will not be able to finish it."

Josephine rubbed it again, but it did nothing to ease the numbing. Jonathan went to say something, but she cut him off.

"No. I need to do this. We can't substitute."

Jonathan sighed, nodding. Aurora gave Josephine another nudge before Queen Matilda called for the two to return to the ring. Josephine patted Aurora on the nose before standing once again in front of King Verner.

She took a breath. His face was fine, but a few bruises were appearing on his arms from where she had grabbed him. King Verner's eyes were calm, but his emotions were telling Josephine a different tale. He was seething. Josephine's eyes narrowed. Verner noticed.

"If you think insulting me by running around dodging me is going to prove anything to anyone, you are wrong, *Princess*," he spat out the words quietly so only the two of them could hear.

"I am simply fighting to protect, not prove anything," she whispered back.

King Verner's glare became even more venomous. "You will never lead us. Fighting is everything to us; even if a warrior loses, if they fought hard to earn their honor in death! That means everything to us! I will not follow someone who is not a true warrior!"

As the queen said, "Start!" King Verner jumped forward. Josephine knew within that second that she was going to lose. She dodged again, realizing that *how* she was fighting was all Verner cared about. Just beating the king was going to do nothing to win him over.

King Verner turned on his heel as Josephine moved and grabbed her arm, and she went flying on the ground. She brought her feet up to block King Verner, to stop him from flattening her. She got up, and the two locked arms.

"Come on, Josephine! Rip his arms off!" yelled Spuck.

Indie did a double take.

"What? All is fair in war and carnage. How do you think I've lived to be two hundred years old? Not like I'm going to say, 'Go, Josephine, give him a big hug'!"

Eve chuckled. Indie shook his head.

Josephine dug her heels into the ground so that Verner couldn't push her back out of the ring, though she knew he would never do that. It was then everything went wrong; King Verner pulled back then forward, pulling Josephine with him. He pinned her down with his thick, muscled arms, pushing down hard on her ribs, knocking the air out of her lungs. Josephine could not move; he pinned both her arms. Her right arm screaming in pain.

The queen called it, "King Verner wins round two!"

Josephine gasped in pain as she got up with Marie's help. Once Queen Matilda had called it, King Verner got up and went back to his spot without even a glance.

This time, Josephine had to sit down on Aurora's foot. Wave took over, poking at Josephine's ribs, making her hiss in pain.

"I KNEW this was going to happen!" Wave snarled.

"Is anything broken?" asked Indie.

"No. He didn't do that," muttered Josephine, wishing Wave would back off.

"No, but he still bruised her bad. Spuck, could you...?"

"NO!" growled Josephine.

"No? What do you mean, no?" demanded Aurora.

"If Spuck heals me, then there is no point in going on."

Wave let out a hiss, but it was in frustration, "If you go on, then there will be no point in an Alliance. Josephine, next time he could break your ribs and that could cause even more problems, like a punctured lung!"

Josephine shook her head. "We won't have the Viken as a member of the Alliance if I let him heal me! They have a warrior code, and I haven't been following it! The only way to gain King Verner's respect and loyalty is to just keep fighting as is."

Wave punched the ground. "That's stupid! Jonathan..."

Eve was the one, though, that spoke, "No, she's right. I wondered why King Verner was still angry even after he won this round. Leave it, Wave, it's the only course that Josephine can take. We thought out the wrong strategy."

Josephine stared into Jonathan's eyes as Eve spoke. He was annoyed, but he understood. Aurora acknowledged Josephine's decision. She took a few breaths and then stood.

King Herlief watched the Dragon Knights talking. He saw Josephine refuse Spuck's help, then stand. He smiled. Josephine met his eye, and he nodded in approval. Honor in the way a person fights their fights was all that mattered to his people, and if Josephine had finally seen that, she had already won.

Josephine stood tall in front of King Verner, who was smirking. He saw her wincing in pain and knew how weak Angliian women were. Most would already be crying from the pain, so he had to give the Dragon Knight leader some credit, but that still changed nothing. She had been fighting like a coward, using her speed to dodge. Well, it didn't work so well in the last round, nor would she have that advantage now that she was so beat up.

Josephine did not flinch at King Verner's glare.

"Are you prepared to give up, woman?" sneered King Verner in a low voice. Josephine's face became a deadly snarl. King Verner blinked at the change of face.

She said nothing but jumped forward as Queen Matilda yelled, "Begin the last round!"

King Verner gasped as Josephine met him head on. He steadied his feet and matched Josephine's furious snarl. They pushed each other a few centimeters back and forth, making no headway. Josephine's ribs were screaming from the pressure that she was putting on them, but she did her best to ignore it. King Verner tried to knock Josephine over by sweeping her feet, but she jumped and swept his feet from under him instead. She was using her superior eyesight to anticipate his moves this time, by watching when his muscles tensed. Josephine and Verner let go for a second so that both could steady themselves. Her focus was entirely on Verner. She didn't even register the dragons' roars. Her heart was beating in her head, her muscles tense.

Josephine jumped at Verner, who dodged her this time and tried to get her arms pinned from behind. Josephine whipped around to stop him from doing that, but she could not dodge his leg this time, falling in a cloud of dust. She coughed, choking on the dust, and then saw out of the corner of her eye King Verner bringing his leg down to crush her skull. Josephine rolled out of the way, then jumped back on her feet as some of the dirt got into her eyes. She furiously tried to get the dust out of her eyes, but it was no good.

King Verner laughed and spoke loud enough for everyone to hear, "Just as I thought, Angliian women are weak and useless. You will never be able to fight along the Viken!"

Josephine snarled again. The sound of his insult finally got to her. She forgot the pain in her sides. Her inner Dragon demanded she tear him apart. Little did the fool know she had been holding back so not to kill him outright with her strength.

Josephine gave up trying to clear her eyes, opting to try instead to feel for the king. She felt him like a gust in a rainstorm. He was laughing, the utter contempt and self-importance rolling off, as well as the shuffling of his bulky feet.

Josephine snarled again, charging at him, landing a punch to his jaw. King Verner yelled out in pain from some of his teeth breaking from the punch. He tried to backhand, but she didn't let him swing his arm even halfway. She punched him in the gut then took his legs from under him, once again pinning his arms, her right elbow in the small of his back. Her growl was lost from the cheering of her friends.

She whispered into his ear, "I am a woman, Verner, but I am also a Dragon Knight. Never forget that. I am proud of who I am and I will never try to be something I'm not. That includes being a *man*."

King Verner stared wide-eyed into the Dragon Knight's eyes. They were thin and furious, and he could see the fire that was behind them. He saw now the warrior that this person was and that he, though strong, was not strong enough to carry the burden that this warrior carried. She had withstood all his insults, making her a better warrior than he. Realizing this, King Verner did not move and said nothing as Queen Matilda called,

"King Verner has lost! Lady Josephine Drageon has won. Let one and all know she won with the honor of the warriors of the Viken!"

Josephine stood up, swaying a little to the left. King Verner jumped up despite his own pain, helped Josephine keep her balance. Josephine smiled and winced at the young king.

"I promise you I will not forget," he said.

He then took a breath and called out to the cheering crowd, "On this day, I, King Verner, swear my oath of allegiance to the Dragon Heart Alliance and its leader, Josephine Drageon. You have my word and my axe, Lady Josephine."

King Verner stepped back to kneel on the ground, the way the Viken bowed. Josephine did the same, despite her ribs screaming in pain.

"I thank you for it, King Verner."

With that, the two stood and grasp arms. All the while, the crowd yelled and chanted,

"Lady Josephine, the mighty, graceful Dragon Heart!"

Chapter Thirty-Seven
Bittersweet Win

S puck ran over and hugged Josephine with a little too much enthusiasm. Josephine winced and said, "Love you, too, Spuck, but my ribs, eh?"

"Oopsies!" Spuck released her, then healed Josephine's bruises.

Aurora tickled Josephine's head with the tip of her nose.

"That was wonderful, Josephine. A true Dragon Knight."

Josephine smiled. "Thank you, Aurora."

King Herlief joined them, smiling as Spuck and Jun were doing a victory dance singing,

"*Josephine kicked the king's butt! Josephine is the best Dragon Knight there ever was!*"

"Come, Josephine, we must drink and be merry. Let us celebrate this victory and those to come from our Alliance."

As they walked off, Indie, Spuck, and Aeolus walked behind the rest and gave Jonathan pointed looks.

Jonathan sighed, "I know! I know! I haven't forgotten! But it would be easier if you idiots weren't staring, you know!"

The three smiled, satisfied with Jonathan's reply.

"Good. Do you want me to go find you a flower?" grinned Spuck.

Jonathan growled, "If it gets you out of my hair, yes!"

Spuck laughed as he disappeared into the twilight. Jonathan glared in the general direction of where the sprite had gone.

"See, told ya he was annoying," smirked Indie as they entered the boisterous hall.

Throughout the evening, the Dragon hearts and their partners enjoyed the celebration that the Viken had set up. Josephine and Aurora were talking with a quiet King Verner about how they should go about coordinating the Viken land forces and the ships.

Not long after that, King Herlief and his sister Queen Alina came over to join the discussion. Jonathan took a seat beside the four but said little. His eyes kept wandering over to the door, waiting for Spuck to come back. Indie noticed this and started to laugh, which caught Eve's attention.

"Why are you laughing like a drunken donkey?"

Indie stopped laughing to glare at Eve for the insult.

"Keep insulting me like a crazy hoyden and I will never talk to you again."

Eve smirked and took a sip of her drink. "Is that a promise?"

"No," smirked Indie, taking a sip of his own drink, "If you must know, I'm watching Jonathan waiting for Spuck to come back from picking flowers."

Eve raised an eyebrow, then both of her eyebrows and her lips went up when she remembered what Jonathan had promised.

"Ahhhh..."

Indie smirked, "He's jumpier than when Alan has done something bad and is waiting for Mango to find out," he chuckled.

Eve giggled. She turned to see Jun playing with Flash and Aeolus, who was obviously taking pleasure in his partner's uneasiness.

"Dunno why he's so worried; Josephine is going to love finally getting a kiss from him," Eve chuckled.

"I don't think it's so much kissing Josephine that's bothering him. I believe it is us," laughed Indie.

The two glanced over to see the prince glaring right at them, showing that he could hear the two's conversation. They raised their goblets to him, which made him roll his eyes.

Spuck snuck in to the hall, tiptoeing to where Jonathan was sitting.

He whispered into his ear as Marie, Jun, Wave, FireWind, Hurricane, and Perun had joined Eve and Indie.

"Okay, got it. One Queen's Cup Lily," the sprite smiled as he tucked it into Jonathan's pocket.

Aeolus grinned at Jonathan. Jonathan glared.

"Oh, wipe that stupid grin off your face."

Aeolus's smile became even wider. "Easier said than done."

Jonathan groaned as he walked over to Josephine, knowing that a certain ten pairs of eyes were watching him. Josephine had finished talking to Queen Alina about her ships when Jonathan tapped her on the shoulder.

"Can I talk to you outside for a little bit?"

Josephine smiled and nodded. "Good idea. This smoke is getting to me."

Josephine and Jonathan walked to the doors. Aurora went to follow, but stopped when everyone in their group waved their hands and heads to stop.

Aurora watched as Josephine and Jonathan left. She then turned to the others.

"What was that all about?"

"Duh, remember what Jonathan promised?" said Perun, laughing.

Aurora smiled and said, "Ah, okay, then. But how are we going to pick on them if we don't follow?"

Spuck floated over, nibbling on some haggis. "Don't worry; we'll pick the sanity out of them later."

Jonathan took Josephine's hand once they were out of sight of their companions. He smiled and led Josephine away.

"Jonathan, where are we going?" giggled Josephine, though she knew what was going on. She may have been talking to the kings and queen, but she could still see the way Jonathan and the others were looking at each other.

"Somewhere away from *them*," he said, gesturing his head towards the hall.

The two slipped through the empty village. Everyone was still at the party. Jonathan and Josephine did not stop until they were a little past the village well, standing under the old ash tree that sat on the ledge overlooking the valley and mountains. Even in the warmer weather, there was still some snow on the highest peaks. The giant barer goats were making soft noises in their pens. The only other sound was of the breeze tickling their hair.

Josephine was smiling at him. She could feel the uneasiness, and she had to admit that she, too, had butterflies in her stomach. She broke the silence.

"I believe you promised me something if I won my match."

Jonathan smiled. "Straight to the point."

Josephine shrugged. "I grew up around boys; they are not known for beating around the bush."

Jonathan smiled broadly, "Opposite with me, royalty likes to beat around the bush. But of course, that's not me. I don't like to hurt plants unnecessarily."

Josephine could feel Jonathan's embarrassment.

"I'd hope not." Josephine chuckled and then she sighed and smiled.

Jonathan, with a light touch, pulled a stray hair away from her face. Josephine blushed at how her heart began to pound painfully loudly. Jonathan's was running just as fast.

He cleared his throat and tried to take a very business-like voice. "Now, I believe I promised you a flower and kiss, correct?"

She nodded, also trying to seem nonchalant. "Yes, you are correct, your royal highness."

Jonathan's mouth twitched as he pulled out the white lily Spuck had found. "Now, I have to give credit. Spuck found this for me."

Josephine smiled as she took the lily from Jonathan. It had a wonderfully soft fragrance.

"Then I thank you, and I will thank Spuck when I see him next."

Josephine leaned over to give Jonathan a kiss on the cheek, purposely lingering. Jonathan let out a sigh, pulling Josephine back closer to him. He leaned into her hair and she felt him breathe in her scent. Josephine took the moment to inch her hands up his arms, and she took in his scent of musk and fresh mountain air. Jonathan opened his eyes to look into Josephine's blue opal eyes.

"And now for a kiss for the lovely Ice Queen."

Josephine slowly closed her eyes as Jonathan leaned forward. How long now had she dreamed of this? Jonathan was a good match for her, she thought, as he closed in. Josephine noticed dimly her palms were sweaty as they touched Jonathan's neck as he hugged her closely. Their noses were just about to touch when a roar ripped through the village.

The two jumped. A large brown Dragon land in the middle of the village.

"That's Sheppard..." muttered Jonathan.

Josephine was paying more attention to the person riding the Dragon. She had long, shimming, silver-white hair.

"And Gazelda!" gasped Josephine, loudly enough in the night for Gazelda to hear.

She turned her head, then cupped her hands to her mouth.

"The City of Tailltiu is under attack — we must leave now!"

"Oh, no," whispered Josephine.

The two ran forward as the other Dragon hearts were rushing out of the main hall to meet Gazelda.

A lone lily lay on the ground, forgotten.

Chapter Thirty-Eight
Flight, then fight!

Gazelda took a warm drink from Queen Matilda. Sheppard, the former and now re-instated Guardian Dragon of Red Rose Castle, was sitting behind her on the stone floor. Jonathan was standing beside him with Aeolus. They escorted everyone out of the hall except Kings Herlief and Verner, Queens Matilda and Alina, and the Dragon Knights.

Once Gazelda was done taking a drink, she spoke in a tired, raspy voice, "I was heading to Tailltiu City when I got a message from Sandra. She and Storm had run into a pair of Shadow dragons and a Shadow magician, which turned out to be the Vanell brothers and Archimago. They attacked, but they got away. Turns out they were scouting the area. A vast company of shadow trolls..."

Spuck choked on his coffee. "SHADOW TROLLS?!"

Gazelda nodded as Eve and FireWind hissed.

"I don't understand it. trolls have their own brand of earth magic, why...?" muttered Marie.

"Why else? So they will have no fear and will be stronger than normal."

"But the trolls will become weaker in a shorter span of time than if they were just themselves," added Gazelda. "Anyway, seems our worries of Cetus having gathered up an army were correct. They are heading right for Tailltiu

City. Ticka and King Kingdor are gathering their forces as we speak, but they will need our strength to make them turn. Dragon heart magic with the phoenix magic will make the Shadow dragons turn tail."

"But we can't use..." started Wave, but Gazelda held up a hand.

"With the crystals, in small amounts, you can. I don't like you doing any elemental magic, but Sandra will be there, so she'll do her best to help. Besides, with the crystals just lighting up like they have been, it'll be enough that you might not have to use your elemental magic. The bulk, hopefully, the dragons can destroy with their fire."

Marie frowned. "But that'll drain our magic faster."

Gazelda nodded, with a bitter expression on her face. "Hopefully, we'll push them back faster before it is a problem."

"Do we know who else is leading the fray?" asked King Herlief.

Gazelda stole a glance at Eve before answering, "Looks to be its Diva and Riagán."

Eve dug her nails into her arms.

"I say half of us go to where Cetus is said to be, and the other half go help the Dananns," suggested Perun.

Gazelda shook her head.

"There is no guarantee. We need all the dragons to help protect the city," answered Josephine at once.

Gazelda nodded in approval. "Exactly."

"So, we need some powerful warriors to invade and destroy whatever gets in their way," smiled Josephine, looking right at King Verner, who replied with a wicked smile.

"It would be our pleasure."

Queen Alina nodded. She shared a similar appearance with her brother, only an inch shorter, with an oval-shaped face and no beard.

"The only problem is, what if there are more than a few dragons there?" Josephine bit down on her lip.

"Then I will accompany them," spoke Sheppard for the first time. "I may be old, but I can fight, or at least distract them from your fighters."

Jonathan didn't look too happy when King Herlief agreed to the old dragon's help, but he did not protest. Sheppard noticed Jonathan's feelings. He nudged him with the tip of his nose.

"I may be old, but I can hold my own. I'm an Earth Dragon; we are sturdy and known to be very stubborn in battle."

Jonathan reluctantly smiled back.

"We will call on the other kings as we go; if Cetus is where Riagán said he is, we will at least make him move somewhere else or at least rethink taking over the Viken villages," Queen Alina said with a wicked smile on her face.

"The only other problem is getting to Tailltiu City," sighed Marie. "There are too many of us for Spuck to get us to the Centaurs."

Spuck took an uneasy breath. "True, but I might be able to get as far as Red Rose City."

Josephine blinked. "Spuck, you can't! It took so much of your energy to move a few of us!"

Marie bit down on her lip then said, "Maybe if we travel to the edge of the Phoenix Mountains first. That at least would shave off a few miles to make it easier, but again, Spuck, that is a lot of your magical energy..."

Josephine did not like doing this to Spuck. She felt the uneasiness in his emotions. Spuck could die from this, and she couldn't do that to the sprite.

"Spuck, I cannot and will not let you do this to yourself. I can release you from your—"

Spuck shook his head, a small smirk on his face. "No. Let me do this, Josephine," Spuck glimpsed over at Gazelda, then back to Josephine, "James tricked me into leaving before the attack. I didn't get to help. Call this payback for tricking the trickster."

Josephine smiled, but it didn't reach her eyes.

Gazelda looked away, a few tears in her eyes.

Josephine reached over to hug the Sprite.

"Thank you, Spuck," she whispered into his ear.

Spuck nodded, then clapped his hands together, "All-righty then! Why are we still standing around? We have a city to save from utter alienation!"

"You mean annihilation, you idiot faerie," sighed Indie as they stood up to leave.

Spuck stuck his tongue out at him and said, "Whatever, Marilyn. Word Warrior."

"Why do I have a feeling they are going to be like that for the rest of our years?" muttered Eve.

As they went to pack up, King Herlief gave them one last gift.

"These are not the best saddles but they should do well for you until proper ones can be crafted," he smiled.

Josephine blinked, shocked. They were all measured out for each dragon, a simple leather saddle. There wasn't much padding, but it they would work much better than the ropes and blankets, and they could even fight with them on the dragon's backs.

All of the dragons and dragon hearts bowed in thanks.

"I humbly thank you for this very precious gift you've given us."

"Consider it as a part of our promise to the Alliance," he smiled.

"And before you go, let us give us give you proper warrior blessings. May you kill many of those who dare to raise their sword against you, and may you show great courage, and if we do not get to share a drink of your victory, at least may we share a great drink to your noble death in the heavenly hall of heroes. May it be not in vain the battle you will fight," spoke King Herlief.

Queen Alina and Queen Matilda spoke similar blessings.

King Verner bowed to Josephine, Anglii style, then added, "You will be great, Lady Josephine. I hope when we fight together in battle, I will live up to your greatness."

Josephine bowed back in Viken style then said, "I hope I can live up to your expectations of me, King Verner, and I thank you for the lesson."

King Verner's eyebrows went up in surprise but he said nothing as the dragons, Dragon hearts, young girl, unicorn, and one sprite kicked up dust, flying towards the edge of the mountains, with Sheppard's roar of "Good luck" echoing through the rocky paths.

It was almost midnight when the dragons reached the edge of the mountains. Jun, Gazelda, Indiana, and Spuck were trying to sleep as the dragons flew.

Josephine and her fellow Dragon Hearts tried to sleep, but their nerves were on edge. Josephine was biting on her lip so hard it was bleeding. This was going to be a massive battle. She was worried that she would lose her head. The only warriors she would have to lead were her own. Even so, she was terrified. Eve caught Josephine's eye and nodded her head once. Eve was as uneasy about this as she was, which made Josephine feel a little better, knowing that even headstrong Eve had concerns.

Aurora snorted, sending a wave of reassurance. Josephine smiled, acknowledging the feeling with a scratch on Aurora's head.

"We're here," muttered Perun. The dragons pulled themselves back in midair to stop. They were at the edge of the desert. Spuck yawned and stretched. The dragons landed on the soft sand, but everyone stayed mounted. The group turned to him.

"Spuck, you don't have to do this," repeated Josephine.

Spuck smiled. "Yes, I do, Josephine. We cannot let the Dananns' city fall."

Spuck then closed his eyes, taking a few deep breaths. He opened his eyes, then said, "I figured out that if I teleport us in two shorter bursts instead of one long journey, I'll be better off, or at least that's the theory. Hold on everyone! Keep your elbows tucked in."

"Just as long as we don't end up in a dung heap," joked Indiana.

Spuck smirked at Indiana, then snapped his fingers. Josephine felt the familiar feeling of Spuck's magic surrounding her and Aurora and the others. Her skin tingled as they disappeared into the darkness. A moment later, their feet slammed back on solid ground.

Spuck shook as he gasped for air. Josephine didn't even bother to see that they were on the edge of Red Rose Forest. Exactly where weeks ago Jessie Bell had called out to Josephine and Starlette. She leaned over to place a supporting hand on Spuck.

"Spuck!" cried Wave, but he held up a hand.

"I'm all right. Just a second."

Spuck waited till his breathing returned to normal, then said he was ready.

"I'll place you a couple of miles away from the city. Like I said before, I was never in Tailltiu, but I passed it on the way to Chiron's sanctuary."

"That is better than we could ever ask for," said Gazelda.

Spuck nodded. "Okay, ready to be teleported into the biggest battle yet?"

"Ready, Spuck," smiled Eve.

Spuck snapped his fingers once more into the night. Josephine and the others found themselves on the edge of the road to Tailltiu City. Spuck could not stay floating in the air. Indie reached over to help the Sprite onto FireWind's back.

"It's all right, our faerie friend. Take a pew," Indie said in a gentle tone of respect.

Spuck said nothing, but smiled at Indie with an amused/annoyed face.

"Yes, Spuck, you've done well. You need to stay here in the woods and wait till your strength has returned," ordered Gazelda, who drew her crystal sword, glaring into the night.

Josephine was so focused on Spuck she almost fell off Aurora when she awoke to her surroundings. The noise of clashing swords and coarse battle cries were ringing in the dark forest, and large fires were just visible over the treetops with smoke heavy like fog in the night air. They could also see the tops of two large, wooden catapults, and hear the twang of the ropes being cut and the wood creaking as it let go of its deadly load. Josephine's stomach quivered as she pulled her sword from its sheath. She heard the others do the same as Jun slid down so she could sit with Spuck, who leaned against a tree for support.

"Stay with him until he is better, Jun. Stay out of sight and do not join in the battle. The night should protect you from attracting attention."

Jun frowned but said, "Yes, Josephine."

Josephine stared into Aurora's left eye.

She smiled. "Shall we now go help our allies?"

Josephine swallowed the bile in her throat. She said in a shaky voice, "Yes, let's go help our friends."

Josephine's determination became stronger when she remembered Ticka was there somewhere and needed her.

Eve yelled out as the Dragons spread their wings and jumped forward into the sky to the city,

"True courage is facing your fears head on!"

Chapter Thirty-Nine
Here They Come to Save the Day

Ticka glared into the spotty darkness. She was leading the main line of warriors and a few of her father's magic wielders to help protect the enchanted gates of Tailltiu City. The large stands of fire were flickering in the wind as the Shadow trolls were climbing or firing at the great wall. Ticka jogged towards the watchtowers that were on either side of the gates. The Danann Princess jumped onto the platform where Bevan and Cori were both standing, giving the archers and magicians directions on where to fire.

Cori's red hair was pulled back into a braid, wearing only her chest armor and leg guards over her chain mail. Bevan was dressed the same, only he was wearing his wrist guards so that he could shoot arrows. Ticka was wearing a jerkin and gloves and saw both warriors glaring at her.

"My lady, you should be wearing your full armor!" complained Cori.

Ticka shook her head. The three ducked as a barrage of flaming arrows came flying over the gates. Most of the arrows missed their targets and bounced harmlessly off the magical barriers. The ones that made it had shadows on their tips. They went through the barriers and into the towers. Ticka jumped up and threw spring water on the arrows before the shadows could slink off them. Ticka placed the cork back on her water bag, then turned to her father's top magicians with a frown.

"I cannot do magic in full armor and you two know it. I don't see you wearing all your armor, either. Don't worry about me; worry about the barriers! The more and more we try to reinforce the magic, the stronger the Shadow trolls become, making our efforts useless!"

"Yes, m'lady. Should we stop trying to save the barrier to focus on the monsters?" Bevan sighed.

Ticka leaned on the railing. There were at least five garrisons of forty trolls attacking Tailltiu's front wall. She shook her head. Normally that number of trolls would never be a problem, for trolls fight amongst themselves. They would never dare attack the Dananns; under normal conditions, they would have them all cleared out. But someone, probably several someones, was using large amounts of Shadow magic to strengthen them, making them more dangerous to the regular army.

Ticka prayed that her father and the rest of the magic guard sealed away most of the inner city, so if the trolls made it through, they would have a hard time getting through to the center of the city.

The people of Tailltiu were being evacuated into tunnels and keeps under the city. Her mother and some of the non-magical guards were assisting. It would take a while to empty the city, so it was imperative for them to keep the horde back.

Ticka swung down and over to the other tower to help cut down some of the scaling ropes that the Trolls had thrown up. Bevan ran up to Ticka as she killed a Troll three times her size with her broad sword.

"Princess Ticka, we've lost two magicians on the other side! They almost overran the wall, but I and a few guardsmen killed them. We cannot go on for much longer — we only have five magicians left, including myself and you, m'lady."

Ticka slammed her fist on the guardrail, "Curse them to the darkest pits! If we only knew what they wanted!"

"Princess?"

"There is no meaning to any of this! If Cetus wanted the city, he would have sent some of his Dragon Knights and many more dark creatures than just shadows and trolls! There is reasoning behind all of this besides just attacking the city... a goal. He wants something in the city, but what? One of us from the royal family, or is it something else completely?"

Bevan frowned then looked over the battle, "Perhaps this is just a distraction, my lady. Or he is trying to weaken the Alliance by attacking us. Maybe the Centaurs are also under siege, and that is why none have answered our messages."

Ticka swore under her breath as she saw five warriors fall to the trolls. She took a few arrows from her quiver and shot all the trolls who had killed her men. Ticka then shot another troll that was crawling up the wall in front of her.

"I dare say the first suggestion is the most likely, but distract us from what? We..."

Ticka felt her stomach turn into ice and her heart rate increase tenfold.

"It's not us they are trying to distract! This *is* just a large trap! Quick, Bevan...!"

But it was too late. A large boom shook the area and everyone, troll and Tuatha Dé Danann alike, grabbed for something to hold on to. The gates were then blown into several large projectiles that killed anything in their wake, Danann and troll alike.

Ticka and Bevan protected those around them by putting up a blanket of protection with their magic. Ticka noticed; however, that she wasn't quick enough, pulling a few splinters out of her arm. She winced as she did so, then searched around wildly for the source of the explosion.

"My lady, the sky!" one soldier yelled.

There were four dragons flying into the city, one black, two red, and one brown. A red fire dragon roared as it flew down to where Ticka and the guards were standing. Ticka cursed and jumped when the red-haired Dragon heart threw a ball of fire at the gates. The others taking down the siege weapons. When Ticka rolled over to get up, she felt a sword against her throat.

"Brother," she said in a calm voice, staring into the eyes of Riagán.

He nodded his head, "Sister."

Ticka watched in anger as Diva, Lupita, Raul, and Cutler came crashing down on the soldiers protecting the city.

She cried out in anger, "*How could you, Riagán?* They were your friends, and I, your kin!"

Before her brother could speak, Diva jumped off her dragon to where Ticka and Riagán were.

"Wisteria, be so kind and kill those who are keeping the barriers up," ordered Diva in a calm voice that sent chills down Ticka's back.

The red dragon, who was much larger than FireWind, bowed her head. "Yes, mistress."

Ticka looked at the Dragon with pity. Its face was long and sad; its voice sounded dead, unlike FireWind, who spoke with fierce love. She, along with Cameron and his Dragon, began attacking those few magicians who were left. Those left jumped away, retreating into the city, but the fire dragon, when they tried to fight their way back into Tailltiu slaughtered two magicians. With those two deaths, the barriers shimmered, then disappeared, leaving the city wide open to the world.

Diva walked up to Ticka with a spring in her step. She drew her sword to shove it under Ticka's chin. Riagán had tied Ticka's arms behind her back with shadow chains.

Diva hissed, "What do we have here, a princess? Well, well, Cetus will be pleased. Perhaps if he takes both children of King Kingdor, he will gain the Danann's support."

Ticka snorted and replied with a voice of ill, "You do not know my father."

Diva sneered at Ticka. "My name is Diva. Typical Dananns, think that they are better than everyone because they are rich. They keep everything to themselves so no one else can take them over. Letting others who suffer to continue to suffer."

She pulled back a little, letting Ticka to see her face more clearly. Diva had full, elegant lips and light skin like white milk. Her red hair was dull and short. Diva's brown eyes glared at the Princess, then turned to call back her Dragon. Diva placed her sword right against Ticka's neck. Ticka could feel some of her blood trickling down her neck.

"I say we kill her and be done with it," snarled Diva.

Ticka glared into her brother's eyes. His face was blank. Diva, too, watched the outlawed prince.

"You are going to do nothing? Have you sold your soul to him? Do you not love even me anymore?" Ticka demanded of him. Riagán remained unmoved.

Diva smiled, bringing her sword up to do the killing stroke. Ticka closed her eyes, waiting for the fatal stroke, but she then opened them when she heard a dragon's roar, then several. Ticka opened her eyes in horror. FireWind, Aurora, and Hurricane were flying right at them.

"NO, JOSEPHINE, IT'S...!" Ticka yelled, but Diva hit Ticka with her hilt to quiet her.

Ticka blinked and tried to sit up. Wisteria was crouched, growling back at the new arrivals. But Ticka blinked again, confused, then she smiled. Riagán frowned at his sister, who glared back.

"Come on, Josephine Drageon! Are you finally here to take the sword that your friend was about to...?"

But then Diva stopped and glared at the Dragons. She yelled, "HEY, WHERE...?!"

FireWind hovered a few inches above the platform with Aurora and Hurricane. Ticka realized that the only one with them was Gazelda in her human form, riding Aurora.

"Surprise!" called out FireWind.

"Not clever now, are you, Diva?" laughed Ticka.

Ticka kicked Diva's legs and swung around her arms, smacking her brother in the jaw. Gazelda jumped off and cut the bindings on Ticka so she could reclaim her sword and properly punch her brother, making him fly back into the railings.

FireWind snickered and then turned to see Aeolus with Jonathan and Eve shoving back Cameron into the open. With a resounding crash, the Dragon heart and his dragon smashed into the gates, breaking them off their hinges completely, falling on top of the two.

Perun came in behind Aeolus, and he, with Marie and Josephine, was fighting Lupita and Raul and their dragons.

Hurricane stayed with Gazelda and Ticka, but FireWind, and Aurora flew back to help Perun. FireWind slammed into Lupita's dragon, and the two roared as they tried to get a grip on their foe's neck.

Ticka and Gazelda both jumped onto the other platform when Hurricane blasted Wisteria with a flame that was mixed with steaming water, sending Wisteria into the platform and destroying it. Bevan and Cori grabbed both Ticka and Gazelda and helped them up. Ticka caught her breath, then grinned at Gazelda.

"Excellent timing and counter strategy, Godmother," Ticka said with a tip of her head.

Gazelda smiled back at her. "Really? You thought I would just go in all out into the middle of the battle, yelling my head off?"

Ticka shook her head, "Not you maybe…"

Both looked up to see Eve and FireWind reunited and wreaking havoc on the Shadow Trolls below, both roaring and ripping anything within reach of their sword and claws.

"Point taken," smirked Gazelda.

Ticka turned to Cori and Bevan, "Tell father that the cavalry has arrived and that the gates and its enchantments are gone, though he probably already knows that."

"And tell him it may be prudent that he and what is left of the magical guard should come up here to help push the Shadow dragons back," Gazelda sighed as she glanced at FireWind and Eve, who in Ticka's eyes seemed to be having quite a large amount of fun ripping trolls apart with the assistance of Indiana and his bow.

"I highly doubt there will be any trolls left by the time he gets back here once Eve and FireWind are done," said Ticka with a grim smile.

Bevan was looking at the aforementioned Dragon heart and dragon with wide eyes. He left while Cori stayed with Ticka. The three women jumped down to join what was left of the guard on the ground to push back the remaining trolls. Their numbers were now half of what they had been because of FireWind's and Eve's ruthless battling along with the other dragons.

Josephine jumped on Aurora's back from Aeolus's and the two flew forward into the fray. Aurora let out a blast of ice-fire, destroying the trolls that FireWind and Eve had missed.

Josephine could only watch in wonder as Eve and FireWind ravaged the invaders. The two showed no mercy. Josephine shivered, shaking her head.

She saw Gazelda and Ticka with another Dannan climbing down what was left of the protective fence. Hurricane and Wave were sharing bouts of fire with Diva and her dragon, while Aeolus, Hurricane, and Perun were fighting with the Garcia twins.

"Ready?" asked Aurora as Hurricane dodged a lick of fire from Wisteria.

Before Josephine could answer, Diva whipped around. Her brown eyes became cold and angry.

"There you are!" Diva snarled.

Wisteria snarled, charging Hurricane, knocking dragon and rider into the trees with her tail.

"Wave!"

Eve and FireWind abandoned their fight with the trolls. FireWind spat fire at Wisteria The fire dragon growled, returning fire, the two streams meeting in midair.

Lupita called out, "Adelita!"

Josephine guessed that was her fire dragon's name, for the dragon tried to go under Wisteria to get to FireWind. But Perun was too fast for Adelita. Perun pushed the fire dragon, only to get bitten by Raul's dragon.

Raul's dragon was massive, bigger than any of the five's dragons, with lethal spikes going down the length of its spine, with a club on the tip of its tail, scales sand-colored and rough shaped like broken rocks. Perun roared and lashed out at Raul's dragon, almost dropping Marie. Aurora and Aeolus both lunged; She went up to help Perun fly back and push off Raul, while Aeolus went down to pull Wisteria's tail so FireWind could right herself. Aurora blew ice at Raul's Dragon to force him to back off.

In the end, it became a showdown; Josephine and her Dragon hearts had their backs against the forest, while Diva and her Shadow Dragons had their backs against the busted wall of Tailltiu City.

Gazelda, Cori, and Ticka killed the last of the trolls and stood at the foot of the wall, watching the showdown. Diva looked around at the slain trolls, then back at them. Diva was the calmest one there. Josephine could feel the tension from everyone, which only increased her own. She tightened her grip on Aurora. Diva then did something that sent shivers down her spine — she started laughing.

"Well, well, we have quite the legend making showdown, don't we?"

Eve snarled.

"Eve," whispered Marie. Marie was holding her hand pointlessly over the gash above Perun's wing joint.

"This was all a ploy to get us to come out of hiding, wasn't it?" called out Josephine. She didn't know why, but Josephine knew she had to keep Diva talking.

Diva tilted her head like a kitten watching an interesting bug.

"Hiding? Ha, we knew exactly what you were doing. Cetus has been building up his strength by practicing his Shadow magic on the barbarians that are the Viken. We knew you would go to them, begging for an alliance."

"You mean Cetus knew," said Josephine, going on a hunch.

Diva's face twitched, "Yes, Cetus knew what was going on."

"Did he get our little message?" smirked Eve.

Diva curled her lip and snorted at Eve. "Yes, in fact, he did. He sends his regrets..."

Josephine felt cold. She tapped Aurora, who flapped her wings to go higher. She could see the others out of the corner of her eye do the same.

At that moment, Jun and Spuck appeared at the edge of the woods.

Spuck pushed Jun back towards to the forest, "Oh, things are about to blow up..."

"What regrets?" asked Indiana.

Diva looked at Indiana in a way that made his skin crawl. Diva laughed, then raised her hands.

Josephine saw Riagán's eyes become wide, and he turned to look at Ticka as though to yell a warning.

"THAT YOU WILL DIE!"

Josephine shivered and watched in horror as shadows crawled up and over Diva as though a shawl. Then there was a massive cloud of shadows, their eyes open and staring wide as they came together in around and twisting up and behind Diva. Josephine noticed, too, that Cutler was cloaked in shadows and chanting. When the cloud reached level with them, it stopped and hung in the air, the thousands of eyes all closed.

Josephine felt the same suffocating, cold, paralyzing feeling when Riagán had attacked her, only it was a million times worse. She could hear the dragons growling from deep in their throats.

"Jun, get down!" hissed Spuck as he pulled her down under the bushes.

For a moment, it was as though time had frozen in place. The only sound was that of the dragons flapping their wings. Then, time broke.

Diva screamed; Shadows broke into two dragons. Little Shadow creatures broke off from the swirling tips of the dragons' tails, wings, and bodies. They crawled around on the ground and went in different directions, their silver eyes blinking. King Kingdor grabbed Ticka and the other two to pull them down out of the way of the massive wave of wind that exploded from when the dragons formed. Ticka, King Kingdor, and Cori made a shield of purple energy to block the charging shadows. Gazelda transformed into her unicorn form, her eyes flashing.

"You three get back!"

The Dananns did as they were asked. Gazelda charged forward, gouging out all the shadow creatures in her path with her gold horn. Ticka and the others drew their swords that were forged with the water of the Phoenix's tears. King Kingdor nodded to the warriors and together they charged forward to either side of Gazelda, hacking away at the creatures.

Josephine let out a yell as Aurora dived out of the way of one of the Shadow dragons. Josephine could hear Diva's high-pitched laughter as they dived. Aurora pulled up, then flew over to Aeolus, taking a bite out of the Shadow dragon.

She spat out the chuck of shadow, and it instantly dissipated.

Josephine felt the necklace under her shirt glow white. She pulled it out, focusing on it. She felt her magic intensify as it flowed through the necklace and out to her hand, making her skin glow with a thin layer of ice.

Jonathan watched and took the cue, focusing on his ring. Eve followed suit with her dagger alight with white fire. Eve shared a look with Josephine, and with that, the three charged while the other two dragons blew lightning and water at the other Shadow dragon to distract it.

Josephine threw out her hand to grab the neck of the one Shadow Dragon. It screamed with a thousand voices as wind, ice, and fire Dragon heart magic cut through it, ignited it like a thousand candles. The Shadow dragon exploded into foul-smelling dust.

Diva yelled out in disbelief. Josephine slumped forward on Aurora.

"JOSEPHINE!" Aurora cried, feeling Josephine suddenly weakening.

"I'm okay... just so much energy at once, I..."

Josephine almost threw up when Aurora lunged to get out of the way of the remaining Shadow dragon as it slashed at them.

Close to the ground, Hurricane and Perun were both injured, their wings slashed, dripping blood. Indie was holding onto Eve to keep her from falling.

"This is just not working," he yelled in Eve's ear.

Josephine was barely hanging on, the same with Jonathan. Aeolus and Aurora were in better shape than

Perun and Hurricane. Gazelda and company were losing numbers fast to the Shadows. She was glowing with her unicorn magic, but Gazelda was only one unicorn, and the enchanted swords would not be enough against the massive number of shadows.

Eve turned to look at Diva. The pair met eyes, anger flowing through both of them. Eve squared her jaw as Aurora and Aeolus dodged another blow from the Shadow dragon. FireWind felt Eve make up her mind and become determined.

"Eve, what are you plotting?"

Eve said, "A way to win."

She turned to Wave and Marie. Perun and Hurricane were flying steadily, but it was hard for them to get higher. Eve nodded her head at Diva. The four nodded.

"What is she up to?" asked Perun, yelling at Marie.

"I dunno, but knowing Eve, it's going to involve kicking their butts and handing them to them, and... lots of yelling," Marie yelled back.

FireWind flew around and turned in on herself to go to Aurora. Eve blinked at Josephine. Josephine took the sign, glancing over to Jonathan, who had not missed the exchange. Jonathan patted Aeolus's side. Aeolus let out a snarl. With that, they broke.

Perun and Hurricane let out jets of dragon fire at Cetus's minions. Aurora and Aeolus snapped at the Shadow dragon, taking turns flashing fire at it. FireWind dived, hard, dodging fire as she flew around, dropping Eve off on the one still whole platform.

Indie watched, trying to sort out what she was planning. Eve flagged FireWind to go help Gazelda. FireWind roared, letting off a long jet of fire on the backs of the Shadow Dragon hearts and dragon, then flew over to burn some of the shadow army on the ground. Eve stood tall on the platform just in time to see Aeolus and Aurora both gain scratches on their faces. To avoid the risk of being knocked out, Jonathan and Josephine attacked the creature with their swords, forgoing their Vanora objects.

Eve's heart sank with guilt.

"Sorry, girls; Sorry, Aunt Nina."

Eve closed her eyes, reaching deep into herself. She felt it, her feral power, her soul.

Josephine screamed when the Shadow dragon lashed out, scratching a deep gash on Aurora's face. Aurora roared, but she kept going, with Aeolus blowing hot wind at the creature, also bearing scratches.

Josephine and Jonathan stared at each other, feeling each other's fear. Perun and Hurricane were at their limit; they couldn't make any more fire from their throats because they had lost too much blood, but they were furiously clawing and biting the enemy dragons.

Even though she was so tired, Josephine noticed that Adelita and the earth Dragon would only lash out if they attacked one of the two siblings. Josephine grabbed on again as Aurora rolled out of the way of a blow. For a moment, everything looked hopeless until a new feeling reached her.

It was... warmth. Like the warmth of a fire after coming out of the rain or a warm bath. Everyone stopped to look; FireWind flew up on the other side of Aurora.

The battlefield became engulfed in an orange–red glow. Josephine's heart almost stopped when she realized it was coming from Eve. Something red was surrounding Eve, just like the Shadows had surrounded Diva. Only Josephine figured out that it was coming *from* Eve. The magic aura wrapped in smooth, gentle curls around Eve's body. At first it had no shape and then suddenly it branched out, first a pair of wings, then what looked like a neck when it snapped its head up, its eyes glowing white with green. Like Eve's eyes. Eve was standing, letting the magic come from her, her eyes closed and her arms at her sides. The dragon looked up and beyond the scene, then looked straight at Josephine. Josephine shivered, then felt something echoing in her mind.

"I'm sorry, please forgive me, brothers, sisters."

The magic aura dragon roared and flew away from Eve, its tail still connected to her. It pulsed and at the same time the dagger did, which was white hot. Eve opened her eyes, glowing white with green.

Indie felt as though someone had stabbed him in the heart, yet at the same time, like someone's arms embraced him.

Eve roared, the spirit dragon lashed out with a bright pulse, ripping the Shadow Dragon, and in the pulse's wake, it turned the rest of the Shadow army to dust.

Diva and the others all yelled out in pain. Diva screamed to her Dragon, and they all fled away from the light. But Josephine wasn't looking at them; she was watching Eve. The dragon that had come from her curled around and flew back into Eve, absorbing back into her body. Eve shared a glance with Josephine, slightly smirking before her eyes rolled back and she fell. FireWind rolled and flew, as Indie reached out and caught her. Indie gripped her tight as FireWind roared.

"EVE!"

Chapter Forty
Love Within

Eve woke up groggy with every fiber of her body burning. It dully hit her why she felt that way and almost shuddered. She blinked a few times to clear her vision and shake off the weariness. She found herself in a bed staring at the ceiling of the Tailltiu City castle. There were a few bandages wrapped around her one arm where she had gotten cut by the trolls.

Eve was able to turn her head to see Indie sitting beside her in a wooden chair. His hair was dark with soot. He had his jerkin off. She noticed his sleeves had burn marks. She couldn't see his face clearly, for he had his face in his hands.

Eve dimly thought that the fact that they were in the castle and in one piece meant that her stupid stunt with Dragon heart magic had worked. Indie shook a little, and that snapped Eve awake. She realized he was silently crying. He was crying? Indiana Phoenix was crying... over her?

Eve swallowed, then whispered, "Indie?"

His head snapped up, giving Eve a full view of his face. Indie's hazel eyes were bloodshot, meaning he hadn't slept and probably hadn't eaten, either, even after all that battling. The surge of annoyance at Indie gave Eve some of her strength back to at least sit up.

"Eve!" started Indie, leaning forward to help her.

"Indie, you stupid, bloody, foolish jerk! Why haven't you eaten or slept? You..." Eve stopped the insult in her mouth. Indie was smiling.

"*Okay, I think the lack of sleep has addled his mind,*" thought Eve.

"Well, if you can throw insults at me, that must mean you're all right," He half-laughed.

Eve shook her head at him.

"Of course, I'm all right, numbskull. I'm breathing, aren't I?" snapped Eve with a small grin.

Indie's smile slipped a little as he took a seat on the edge of the bed. "What was that you did, Eve?"

Eve sighed. She knew he didn't care so much about what she did, as it was the fact she had done something that had almost killed her.

"I did the Dragon Soul spell. I didn't know what else to do!" grumbled Eve, "I couldn't think of any other way to protect you..."

Indie stared.

"And... er, the others," blushed Eve.

Indie pulled her into a hug. "Promise me you'll never do that again," he said.

"That goes double for me!" came Gazelda's voice.

Jun had peered in to see Eve talking and had run to get the others. Gazelda walked into the room in Danann form, anger flowing off her. Eve gulped. Indie moved back a little, but he squeezed her hand.

Josephine and the others filed in. FireWind and the drag-ons were gathered by the narrow doorway. FireWind poked her snout in. Eve smiled. FireWind was mad, but more so, relieved. Eve reached out to pat her on the nose. She smiled and purred. Eve noticed that Josephine almost laughed at the sight of Indie with his hand on her hand, but before Josephine could, Gazelda yelled at Eve.

"What were you thinking? You can't do elemental magic, but yet you do the Soul spell! Of all the bloody thoughtless things to do! You could have died, you know, exposing yourself like that!"

"You know, I've seen a lot in my lifetime, Dragon heart magic included, but I don't think I've ever seen that one. Care to explain?" spoke Spuck.

Gazelda sighed in frustration. "That was the Dragon Soul Spell. She separated her soul from her body, her spirit of pure magic and heart. No Shadow creature can ever stand up to the power of a Dragon heart's pure soul. Eve, how could you do that?"

Eve stared back at Gazelda and said in a soothing voice, "It was the only way. Everyone was near their limits, and you even were losing. I just couldn't stand by and let you get overrun."

Gazelda glowered at Eve. Josephine had never felt so much anger rolling off Gazelda. Josephine shared a look with Ticka, who was also surprised at Gazelda's reaction.

"I still had some magic of my own up my sleeves..."

Spuck let his lips curl into a smirk. "Uh, well, technically, you were in your unicorn form..."

Gazelda glared at Spuck, who quickly stopped talking.

"I understand why you did, but..."

Josephine's and everyone's eyes went wide when Gazelda started to tear up.

"I forbid any of you to ever do that! You could have easily died. Unless you are in a in which you are going to die, then fine, but other than that I forbid it! I will kill you myself if you survive!"

Gazelda then turned away without looking at any of them, cursing and crying. Queen Andromeda and King Kingdor both entered the room.

"Forgive her," said Queen Andromeda.

"Why...?" started Jun, but King Kingdor spoke before she finished her question.

"James did that same spell during the Last Battle. His magic had reached its zenith, we think, because he did that. James could never do his elemental magic proper after that day."

Eve let out an uneasy breath. "I know, because Great Aunt Nina told me all about it. That's how I knew sort of how to do it. Aunt Nina explained the basics, and I went from there."

Eve shrugged at the displeased looks on Marie's and Wave's faces.

"It was the only way. I don't care what Gazelda thought. There was just no way we were going to win without something like that." Eve turned to Josephine. "I know I broke a rule about doing magic. So, what is the verdict?"

Josephine chewed on her lip. "Well, because of the extreme battle situation, I think I can let it slide this time," Josephine smiled, "But next time, you will lose second-in-command status, understood?"

Eve smiled and nodded.

Josephine looked at Queen Andromeda. "Should we...?"

Queen Andromeda shook her head. "Let her be. She'll be fine. Just let her get it all out."

"All right then. Eve, rest. We'll talk about what happened once Gazelda is better. For now, we all need to recover."

After two hours, Josephine and Aurora searched for Gazelda. They found their teacher standing in front of the Phoenix statue. Josephine knew Gazelda could hear them, but said nothing. She stood behind her teacher.

Gazelda sighed. "I am sorry for the way I acted. I was not acting like a proper teacher."

Josephine smiled, "King Kingdor explained. It's all right, Gazelda. I can sympathize."

Gazelda smirked. "Thanks to Eve, you can."

Gazelda snorted, turning her gaze back to the statue. "I shouldn't have been so harsh. Eve did what she had to do to fight and protect. That is the oath that those of the Dragon hearts take. As do the warriors," she turned her head to look at Aurora and Josephine.

"You look so much like him, Josephine."

Josephine bowed her head. "I'm his great granddaughter, aren't I? That's what Dejen meant when he said about it being in my family line? And that day when we arrived here and King Kingdor remarked I looked like someone he knew?"

Gazelda laughed, "Oh, heavens, yes, in more ways than one. Aurora... Josephine."

The two looked at her, waiting.

"You know this was a distraction to take you lot out of commission. He has something planned, and he did not want to risk you showing up. I know I am being cliché when I say this, but... tread lightly, my dear. You are going to be tested even more so than you just were. There may be no way..."

"That we'll make it back alive," finished Aurora.

"We know, Gazelda, but I have to fight. It's in my heart to fight," said Josephine, placing her hand on Aurora's neck. "I'm uncertain what will come next, but it will be as twisted evil as those Shadow dragons. We're unprepared, yet here we are; I've struggled internally, but now I know I must use my gifts to protect; if killing is necessary, I will. I will not show weakness to those who kill without remorse. We are all there is, so..." Josephine sighed, as did Aurora, who finished the sentence.

"We fight."

Gazelda nodded, "Ah, how we, the old, forget the prowess and stubbornness of the young and that they, too, can be wise and see what we, the old, have overlooked."

"That's why the old and the young have to learn to listen and work together," smirked Josephine.

Gazelda matched it as well as she could as a unicorn.

"Do we have any idea how they stopped the messages from the Dananns to the Centaurs?" asked Gazelda, moving her gaze back to the statue.

"From what King Kingdor could figure, Diva and the others were sitting and waiting for the messengers. They..." Josephine shuddered, but Gazelda didn't bother to ask her to say anymore.

"How did the warriors fare?"

"They lost nearly two-thirds of their front guard and there are only now seven magicians left, counting the King and Ticka, not counting the one that is with the Centaurs."

Aurora growled, "Gazelda, you wouldn't have any ideas on why they....?"

"AURORA! JOSEPHINE! GAZELDA!"

The three turned to see Ticka running towards them.

"Just got word from Red Rose City. Cetus has been spotted."

Eve and Indie were walking quietly through the gardens behind the castle. Indie then helped Eve sit down on the bench. Even as they sat down, Eve did not remove her hand from Indiana's shoulder. She then leaned her head against him. Indie kept staring straight ahead into the daffodils. Both said nothing, but their minds were raging.

"I want to tell her so badly, but do I dare? I know she cares for me, there's no doubt of that, but in that way... that I do for her..." thought Indie.

"Is he ever going to say anything? I know he has feelings for me. I can sense them, but he feels so confused right now.

Come on, Indie, you never have problems telling me what's on your mind any other time of the day," wondered Eve.

Indiana sighed, figuring he'd best say something. He turned to look into Eve's fiery green eyes.

"I have a recovery gift for you."

Eve raised an eyebrow as Indie reached into his bag and pulled out the piece of wood that he had been carving since Mango's. Only now the piece of wood was shaped like Flash. She smiled, hugging the little figure, then showed it to its model. He had slipped into the garden, chasing fireflies. Flash sniffed at it, then slipped off to chase more bugs. Eve smiled and wrapped her arm around Indie's shoulder.

"Thanks. I would have never guessed you as the crafty type."

Indie smirked and wrapped his arm around Eve's shoulder. "I was making it for the squirt, but I thought you needed a little something."

Eve grinned, and then the two went back into a slightly awkward silence. Indie tried once or twice to say something, but the words wouldn't come out as anything more than sighs. Eve had to bite her tongue before she sighed. Indie was nervous. Eve wasn't much for waiting. So, she decided to help him a little.

Little did she know that at that moment, FireWind and Jun had walked into the garden on a whim to discover the two.

Jun stopped FireWind when she noticed the couple. They hid as far back as they could in the trees that surrounded the garden. FireWind went to say something, but Jun placed her hand on FireWind's mouth, a finger to her own.

Jun tried not to giggle as Eve said, "Indie, you know what I think about you?"

Indie's eyebrow went high on his forehead and in a nervous voice said, "Uh, a good friend, right?"

Eve let out a snort. "I think you are an overbearing, self-absorbed, sneaky, cocky, obnoxious boy, and one of the greatest warriors I've met. At least, currently. And somewhat sweet when you want to be."

It took Indie a moment to absorb that little piece of information. Eve's smiling face was making it hard for Indie's mind to focus.

Once he got his brain to work again, he smiled wide, and he found his voice again, "Oh, really?" he smiled with a cheeky expression that Eve had started to really like, "You, Eve Grace, are a hotheaded hoyden, and just as overbearing; also, a narrow-minded, loud, elegant, kind-hearted, powerful knight... and those are the reasons why I... love you."

Indie whispered the last part, standing up and taking Eve's hands. Eve stood with him, matching his smile. Indie almost laughed; he had always imaged that Eve would stare at him funny, raise her eyebrows, heck, maybe even punch him, but she was smiling at him. Then she did something that was not in Eve's range of normal reactions. She hugged him tight, then teared up. Indie was a little dazed as he hugged her back.

"Confused, huh?" she laughed.

"Yeah, guess you would know that."

Eve sighed, "When my spirit left my body... all I could think about was all of you. Especially you. If I had died..."

Indie squeezed her back. "You didn't, though. But I am warning you right now, if you become my..."

Eve glared at him, warning him to watch his wording.

"Beloved," he paused. She smirked instead of wearing her normal look of distaste. He continued, "That you can't sacrifice yourself like that every time we get in a tight spot."

Eve nodded, "But you must understand, Indie, that I won't put up with any of the protecting the woman crap. I want a man to fight with me. We fight side by side, not in front of me nor me in front of you... If we are going to do this, we do it together as equals, in battle and everything else," she said, reaching her hand up to stroke his nose.

Indie leaned down so she could do so. For a minute she did that, and then she let her hand drop. She gazed back into his bright hazel eyes as he pulled back her fiery hair. He leaned close to her face. When they were a quarter of a centimeter from touching their lips, Indie whispered,

"Eve..."

Eve shushed him. "Just shut up and kiss me, you nitwit."

Indie did as he was told; he wasn't going to argue with a hot-headed Dragon heart.

Jun's jaw dropped. FireWind smiled, showing all of her sharp ivory teeth.

"Spuck won the bet!" Jun whispered.

FireWind didn't really hear Jun; she was focusing on the pure love and joy emanating from Eve. They had spoken about Indie so much. She was happy that Eve finally admitted her feelings to herself and Indie.

The two watchers smiled when Indie pulled Eve up and placed her feet on his own. That was when the two watchers got into serious trouble. Jun's foot slipped from FireWind's head, hitting the rose bushes with a loud rustling sound. Both froze, staring at the kissing couple. Eve pulled back with a confused look on her face.

"Did you hear something?"

"*Crap!*" thought Jun and FireWind.

"Hmm?" said Indie. He was too busy enjoying Eve's perfume and the kiss.

"Eh," Eve shrugged and returned to Indie.

Jun and FireWind paused, and upon realizing they weren't going to be flung across the courtyard, exhaled in unison. FireWind figured the two had pushed their luck to the maximum, and with measured steps, backed up and left the garden. As the two were leaving, Wave and Hurricane came rushing towards them.

"Wave, what's wrong?" asked FireWind.

Eve and Indie pulled apart, listening. Eve could feel the fear in Wave.

"It's Red Rose Castle — they're under attack!"

Indie and Eve did not hesitate; the two ran out and together the friends ran up the steps of the castle.

Chapter Forty-One
Good Ol' Loop Holes

E veryone gathered in the throne room. The last to enter were Eve, Indie, and FireWind, the latter two helping Eve walk. Well, they didn't really need to, as Eve had a cane that Ticka had given her, but Indie needed an excuse to hold her waist, so she pretended to have left it in the garden.

Josephine and Aurora noticed that Jun and FireWind were a bit on the scared side, while Indie and Eve were acting strangely calm and supportive. When Josephine gave the young girl and dragon a quizzical look, they shrugged. Josephine raised her eyebrow at Aurora, who also shrugged.

Gazelda walked forward and stood beside King Kingdor, who had a letter in his hand.

"What is going on, your majesty?" asked Perun.

He sighed. "It appears we were right about the distraction. I just received a message from Sandra Heartwell."

Gazelda glared, "What...?"

Kingdor held up his hand. "She is at the Centaurs."

Gazelda did a double take. "What? She's supposed to be guarding the queen in Red Rose City! How...?"

King Kingdor explained, "Apparently, she got a message from you, Gazelda, telling her that Sheppard was returning to Red Rose Castle and that she needed to report to the

Centaurs. She says here it was your handwriting as far as she could tell, and so she and Storm left. When they got to the Centaurs and Jabari told her about us being attacked, she sent this off right away."

Gazelda rubbed her forehead. "He must be after the shrine. That is the only reason he would really have to attack it."

Jonathan's head snapped up. "You mean that giant stone tablet that sits in the middle of the garden?"

Gazelda nodded. "The elemental tablet. Part of the reason King Joshua Falcon chose that particular spot to rebuild the kingdom was because of the tablet. Taranis placed it there with the original five Dragon hearts."

"What is it for?" asked Indie.

"Part of my duty as guardian of Red Rose Castle was to guard that shrine, as well as the dragon and wizard of the castle. The tablet was created by Taranis, Quickstrike, and the others after the last battle of the first Shadow War. That tablet marks where the six stood with their dragons standing behind them. The witch who created the stone engraved it with the Dragon language, not the written language but the actual spoken language of the Dragons, onto the tablet. The spoken language holds the most magic."

Jun tilted her head in confusion. "How can the spoken language be more powerful?"

Gazelda smiled, "Words are powerful, Jun, but only when someone speaks them is when they hold meaning. Reading a word and actually saying it aloud are two different things. The way it is said can hold as much power as the word itself. The Dragon hearts stood in that spot using..." Gazelda's lip curled.

"The Dragon Soul spell," said Josephine, remembering that passage now.

Gazelda nodded, "Yes. You saw what Eve's soul did to those shadows; well, imagine ten times the number of Shadows ordered around by a much more powerful magician Zankeno, then times Eve's power by six with the help of Dragon Magic."

Spuck let out a whistle. "That must have lit up the place."

Ticka smirked. "According to the *Dragon Heart Chronicles*, the light was greater than ten suns. Anything that was possessed by a shadow was destroyed. Many souls were saved that day from shadows, thanks to the ancient Dragon hearts."

Gazelda added, "After the Red Rose Kingdom was established and the Dragon Knight Alliance founded, they placed another spell on it, a protection spell. As long as there is a Dragon an/ or a Dragon heart on the grounds of Red Rose Castle, shadows cannot enter. Even after all these centuries, the power that Taranis and the Dragon Knights gave off still saturates the earth. It has a small level of protection. If a dragon is there, it strengthens the spell. But without either..."

"The spell is weakening to where, if the Shadow is strong enough, it can enter the castle. It is the only spell left on the castle. The various other spells that were there to guard the home of the Alliance were weakened and/or gone once the king got rid of the Marvel twins," said Marie in a sour voice.

"So that's why Father kept Sheppard," said Jonathan, but that confused him further, "But if Father was on Cetus's side, then why he didn't send away Sheppard so that Cetus could enter?"

Josephine frowned, then said, "He may not have been on Cetus's side. Your father distrusts magicians, you said? So perhaps he did not trust the Marvel twins and was worried about Shadow Magicians, so he kept Sheppard around to protect against them. Bet he figured that if he couldn't order Sheppard around, he could just order the warriors to fight him."

Marie then interjected, "Yes, that and the fact there is a pact with the guardian Dragon to always follow the king of the kingdom. Also remember you were born there Jonathan, and you living there would have kept the magic steady."

"Yet, wouldn't it work if he was with his dragon or any of the others? Shayla doesn't have Shadow magic..." muttered Eve.

"I have a theory on that," said Gazelda.

"This is all fine, but can we go now?" asked Jonathan.

Josephine gave him a sympathetic face.

"Yes, we need to leave now. I'll send for Sandra to come as fast as she can to help us. Sheppard is out of range, but I will call on Turku to see if there is any way he can help."

Queen Andromeda frowned. "What about Mina?"

Gazelda's face became dark. "She will not help us, nor could she if she wanted to."

Her mood had become dark and resentful, so no one asked anything more.

"Okay, then I'll just go and..." started Jun, but Gazelda cut her off.

"You are not coming. In fact, you, Spuck, and Indiana should stay here."

The three instantly protested.

"I understand why the squirt has to stay–" – "Humph," muttered Jun, "–but no way am I staying. I am a warrior, and I'm coming."

Josephine smiled. Indiana had taken the oath of a Dragon Warrior the moment they had been told that Eve was going to be fine.

Gazelda shook her head. "Regardless, this will be a battle of the Dragon hearts. Cetus is going to use his Dragon hearts to corrupt the tablet so that can increase their powers. There was a reason the naming ceremonies took place there, for a Dragon heart's and dragon's powers are slightly increased when they stand there. You wouldn't stand a chance against those shadow creatures even with your sword, Indiana."

"Okay, fine, but what about Eve? If I can't, she shouldn't."

Eve glared at him.

Josephine said, "We are going to need all the Dragon hearts we can get. Eve, do you think you can fight?"

Eve leaned away from Indiana so she could stand straight. "Yes, if I have to, I will."

Gazelda frowned. "I don't think you should, but it is in the end your call, Josephine. What say you?"

Josephine glanced around at each of her friends' faces. Josephine saved Aurora's for last. Aurora was radiating confidence, which gave Josephine confidence in what she decided.

"Indiana, Spuck, and Jun will stay here. Red Rose Castle is going to be crawling with shadows, and you three do not have the magic to protect you."

The three all looked at Josephine angrily, but said nothing. Gazelda nodded, as did the others.

"All right then, let's pack up and get out within the next hour; we have a castle to save."

With that, they gathered their things. Ticka, with Cori and Queen Andromeda's help, made sure that their weapons were in working order and gave them half-armor. It would be too much weight if they wore full armor, as the dragons weren't that strong yet to take the weight. Josephine found that the Danann's armor was rather light, and it shimmered, showing that it had been made with Phoenix Spring water.

While Josephine and the others were packing, Spuck, Indiana, and Jun all tried their best to convince the dragons and Dragon hearts that they needed to come.

"Come on, Eve, you know you aren't going to be able to fight without me. You need someone to cover your back. You're barely healed," pleaded Indie as Eve was packing her battle gear. She sighed as she plopped on her bed to change her shoes.

"Indiana, normally I would agree with you, but the amount of Shadow Magic..."

Indie snorted, "Eve, if I am going to be a part of this little quest for justice, you know that I am going to face tons of Shadow Magicians, and what is the point of being a Dragon

Warrior if every time you face Cetus, you leave me somewhere to tap my foot and babysit Jun!"

Jun, who was following Wave around, heard Indie and
stuck her head in and said, "Hey, nobody is babysitting me!
I..."

Indie and Eve glared at her, which motivated Jun to move
on. Once she was out of earshot, Eve jumped up to grab her
hunting knife and strapped it to her leg.

"Look, Indie, I just..."

Indie grabbed Eve to make her look him in the eyes.
"What were you saying earlier about fighting side by side as
equals?"

Eve closed her eyes so Indie's eyes would not pull her will
down any further.

"Indie, I do want you to come, but Josephine's order is final.
I can't break it, nor can you!" she said, raising a finger at
him when she felt his frustration to her answer, "Next time,
I promise," she said, pulling his face down so she could kiss
his bottom lip.

Jun was not having any better luck with her guilt trip. She
tried Wave, but Wave would not have it.

"Jun, I know you have lived on the streets since you were
little and that you are tough. We know that. But Jun, you
don't have enough experience, not to mention the Shadow
creatures."

Jun muttered something under her breath that Wave
didn't hear, fortunately, and went off to find Josephine and
Aurora, only to bump heads with Spuck.

"OW! Spuck, watch it!"

Spuck sighed, "If you are going to try Josephine, give it up. Before I could even open my mouth, she yelled me out of the room, saying that her order was final. Honestly, what good is being two-hundred years old if you can't show off your cultivated wisdom?"

"Pulling pranks is your idea of wisdom?" asked Jun, raising an eyebrow.

Spuck snorted, "I'll have you know pranking is a very refined art. It takes planning..."

"More like an underhanded art, like the art of the kageshi," smirked Eve, coming out of her room with Indiana on her heels.

"I resent that! Kageshis knows nothing about being subtle and ironic," said Spuck, folding his arms and legs in midair.

"Oh, yeah, Spuck, you're really subtle, I'll give you that," snorted Jonathan with Aeolus as they came up behind the sprite.

"Jonathan..."

Jonathan shook his head.

"If you really want to help, stay here. We have to leave now," he said, turning to Eve and FireWind.

"Right."

Eve gave Indiana one last harsh look before she and Jonathan left with FireWind and Aeolus behind them.

Josephine and Aurora were sitting near the remains of the gates of Tailltiu City. Debris was everywhere, and the ground was scarred with burned patches of grass. The smell from the battle still lingered in the air, making her stomach churn.

"Terrified?" asked Aurora in a casual voice.

Josephine laughed.

"Don't suppose a dragon would be?"

Aurora smiled. "Not really. From what I saw, their Shadow magic has weakened them and that the bond between the dragons and their partners is weak as well. Not only that, I enjoy fighting. You forget that dragons, as intelligent as we can be, are also ruthless monsters."

Josephine looked at her dragon partner with skepticism. "Ruthless monsters?"

Aurora shrugged, "Okay, maybe not monsters, per se, but you saw Eve and FireWind. We dragons and Dragon hearts were meant to fight. If we weren't, we'd be fluffy little bunnies or tiny salamanders."

Josephine laughed as the others came out to join them. She exhaled when she saw Indie, Jun, and Spuck. Jun glared at Josephine, then ran over and hugged her.

"Please?" she whispered.

Josephine sighed again, finally understanding her aunt and mother a little better when it came to things like this. Though the most Josephine had asked for was to go with father on hunting trips, not battle against the betrayer of the Dragon hearts. Though, as she thought about it, that was exactly what leaving with Dejen was all about.

"No, and you know why."

Jun nodded and slipped back; her head bowed in defeat. Gazelda came by at that moment in her human form. She was dressed in a simple green linen gown, her choker shining in the sun, her sword at her side.

"Aren't you going to...?" started Spuck, but Gazelda shook her head.

"No point in wearing armor. It's not like clothing, and I'll need to be able to go back into my normal form on the fly." Gazelda smiled at the sprite, kissed Jun on the cheek, then sighed at Indie. She patted him on the shoulder, then jumped on Aurora's back.

King Kingdor came out to see them off. "As soon as we can secure things here, we will come at once," he said.

"Ready?" Josephine asked, not really sure that she could say she was.

Everyone said yes. With one last look at the trio being left behind, the dragons unfurled their long, leather wings and jumped into the air, soaring over the forest, out of sight. Josephine felt as though her stomach had bottomed out and it wasn't from the take-off.

Gazelda gave her a squeeze and whispered as though she sensed Josephine's emotions, "Don't worry, we will stop them."

Josephine patted her teacher's hand, but that wasn't really what she was worried about. Aurora blinked one eye at her as they flew. Josephine stared at the backs of her new friends, worrying what it would cost them to stop him.

Spuck, Indiana, and Jun watched as the five dragons disappeared over the forest's horizon. Spuck pursed his lips.

"We should be going with them."

Indie snorted, "For once I agree with you, faerie."

Jun was rubbing her eyes and glaring.

Indie noticed, "Jun, even if Spuck and I could go, you know you would have to stay behind."

Jun glared at Indie. "Don't tell me, because I don't have enough training? They don't either, you know. I could tell Josephine was worried that they were going to face Cetus with so little training. Heard her telling Aurora so. I want to help fight in any way I can. Besides, I've gotten good with that whip that Ticka gave me, and if I used a few of Spuck's little bits..."

Spuck smiled. "You got a warrior's spirit, kid. I'll give you that. Whatever clan you are descended from had to have a lot of what I call 'warrior's spunk'."

"Yeah, well, there isn't enough 'warrior's spunk' between the three of us to get to Red Rose City."

Ticka walked up beside Indiana. "I know what you mean. I'd go myself, but I'm needed here. Josephine needs you three."

Indie smirked, "Think so highly of yourself to think the three of us make up just one of little old you?"

Ticka rolled her eyes. Jun stomped her foot.

"Well, I'm going!"

Spuck sighed. "And how are you going to do that?"

Jun glared at Spuck. "You are going to take me."

Spuck sighed again, rubbing his forehead, "Kid, I swore an oath to Josephine that I would follow her orders. I can't do that, and Indie swore a warrior's oath to Josephine, too, so we're stuck."

Jun blew a raspberry. "But I didn't!"

Indie laughed, "Jun, I doubt that makes much of a difference. She's your 'mom'; I think it's a given that you are supposed to obey or else."

"Not always true," came a voice from behind them. The four turned around to see Sandra Heartwell and Storm walking towards them.

"Dragon Master Heartwell," said Ticka in a shocked voice.

Sandra smiled, bowing her head. "Princess Ticka."

Indie did a double take. Gazelda, of course, had mentioned the last apprentice of James Dracolus, but to see her was something else. She had the appearance of someone in her late thirties, with minimal wrinkles. Her mid-length blonde hair pulled back into a ponytail. Sandra was wearing a chest plate along with arm and leg guards. The chest armor was decorated with the symbol of the Dragon Heart Alliance, while the leg and arm guards were embossed with lightning bolts done in a relief design.

Spuck jumped on her.

"SANDRA! STORM! HOW I'VE MISSED YOU!"

Sandra stood in shock for a moment, then patted the sprite on the head.

"Spuck the Sprite Goodfellow, long time no see. Didn't know you had come out of your old haunt to help."

Spuck was still hugging Sandra, who pulled him off. Spuck blushed. "Sorry. Just nice to see a really old friend. And you smell nice... peaches and vanilla..."

Sandra rolled her eyes. "I will take the more flattering interpretation of that first statement. Thanks, Spuck."

Sandra smiled and turned to Indie and Jun. "So, you must be Indiana Phoenix and Jun, Josephine's ward, am I right?"

Jun went wide-eyed at the Dragon heart master.

"Yeah, that would be us," smiled Indie.

"How do you know me?" asked Jun.

Sandra smiled at Jun. "Josephine told me all about you and the fun you lot had at Drake City. But, more about past excursions later. We have a castle to save. Won't be the first time for me nor, I have a feeling, the last. So..."

Indie raised his hand to get Sandra to stop talking, "Wait a minute, there is no 'we'. Josephine ordered us to stay here. The two of us," Indie pointed to Spuck and himself, "Swore oaths, and we can't break the orders that Josephine gave us."

Sandra let out a whistle and smiled as King Kingdor and Queen Andromeda came to join them.

"Okay. Well then, let's get moving," said Storm.

Indie stared at the lightning dragon, then his partner. "What part of 'we have to follow our oaths' do you two not get? You were part of the old Alliance; you know the consequences."

Sandra looked at King Kingdor, who shrugged. Queen Andromeda grinned.

"Think about it. You swore an oath to protect the Dragon Heart Alliance, right?"

Indie and Spuck looked at each other. "Well... yes..."

Sandra said, "In order to protect the Dragon Heart Alliance, you have to be around the Dragon heart leader, right? To protect its functioning? And if said leader gives you an order that counters the protection of the Alliance, then the warrior can see fit to… circumvent the order."

Spuck grinned, "Hahaha, I knew there was a reason I liked you, Sandra. Quite the devious mind."

Sandra pouted at him, insulted, "I am not devious; I am just well-read in the laws of the Dragon Heart Alliance."

King Kingdor leaned to his wife and whispered in a loud tone, "James' theory was right; she was a lawyer in another life."

Sandra rolled her eyes. "Funny, he didn't believe in reincarnation of people's souls, but whatever."

"Why do I have a feeling that you know that loop hole well?" smirked Indie.

Storm cleared his throat. Sandra glared at him. "We are wasting sunlight here, warriors. Let's move out."

Indiana, Spuck, and Jun smiled and then looked at Ticka, who looked at her father.

"Go. We can look after things here. I doubt there will be any more attacks, and Jabari's warriors should arrive within the hour."

Ticka nodded.

Storm sighed. "I know I am a strong dragon, but I'm built for speed, not a warrior delivery service."

Spuck smiled widely. "I got that covered. I'm better now that I've had a good, long nap."

Indie snorted, "Nice, long, loud nap. You snore like a troll."

Spuck rolled his eyes.

"Spuck, could I use some of your weapons?" asked Jun. Spuck glanced at Indie, who shrugged.

"Jun, you really shouldn't…"

Jun's eyes narrowed. She had heard enough of their protests. She grabbed Spuck and put him in a headlock and began rubbing his head hard.

"I–am–going–so–just–give–me–some–stuff!"

Spuck looked at Indie, who rolled his shoulders again. He really didn't think it was a good idea to let the young girl come, but either way, she was going to come, so they might as well accept it.

"Thanks for nothing, Indie," he gasped, finally being released from Jun's steel grip. "Fine, but if she gets into trouble, I'm blaming you."

Spuck snapped his fingers, and the trunk that Josephine had seen in Spuck's home appeared. He unlocked it, then pulled out a belt and started hooking things to it.

"Okay, smoke shots, net shots, curry power, and my personal favorite when dealing with rogue dragons and Dragon hearts..."

Sandra and Storm both groaned, putting their hands and claws over their respective noses.

"Essence of Dragon Arum," Spuck smiled, "Been annoying and overcoming Dragon/Dragon heart senses for years."

Spuck placed the glass vile into his pocket and magick'd away his trunk, then gave Jun some of his shots.

"Okay, ready to go?"

The four nodded.

Sandra rubbed her hands together. "Good. Okay, let's go. I owe an old friend a swift kick in the nether regions, and I'd rather not be any later. It's long overdue."

Chapter Forty-Two
Creeping Shadows of Red Rose Castle

It took them a few hours to reach Red Rose City from Tailltiu City. None of them said a word as they flew, not that they would have been able to anyway, as the wind was whipping into their faces from the dragons flying at high speed. Perun, being the fastest, was the head point of the group. Josephine was trying not to think about what was waiting for them at the Red Rose Castle, but she knew Jonathan was — the worry and tension was rolling off him.

The castle came into view on its solitary hill. The Dragons skidded to a stop mid-air.

"No," whispered Jonathan.

There was black, thick smoke bellowing from the castle. Aeolus flapped his wings, dived, and then evened out, heading to the castle.

"Jonathan!" yelled Josephine, and the rest of the dragons followed Aeolus while the girls drew their swords. Their blades shimmered in the orange sunset.

"Forget strategy, Ice Princess," said Eve. "This is killed or be killed."

The smoke became thicker in the air as they went along, clogging their noses and making them sneeze, even the dragons. Josephine could hear shouts of alarm along the wall as they flew closer.

"It's just like before," muttered Gazelda.

Josephine realized with a jolt that Gazelda was talking about the last time Cetus had attacked the castle. Perun reached Aeolus with FireWind and the others a few feet back.

Jonathan and Aeolus passed over the half demolished front barrier wall of the castle when out of nowhere, a massive wave of Shadows grabbed Aeolus around the middle and pulled Jonathan from the Wind Dragon's back. Aeolus roared and started biting the churning black chains. As soon as Aeolus was free, the chains reformed, so the dragon began trying to drive them off with fire. Jonathan was struggling, trying to reach for his sword, but he was completely immobilized.

Josephine's necklace flashed brightly, as did Jonathan's ring. The shadows recoiled at the bright light, dropping both knight and dragon. Aeolus unfurled his wings, flying downwards as Jonathan scrambled back on while Aeolus leveled out. Perun stopped behind them.

"Look!" yelled Marie.

Claudette, the Shadow magician, appeared on the wall; arms outstretched from under a black cloak. She smiled at them.

"*Bonjour*, my dragons. Welcome to your DEATH!" she yelled, and a massive wave of shadows curled up above her.

"Let me handle her," whispered Gazelda in her ear.

Aurora snorted, then flew forward, dodging the bat-like shadows that were flying straight at them. One came close to biting the side of Aurora's head, but Josephine lashed out with her sword, cutting the creature in half.

Gazelda leaped off Aurora. The ice dragon stopped flapping her wings to pull herself back away from the wall.

With her sword unsheathed and necklace glowing, Gazelda jumped down upon Claudette, slashing at her cloak. Josephine then realized with another jolt to her stomach that the cloak was really made of shadows.

"Aurora, let's get rid of Claudette's shadow minions," said Josephine.

Aurora roared, unleashing a jet of ice-fire on the creatures. FireWind, Hurricane, and Perun added blasts of white lightning, orange fire, and jets of boiling water fire. Within that second, Josephine realized Jonathan was nowhere in the mix. She whipped her head around in a panic to see Aeolus blasting away shadows before entering the front courtyard of the castle.

Josephine tried to yell to him, but she couldn't, with Aurora flying around. Her voice was lost in the smoky air. Wave noticed what happened. She nudged Hurricane to fly beside them. She leaned over to speak right into Josephine's ear.

"Come on, let's follow him. Gazelda has Claudette. We've slowed down her shadows. We can't let Jonathan go in by himself."

Josephine waved her arms at the other four. They paused. Josephine pointed toward where Jonathan had gone.

Gazelda paused long enough to tilt her head to say, "Go," before taking another lunge at Claudette.

Each Dragon let out one more blast of elemental power on what was left of the shadows then flew right into the courtyard of the castle. The ornate stone fountain that sat in the middle of the yard was demolished into a pile of rubble.

Perun, Aurora, FireWind, and Hurricane landed just beyond the fountain. The doors of the castle were in pieces and cracks were all over the grounds and the grass was charred. Jonathan and Aeolus were not to be found.

"Where are they?" growled FireWind.

With a bang, a body flew out of the castle and crumpled into a pile on the grass. The girls grabbed their swords, only to realize that the person was an unconscious Archimago. They blinked, then looked up to see Mango. She was wearing a long moss-green colored dress with a sour look on her face. Josephine thought she knew why Mango was cross — her lovely hair was smoking.

"Can't believe I let him get close enough to light my hair on fire," she muttered.

Mirage flew in at that moment, landing on the witch's shoulder. Alan appeared beside Mango. She walked over to place the heel of her boot on Archimago's neck. Mango curled her lip at him, then finally looked up to notice the girls and Perun.

"Oh! Josephine! About time you lot showed up! Cetus tricked his way in. I wasn't able to keep the magic up for long. This thing..." Mango kicked the insensible Shadow Magician in the head, "stormed in, trying to take the queen and the prince Jeremiah. "

"Fortunately, Mango is as skilled as she was in the days of the old Alliance," came a voice behind Mango.

Mango smirked as the queen and the second eldest son of the Red Rose Kingdom walked out. Queen Adriana was wearing a simple blue dress, a short sword at her hip. Beside her was Jeremiah. He had a broadsword in his left hand, wearing black-rimmed glasses. Josephine in an instant saw the resemblances between Jonathan and the two Falcons in front of her. The queen had the same brown eyes and nose, and Jeremiah was almost as tall as his brother and had a similarly shaped face.

"Good thing I sent my other two children away, or we would have even more problems. The guards are dealing with shadows all over the castle as we speak."

Josephine and the others bowed as Queen Adriana walked to them. The queen smiled at her.

"Worry about formalities later, Lady Dragon heart. You are the one named Josephine?"

Josephine smiled as she straightened up. "Yes, your majesty. Did you see your eldest son fly past?"

Queen Adriana frowned, "No, I did not. I heard someone yelling, but the voices disappeared into the back courtyard."

"*I KNOW WHERE HE IS!*" yelled a singsong voice.

They all tensed as they looked up to see Diva sitting on the roof of the southern tower. Wisteria was curled around the tower, her head resting on the tip. FireWind let out a deep-throated growl.

"Cameron has his friend Jamard, or so he told him. He's gone to the garden. I am supposed to kill all of you," Diva smiled, looking at Eve.

"Leave Diva to me."

"Eve, you haven't recovered..." started Wave, but Josephine cut her off.

"Go. Mango, your majesties. I believe it would be best if you go back into the castle."

The queen rolled her lips, but she nodded and pulled Jeremiah backwards into the castle. Mango snapped her fingers and green energy encircled Archimago. An invisible force pushed him aside into the wall, where he slumped to the ground.

Mango frowned. "Beware, all the protective magic has been broken now. There is nothing left to expel the shadows if that wasn't already obvious. When he was here last, Cetus stripped some of it and whatever magic he used has now dissolved what was left before I could repair it. Most of the troops are fighting in the castle, trying to dispel shadows."

She nodded to Josephine and followed the Falcons into the castle with the Marvels in her wake. Josephine and the other two mounted their partners and flew past Diva.

Diva watched the six of them fly off with a look of indifference. Once they had flown past, Diva jumped down on the windowsill, then to the ground. Wisteria stayed where she was but slithered further up the tower.

"Well, well, old friend, we finally get to fight in battle," she grinned.

Eve said nothing, felt nothing as she took a stance. FireWind did the same behind her.

"You are going to die," Diva laughed.

Eve rolled her eyes. "Well, duh, of course I'm going to die. FireWind, you, and your little pet salamander, we're all going to die. Just a question of when and, Diva, if I were you, I'd start praying."

Diva curled her upper lip and growled.

Eve smirked, "Here, doggie, doggie."

Diva pulled her sword out. The two swung at each other as the dragons let out earth shattering battle roars.

Josephine's spine shivered as she heard the fire dragons' roaring. Wave was trying not to cry.

"It's okay, Wave. Eve is a big knight, she can..." Marie yelled out as, out of nowhere, Adelita attacked Perun, pushing him through the air.

Aurora grabbed wildly at Adelita's tail, digging her claws in deep, breaking some of the orange scales and drawing blood. Lupita slid down Adelita's back to slash Aurora's claws, making her let go. Hurricane fired a gush of firewater into Adelita's face.

Adelita roared in pain and crashed onto the roof of the castle. Lupita jumped off and hugged Adelita's face. She shook herself like a dog shaking off water, then stood back up. Lupita's panic disappeared. She jumped back on her partner's back.

Josephine and the others then turned to see Cutler. He frowned.

"Aw, is Eve fighting with Diva?"

"Josephine, go, find Jonathan. We'll take care of these two," said Hurricane.

Perun and Marie growled in agreement.

"But you'd..."

"They will kill Jonathan faster if you don't back him up," interrupted Marie, her yellow eyes on Cutler.

"Just go, Ice Princess, we've got speed on our side," said Perun, running his tongue across his teeth.

"Right," said Aurora and dived.

Cutler went to follow, but Perun rammed into him and his dragon while Hurricane dived at Adelita, mouth spewing out streams of water.

Aurora lashed out her tail at Cutler's dragon's head as they passed, giving Perun the chance to bite the red dragon's neck.

"Aurora, let's find them alive," Josephine whispered as they flew to the gardens.

"Agreed," whispered Aurora back as they reached the garden.

It was massive, at least as long as the castle, maybe even twice as long. Large green hedges with little red berries fenced the garden off. Flowers of all sorts were blooming in geometric patches with various little statues in the middle of it all.

Josephine jumped off, searching around, not seeing anyone, but then Riagán appeared from behind a yew tree. Dressed entirely in black, his baggy shirt revealing the top of a heart tattooed on his chest, a lightning bolt puncturing it. Riagán appeared thinner to Josephine since she had last seen him, his cheeks sharp and arms thin. There were dark circles under his eyes.

Josephine pulled her sword, growling at him. Aurora also growled at the former prince.

"Come, Josephine, we have Jonathan and Aeolus. I am sorry to say that if you don't come now, they will die."

Josephine pointed her sword at him. "I'm not stupid, Riagán. Especially after you tried to kill me."

Riagán sighed. "Please, or else he will activate the stone sooner. I want many things, Josephine, but not the evil he wants to bring forth."

Josephine stared at him in shock.

"You truly don't want this, I can feel it," frowned Aurora.

Riagán gave a nod, pointing his sword towards the shrine. Josephine and Aurora paused. They knew Cetus was the one they had to fight, not Riagán. After the look that Riagán had had on his face when Diva created those Shadow Dragons, Josephine figured it was worth the risk.

She took a deep breath and walked forward; shoulders squared. Riagán let her pass before following her, Aurora behind the two. They walked down the stone path; the gravel crackling under their feet and paws. Josephine's heart was beating harder as they went, in fear of what was going to be over the next horizon. Aurora was worried as well, which did not make Josephine feel better. Finally, the bushes cleared. Josephine let out a small gasp at what met her eyes.

Claudette was now fighting Gazelda with a dagger and her sword. Gazelda was dodging more than attacking.

"I knew Cetus was exaggerating when he said you were a great warrior, *Fair Lady*," Claudette said Gazelda's name in a mocking tone.

Gazelda sighed, "Like an old friend of mine used to say..." Gazelda's necklace shined and blinded Claudette, long enough for Gazelda to jump forward with her crystal sword, to disarm the Shadow mistress, elbow her, and knock her out, "Don't underestimate your enemies."

Gazelda glanced around, trying to sort out how to get down. She saw a rope that ran down the length of the wall. She inwardly sighed and muttered to herself in her mind,

"True courage is facing your fear head on. And being a unicorn, heights is definitely one of them."

Gazelda bent over to pull up the rope when she heard something scraping the stone floor. She paused; a Shadow creature in a shapeless form lunged at her.

A bolt of lightning fire struck the beast, evaporating it.

Gazelda whipped around to see Sandra and Storm with Jun, Indie, and Ticka holding on tight to Storm. Spuck floating in the air beside the dragon.

"I believe the rest of that line goes, 'and don't overestimate your own strength'," Sandra said with a cocky smile.

Gazelda shook her head, glaring.

"Who invited you?"

"No one did. We're cutting into this dance," chuckled Spuck.

"More like crashing," snorted Gazelda.

"You're glad we're here, don't deny it," smirked Storm.

Gazelda shook her head. She narrowed her eyes, noticing three figures coming up the road of the castle. As they got closer, Gazelda could identify who they were. Her heart grew lighter in relief.

"Yes, I am."

Chapter Forty-Three
Old Fashioned Showdown

J osephine swallowed back the bile from her stomach. Cameron had his sword on Jonathan's neck. Jamard was standing on the other side with his sword drawn, his eyes dark with shadows. Jonathan was tied up in shadow chains and gagged. Shayla was holding Jonathan's ring.

"Well, that explains why Jonathan can't break free," thought Josephine, but she couldn't understand why Jonathan would have given it up. Josephine moved her head to see beside Jonathan, Cameron, and Shayla.

Cameron's Dragon was overlooking the chains that were binding Aeolus to the ground, flat on his stomach. Beyond the two was a large stone tablet. It was circular and the color of a heavy storm cloud. Josephine felt colder as she stared at it, but comfortingly. Dragon language engraved along the edge of the full length of the tablet.

Josephine felt some of her courage return to her from staring at the shrine. She smiled with a wicked glint in her eye.

Past Raul, his dragon, and Riagán, stood Cetus. His square face was cleaner and fuller than the last time she had seen him. The scabs from all over his body were also gone. His ice-blue eyes were narrowed in curiosity and smugness, as Josephine could feel his emotional aurora. His black hair pulled into a ponytail, wearing half-armor with his sword sheathed. Cetus smiled warmly, which made Josephine nervous. He walked forward with arms open wide.

"Ah, here she is, the new leader of the Dragon Heart Alliance, Josephine Drageon. Yes, my dear, what stories I have heard."

Josephine looked back into Cetus' cold eyes and realized that Cetus was... hungry. There was something he wanted. She couldn't quite understand or place the feeling — it almost felt like an obsession.

"I can see that you are wondering why young Prince Jonathan gave up. He was fighting well, him and his dragon..." Cetus glared, irritated at Cameron's black eye, and the long gash that Cameron's dragon had across his muzzle.

"But when he saw I had his friend Jamard and his family inside the castle, he gave up. Of course, he didn't realize that Jamard is fully under my control." Cetus snapped his fingers to have the young soldier stand beside him.

"What do you want, Cetus?" asked Josephine.

Cetus smirked. "Did you know I was a seventh generation Dragon heart, Josephine?"

"Yes, I did." Josephine waited for Cetus to get to the point.

"I lost both my parents, who sacrificed themselves for the greater good."

Cetus tilted his head to look at Jamard. "You ask what I want, Josephine? Well, I wish for life to be good again. For so long, people fought against the Shadows. I realized during my training that we Dragon hearts have the power to bridge the gap."

Cetus moved his wrist in a circular motion to create a shadow snake that curled around his sword. "Dragon Hearts have vast amounts of power to help control the people, Josephine. I can sense that power in you so much more than even Master James; I don't think he had as much inner strength as you do, young girl. With this tablet, all will fear me and will realize that their lives will be safer with me at the head of their lives. Share and share alike, no more rich or poor."

Josephine's eyes widened, then narrowed. "That's not true; if you are in charge, you will have all the power. No one has the right to tell another what to do like that. No one has the right to determine who should and shouldn't have something."

"But they cannot control themselves, Josephine!" sighed Cetus, "They are not smart enough to not steal and murder, only I and the others who share the vision know how to control ourselves and our power," Cetus waved his hand at the ones gathered behind him.

Josephine could feel, though, that was not the case. Shayla and Alcyone, in particular, were both feeling a bit of condescension at Cetus.

"That's not true. You're just power hungry. I can feel it, Cetus," said Josephine. Aurora growled in agreement.

"You think you are a god, that you can tell people how to live."

"I do know better than most, but I don't necessary to think myself as a god," Cetus laughed.

"Come, Josephine, Aurora, you two are smart; let us rule together, with our dragons and shadow powers."

"Your former partner did not see the wisdom in you, and nor do we," said Aurora.

Cetus flinched. Josephine saw the hurt in his face. "I do not begrudge her wishes. She fought beside me for a long time; I would not force her."

Josephine glanced at Aurora, who eyes narrowed. Cetus was calm, but the small surge of anger tipped them off.

"You are lying. I can feel it. She was the one who left; you never asked her if the path you were going on was okay. You never treated her like an equal, just a means to an end. She fought back, left you, and broke the bond the two of you shared."

Cetus sneered, "I see you are young, but foolish. Most of the young know so much more than most of the older generations. It is their fault the world is the way it is. Always fighting, never compromising."

"Sometimes you cannot, should not compromise, Cetus, especially with evil," Josephine whispered.

"You have to fight for what is right with all your heart, lest you become as dark as your enemy. You have set the rules, Cetus, so I will fight like you."

Cetus laughed, "Oh, I doubt that highly." Cetus whipped around to stab Jamard in the heart.

Jonathan cried out as his best friend fell to the ground, dead. Cetus pulled his sword up and out, then pointed it at Josephine, Jamard's blood dripping down the blade.

"Sometimes you have to trim off some limbs in order to make things pure. Kill those two,"-Cetus pointed at Aeolus and Jonathan- "then Shayla, Alcyone, get on the tablet. You too, Cameron and Boudica. We need to get things in motion;

soon Shadow magic will be the ruling magic when either Diva or Cutler makes it back. One of them can stand for the fire element on the stone. Better yet, do that first."

Josephine dared to look away from Cetus to look at the tablet. There were six symbols to represent each Dragon element, along with a precious stone in the innermost circle of the tablet. It was a mistake though, looking away, for Cetus snapped his fingers and Josephine and Aurora were lifted off the ground and entangled in shadow bindings. At that moment, Josephine could hear yelling and screaming. Josephine prayed it wasn't Eve and the others dying because of her. At that second, she felt calm, even as Shayla and Cameron walked toward the tablet, as the shadows were tightening around Aeolus and Jonathan, squeezing out their breath.

Shayla stood at the ice marking with Alcyone behind her, and Cameron stood on her left side with Boudica behind him. For a second nothing happened, and then without warning, white sparks came off the tablet, burning Shayla and Cameron along with the Dragons. The four yelled, leaping off the stone. Cetus whipped around to see what was going wrong when an arrow punctured his arm.

The necklace flash, releasing Josephine and Aurora from their bindings. Josephine turned her head to see Eve and FireWind with the others and a few additions, including, to her displeasure, Spuck, Indie, and Jun. Gazelda walked forward in unicorn form. Ticka helped Josephine get to her feet. Josephine glanced to see where the arrow had come from.

Nathaniel was at the ready, with other archers in several of the windows and along the wall. Gazelda walked until she was a few feet from her former student. She said nothing as Cetus broke off the shaft of the arrow from his arm, making Josephine flinch.

"Fair Lady, I see once again you bring the best of the best with you," he commented as he fixed his shirt.

Cetus's eyes lingered on Sandra, who was glaring at him, and a tall, black-skinned woman that Josephine had never seen before, as well as a young woman with light brown skin. Ark let out a low growl.

"Give it up, Cetus. As your little toadies just discovered, the spirits of the original six Dragon Hearts and their partners still live here in the tablet and all around, which is its strongest," Gazelda glanced up into the early night sky, "-when the Dragon Star is in the night sky. The magic is reacting to the Dragon hearts of the prophecy. It will not take your students who are impure of heart."

Cetus glanced at Shayla, who was nursing Alcyone's burns with breaths of ice. Cameron was nursing his own burns along his arms. Cetus then glanced into the woods.

"Let Jonathan go or, well, you can guess what will happen. You weren't smart, Cetus, but you're not stupid, either," Gazelda sneered.

"I'm afraid I will have to decline your offer of kindness, Gazelda. I see now that I can never take this tablet over, but at least I can take down one of the royal dragons."

As Cetus raised his arm, Lance appeared out of nowhere, a familiar popping noise in his wake. Lance stabbed Cetus below his heart. But before Lance could do anything else, a black and red spider the size of a horse with an almost human-shaped face appeared from nowhere. He stabbed at Lance, sending him flying.

Cetus growled, hissing in pain as he removed the sword. The shadows came at once to heal the wound. He then let forth a large barrage of shapeless shadow creatures. Nathaniel shot another arrow, this time with the other royal archers helping. But the shadow creatures forced them back.

Josephine jumped forward, past Jamard's still body, to get to Jonathan. Cetus swung at her, but Sandra appeared, sending him flying with a right hook, sparks flying off her. Josephine reached out to Jonathan, and the necklace lit up, dissolving the shadows.

Jonathan let out a gasp then turned, pulling out his sword to break the bonds holding down Aeolus. Boudica jumped at Aeolus, who roared, flying into the air out of her reach and made her follow him to get the dragon away from Josephine and Jonathan. The two grabbed Lance and pulled him to safety. Josephine, with as light a touch as she could, laid her hand on Lance's wound. He was out and breathing hard. Josephine closed her eyes and let the ice magic shift from her hand onto the wound. Josephine gasped and shook her head when Jonathan wrapped his arm around her.

"It's okay; it was hard keeping it all back. I froze the wound so that he won't bleed out, but I don't know if it'll do much good."

Jonathan turned around to see Aeolus and Aurora fighting with Alcyone and Boudica. "It's all right, Josephine. Let's go help the others."

Jonathan regarded his old mentor.

"I'm sorry," he muttered.

Josephine didn't understand why he said sorry, but didn't bother to ask why.

As she moved to join the fray, Josephine heard something in the garden. She spun around, but she neither saw nor felt anything. She waited one more second before running back towards the fight.

Indie was dueling with Cutler, who was letting off sparks, trying to set Indie on fire. Indie was too fast for the Shadow Dragon heart. Josephine jumped in, helping Indie to drive Cutler back. Josephine scanned the battle for Jun, but she didn't see her ward.

"Where's Jun?" demanded Josephine as Indie took a punch at Cutler, breaking the Vanell brother's nose.

Indie glanced over at Josephine as Cutler yelled in pain, "She was over by the garden! That Kageshi girl was taking potshots at Ticka with some shooting stars."

"WHY DID YOU LET JUN COME!? YOU LET A THIR-TEEN-YEAR-OLD COME TO A BATTLE?!" Josephine yelled in frustration as Cutler tried to hit Indie.

Indie ducked, then kidney punched Cutler, making him drop to the ground.

Spuck paused for a moment from throwing smoke bombs to flinch with Indie at Josephine's yelling.

"Josey, come on, we tried to leave her, honest!" muttered Indie.

"Yeah!" said Spuck, "She bullied us into letting her come! She put me in a headlock and rubbed my head hard!"

Josephine glared at the two, then punched Cutler, who was trying to grab at Indie's ankles.

"Nice punch," commented Indie.

"You two are *in so much trouble*," growled Josephine.

"I have a feeling we won't be babysitting ever again," said Spuck.

"Amongst other things, if we live through this," muttered Indie.

The three looked up in time to jump and roll as the spider creature crashed down on them.

Spuck did a double take.

"Anansi!"

The spider turned its many-eyed-head in Spuck's direction. "Ssspuckkk. How gooood to sssee you, old friend."

Spuck sneered, "You dare call yourself a trickster."

The spider shrugged, then spat at Spuck. He jumped high in the sky to dodge the yellow liquid. Indie watched as the poison melted a marble dragon statue.

"Ex best bud?" asked Indie to the Sprite.

Spuck pulled out a small dagger. "Yep."

Indie sighed. "A lot of that happening lately. Would you like my assistance?"

Spuck smirked, "Sure. You get his legs; I'll get his bug eyes. Be careful, that's not his real form."

Josephine left the two to fight the spider trickster. Josephine searched frantically around for Jun, only to come face to face with Cameron. Cameron brought his sword down to cleave Josephine in two, only to find that he could not move. Ticka smirked as she used her magic to yank Cameron's feet from under him.

"Don't worry about Jun; a friend of Gazelda's and Wave went after her. Go help Sandra and Gazelda," Ticka yelled to her.

Josephine turned to see Sandra and Gazelda fighting Cetus. Claudette had somehow regained consciousness. She was sneaking up behind the two women.

Josephine weaved around the other fights. She jumped onto the Shadow magician with a yell, cutting Claudette across her ribs. Claudette muttered a few words as she held her hand to her wound. Some Shadow foxes appeared surrounding Josephine.

Josephine dueled with Claudette, waiting for the right opening and got it — Claudette tried to side swipe her. With two strokes, Josephine blocked it, then shoved her sword right through Claudette's stomach. The Shadow magician yelled. The shadows lost their shapes, then descended upon Claudette.

Josephine did not watch. She ran past Claudette. As Cetus blocked Gazelda's sword, Josephine swung down hers, aiming for his head. Cetus retreated to evaluate the new threat, also seeing that Claudette was being eaten by her own Shadow creatures.

"Give up, Cetus," muttered Sandra.

Aurora and Storm landed at that moment, blood all over their faces and both growling. Shayla push back Marie and jumped up onto Alcyone's back so they could fly off. Cutler was badly injured and his dragon's face was covered in long gashes. Cameron had numerous cuts as well. He was forced to back up to where his dragon was as he dodged Jonathan's large swings.

Jonathan had in the battle's confusion, picked up the Vanora ring again. It flashed as he swung his sword at the Vanell brother. Ticka shoved Riagán back into Shayla's dragon while Anansi was tangled up, thanks to the efforts of Indiana and Spuck. Shayla locked eyes with Josephine, then glanced at Cetus, her eyes wide with fear.

"Then, I guess I have but one option," Cetus growled.

Gazelda blinked, "CETUS, NO!"

Cetus roared into the night sky and was answered by many more roars.

Chapter Forty-Four
Dragon Souls

Jun ended up in the northern part of the garden, fighting the Kageshi girl, Daiyu. Jun repeatedly swung her whip at Daiyu's leg, but kept missing, and had to straighten it out each time.

Daiyu skidded to a stop, then turned on her heel to kick Jun in the face. Jun ducked then tried to grab at Daiyu's leg, but she swung her other leg around, kicking Jun in the face. Jun fell back, blinking furiously, trying to clear her vision as pain racked her head.

Daiyu smirked. She went to bring her leg down in a smashing blow when Jun's instincts kicked into overdrive.

She brought her arms up to block the kick. Daiyu staggered, trying to pull her leg free, but all the training from Indiana and Jonathan made her grip strong and tight. Jun heaved on Daiyu's leg to knock her off balance and onto her butt. As Daiyu got up, Jun punched the Kageshi with all her weight, just as Jonathan had taught her.

"MY NOSE, YOU LITTLE BRAT!"

Jun smirked as Daiyu tossed a smoke bomb to disappear. Jun glanced around, but the only thing around was the smell of black powder.

"Coward and a wuss," chuckled Jun.

Jun did not see Archimago was creeping up behind her. Upon waking, he discovered everyone had left for the shrine. He was sneaking around when he spotted Jun. Aware of the brat's importance to the Dragon heart leader, the shadow magician moved to snatch her, but his body froze.

Jun spun around when she heard a gagging noise to see Archimago. She jumped back, her hand going to her whip. Archimago was paralyzed. He flailed against the shadows holding him. Before Jun could sort out why the shadows had gone against his will, she realized it wasn't permanent; the shadow's grip slipped down from his shoulders a centimeter.

"JUN!"

The girl turned to see Wave running towards her. The Dragon heart pulled her away from Archimago.

"What are you doing? Lucky, I saw you run off! Come on, we need to get back..."

Jun yelled as Wave turned too late to see Archimago swinging his sword down. Wave's hand was on her sword hilt, but there was no way to stop Archimago. Then, in an instant, a long, curved sword cut through Archimago's chest. The wielder then removed it, pushing Archimago's dead body to the ground.

Wave and Jun stared at the new-comer. She had light brown skin, with full lips and a heart-shaped face. She was wearing a plum and maroon silk dress that was wrapped around her tall frame, a strange motif tattoo on her upper arm. In her hand was a two bladed staff that seem too heavy for the girl holding it. Her ink black hair was in a braid. The young woman stared at Jun, with dark eyes that were wide with disbelief.

"Uh, thank you..." said Wave, unsure what to say and unsure why she was looking at Jun in such a way.

The Indra girl blinked, shook her head. She smiled, "Mandara Taradon, Sorceress."

She gave Wave a hand up, for Wave had tumbled backwards when Archimago had been stabbed.

Hurricane came running over, yelling, "Wave, quick! Cetus..."

The four jumped at the bang that came from the shrine.

Mandara pushed Wave forward, "GO! Help Josephine; I will look after her."

Wave jumped on Hurricane's back as Mandara grabbed Jun to pull her back towards the castle.

"No, wait, I want to help!"

Mandara glanced at the dark aurora that was drifting around the garden. "You have done as much as you can, my dear. It is up to the Dragon hearts now."

Gazelda pulled Josephine and Sandra back, but then the three flew backwards as the area around Cetus exploded.

Eve and FireWind jumped forward to help the three women back on their feet. Everyone tensed as Cetus's dragon soul was entwining with shadows. Diva and Wisteria appeared at that moment beside their leader. Diva was grinning from ear to ear, her eyes pitch black.

Cetus's black soul turned and stared right into Josephine's eyes, making her shudder. His eyes were snow white. Cetus's body had been completely engulfed in shadows. The soul curled like a thin cloud, pulling together to make a dragon shape. It was not stable; the shadows kept screeching and flinching against his dragon soul, which was also flinching against what it normally would repel. All the warmth in the air had been sucked away. Josephine gasped, trying to breathe against the overwhelming sensation.

"Gazelda," whispered the dark-skinned woman. She had a rich accent, deeper than Marie's.

"We need to get them to the shrine; the magic will protect their spirits."

Gazelda glared at the woman.

"You mean use the Dragon Soul spell?" whispered Josephine. She did not have to look at the others; they could feel Josephine's conviction. She was terrified, but so were the others, and their fear would not stop them.

"One problem, how..."

"It's instinctive: let your senses guide you."

"Diana..." hissed Gazelda, but the woman shook her head.

"Not scared of me, are you?" mocked the soul.

Josephine did her best to resist the urge to flinch.

It was at that second that they broke. The dragons roared, shooting flames at Cetus and the others, making the group scatter. Cetus's body, with its corrupted soul still attached, its tail like an anchor chain to his back. It stood still, then its wings opened. Roaring, black ice broke through the ground to surround Cetus to stop the elemental fire.

Aurora and Josephine jumped past, with the others right behind them.

Diva slashed at Eve, making her tilt backwards. Diva made a grab at Eve's belt, taking the Vanora dagger, belt, scabbard and all, her dragon fire covering her hand touching the dagger. Diva's crows slashed at Eve's arms.

A silver dagger flew through the air, slicing through the crows, embedding itself in Diva's arm. She screamed, pulling the silver dagger out, then calling her Shadows to pull her to safety. All the while making sure that she was holding the Vanora dagger by the scabbard, her hand still aflame.

FireWind used her nose to scoop up Eve, then jumped over to the tablet.

The second the five's feet touched the stone tablet, each felt warm as their elements trickled up over their skin, enveloping their bodies. Josephine took a stand where the opal was, with Jonathan at the diamond, Wave the sapphire, Marie the citrine, and Eve the ruby. The spot with the amber stone left empty.

Josephine could feel her soul-stirring inside of her, wanting to be free to fight, the feeling of her ice powers crackling and forming along her skin like frost dancing on a window-pane. Aurora touched Josephine on her back, and within a half of a second of her doing so, the Vanora necklace and ring lit up.

Josephine felt herself escape into her mind when her eyes closed. The sensation of flying into the air, the wings from her back opening up, overcoming her.

Josephine opened her eyes to the night sky. It was of many colors; the stars were brighter than she had ever seen them. She could feel her wings flapping. Josephine stretched her long neck to take in her surroundings. For a few seconds she could see the others, the colors of their elements—fire, wind, lightning, and water rolling off their bright souls. Josephine felt a pull at that moment, something cold. It was Cetus's pitch-black soul, its wings unfurled, snarling up at them.

She felt the urge to rip him apart, to send him away from the hallow grounds of the Dragons and Dragon hearts. Josephine roared, as did the others. She felt herself flying forward, snapping at Cetus.

Cetus tried to fight back, but he was not strong enough to fight them all off. Josephine flew around once, then back again at Cetus, seeing him weakening after every pass one of them made. Josephine flew to him and, with her snout, she touched Cetus's smoky, coal-colored soul with her ice fire.

Cetus screamed, and the Shadows exploded and dissipated, whirling around where Cetus's body was standing. For a confused moment, Josephine saw something shining dimly in the shadows, but it was as gone as soon as she saw it. Josephine raised her head towards the sky, wanting to fly higher now that the threat was gone, but she heard Aurora's voice echoing in her mind.

"Josephine, come back, Ice Princess. All is safe now."

Josephine closed her eyes and when she opened them, she was back in her own body. She could see the others in her peripheral vision opening their eyes. Within a few seconds, Josephine felt her legs give way under her. She collapsed on the tablet.

Josephine thought maybe she had been knocked down, but she blinked twice to see she was still on the tablet. She lifted her head to see that the tablet was cracked. The place where the Earth Dragon heart should have stood broke off from the rest of the tablet.

Josephine moaned; her head was like it was being hit repeatedly by a troll. Josephine felt a warm, gentle, human hand helping her up. She lifted her head to see it was Gazelda, smiling, radiating relief. Josephine placed her left arm over Gazelda's shoulder as she helped Josephine stand.

Jonathan was being helped by his brother and mother, while Indiana was helping Eve stand. He glared at her, but it didn't last when she hugged him. The two then turned to help Wave up. Marie, who was leaning against Perun, looked pointedly at Spuck, who shrugged.

Jun ran over to Josephine. To Josephine's relief, she was in one piece, with just a few tiny scratches. She grabbed her in a rib-breaking hug.

"It's okay, I'm fine."

Aurora snaked her head over to nudge them, knocking them over and making them laugh.

"Is everyone in one piece?" chuckled Storm.

"I'm afraid not," whispered the woman, Diana. They all turned to see Diana standing with Lance. Josephine could tell he was already gone. The Falcons walked over to stand over him. Jonathan kneeled beside him.

"Thank you, Sir Lance," he whispered.

Josephine walked over and embraced him. Jonathan then turned to Jamard. Nathaniel walked forward and kneeled beside their childhood friend, to close his glassy eyes. Jonathan reached over to touch Nathaniel's shoulder, who nodded to Jonathan. The dragons all stood side by side, then all together they roared into the night to let the stars know that two warriors were joining the other fallen.

Epilogue
A New Horizon

The royal family held special funerals for both Sir "Horseman" Lance and Jamard Pierce. Jonathan was somber before and after the funerals. The tall, dark-skinned woman named Diana left after Lance's funeral, before Josephine could speak with her. When she asked Mango about Diana, her face turned into a scowl.

"Diana Rook is an annoying, self-righteous, pigheaded magician. Don't worry yourself about her. You have me to repair all the deep magic that was destroyed."

At that moment, Sandra came in laughing. Mango glared at the lightning Dragon heart then stomped out. Josephine looked at Sandra for an explanation.

Sandra tilted her head and sighed. "I don't know the story myself, but as long as I can remember, those two have never gotten along. They both know each other from a long time ago, before even James's Master Ming came to be the leader. Mango joined when Boon became the head of the Alliance. Story goes that he had heard of Mango's healing abilities and wanted her to do just that. Mango, however, wanted to be a warrior. She challenged him on the terms that if she won, she would be a warrior with a few healing duties."

Josephine and Aurora grinned; they didn't need to ask how that fight came out. Sandra smirked at their faces, then sighed again.

"Diana joined not long after that. The two got into a spitting contest, and I mean a spitting contest. The two were at each other like fire on a dry field. James, Shoney, and Maynu had to stand between the two to keep them from ripping each other apart. Which is saying something, seeing how the three were only about twelve. Ever since, the two asked that they never have to work together. Some kind of blood feud or something is going on, but don't worry, the two know when to not start something, like now. They are respectful of the fallen. I am sure once Mango goes back home, Diana will come back to swear allegiance to you."

Josephine nodded, but when Sandra mentioned the fallen, her mind wandered to Jonathan. Sandra and Storm shared a look.

"Go talk to him. He'll need you. Jonathan is barely eating from what I heard from the queen. From what I can feel from him, it's guilt."

Josephine frowned, "Guilt? But he…"

Sandra chuckled and waved her hand. "Tell him, not me. I have to go talk to Sheppard about the Viken and what their plans are. Go for it."

Sandra waved; Storm nodded his head as they parted.

Josephine looked at Aurora.

"Come with me?" she smiled.

Aurora nodded her scaly head. "Of course."

They found Jonathan at the elemental tablet. He was staring into space, with Aeolus sitting at his side. Aeolus noticed the girls and smiled in a greeting. Josephine took a spot beside Jonathan.

For a few minutes, neither said anything as they stared at the tablet. Mango and Gazelda theorized the tablet broke because the sixth royal Dragon heart was not there. Even so, the magic had probably destroyed Cetus. And yet, Josephine still had a gut feeling that this wasn't over. The glimmer of light was still bothering her, but no one could say for sure where it came from, for everyone else's eyes were closed because of the exploding Shadow creatures. It was just as he had escaped in the mines, making Josephine believe there was another Shadow magician under his command.

Josephine felt the urged to touch the amber stone at that second. It felt cool to her touch. She saw in her mind's eye a tall, dark-skinned teenage boy and a large, spiked, earth-brown dragon. Josephine quickly withdrew her hand. Jonathan stared at her, puzzled.

"What's wrong?"

Josephine shook her head. "Just the Dragon spirits show-ing me something."

Jonathan smirked, "Speaking of showing, is Jun going to go with Mandara?"

Josephine sighed. Mandara had come to Josephine, asking if she could take her ward with her to train. Josephine and Jun both asked why and Mandara said,

"She is an Xian."

Mandara explained that Jun's natural flexibility and fighting talent meant she had to be a member of the long-lost Xian clan. Mandara knew one of the last remain-ing members of the clan and wished to take Jun with her to meet the woman. Jun knew maybe what her parent's first names were, and it could help narrow down if she was Xian or not. With the thought of perhaps meeting a family member, Jun became tearful.

"I know, Jun. Mandara can train you and help you find out who your ancestors were."

Josephine let out a ragged breath and jumped, realizing she was crying.

Jonathan rubbed her back. "She'll come back a great warrior and with a family history."

She smiled, wiping the tears away.

Jonathan tried to lighten the mood. "Marie and Wave are practically stalking Eve and Indie. Has anything happened?"

Josephine chuckled, then clicked her tongue, "Nope. The two are back to snapping at each other. Marie and Wave are sure something would or will happen, though. Eve found the two following her to the garden yesterday. She yelled at them for an hour about letting her have five minutes of peace. She was fully recovered and didn't need her friends to be nagging nannies. Good thing; it means she doesn't know about the bet, so for now they are safe. Spuck is sad, though; he could have sworn he was going to win it."

Jonathan laughed. She wrapped her arm through his.

"Nice to hear you laugh again."

Jonathan stared at the tablet again with an unemotional face. Josephine waited as he gathered his thoughts.

He then said after a minute, "It was my fault, you know. I rushed in without thinking of anyone else but me. I didn't stop to see what you wanted to do; I just had to make sure that Mum and my brother were safe. Sir Lance would have been furious at me."

Josephine shook her head before he had even finished talking.

"You care about your kingdom and kin. No shame in that. I really didn't have a plan anyway, so in the end it didn't matter. Red Rose in the end is your home, and it was your right to charge in."

Jonathan didn't look ready to give the guilt up, so Josephine pushed on. "You did what you thought was right. We were flying blind into a battle. I didn't give any orders, nor did Gazelda. You were trying to save Jamard, but Cetus was already using him. You know you are not the only one who feels guilty; Jeremiah is feeling bad because he was the one who let Jamard into the castle."

Jonathan breathed, "I'll talk to him again. He is not to blame."

"Nor are you, Mr. Wind Prince," whispered Josephine.

Jonathan's lips twitched into a tiny smirk. Josephine could feel the last of his guilt dissipate. She relaxed, leaning against him.

"Jabari and Kingdor will be here soon to discuss what do about Diva and the others. They are still running around, so we will have to coordinate to capture them. Eve is furious about Diva taking the dagger, so no big surprise, she wants to head that hunt."

"What about Riagán?" asked Aeolus.

Josephine knew, though, that it was really Ticka he was asking about.

"Ticka is going to go back home to help with rebuilding. Riagán will be captured and brought to trial. Ticka will be fine. She understands he made his choices."

Jonathan nodded, and they fell silent. The sun was retreating behind the horizon. Josephine glanced up to see the Dragon Star winking down at her. Then Josephine looked back at Jonathan, feeling the change in his emotions.

"What is it?" asked Aurora.

Jonathan grinned. "If I recall correctly, I still owe you a kiss, Ice Queen."

Josephine beamed as the two dragons chuckled.

"Yes, I believe you do."

As Jonathan took her hand, Josephine felt the same calm as she had when she stood on the tablet, the calm feeling of love and the knowledge that she was not alone in the battle raging before them.

Josephine leaned forward, the Vanora necklace turning red as they kissed. As they embraced, the two dragons wrapped around them. The four of them watched the sunset fall, marking the end of one quest and the beginning of another.

The End of Book One

Bonus Chapter
Death of the Traitors

C etus was gripping the armrests of his chair. The burns ached, ripping at him while pus kept oozing out and down his arms. The Dragon magic that the five young Dragon hearts had was overwhelming. Cetus growled at the thought. He tightened his grasp, and the burns on his arms protested as his muscles contracted. It would be weeks before he could use shadow magic again. It was as before with Master James, only it was but one man. This time, it was five young knights with untapped potential. If it had not been for his Shadow stone and his loyal servant, Cetus knew that the Vanora Crystal would have killed him this time. The Vanell brothers were standing in front of Cetus. They glanced at him. Cetus had donned black attire to cover up his burned face and body.

"My lord?" asked Cutler. Out of the three Vanell children, Cutler was the most loyal. Cetus sighed, feeling Cutler's unease.

"Need not fret, Cutler. Be patient and watchful unless you wish to become worse off than I?"

Cutler's eyes widened, and he turned back to face the entrance of the cave. Cetus cursed the Viken for pushing him further into the Mayni Mountains. He had not gotten a chance to capture a phoenix to study. But it was not of any worry of importance. For now, he needed to focus on overtaking a kingdom. Red Rose was out of his reach now, but no matter. WarWink would do just as well, but first, some unfinished business.

His loyal servant entered the cave with the two subjects. The servant pulled back his cloak to reveal the youth's face. The young man's hair was as dark as the sky of a new moon and his eyes were the darkest shade of indigo blue.

"Ah, Gabriel, you've returned with the prisoners, King Justin and Lord Wilson."

Both men were on their knees, bowing to Cetus. They were tied up with shadow chains. Lord Wilson bowed lower to the Shadow Dragon heart, but King Justin said nothing, nor did he move. Both men's royal attire was dirty and torn in places from weeks of captivity. Cetus smiled. This was going to be satisfying.

"King Justin Falcon and Lord Wilson, how good that you've decided to join me," Cetus, despite his injuries, stood up from his chair and walked to face the two men.

"Lord Wilson, you failed me."

Lord Wilson winced and muttered to the ground, "I–I did my Lord...?" He said it as though Wilson did not know if he should question the statement or agree.

King Justin's lip curled. Cetus smiled as he said to the Lord in a condescending tone,

"Yes, you did. Your use of fay charms was sloppy, and the King here," Cetus and King Justin shared a glance, "Was able to break it several times. You failed to stand your ground, and the queen took back the castle before I could get to the shrine and finish stripping the magic on the castle.

The Dragon Hearts Royal were able to get on the shrine and reduce me to this."

Cetus showed one of his charred arms. Lord Wilson flinched. King Justin's eyes sparkled, but he remained silent. Cetus noticed.

"Proud of your son, Justin?"

The king closed his eyes. Cetus smirked, feeling the melancholy feelings coming from the defrocked king.

"Yes, He has the will that I have not."

Cetus grunted. "Stubborn, most definitely."

"Not to mention it looks like he has gotten himself some nice tail," laughed Cutler.

"Now, now, speak respectfully of Josephine. She is the leader of the Dragon hearts, after all," Cetus said without taking his eyes from King Justin's.

"Any last regrets, your majesty?" Cetus smirked.

"Just that I could not protect. That it is now on their shoulders," King Justin replied.

Cetus grunted in surprise. He could feel genuine regret from him. Cetus's own father died before he was even able to walk, and his grandfather had no real love for him as he raised him. Grandfather made it clear that the Cyprus name was the only important thing to him. Love was not important.

Cetus viewed Justin as the same type of man as his grandfather, so it was interesting that he had such feelings.

Cameron glared. "What kind of lame, crappy last line was that?" He asked.

Cetus said nothing. He turned his back on the King and sat back down on his throne. Gabriel was standing on the dusty floor of the cave behind the two prisoners. Cetus locked eyes with him.

"Gabriel, please get rid of them."

Gabriel's face was blank as he walked towards them. Lord Wilson was blubbering. King Justin stood up straight, waiting. Gabriel faced the king and stared at him; his eyes tight. Cetus could not see Gabriel's face, only his back.

Gabriel let shadows gather on his sword. He was not going as fast as Cutler thought he should.

"Oh, come on!" smiled Cutler.

The Vanell brother pushed past Gabriel and thrusted his sword into the King's chest. He fell with a defiant face, a prick of regret and sadness coming off him.

As Lord Wilson's foot touched past the threshold of the cave, a large flaming spike penetrated the Lord's body and it fell down the stone steps into the snow. Shayla walked forward to glare with disgust at the fat lord. She looked up to see Gabriel, his eyes tight with equal distaste. The two shared unease. Cetus had not noticed her disgust, nor Gabriel's hesitation. He laughed from his throne as Cutler smirked.

"Now that I have sacrificed a few pawns, the real warriors can take the board."

Book 2 Preview

The Epic adventure continues in Book Two of the Dragon
Heart Chronicles:
Quest for the Magic
Special Preview
Chapter One
In the Blanket of the Night

It was the stench that he hated the most. Dressed in all black, his traveling cloak swayed in his wake as the Shadow magician slipped through the dung ridden streets. As he paused in front of the oak doors of the castle, footsteps echoed from behind him. The young man stiffened, then relaxed when he saw who it was.

"Well, what brings you here, Gabriel Lucas?"

"Your father's mistakes, Lady Shayla Vanell."

He turned to the blonde-haired girl. She leered at him with her dragon-shaped eyes, though light colored, were dark with bitterness.

"Rubbing salt into the wound, Gabriel? You need not remind me of my father's stupidity."

Gabriel's face remained passive. A black dragonling crawled up Gabriel's back and sniffed Shayla from his shoulder. Shayla smiled and patted the little dragon creature on the head, and it thanked her with a purr.

"*Hello, Isaiah,*" she said in Dragon language.

"I am sorry. It was not my intention, Lady Shayla. I was answering your question."

The Vanell girl raised an eyebrow. "Fair enough. So besides cleaning up my father's mistakes, what else would bring you here to this god-forsaken City of Warwink?"

The boy's deep indigo eyes became tight.

"Doing our master's will," he muttered, wishing the accursed wind would blow in another direction.

Isaiah looked at Gabriel with a sad expression. He nudged his friend's hair.

"He is your master," Shayla whispered, glancing around to make sure no one else was nearby. Gabriel did the same, though he knew that either his Shadow magic or Isaiah would have alerted him if anyone was nearby. Once the two were sure no one was around, Shayla asked him with no actual concern.

"So how is the Lord? I know he was not still fully recovered when I left for here a few weeks ago."

"He is better, but not to where he wishes to be. His shadowed soul was subjected to pure Dragon Heart magic. It drained him. His shadow stone has helped little with speeding up his recovery this time. Cetus's own dragon magic has been pushing away the shadow magic all in due part to the Royals' attack on his bare soul," Gabriel informed her. His tone was equally unconcerned for the man they worked for.

Shayla nodded and then pulled back the young man's hood so she could look at him properly. Gabriel was a handsome boy, with a pleasant round face and remarkable dark blue eyes. But they were cold and empty from years of being a servant to a man who himself is cold and dark.

"Gabriel..." she whispered, leaning forward, "How much longer do you truly think your 'master' will keep you? Your ailment is getting worse by the day, and your magic is stronger than his. Cetus's distrust towards you and me has grown since Riagán fled."

Gabriel's eyebrow arched. But then, as though to emphasize her point, Gabriel went into a small coughing fit. It went on for a minute, shaking his whole body with pain. He wiped a small trickle of blood from his lip with a handkerchief from Shayla.

Once he had recovered, he said, "From what I can get from your tone of voice, you have a plan?" He scowled, pulling his hood back up.

Shayla gave him a sad face, then put a hand on his arm.

"Who would I go to?" he whispered, pain and uncertainty leaking into his practiced monotone voice.

"To the enemy," she chuckled.

Gabriel glared at her, not appreciating the joke. Shayla noticed his mood and stopped. She gave him a stern expression.

"Gabriel, you deserve more from life. You can be free if you but chose a better path. I was not joking."

Gabriel stared at the young girl with disbelief and appreciation. She was the only one in the group of students whom he could even tolerate to the point he somewhat liked her. Her brothers and Diva were unbearable to be even within ten feet of. Archimago had been barely tolerable, while Claudette had been almost as bad as Diva. He knew Shayla felt the same way, so when he asked the next question, he said it with deep sadness and little hope.

"What are you going to do, Shayla?"

The ice Dragon heart's smile became fierce. She whispered into Gabriel's ear, "I am going to the underground. I have to fight him my way. The light shall come soon looking for the crystals of the Dragon Knights—the crown and the dagger. Not only that, to rekindle an alliance. We both know that will not happen. At first chance, slip away as soon as you can. Be quick, for it will not take Cetus long to figure out our plan. Go straight to Red Rose City and speak to Josephine Drageon."

Shayla walked away.

"Wait, Shayla, what will I say to earn their trust?"

She tilted her head and said, "Tell Josephine Drageon, the one who loves the rain that washes her chains away, sent you. She will understand."

With that, Shayla Vanell disappeared into the blanket of the nightly shadows.

Gabriel turned his head to his dragonling's yellow eyes.

"Come, Isaiah, it seems we are on a tighter schedule than I thought."

Despite his normal demeanor, he let a small, quick smile show on his full lips as he entered the courtyard of the castle. He walked into the castle itself, traveling down the velvet rug of the castle hall, the paintings of monarchs long dead staring as though silent witnesses to his invasion.

Gabriel let himself into the main throne room after knocking out the guards with his shadows. Occupying the room's center were golden thrones draped in the finest silk curtains. A bowl of fruit sitting on a small table beside the current resident of the grand estate.

"You've come for what reason into my domain?" demanded the man sitting on the throne. He wore extravagant blue robes that seemed a little tight around the middle as he stood to his full height. His dark brown eyes were full of rage.

Gabriel bowed his head and answered, "I, Gabriel Lucas, came on behalf of my Lord to ask if you wish to make official your alliance to him, King Charles Castel of the WarWink Kingdom."

The fat king glared and stood. He yelled,

"And who would your lord be to ask such a question?"

Gabriel leveled his gaze at the king and replied in a flat but distinct tone,

"My Lord, Cetus Cyprus."

Other Works

As you wait for *Quest for the Magic* make sure to check out:

Never Alone
YA Murder Mystery

About the Author

Kathleen Shay is a graduate of Clarion University of Pennsylvania, with a degree in secondary education English. She is passionate about literature, especially the Young Adult Fantasy genre – an interest that was sparked by the *Harry Potter* series by J. K. Rowling. The *Dragon Heart Chronicles* is her first published work.

She currently resides in rural western Pennsylvania with her family and enjoys writing, reading, listening to music and playing with her cats.

Written by Author's Best Friend, Meghan Schill.

Social Media

Visit the official Facebook Dragon Heart Chronicles Page:
https://www.facebook.com/DragonHeartChronicles

Or Website: www.dragonninjawriter.com